The Watchful Eye

By

WESS REED

This book is a work of fiction. Places, events, and situations in this story are purely fictional. Any resemblance to actual persons, living or dead, is coincidental.

© 2003 by Wess Reed. All rights reserved.

No part of this book may be reproduced, stored in a retrieval system, or transmitted by any means, electronic, mechanical, photocopying, recording, or otherwise, without written permission from the author.

ISBN: 1-4107-7519-4 (e-book)
ISBN: 1-4107-7518-6 (Paperback)
ISBN: 1-4107-7517-8 (Dust Jacket)

This book is printed on acid free paper.

This book is dedicated to my lovely wife, Heather, for her encouragement, friendship, love, and unending support. Without these, this book wouldn't exist.

And to Joyce Hachadourian, for all your hard work, honesty, commitment, and brilliance in seeing this grueling process through.

Freedom is a right given by God.
The right to express that freedom is taken by man.
Boots

Chapter One

After working all day behind the sales desk, Adrian Jacobs decided to have a little fun on the newest late model computer.

Tilting his head back and closing his weary eyes; he took in a deep breath and then slowly exhaled the monotonous torment of the day while running all ten fingers through his dandruffy brown hair. As usual, he was in desperate need of professional grooming.

Adrian walked over to the front entrance and removed a small rubber stopper from between the carpet and the door, which allowed it to swing freely.

A small brass bell, aged, tarnished and hanging from an exhausted length of faded red yarn, rattled against the glass sounding off closing time with its metallic chatter. Adrian slowly closed the door and locked it in place.

Looking out into the stale evening he saw nothing more than broken promises in the form of worn down buildings similar to his, most of which had seen their better days.

In the glass reflection staring back at him he saw tired brown eyes sunken deep into a face that had aged at such a fast pace that it was hard for even him to recognize any trace of the promising young lad that a once joyous life had left behind. Crowding most peoples' shoulders at five foot five he wasn't a very tall man, or even muscular, at most, he weighed one hundred and thirty-six pounds soaking wet. Nevertheless, none of that mattered once he sat down at a computer. After all, computers control the world and he was the master.

Four years ago, Adrian had fought to improve his life with the help of small time embezzlement. At first, he had learned how to hack into bank records moving small transactions through various mazes that eventually wound up in his own personal account. This had been a tedious process with little rewards. Seeking more, he had then taught himself to hack ATM processors. By programming timers into a machine's data bank, he was able to release funds at a time he had scheduled, from several bogus accounts.

After only his fourth successful theft he had noticed a patrol car parked across the street from his targeted ATM. Choosing not to risk getting caught, he left the money for a soon-to-be innocent victim, and drove away. Paranoid or not, he wasn't willing to take the chance.

Soon after, he had found the answer he was looking for in the form of credit. With a few final strokes on his keyboard, after hours of hacking, he had approved himself four major credit cards.

Weekly, he would enter the creditor's computer program and wipe away all proof of his purchases, shortly after they were paid for of course.

Now, four years later, Adrian owned a small computer sales and service company that he had purchased mainly with his talent for illegal funding. For the most part, he now allowed his small business to pay the bills, however, when business was slow he never hesitated to make up the difference with the use of his illegitimate skills.

Lately business was booming. Computer sales were on the rise, which in turn increased service demands. Adrian

The Watchful Eye

was always happy to trouble shoot software problems for the inexperienced customer, as long as it involved money. Furthermore, the customers were always pleased with his performance and happily paid for his expertise. Little did they know, the majority of glitches they were having problems with had been planted into the software prior to purchase.

In the evenings Adrian spent most of his spare time on the computer trying to find a new scam. Night after night he assiduously prodded the world from behind the safety of his sixteen-inch monitor, searching for anything that would pay big and allow him the freedom of never having to work again. Unlike most people who spent their evenings glued to a television set, Adrian saw every minute of the day as an opportunity to make himself rich.

Five days ago while trying to find the big scam, Adrian had stumbled across a government project cloaked within a child relief program. Without hesitation he had begun trying to hack it. Although it didn't appear to be a possible gain in wealth, Adrian had never been able to pass up an opportunity to test his computer skills, especially against good old Uncle Sam. This would be the fifth night he had tried to break into the program and was determined that tonight, he would accomplish his task. There was nothing in the actual program itself that would interest him, he was sure, but he simply couldn't resist the challenge.

With firewalls unlike any he had ever seen before; the program obviously employed the latest technology in computer security.

Adrian, eyes fixated and heedless to his surroundings, pounded the keyboard with cold determination. Nobody, including government mental wizards, could build a security system tight enough to keep him out!

Matter of fact, he thought, once he did get through their massive security, he was considering the idea of scrambling their precious program. Maybe, if he could muster up enough courage, he would even leave an untraceable calling card just to let those uptight government jerks know who the amateurs really were.

Rattling the keyboard with lightning quick reflexes, his fingers seemed to have a mind all their own.

"Come on, here we go!" tap, tap, tap, ta-dap.

"Open up sweetheart, come on let me in, you know you can't hide forever." Tap, tap, ta-dap, tap, tap.

"Oh yeah that's a good girl, just a little more." Tap, ta-dap, tap, tap, tap.

"Voila`!"

The screen opened into a cryptic looking display with bright red text in which were displayed numerical sequences resembling social security numbers, however, these contained eleven extra digits. As far as Adrian could tell, it didn't look similar to any language or encryption that he had seen before.

Without knowing for sure what he was looking at, a hercularian pride swelled his cranium to an X-Large. After five frustrating days of hacking, including four hours of mental meltdown tonight, he had finally broken through the nearly indomitable security. "I am the best!"

A quick glance at the clock revealed how late it was. Without warning, fatigue quickly settled in and overthrew the celebration of this newest accomplishment. He had completely lost track of time.

Adrian opened a drawer, pulled out a new disk, and slid it into the processor with intentions of saving the information. Later, at his convenience, he would be able to study the columns of numbers. Right now however, it was late and he had a date with the sandman.

Adrian clicked on the save menu, looked once more at his greatest accomplishment, then clicked save.

The second Adrian depressed the mouse key, the screen went black. Two seconds later it lit up again showing an aerial view of the globe.

The Watchful Eye

"Bleep" The screen flashed. He was looking at what appeared to be a land formation.

"Bleep" The screen flashed again. This time it was showing an aerial view of a city.

"Bleep" Next was a building. "Oh-Shit!" Adrian said out loud voicing his astonishment.

Steadily building fear, exploded into perplex emotional shrapnel as he read the inscription on the side of the building over and over again. It read A.J. Computer Specialists. He was looking at his own business!

Immediately, Adrian shut down his computer. His heart began to race; he could feel its reverberation resonating within his rib cage. He had just hacked himself into some major trouble! Either the program itself, or a person operating it, had pinpointed his exact location in a matter of seconds. How could that be possible? He had used all the tricks in the book, and built his own firewalls along the way. It should have been impossible to trace him. Stealth was his specialty.

The phone rang.

"Oh my god, what have I done?" Adrian stood staring at the now blank monitor.

The phone continued to ring. He didn't answer it. He didn't have time or the mentality at the moment to walk somebody through a stupid software problem. Besides, who the hell had the nerve to call at this ungodly hour? He had to think fast.

The phone continued to ring.

As hard as he tried, he was unable to control the circular pathway of his thoughts. He couldn't clear his head of the chaotic mess that allowed any possible solutions to elude him.

"What kind of trouble have I gotten myself into? Just think Adrian, come on you have to think! Oh jeez, I don't want to go to jail!" he said aloud, although nobody was around to hear him.

Frustrated, Adrian grabbed up the phone, "Sorry I'm closed!" and slammed it back down on the receiver. He heard an uncontrollable fear quivering in his own voice.

"Okay, slow down and think, maybe there's a way I can get out of this somehow."

He knew that if he were arrested for hacking, *ALL* of his illegal computer activities would surface.

Adrian considered booting up his computer again. Maybe he could get back into the program and delete any proof of his earlier presence.

The phone rang.

Adrian's pacing came to a dead stop. Slowly he turned and stared at the ringing phone as if it were an instrument of hell and the devil himself was impatiently waiting for him on the other end. The reality of his present situation smashed through him like a ton of bricks. He stared at the phone not knowing how deep he had sunken into trouble's murky depths. Who could be on the other end? His throat felt as though it was constricting tighter and tighter, eventually threatening to close up completely.

He picked up the phone and listened.

"Don't hang up Mr. Jacobs!"

"How do you know my name? Who are you?"

"I know a lot more than your name Mr. Jacobs, and I'm learning more and more as we speak. As for who I am? Well, that simply changes to meet the demands, but right about now, I'm your worst fears come true! You shouldn't have been poking around where you don't belong!"

"I don't know what you're talking about. You must have the wrong number!"

"I believe you know very well what I'm talking about Mr. Jacobs."

"What do you want from me?"

"I want to know what you thought you could accomplish by snooping through my program."

The Watchful Eye

"I still don't know what you're talking about, and I don't have time for stupid phone games!"

Trying to run from reality, Adrian hung up the phone. He had never been this scared in his life. Reaching over, he tried to power up the computer. Nothing happened.

The phone rang.

"Hello."

"I told you not to hang up Mr. Jacobs. We're really not getting off to a very good start here!"

"Listen, I already told you, I don't have time for childish phone games. Now if you don't stop bothering me, I'll have no choice but to call the police!"

"I don't believe calling the police would be a very wise choice Mr. Jacobs. After all, if they had any idea of what you've been up to lately, I'm quite positive that you'd be locked away for quite some time, don't you think? Tell me Mr. Jacobs; Do I have your attention now?"

"Okay, I'm listening"

"Well, that's much better. Now, I want to know exactly who you work for and whether or not you managed to make a copy of my program!"

"Who I work for?" Adrian asked in his confusion.

"Don't play with me Mr. Jacobs. Who do you work for?"

"Myself! I mean, nobody. I run my own computer store."

"If you've managed to make a copy, I need to know about it!"

"No, I didn't make a copy. Now tell me who you are and what you want with me?"

"I don't believe you're in a position to be making demands Mr. Jacobs! If I were you I'd stop with the lies and start listening."

Again, hoping his troubles would simply dissipate, Adrian hung up.

Balance is the center of the universe. It is a fulcrum that caresses good and evil, winners and losers, life and death. It is our human desire that good inherently win over these physics of life.

H.R.R.

Chapter Two

Jack Kurts had a long-term love of the martial arts. In his line of work, being physically fit, a positive side effect of all the strenuous hours of practice, was a necessity. In addition to an extreme workout, martial arts also provided an excellent opportunity to free the mind and strengthen the spirit. Jack's knowledge in the arts included military hand-to-hand combat, Shito-ryu, Taekwondo, and Aikido. Aikido was where he found his strength.

Along with his martial arts he loved to run. Jack demanded a lot out of his body and at age thirty-six, with the exception of some gray mottling through his dark brown hair, he was a well-oiled machine.

His eyes, the pathway to his soul, were ocean blue. He kept a nice tan during summer months and his skin, without aid of lotions and oils, had a healthy glow.

Jack stood about five foot eleven and kept himself well groomed. He liked to be clean cut. Although he didn't consider himself to be a handsome man, his face and body were nicely chiseled.

Four times a week Jack started his day with a three-mile jog across Venice Beach. He chose the location for two reasons; the view of the Santa Monica Mountains peering over the ocean took his breath away, as did running across the sand next to the boardwalk.

Running gave him a great sensation of freedom. He also felt a sense of satisfaction while running; witnessing others, through sweat smudged eyes, enjoying their liberty.

Venice Beach drew crowds from all walks of life, expressing themselves through art, culture, religion, music and anything else a person could do to occupy their time under the sun.

Nature's wonder entranced his mind, while its thick granular surface challenged his body. The world around him, though heavily overcast, overflowed with enthusiasm. He joyfully exerted himself while taking in the beauty of life.

Humidity's giants were assembled and preparing to unleash a tempest. The ocean stretched up toward the mountains with roars of laughter, as if trying to taunt the ever-motionless peaks. He could taste its salty hiss.

This morning, while nearing the end of his run, Jack basked in the day unaware of events soon to unfold.

Thirty feet away and to his left, two young men both in their mid to late twenties, closely watched as Jack approached. One, the skinnier of the two, had long stringy hair soaked with enough grease to fry an egg. He wore black jeans that appeared to have been executed by a firing squad on several different occasions and a faded black T shirt that boasted tour dates of a heavy metal group. The other was a foot taller and about sixty pounds heavier than his wasted youth colleague and shared the same taste in casual attire. He sported a razor kissed head with a tattoo that covered his massive skull from front to back, both ears included.

The Watchful Eye

Earlier that morning, the trouble craving duo had been hanging out on the boardwalk sporting a high and ogling the few chicks that were out and about, when a man had approached them wearing a black military type uniform.

"Hey dude," Preston said to his larger companion Scott, "check out GI Joe there." He pointed out the man approaching in fatigues.

"Whoa, looks like he's lost. What the hell does he think he's doing wearing my Uncle Sam's clothes to the beach? There's no war here."

Preston couldn't help but laugh at his partner's remarks. Maybe they could have a little fun at this idiot's expense.

"Hey Scott," Preston said trying to provoke his friend, "why don't you go over there and point his dumb ass over to the Middle East. Tell him to get back to work. While you're at it," he added, "maybe you could talk him into reimbursing us for all of our tax dollars he's been wasting."

"Looks like he's coming over here, why don't you tell him yourself."

"Tell him? I'm gonna order him. After all, my tax dollars pay his salary. That runt works for me and he damn well better do as I say!"

With the mixture of drugs and jokes, they both chuckled uncontrollably like small slaphappy children.

Closer now, they saw nothing but coldness in the eyes of the tough looking uniformed man. The laughter stopped immediately.

Very stocky and probably in his early thirties, the towering man not only carried an extreme air of confidence, he looked downright mean.

Without the slightest of introductions the man got right to the point. Presenting them with a couple of photographs, he asked if they were interested in doing a job and making some quick money. It was risky and they could get hurt, but he assured them that they would be doing a good deed for their country and would not be held accountable for their actions if things didn't go as planned.

Neither of the two could care less about doing the good deed, however, the envelope was stuffed with enough cash that they both quickly agreed.

After a few more minutes of discussion and the exchange of the large sum of money, the man walked away.

✯✯✯

Finishing his run, Jack's mind was free of all thought other than the rhythmic unanimity between his heart, lungs, and legs. His comfortable strides felt as if they were in perfect harmony with the cloud-blanketed ocean's periodic slapping of the sand. Jack shifted his direction across the beach and over to the asphalt toward a corner street where he had parked his car earlier that morning.

Halfway across the asphalt, Jack noticed the two young men walking toward him, at a glance they appeared to be harmless punks.

Changing his direction slightly to avoid a collision, Jack was passing by when the larger of the two, without warning, swung a wholehearted punch. Slamming Jack in the chest, the punch felt no less solid than would a three-pound sledge hammer in full swing. Not only did the assault catch Jack completely off guard, but he also took the full force of the blow during the end of an exhalation.

Looking up from a pain induced crouch, both hands on his chest and gasping for breath, Jack's first reaction was to yell in anger, however, before he could catch his breath and spit out any words, the bald headed lunatic was in mid-swing with another punch. This time, he was aiming for Jack's head.

Moving as quickly as possible, Jack avoided the worst of the blow but managed to take a healthy scraping of

The Watchful Eye

knuckles against the back of his left ear. *What the hell is this madman trying to do!* he thought to himself.

Before the bald man could get off a third swing, Jack stepped in close, grabbed him by the shirt collar, and jerked him forward in a circular motion with all of his might.

Off-balanced, the oversized punk didn't have half a chance of blocking the roundhouse kick that connected explosively against the side of his neck and the base of his colorfully tattooed skull. He went down hard.

Jack stood over him for a minute while trying to catch his breath. At the same time, he searched his mind for the slightest explanation of what had just happened and why? While trying to find the answer, he realized that amidst all of the commotion and his confusion, he had forgotten about the big, bald man's longhaired companion.

Turning around and finding him, he ducked in the nick of time to avoid the sharp end of stainless steel six-inch blade. The longhaired guy had a knife.

Fully intending on sinking the blade into Jacks exposed back, the longhaired punk quickly lost his confidence upon seeing anger and determination in Jack's eyes.

Fear flowed through the smaller man's veins, showing its cowardly colors in the punk's fright widened pupils and the ghostly whitening of his skin.

Although boldly swinging the knife in an effort to hold his ground, his face clearly showed his terror in having to face the consequences of his actions.

Looking around frantically in hopes of finding an escape, the longhaired grease-ball grabbed hold of a nearby woman and pressed the knife against her throat.

"Stay away from me!" he shouted at not wanting to be the devastated loser in the already heated confrontation.

"Stay away or I'll hurt her!"

The woman began to struggle.

"Let her go," Jack said calmly as he took a couple of steps back.

The woman's screams and struggles grew hysterically. This was not what the punk had intended on. He had hoped that she would provide him with a safe retreat from the beach, and more importantly from Jack who was looking intent on disfiguring him.

Having a hard time holding on to the woman, and becoming engrossed with maintaining the control that he knew he was quickly losing, Preston turned his focus completely away from Jack.

"Hold still bitch or I'll cut your throat out!"

Jack saw the opportunity opening up and moved a few steps closer.

In the process of trying to keep the woman under control, the longhaired lunatic accidentally thrust his knife into the woman's shoulder.

Swiftly, without conscious thought, Jack launched himself forward and struck the man with an elbow and knocked him down. He had targeted the creep's temple with pinpoint accuracy.

The moment the impact was received, Preston's vision clouded under a blanket of white twinkly lights, his thoughts were instantly numbed, and then everything faded to black.

Before Jack could assess the damage he had caused, he was grabbed from behind. The big guy had gotten back up.

Acting purely by reflex, Jack dropped into a squat and shot his palms toward the sky with all his might. The bear hug from behind was broken. He then twisted counter clockwise covering his left fist with the palm of his right hand for reinforcement, and drove his left elbow into the larger punk's ribs. With the bald man still behind him, he side stepped left and swung his right fist down toward the outside of his thigh and into the large punk's groin. With a final spin counter clockwise, he planted a back fist into the previously battered and swollen area of the punk's fleshy modern art. The colorfully bald man hit the ground with a

The Watchful Eye

thud. As though it were leaking, blood slowly began to flow like ink from his cranial tapestry.

Jack stepped over to the longhaired punk. Lying unconscious on the pavement, he looked like nothing more than a harmless grease mop. He kicked the knife from his immediate reach.

The woman looked dizzy. She was slowly beginning to fade.

At that moment, as if on cue, it began to rain.

★★★

The following morning Jack woke early. After showering and dressing for the day, he sipped coffee while waiting for toast to pop up. He thought about the woman. The wound she had suffered appeared as though it might have been serious. Why couldn't he have acted sooner? He couldn't help but feel somewhat responsible for what had happened to her.

What the hell was wrong with those two men? Even though he had thought about what had happened until late last night, he couldn't come up with any reasons for his being attacked.

With the help of a few bystanders, Jack had done his best to stop the woman's bleeding until the paramedics had arrived, after which, he continued to stay by her side until they drove away. Jack didn't leave the scene until after the authorities had been satisfied with his statement. At least this time, unlike most crimes, the bad guys were apprehended and off the streets.

While reflecting on what had happened and the possible intentions of the attackers, Jack's focus inadvertently drifted back to the woman. Holding pressure on her bleeding wound, Jack had spoken softly to her in an effort to keep her calm. Even when her eyes swam out of focus, he had continued to talk to her with a reassuring voice. During that time, he couldn't help but notice how beautiful she was. Maybe he noticed her beauty because he was looking down on her with compassion. Nonetheless, he had never seen a woman look so soft, innocent and lovely. Sliding in and out of consciousness, she had managed to tell the paramedics her name; it was Sharon.

In her mid thirties and very attractive, Sharon was about five foot seven with sandy blond hair that softly quilted her shoulders. He also recalled her slender shape, the delicate curves of her face, but most of all her eyes. They were dark emerald green with a slight hint of sapphire. She was breathtaking.

✯✯✯

At work, later that day, Jack found himself daydreaming again about the beautiful woman named Sharon. He still couldn't help but feel responsible for her involvement in the incident yesterday at Venice Beach.

Getting up from behind his desk, he stepped outside his office and into a short hallway where he knocked on an entrance three doors down.

"Come on in!" yelled a voice from behind the closed door.

Jack entered into a room filled with a mass of various components of computing hardware. The room *bleeped, flashed, twinkled, and hummed* as if it were ready to blast itself into orbit at any given moment.

Don McConnel sat in the cockpit of intelligence. There was a faint glow from the duel monitors, reflecting across his hazel eyes. Staying in his seat, he twisted at the waist in order to look at his superior, but managed to keep his fingers flickering relentlessly as though they were magnetized to the chattering keyboard.

"Good morning Jack, what can I do for you?"

The Watchful Eye

Jack liked to keep his personal life just that,...*Personal!* The people he worked with, and for in his opinion, had no reason to know him other than in the professional manner it took to get the job done effectively and efficiently. Up until this point, he had not mentioned to anyone, the events that had taken place the previous day regarding himself or the woman.

Today's visit *was* personal, as he was hoping to dig up some information pertaining to the woman and his attackers. He replayed the events to Don.

"Wow!" Don said. His reaction to the story overflowed with genuine interest and excitement. "Are you okay?"

"My chest is still a little sore, but other than that I feel fine."

"How about the girl, is she okay?"

For a moment, Jack reconsidered his intentions. Being quite the professional, he didn't like the idea of using the agency's unlimited resources for personal gain. Then again, maybe he was being a tad bit too anal? He continued on the path of his first intent.

"Well, that's part of the reason I'm here," Jack answered, carefully measuring Don's expression. He still didn't feel right in asking but continued anyway. "If you have some extra time and don't mind, I was hoping you might be able to dig up some information for me."

"No problem!"

Grinning, Don cracked his knuckles in a festive attempt to brag about what his priceless digits and the organic super computer they were attached to could do.

"Anything you want! If it's in here," Don said referring to his computer system, "I can find it. Where should I start?"

"First," Jack said, "I'd like to know about the woman, her name is Sharon, but I don't know her last name, birth-date, or social security number. Search all of the local hospitals for any woman with the same first name. She was admitted yesterday by ambulance. I believe she's in her mid thirties. If you can find her, I'd like information regarding her condition." Trying not to sound too personal he added, "you know, just to make sure she's alright."

Jack was concerned with the victim's health and well being, especially since he, himself, had somehow been the main target in the skirmish. He was the reason she was involved in the first place.

"Next, I want to know who those two men were, what they're going to be charged with and anything you can find that might explain a possible motive."

Don could hear a subtle hint of anger weighing slightly in Jack's otherwise unequivocally docile voice. Although it wasn't much, it was enough to make him thankful to be on Jack's side.

"For sure!" Don said, "It's a tricky process getting into LAPD records and it'll take a while, but I can probably have it to you by the end of the day. The rest is gonna be gravy!"

Smiling, as he did every time he was presented with a chance to show off his skills, Don turned back around to face the monitor, "just give me a second here..."

Jack interrupted. "There's no hurry. If you're busy, I can always come back later."

Slapping rhythm into the keyboard, Don persisted, "Not a problem boss, I have plenty of time. Besides, this is the stuff that makes my job enjoyable"

Don closed the file he was previously working on, pulled up a different screen with which he was required to enter a password, entered it, and then scanned his system for what he explained to Jack as static trace.

After a few seconds of what appeared to be simple typing on the keyboard, Don was into the telephone company's computer system. From there he was able to access all local hospital computer files. One by one, he checked hospitals in the Los Angeles area.

The Watchful Eye

Previously, Don had worked for more than ten years as a computer specialist for the DEA. He was an expert at hacking into well-protected systems, as well as finding and tracing activities of other hackers. After a meeting with Jack and the Director of Central Intelligence two years ago, Don had quit his job with the DEA. A few days later, he began his career with AFA. As with Jack, his life from that point had been changed forever.

Within five minutes Don was able to provide Jack with all the information he had requested regarding the woman. Sliding himself aside, chair and all, he gave Jack a better view of the monitor.

"I think you'll find everything you're looking for right here!" says Don while grinning with the pride of a first time bicyclist.

Jack stepped up to the screen to have a better look.

According to the records, three women named Sharon were seen in Los Angeles emergency rooms by way of ambulance the previous morning. Among names, were brief descriptions of the patient's diagnosis and personal information submitted alongside insurance claims.

One, a sixty-three year old renal patient, had been admitted for a clotted internal jugular catheter. She was scheduled to be de-clotted with Cathflo Activase.

The second one was a twelve-year-old child who had been hit by a car while riding her bicycle. She suffered a broken femur, two fractured ribs and a few minor cuts and abrasions.

The third woman, thirty-two year old Sharon Andrews, was an intensive care patient at St. Francis. There was no further information regarding her condition.

"This must be her?" Jack said referring to the last entry. "It has to be her," he repeated although his voice lacked certainty. "Why isn't there anything regarding her condition on file? Can you find out more about her?" he asked, staring at the screen through puzzled eyes.

"That's strange?" Don slid himself back in front of the monitor. "Her file should be filled with a similar amount of content. Let me try something different."

Don began hammering vigilantly on the small keys. Within no time at all, he was into the Motor Vehicle Department where he pulled up a file for Sharon Andrews.

"Is this her?" he asked sliding out of Jack's way once again.

"Yeah...it sure is...thanks Don," Jack answered imperviously, while concentrating on the data that had been pulled up from the state.

"Damn she's good looking! I can't say I blame you for wanting to check up on her. I would too if I were you. Matter of fact," Don continued, "If you think you'll need some help..."

Jack cut him off before he could finish his sentence. "It's not like that. I'm just concerned about her well-being okay, that's all there is to it."

"Okay." Because of Jack's serious tone, Don refrained himself from any further banter.

Without much contemplation, Jack decided to pay a visit to St. Francis. After all, it was very possible that he had saved Sharon's life, surely it wouldn't hurt to check up on her.

"Thanks for all your help," Jack said as he turned to leave the room.

"Hey boss?"

"Yeah?" Jack turned back toward Don and his space station of a computer to see Don's face fully clad with an impish smile that stretched from ear to ear. "Good luck Sir!"

Reluctantly, Jack entered the hospital. Thinking about his mother and father, hospitals seemed to be a place where

The Watchful Eye

people go, not to be healed, but to die. That's what had happened to his mother while giving birth to him anyway.

As a small child, Jack had never understood the details pertaining to his mother's death. Furthermore, when he had grown old enough to understand, his father had still been too reluctant to talk about it. Then, when he was fourteen, he lost his father to a hospital as well.

His dad had been driving home from work during a major rainstorm, when up ahead, he caught a glimpse of a lady and her three children stranded in the middle of the road with a flat tire. She had never thought to pull off the road and onto the shoulder.

By the time his father had seen the car it was already too late. Swerving to miss the vehicle, his only option had left him trapped in his car and upside down in a swift moving wash. An officer headed in the opposite direction had missed the collision by a fraction of a second.

Quick to act, the officer had been able to pull Jack's father from the sunken car and administered CPR. With the help of a hero in uniform, against unimaginable odds, Jack's father had survived the incident with only a few minor scraps and bruises.

Everything seemed to be fine when Jack's father was released from the hospital hours after the accident. Three days later, however, he was admitted back into the same hospital with pneumonia.

As a result of the storm's runoff, harmful microorganisms had seeped into the river water, in the form of raw sewage, and had settled into his father's lungs causing pneumonia, or in his case *Secondary Drowning*. His father had been placed on a medical floor in a semi-private room containing two beds. Jack's father occupied one and the other held a man suffering from a diabetic complication called DKA, otherwise known as Diabetic Keto Acidosis. This was an acute life threatening side effect of uncontrolled diabetes.

WESS REED

One night, while extremely shorthanded, the medical staff had been scrambling vigorously trying to accomplish their assigned tasks. Jack's father lay in bed waiting to receive his Ceftriaxone. This was an antibiotic meant to heal his pneumonia. He was also getting an IV drip of Normal Saline to aid in re-hydrating his fevered body.

Shortly after a nurse had entered the room to hang his father's antibiotics and a fresh insulin drip for the diabetes-crippled man, a code blue was called out over the intercom. Medical staff rushed down to a nearby room and struggled to restart the heart of a dying man.

Paying a minimal amount of attention to her present duties, the nurse quickly hung the medications, started the infusion pumps, and then left the room to join in.

Hours' later, cold and breathless, his father was found dead lying in a pool of sweat soaked sheets. The insulin drip intended for his diabetes suffering bunkmate, had been hung on his father's saline pump at a rate of two hundred and fifty cc's an hour. The diabetic man, who in turn had been treated for pneumonia, somehow managed to live through the whole ordeal.

Because of negligent medical care, *"twice,"* Jack had spent the remainder of his childhood without a family. As of that day, he had never felt comfortable in the presence of a hospital.

From the moment Jack walked through the front door at St. Francis, he felt as if bacteria were slowly depositing its filth on his skin and clothes. Off-white ceiling tiles swallowed the mild clatter of traffic moving down the spit-shined vinyl highway, however, Jack could sense diseased exhaust floating heavily overhead. Patients commuting from one hallway to the next left behind their infectious fumes.

The Watchful Eye

Fluorescent lighting gave the sunless corridors a sickly yellow glow. Even if only in his imagination, Jack smelled death soaked in antiseptic. He approached the front desk feeling mentally queasy.

The receptionist was a kind elderly lady with thick bifocals. Her demeanor was quite pleasant, reminding him of his grandmother. Looking up from the desk over the rim of her glasses the lady asked, "May I help you?"

"Yes, can you please direct me to Sharon Andrews room?"

Looking over the top of her glasses, the receptionist punched the name into a computer.

"I'm sorry sir, Ms. Andrews was discharged yesterday afternoon."

Jack could feel disappointment and confusion taking control of his face. *That couldn't be possible,* he thought. *People aren't transported to the ICU under emergency conditions and then get up and walk out all in one day.* He forced a smile for the receptionist and thanked her for her time.

"Have a nice day sir." The receptionist smiled back pleasantly.

Jack walked back to his car and returned to work.

Chapter Three

Thirty minutes had passed since Adrian hung up on the stranger. With the exception of his periodic emotional outbursts, the room had been silent.

Frantically, Adrian searched his mind for the best possible solution. He had worked too hard to build his house into the business it was today. He didn't want to run, besides, he had nowhere to go. What he wouldn't give at the moment to be able to turn back time. Sweat trickled across his brow and down his temple.

Easily able to squeeze money from the world via phone line, Adrian had never considered saving any of what he stole. On the run without a computer, he would surely perish. How could he make it through life as a fugitive without cash?

Shuddering with fear and extremely close to a panic attack, Adrian wiped his clammy hands down the front of his pants.

He did have credit cards and had thought about using them. At the least he could get by for a couple of months before they were cancelled. Then what? Starve? Live in a box? Without his computer he wouldn't be able to clear away his debt. Furthermore, he knew that by living on credit, if even for a short while, he would leave a smoking trail for anyone who knew what they were doing to follow. It wouldn't take long before they found him, and then what? Kill him?

Adrian couldn't stop pacing. What had he done, and what was he going to do now? What did these people want with him and how powerful were they? These questions swirled around in his head burning a path through his mind no different than his pacing, through time, would eventually wear a trail across every thread of carpet in his small business.

How was he going to get away? And if so, where would he go? What would he do?

Adrian was about ready to lose himself in a tantrum for lack of a solution, when it hit him. Laptops! There were two of them still in boxes in the back room. As long as he checked into hotels that were equipped with Internet, he could not only erase charges to his credit cards, but also erase any electronic proof of the transaction. Relief rapidly washed through him and cleared his flustered mind. Once he was at a safe distance, he would then decide what his next step would be.

Under the sales counter, Adrian retrieved all the software he would need to beef up the laptop to meet his needs. Then, after packing a few changes of clothes and the portable computer, he would find another life somewhere else, somewhere safe.

Like the haunting screech of an owl, piercing the stillest of nights, his new train of thought was immediately shattered when the spiritless phone came noisily back to life.

Adrian chose not to answer it in hopes that silence would again defeat the phone's tormenting ring and potentially, the anguish brought with it. *Eventually it will stop*, he thought to himself. After about five minutes, which was all he needed to throw a few clothes and the software into a suitcase, Adrian couldn't take it anymore. He set everything down in a pile on the floor and marched over to the phone. It was time to end this insane mess. Surely, whoever was on the other end would be able to reason with him after realizing that he was actually a nobody who happened to breach that stupid program purely on accident. If not, they could kiss off, he was packed and ready to go!

Adrian picked up the phone, but before he could say anything he heard screeching tires and the roar of an engine out in front of his house. He dropped the phone and ran over to the window.

A handful of large men wearing black military type outfits, poured quickly from two dark SUV's. Armed with automatic weapons of all sorts, they wasted no time charging the building.

Adrian's heart pushed its way up into his already constricted throat. He turned and ran for the back of the building. Halfway to the doorway that would lead him to the back, an earsplitting *"BOOM"* shook the building rattling windows and shattering glass in the largest of the three that faced the entrance. A grenade shot past Adrian, hit a wall and then bounced back toward the middle of the room. Already running as fast as he could, he was able to make it through the doorway and into the supply room a split second before the grenade exploded. With a blinding flash of light, Adrian felt a pounding rush of hot air, quickly followed by a brief absence of it, in his lungs. His ears popped from the transient change of pressure.

Although not as loud as he would have imagined, the manmade thunder emitted from the detonating grenade stunned his eardrums' leaving him temporarily hard of hearing, if not permanently deaf.

The walls were still standing, and there was no flying debris following the explosion. The grenade should have remodeled the building, demolishing him and his business into nothing more than a worthless pile of smoldering rubble. There was no time to think about it. Adrian at this point was simply glad to be alive.

Still running, he made it safely to the back of the building and reached the exit in one piece.

The service door to the alley swung open with little effort. Although his arms were meek, built for no more than overpowering a computer keyboard, his adrenaline-bloated body would have allowed him to rip it from its hinges.

He ran out into the night and down the alley as fast as his legs would carry him. He couldn't hear anyone pursuing him, though he knew they would be. Considering the fear and confusion storming in his brain, not to mention the close call with a grenade, he wasn't sure if he could trust his hearing. Nonetheless, he was sure that they would soon be on his heels, if not already close behind.

Maybe they were still in the building searching for him. Surely it wouldn't be long before they found the service entrance connecting to the alley. Only two doors allowed passage in and out of the building, and they knew he didn't exit from the front.

Fearing for his life, he continued to run for all he was worth. The alley didn't provide much for hiding places, therefore, Adrian looked desperately to find a way out as soon as possible. He thought he heard a noise behind him and tried to quicken his pace.

Thoughts of being shot in the back entered his mind forcing him to push even harder. How could this have possibly happened? Adrian, like most people, never dreamed that he might be running for his life someday.

His chest churned up more pain with every stride, as his heart pounded against his rib cage competing for more space. Between gasps for air, he was sure he heard footsteps behind him. They were coming!

Darkness reluctantly gave way to the neglected glow of a distant street lamp. Adrian glanced quickly over his shoulder hoping for a glimpse of his followers, or better yet,

The Watchful Eye

an absence of them but his eyes were not yet adjusted to the night.

Frosted by the moon, cold humid air spiraled down into the alley and incinerated his lungs.

Broken glass and gravel grumbled, sharply protesting the disturbance caused by his fleeing footsteps. Twice he almost fell, misjudging potholes for smooth solid asphalt in the dark.

Thick sticky saliva began to coat his tongue while his raw and cracking throat pleaded for moisture. Exceeding its capabilities, his thundering heart seemed ready to burst. Pushing harder and harder his weary legs pumped furiously, trying to distance himself from his pursuers.

The fear of death pushed him far beyond his limits. He knew his merciless hunters were closing in.

At the end of the alley now, he ran through an opening to his left and ducked into a four-story parking garage. Severe cramps twisted relentlessly in his abdomen and knotted his gut.

Weakened, his leg muscles quivered violently as he quickly climbed up a cement staircase to the second level of the garage.

Alone in the concrete ceiling, an old unprotected light bulb flickered hopelessly, fighting for its last few hours of life. Weathered urine and stale cigarette butts left behind their pungent fumes.

Exiting the stairwell, Adrian took refuge behind a full size sedan parked along a shadow smeared brick wall. A restless breeze entered the garage and softly stirred the oil soaked atmosphere. Only his hammering heart interrupted the morbid silence.

Adrian listened for any noise that might inform him as to whether or not someone had followed him up the stairs and into the huge parking structure. Fed by fear, his mind began to play tricks on itself. Fictitious demons crept at the edge of his vision. When he turned to look, they all but melted into the shadows. Was someone in the garage with him? Although listening carefully, he couldn't hear past his thundering heart. From the corners of his eyes, he continued to see movement. Not sure if what he was seeing was real, he questioned his imagination for playing tricks on him.

After quick contemplation, Adrian decided he would be better off if he continued to move. He felt as if he were a sitting duck waiting to be taken from life unexpectedly.

Getting as far away as possible was the best thing he could do at the moment. But, what if they're somewhere close and he revealed his location. Maybe he'd unknowingly run right into them. He decided to stay where he was for a while longer, until it was safe to move. Soon they'll decide that they've lost him and leave the area. But then again, they might sneak right up behind him and transform his skull into a lead garden.

Adrian was just about to get up and try to make his way to safety outside of the parking garage, when a car slowly turned up the ramp and onto the second level.

Chased by its headlights, curious shadows scampered across the brick walls. Maybe this was his chance for escape.

Although still unidentifiable through the glowing beams of its headlights, Adrian's fear was slightly relieved when he determined at a glance that the approaching vehicle was a car, not an SUV.

Light reflected back to the vehicle from the windshield of a parked car, revealing blue and red emergency lights on top of the cruiser. Another reflection of light permitted Adrian to read the decal, Virginia State Police.

A feeling of security quickly overcame his fears. The policeman would be able to help him. He could take him from the garage into the safety of numbers. Even if he went to jail, anything beats dying scared and alone in a cold and

The Watchful Eye

smelly parking garage. He stood up to wave the officer down and immediately realized his mistake.

As soon as he stood up, another reflection of light hit the passenger's window of the slowly approaching cruiser. It was smeared with blood. Adrian tried to hide again, but it was already too late. The driver had spotted him and the cruiser came to an abrupt stop. Adrian's hopes for escape were somberly washed away in the drowning beam of a spotlight. As he turned to run, a stern voice crackled over the police car's P.A. system.

"Stay where you are! Take two steps and you're as good as dead!"

A tower of a man stepped out of the car wearing a black military uniform, he had a .50-caliber desert eagle equipped with a laser sight, and it was pointed directly at Adrian's thumping heart. Keying a handheld radio, he approached Adrian.

"657, I've completed and can deliver!" Following a static induced hiss, a stern, apathetic voice crackled back through the radio, *"Bravo Zulu, hold strong ETA five minutes!"*

Adrian considered running for the exit but knew he would never make it. The towering man in black fatigues recognized his thoughts and warned him sharply.

"Don't even think of it! If you so much as lean in one direction or another, I'll put a hole through your chest the size of Miami!"

Adrian looked deep into the man's callous eyes, seeing only that they reinforced his threatening words. With a resonance of consternation, Adrian asked, "Who are you and what do you want with me?"

Lacking any sign of pity or remorse thereafter, the man thrust the barrel of his .50-caliber cannon into Adrian's forehead, nearly knocking him over. Pain shot across Adrian's scull like a high voltage current, leaving a singed wave of nerves in its wake. Adrian felt nothing but cold fearless hatred overflowing from his captor. It only helped him to realize that there was no possible chance for escape.

"I would love nothing more than to kill you right now! So why don't you keep your mouth shut and relieve my temptations," the man said. Repulsion surged throughout his voice.

Adrian couldn't believe this was actually happening to him. It has to be a bad dream, yet he could already feel the painful indention throbbing on his forehead.

Reduced to groveling, for fear of losing his life, Adrian's body started quivering uncontrollably. Somehow he knew this wasn't just a show. He had pissed off the wrong people and was fixing to pay for it with his very existence.

"I'm sorry for whatever it was that I did! Please, just tell me what you want, I'll do anything. I don't want to die!"

Hatred swelled out of control in the man's malevolent eyes. Before Adrian saw or felt what had happened, he fell to the pavement with an excruciating thud. Sharp twisting pain shot bullet-like through his right leg. The ruthless tower dressed in black had kicked his feet out from underneath him, intentionally shattering his kneecap in the process.

"I've told you for the last time, Shut up!"

On the cold hard cement, quivering in pain, Adrian watched helplessly as another vehicle rounded the corner onto the second level of the garage. Screeching tires protested the speed at which the vehicle was handled. The black SUV pulled ahead of the police car and came to a stop. Two more men in black fatigues piled out of it carrying with them what appeared to Adrian to be fully automatic weapons. One of them, the smaller of the two, rushed over to where Adrian was laying on the concrete and began to search through his clothing.

"Nothing! Looks like we have the only copy he made."

The Watchful Eye

Melodically thumping sounds slowly arose in the distance and gradually became louder. Adrian recognized the pounding swish of a helicopter's rotor blades slicing through the night air outside the parking structure. Minutes later another vehicle, the second SUV, rounded the corner and came to a stop.

All three uniformed men stood at attention as an elderly looking man wearing a crisp new suit stepped out of the SUV. Nicely aged and quite distinguished looking, he had a full head of silvery-gray hair. His eyes were of such a light blue and gray that they nearly matched his hair and boldly displayed perspicaciousness from deep within their penetrating stare. The driver of that vehicle, also a large man in uniform, followed him over to where Adrian was laying on the hard oily concrete.

"At ease."

"Yes, sir'."

The four men watched closely, as the elderly looking man approached Adrian.

"Well Mr. Jacobs, looks like we finally get to meet in person. I have to say, you don't look as bright as I would have imagined, especially not now!"

"Who are you?" Adrian asked in a voice that trembled with fear.

Ignoring the question and looking less pleasant by the second, the man began to yell.

"Do you not have any idea the depths of your troubles Mr. Jacobs? What on earth did you think you were doing?"

"I'm truly sorry for whatever it was I did. Please believe me. I didn't mean any harm! I'm sure I can fix any problems that I've caused if you'll only let me."

Perturbed by Adrian's response the man shouted, "Cut the crap Mr. Jacobs, who are you working for?"

"What do you mean? I told you, I don't work for anybody. I work for myself."

"Then why were you snooping through a classified government project?"

"I don't know, I just thought…you have to believe me. I didn't mean to cause you any problems. I promise, I'll never do it again!"

Laughing with derision, the elder man replied, "Do you really expect me to believe that this is just some sort of silly coincidence? Nobody without reason would take the time and effort required to enter that program! You're running out of time Mr. Jacobs, this is your last chance, who do you work for!"

"But I've told you already, I work for myself. Please, you have to believe me!"

Looking to the smallest of the four soldiers', the one that had searched Adrian previously, the elderly man asked, "Have we received any more information yet?"

"Yes, sir', he's clean, however, they found a disk in his computer. It contained evidence that he was in fact trying to copy the eye's tracking function. Our men have already eliminated the disk and destroyed the hard drive. We're completely clean Sir."

"Well Mr. Jacobs, looks like we're all finished here, no harm done after all. I suppose we can all just go home and forget that this little misfortune ever happened."

Adrian felt a slight sense of relief. The elder man turned toward the SUV he had arrived in and started to walk off followed closely by the man who had driven. Stopping, he looked at the soldier with the desert eagle that had detained Adrian prior to his arrival. He then looked at the patrol car with its crimson smeared window. Chuckling in his amazement through a proud but disbelieving grin he said, "You never cease to amaze me Sgt. Stalls. I presume you killed the officer?"

"Yes, sir."

"Just for the car,…to lure Mr. Jacobs here out of hiding?"

"That's affirmative Sir."

"Fine work soldier. Now, make sure you dispose of this mess properly. I don't need any more paperwork than is absolutely necessary," he warned.

"Yes, sir. What would you like me to do with him?" he asked referring to Adrian.

"I wouldn't want to think the fine policeman died in vain, would you?"

"No sir."

"Good, dispose of him as well."

"Yes, sir."

Hearing his execution ordered, Adrian's bladder released involuntarily. His tears quickly followed, leaving his mind to sink inside itself.

The gray-haired man in the crisp suit returned to the SUV where the driver was holding the door open for him. He climbed in.

As the SUV drove off on its way back to the waiting helicopter, the older, gray-haired man heard the ferocious thundering emitted from the hand-held cannon. The sound of death rumbled heedlessly through the parking garage.

Chapter Four

Eight days had passed since the attack at Venice Beach. Sharon Andrews sat at her father's kitchen table and took a long hard chug of ice cold beer.

Her shoulder had required a three-hour surgical procedure and a total of eight days in the hospital to repair the damage that had been inflicted during the attack.

"I'm so thankful you're okay. You could have been killed."

Swallowing another mouthful of beer, she sat at the kitchen table listening to one of her father's seldom lectures. He was not just her father, but one of her closest friends as well.

Twenty two years ago, when Sharon was a small child of ten years, her mother and father had divorced. Her father had been busy with his career, which at the time was moving forward with large strides. Her parents had slowly drifted apart. One bleak morning, after they had spent the majority of the previous evening in a long heated argument, her mother simply left. Without having ever looked back, she packed up all of her personal belongings, emptied their bank account, and abandoned them both forever.

Since then, Sharon and her father John had grown very close. Even during her teen years when her body had begun its transformation from young child to young woman, she had never felt uncomfortable or out of place when talking to him, no matter how awkward the topic of conversation was. John, her father, had always listened to what she had to say and in her eyes, had done his very best to help her see through life's problems without ever passing judgement.

Raising a daughter with only bits and pieces of advice from household staff members wouldn't have been an easy task for any man. Nonetheless, John had managed to be a very stable father, and at the same time, a supportive and loving friend. With his busy and demanding job as a U.S. Congressman, he had always managed to be there for her through thick and thin. Sharon knew she could count on him even if it meant canceling very important meetings, although she would never have asked him to. Now, Sharon wondered what her mother might say if she were still an active part of the family.

"Yeah, I'm really lucky I guess. It could have been a lot worse." Sharon said. The thought of what could have happened sent a brigade of chills marching directly down her spine.

"I can't believe you didn't call me and let me know that you were hurt," her father said with a look of disappointment.

"I'm sorry Dad. I just didn't think you needed to worry about me. Besides, I know you're busy and I didn't want you to think you had to sit in the hospital and baby-sit me. I took full advantage and used the time to catch up on my sleep. Besides, I was doped up on pain medication most of the time and wouldn't have been very good company anyway."

"You're the only family I have. What on earth would I do without you?"

The Watchful Eye

"It was no big deal dad, but next time I'll make sure and tell you."

"Next time? What do you mean *Next Time?*"

"All I'm saying is that I've learned my lesson and that I should have called."

"Speaking of calling, have you contacted that man yet, the one that helped you? You really should thank him for what he did," her father said in a suggestive manner. "Maybe you could send him a card with some flowers. I'm not really sure what would be appropriate. I suppose it doesn't matter as long as you do *something* to show your appreciation."

"I was thinking of contacting him tomorrow and asking him to lunch or maybe even dinner."

Having thought about it prior to her father's suggestion, she had already picked up a copy of the police report that morning. According to the report, his name was Jack Kurts. She had felt a strange connection to him when she read his name, like she had met him and actually knew him sometime in her past. After giving it more thought, she finally decided that she had never met him before, but still couldn't alleviate that weird feeling of being connected to him somehow.

With the exception of Mr. Kurts, events that had taken place that morning, including most of her stay at the hospital, had literally left her with a blurred and confused memory. The whole week seemed to be out of place. It almost left her feeling like she was an outsider that had been looking in on someone else's life. Even considering all the pain medications she had been on during her hospital stay, she figured the day of the attack itself would at least have more substance than an old dream.

Another thing that struck her as odd was that even though she could hardly remember what had happened, she clearly remembered Jack as though she had just seen him five minutes ago. Of course there had been so much happening so fast that day, that her brain had probably blocked some of it out as a means of protecting itself, a type of coping mechanism. The whole week seemed to be nothing more than cluttered memories that were scarce and incomplete. Memories weren't even the correct description for what she was feeling, it was more like she was revisiting the scattered remains of a bad dream.

Then again there was Jack. Through it all, she could somehow recall exactly what he looked like with extreme mental clarity, as if her memories of him were from some other time or maybe even some other place. She couldn't quite put her finger on it.

Even stranger, she also felt as though she not only knew him at some other point in her life, but had been very close to him and was comfortable with his personality. This feeling pulled at her with tremendous strength.

If she had known him a long time ago and shared whatever bond she was feeling at the moment, how could she have possibly forgotten? Unless they were small children at the time, which might explain it. Could she have known him in kindergarten or elementary? No, she was grasping at straws.

Deep down she somehow knew, although she could close her eyes and see his face vividly, that she had never met this Jack Kurts before that horrible morning eight days ago. She was merely reacting to the fact that he had saved her from that weird little creep, and felt a strange closeness to him based solely on his bravery at a time of need. Nonetheless, when she did think of and picture Jack's face, it was all too real. De'ja'vu struck her hard.

"Make sure you thank him for me as well. I can't imagine what I'd do without you."

"I can," she said trying to redirect her thoughts along with the conversation. "You'd probably have time to find a female companion, maybe someone to spend time with other than your daughter."

The Watchful Eye

Her father stood up from the table and walked over to the fridge.

"I'm not talking about this with you again," he stated trying to avoid a repeat of several conversations they had had in the past. "I'm simply too busy. I just don't have any extra time to dedicate to a relationship."

"It doesn't have to be a relationship. What's wrong with a friendship?"

John popped the tops off of two more beers and handed her one. "I said I'm not talking about this anymore!"

"Sorry Dad, I just thought…"

"Sshhshsht!"

"But."

Sharon was cut short again, this time however, it had only taken a sharp daring look from her father's severe but loving eyes.

"How does your shoulder feel now? Did they give you any good pain killers?" Sharon lifted her shirtsleeve allowing him a chance to examine the wound again. "Yes, but I haven't needed any lately. It looks and feels a lot better than it did."

"It looks quite painful to me," he said grimacing at the wound.

Her shoulder was still badly bruised, and actually quite sore. "It really looks a lot worse than it is. Besides, after a few more of these liquid pain killers," she said referring to the beer, "I won't feel a thing."

"Do you have time for dinner? If you don't mind waiting, I can have it ready in about thirty minutes."

"Sure that sounds great, but don't think I need to be pampered! I'll stay only as long as I can help prepare it."

"Well there's no sense in arguing about it," said her father with a scampish grin, "Would you like to dial or place the order?"

Laughing, he picked up the phone and called in a pizza. They talked, laughed, drank beer, and ate.

Chapter Five

Getting out of bed took a little longer than usual. Not only was her head aching and slightly pounding behind each eye, but Sharon still felt tired enough to sleep in the rest of the day.

Sharon sat up on the edge of her bed anyway, dug her toes into her favorite slippers and slowly made her way to the kitchen.

"I have to have some coffee," she mumbled speaking only to herself. Her slippers gently sanded the hardwood floor as she trudged over to the coffee maker.

United by arcane threads, shadows of leaf puppets leaped through the window and danced across the sun lit room, cheerfully displaying nature's morning mood as the wind blew softly through the trees outside.

Today, Sharon decided to get herself "mentally" back into the everyday grind, as soon as her hangover wore off anyway. Eight days in a hospital would be enough to make anyone forget where they had left off. Nevertheless, it was nice to finally be back home.

Although she had been discharged just yesterday, the memory of her stay was still worn just as thin as if it had already aged five years. Maybe she was still in a haze from all the pain medication that they had pumped into her, not to mention the alcohol she had consumed last night with her father.

Bubbling and burping, the coffee maker filled the kitchen with its heavenly aroma. Sharon massaged her scalp, rubbed her eyes, and then poured herself a cup of hot Java. Usually, cream and sugar were her preference, this morning however, she welcomed it as black as the coffee maker would allow; her brain needed a bit more coaxing than usual.

Walking over to the kitchen table, Sharon noticed a flashing light on her answering machine indicating that she had new messages. Ignoring it, she sat down at the table and slowly sipped her steaming hot coffee.

After she had reached the bottom of her coffee mug twice, she walked over to the machine and hit play.

Two of the five messages were from her art dealer. The first was to remind her of an auction that she had already missed. To this point she had completely forgotten about it. Perturbed, she couldn't believe that she had missed it while in the hospital. The second call was from the same gallery. Her dealer sounded excited. This time he had called to tell her that two of her paintings had sold twenty-three prints altogether. Hearing the message, Sharon's mood lifted drastically. This was great news.

When Sharon heard the voice on the third message, the first two calls were quickly disregarded as a slow-moving chill swept down her spine and settled in her abdomen.

"Hi, this is Jack Kurts. We met...well something like that, at Venice Beach. I feel a little funny calling you, and I know we didn't meet under the best of circumstances, but I'm having a hard time putting what happened behind me. I just wanted to get in touch with you and make sure everything is okay." Then, he had left a call back number.

Next there was a message from St. Francis hospital, something to do with her insurance?

The Watchful Eye

The last message was from her father. He had called to make sure she had made it home safely, claiming that she had had too much to drink and wasn't in a position to drive. Worried about her, he had tried to talk her into staying the night in one of the guestrooms. Even though she probably shouldn't have, Sharon had decided to go home so she could try to get a fresh start in the morning. After the recent events, she felt as though she needed to work at getting back into the swing of things.

After listening to all the messages, Sharon decided to call her father first. Without realizing that she had even picked up the phone, she was listening to the other line ringing. Before it was answered, she quickly hung up.

What was that? she thought. She didn't remember whose number she had dialed or even picking up the phone to dial for that matter. Last thing she knew was that she was standing in front of the phone, and then all of a sudden she was holding it to her ear waiting for someone to pick up. Sharon shook off a chill.

It was like someone or *something* had cut time in half, and then tied it back together with a piece missing. "Uh! Pull yourself together!" she said to herself at a loss for an explanation of what had just happened. She walked back to the coffee maker with her cup in hand.

After pouring her third cup of coffee and using it to wash down a couple of aspirin, Sharon made her way down the hallway of her three bedroom house to the bathroom where she could wash her face and hopefully wash away some of the haze that she had seemed to be in since her discharge from the hospital.

How embarrassing it would have been when the other party answered the phone and she didn't know to whom she was talking too, or why she had even called. Surely that party would think she had lost her mind. Was she losing her mind?

She had never been operated on before in her life and had never exposed herself to drugs of any kind in the past. She couldn't help but wonder if this was a side effect of all the pain medication she had been on.

In the bathroom, Sharon reached into the cupboard and removed a washcloth. With it she washed her face and the back of her neck with cold water. After thoroughly scrubbing away her drowsiness, she dried her face and hands on a soft fuzzy hand towel and returned to the kitchen.

Without much more thought she finished the remaining coffee in her cup and then again picked up the phone and dialed her father. On the third ring someone answered.

"Hello." The voice didn't sound familiar.

"Good morning," she said a bit hesitantly, "is John there?"

"No, I don't believe..."

"Oh forgive me," she cut in. *How could I have done it again?* she thought. "I'm sorry. I must have dialed the wrong number." She was about to hang up when the voice at the other end asked, *"Ms. Andrews?"*

His voice was soothing, but she still didn't know to whom she was talking.

"Yes...who is this, and how do you know my name?" She felt ridiculous asking those questions when she was the one who had actually called.

"This is Jack Kurts, I saw your name and number on my caller ID. How are you?"

She was as completely embarrassed as she had imagined she would have been only seconds ago.

"Oh, hello. I'm sorry, I thought I was calling my father's house but I must have dialed your number on accident." *That really sounded stupid!* she thought to herself. "I hope I'm not disturbing you this early in the morning,...how are you?" She not only felt awkward, but like a bumbling fool as well.

The Watchful Eye

"I'm fine. I've wanted to talk to you for a few days now, make sure everything's okay. How's your shoulder?"
He sounded genuinely concerned, which immediately put her at ease.

"Oh, I feel fine, it wasn't as bad as it looked. Thanks for helping me, by the way. Who knows what might have happened if you weren't there."

"Oh, it was nothing, I'm just glad I was able to."

"Well Mr. Kurts, that's a very modest opinion, spoken like a true hero."

"Most people would have done the same. I'm just glad to hear that you're okay. I was worried. After all, that cut on your shoulder looked pretty bad."

Sharon paused for a minute to collect her thoughts and then asked, "If you don't mind and have the time later today, I'd like to buy you lunch or maybe dinner. I know it's not much after what you did, but it's the least I can do to repay your kindness."

"Well, I don't believe I deserve the hero's special or anything. I'm sure anybody else would have done the same thing but that sounds like a wonderful idea, I'd love to have lunch with you. How about Getario's at twelve o'clock?"

"That sounds great. I'll meet you there. Thanks again Mr. Kurts."

"You're very welcome, and by the way, you can call me Jack. See you this afternoon."

Sharon hung up the phone confused.

She was almost certain that she had dialed her father's house. Not only that, but now that she thought about it, she couldn't even remember the number that Jack had left on her answering machine.

Not just once, but after what had just happened she was almost certain that she had called him both times. She had planned on talking to him later in the day, but after hearing his voice on her answering machine, it was almost as if her subconscious had dialed his number for her.

Sharon poured another cup of coffee and sat back down at the kitchen table to think it over, looked at the clock and then panicked. Unless the clock was wrong, she was to meet him in an hour and fifteen minutes. How could she have assumed it was still so early? She must be going crazy. There would be no more of those liquid painkiller evenings for a long time to come.

Rushing back to her room, Sharon fumbled through her closet trying to find the right outfit, climbed into the shower, and began to get ready for her lunch date. She would have to hurry in order to make it to the restaurant on time.

★★★

After ending the conversation with Sharon, Jack pulled into the parking lot at High Velocity Total Fitness. The huge fitness center stood four stories high and was packed with any and all the exercise equipment a health nut, including Jack could possibly dream of.

As soon as he walked in the front entrance, Nancy met his eyes with a buoyant smile bright enough to melt through a pair of Oakleys.

"Good morning Jack. How are you today?"

"Not bad thanks, and you?"

"So far so good!" she said.

At first, Jack had hired her not only because she was qualified for the job, but also because she was very beautiful, extremely fit, and seemed to have the confidence of all three Musketeers.

When potential clients entered the fitness center, having her at the front desk was an excellent marketing strategy. Either they would want to look like her, or simply just look at her. Whether it was the former or the later, both were good for business.

The Watchful Eye

In the three years following her start date, Nancy had never once missed a day of work or shown up the least bit tardy. In this Los Angeles day-and-age those qualities were extremely rare.

Looking at Nancy, Jack thought back to a few weeks after he had hired her. He had been pulling out of the parking lot on his way home when he noticed her walking away from her old beat down car. It looked quite hopeless with its two flat and totally bald tires. The other two were just as worn and wouldn't last much longer.

Feeling sympathetic, he had pulled over and offered her a ride. On the way to her house they stopped by her babysitter's to pick up her three-year-old daughter and from there he drove them home.

From the outside, the house looked as though it should have been condemned years ago. Weathered duct-tape held four of its five windows together. Two of them appeared to have been shattered by high-speed lead. The rest of the small house, although not as fragile as the shattered glass windows it struggled to maintain, was battered by life, rough and unforgiving.

Inside Jack sat on an "Antique," as she called it, tattered pink couch with stained stuffing peering from a seam where an old zipper had at one time proudly held it together. The carpet, or what was left of it anyway, was heavily stained and worn clean through in many places. Nonetheless, it couldn't have been any cleaner had it been brand new.

Sitting on the couch in front of a makeshift, cardboard box coffee table draped with a beautifully crafted homemade tablecloth, Jack had suggested helping take her car to the tire shop and getting all four tires replaced.

This idea, although constructive, was met with a look of layered emotions consisting first of shattered hope and then quickly smoothed over with pride.

Although she had tried to be tough, and was determined to make it on her own, the offer of help was enough to bring tears to her eyes. Heretofore, she had managed to hold her emotions together, but now, with the help of two flat tires, she wasn't able to maintain control of them any longer. She simply didn't have the money for tires.

Nancy had moved to LA with the father of her unborn child when she was eight months pregnant. They were both chasing dreams, only she had believed that they were doing it together.

Travis, her boyfriend of two years, had talked her into moving from Lafayette, Louisiana, where she held a successful job managing a small rent-to-own furniture store. He had told her repeatedly about his dreams of the two of them having a family together in sunny California where he would get a job as a stuntman for the movies and they would live happily ever after.

Although the pregnancy was an accident, a very irresponsible accident at that, Nancy had loved Travis with all of her heart and believed in him every bit as much. The thought of getting married as soon as they could afford it, and "making things right," as he had told her repeatedly, was eventually enough to coax her into draining what little savings she had in her bank account and finance a one way trip for two to the West Coast.

Shortly after they had arrived Travis found what he was looking for and was hired as a stunt double for a major motion picture. Soon after that, however, Nancy found herself abandoned, broke and only days away from delivering her child.

After having a daughter, whom she had named after her mother, Jennifer Amber, Nancy had somehow managed to stay on her feet. This proved to be an everyday battle.

She didn't have extra money at this point to replace or even fix the tires, yet she had to have her car in order to commute back and forth to work. Without a vehicle she wouldn't be able to bring home groceries, take her daughter to the sitter's house, or even to a doctor's office if the need

The Watchful Eye

arose. Without the use of a car, how would she possibly hold down the job that was required in order to break the cold, cruel cycle?

After talking a while longer, and trying to convince Nancy that everything was going to be all right, Jack informed her that she didn't have a choice but to let him help her with her car. "After all," he told her, "I need someone to watch the front desk and you were hired to do it. How are you going to do that without a car?"

The next morning, her car was parked in front of her house with four new tires, a full tank of gas, and a small note placed under the windshield wiper that read "Don't let the little things get you down. All of us need help once in a while."

Later that day, when questioned about the car, Jack had refused to be paid back for his kindness asking only that she return the favor in the future to another down on their luck.

Since then, she had been one of the best employees at the center and he couldn't help but carry a great deal of pride for her as a father might feel for his own daughter.

Not only was she grateful for his kindness, but she had worked hard to move herself and her child into a nice little house that was located in a much better neighborhood. She was, in Jack's eyes, one of the nicest, most responsible people he had ever met.

"I'll only be here a while. If I have any calls could you please take a name and a number?" he asked while continuing through the front lobby.

"Sure, I'll just put any messages I have for you on the board," said Nancy still smiling brightly.

"Thanks."

Walking across the ground level where all of the Nautilus equipment and free-weights were contained, Jack stopped to praise a few regulars on their physical progress. After chatting with them for a while, pumping their heads as big as their biceps, he walked over to the elevator, stepped in, and waited for the door to close.

Jack punched a seven-sequence code into the elevator's control panel using the four existing floor buttons. Then, all function buttons began to blink in unison giving him exactly six seconds to quote a phrase into the voice recognition system before the panel completed a reset program. As soon as he quoted his phrase and his voice pattern was verified as a match, the elevator shuttered and began its decent to the underground portion of the center.

This portion of the center was known by only two other agents and was not an available choice on the elevator control panel for customers or the center's staff for that matter.

Thirty feet below the fitness center stood an undercover U.S. intelligence unit called the American Freedom Agency.

Started as the first of fifteen units now established in the United States, High Velocity was nothing more than a cover for the agency founded by Congressman, Jonathan Morgan, less than five years ago.

After a congressional hearing, Mr. Morgan had accidentally happened upon a conversation, without being noticed, in a restroom occupied by two extremely powerful officials. They were discussing legislation that would eventually be put into place ensuring the American people a great loss of their rights as they knew them today. After witnessing the conversation and then piecing it together with laws that were in the process of being passed, an overwhelming fear brought the Congressman to the point of doing something about it.

Congressman Morgan told his story to an old friend, Frank Thomas. Frank happened to be the director of intelligence for the CIA. The two of them had been friends

The Watchful Eye

since Vietnam where they had both served their country proudly.

Congressman Morgan believed that many laws were being written with a completely hidden and evil agenda, laws that couldn't possibly be passed without the help of some extensive log rolling in the highest arenas of the government. These laws, if passed, would certainly pave the way for the destruction of democracy in a country he grew up in and had fought so hard to protect.

Together, after some exhausting research on the Director's part, the two of them had secretly started this new agency they called the AFA.

In the beginning, Congressman Morgan had opened the first three of the now fifteen units in the U.S. with the help of semi-illegal campaign contributions and a great sum of his own money. Never having taken illegal funding before in his life, the Congressman needed a great deal of money to break ground with this new organization, and if his assumptions were right, why not use funds intended to pass these horrible laws against the people who were trying to pass them.

The intentions behind starting the AFA were to develop an agency that would be able to work under the full power of the United States government, but would not be accountable for its operations as a governing body. It was an agency designed to keep tabs on big brother.

By dividing the organization into many small multitask units and then hiding those units within successful businesses like High Velocity, the AFA would be able to perform intelligence operations with complete self-funding capabilities. This allowed the organization the ability to conduct all of its operations without the burden of red tape while also allowing it the ability to function virtually undetected.

Furthermore, by splitting the agency into multiple three man units verses one large organization, the agency could function with little loss if evidence of a single unit's existence were discovered which would reveal the unit for what it really was. If so, the remaining units would still be able to function with little to no loss.

After deciding to put their plan into action, Frank Thomas, the Director of Central Intelligence, had recruited Jack. At the time, he was one of the CIA's best field agents.

Jack had started his career in the U.S. Navy where he had enlisted with hopes of becoming a Navy Seal. With strength to find courage and the courage to find strength, he had made the elite Seal Team with flying colors. Shortly after, he had been promoted to Gray Sail, a highly classified Seal detachment.

Upon being discharged from the service, Jack had been accepted into the CIA where he took part in collecting intelligence on foreign affairs. Three years later, Frank Thomas had approached him with an opportunity to do more for his country. Frank offered him a position running the AFA.

Eventually, with careful consideration, the Director, along with Jack's help, had recruited sixty-five highly trained government employees. Most operatives for AFA had been recruited from within the CIA, FBI and DEA.

When the elevator stopped and the doors opened, Jack stepped into the small meeting room. This room was well lit and quite comfortable as long as you didn't mind the absence of windows and the natural light that accompanied them. Four offices were connected to the meeting room via a short hallway, two on each side. The entire unit was completely concealed in the underground section of the fitness center.

Jack was the highest-ranking agent in the AFA and commanded the actions of all fifteen units. He worked under the direct orders of Frank Thomas, but was never aware that a single Congressman had started the organization or that one had anything to do with it

The Watchful Eye

personally for that matter. The Congressman, under the Director's strong suggestion, had been kept out of the loop for security purposes.

Jack sat down at his desk and looked over a few papers containing information that Don, his computer specialist, had delivered to him earlier that day. The papers contained important information that had been gathered from a sister unit currently in the process of monitoring foreign trade.

While looking over the paper work, a short three-burst alarm sounded as a red warning light flashed on the security control panel. A small monitor lit up showing the inside of the center's elevator compartment. The alarm sounded any time the lower level was accessed from the fitness center.

Jack looked over to the screen and saw Ted. Ted began working for AFA three months after the fitness center was established. He had been recruited from the FBI where he was assigned to the Foreign and Domestic Relations department. He specialized in interrogation of captured terrorists.

Jack, alongside CIA Director, Frank Thomas, had watched videos of Ted at work interrogating. Ted seemed as though he thoroughly enjoyed his cerebral though sadist type employment and was quite efficient at it as well. The Director had been very impressed and insisted on his recruitment.

Thinking back to the video and remembering the ease at which Ted had tortured his subjects, Jack couldn't help but feel somewhat disquieted in Ted's presence.

As a part of being recruited into the AFA, Ted had been promised the opportunity to interrogate for the agency some time in the future as creatively as he saw fit.

He was a large man, more than six feet tall and weighed around two hundred and thirty pounds. He was solid muscle. His face looked to Jack as though it had been chiseled from a block of concrete and most often was just as expressionless. His eyes boasted very mysterious irises that were dark brown in direct sunlight, however, in the slightest of shadows or even under manmade lighting for that matter, they were as black and cold as the pupils they imprisoned.

When Ted wasn't busy with work, which frequently took him many places in the world, or lifting weights in the center, he could usually be found with his head buried deep in a romance novel.

To Jack, Ted didn't seem capable of romance. When Ted actually spoke, which wasn't often, he said only what needed to be said, nothing more, nothing less. This also made Jack a little uneasy.

Ted wasn't stupid by any means, according to his IQ scores he was actually quite intelligent. For some reason, he just seemed to want to keep himself apart from any type of social connection at all. Jack believed Ted's mannerism to stem from some dark unspoken past.

The door opened and Ted stepped into the room.

"Eleven o' clock, right on the button," Jack said trying to pull some sort of expression from his flat affect co-worker.

"I'm never late sir, you can count on that," said Ted with less feeling than Jack had imagined he would get.

"I have some Intel' I need to deliver," Jack stated referring to the paperwork he had been looking over prior to Ted's arrival, "If Don pulls any updates you know how to reach me."

Jack stepped into the elevator and left the center.

He would make the drop providing the Director with his unit's latest findings, along with those of Unit Eights', and then meet Sharon Andrews for lunch.

Chapter Six

Not wanting to be late, Jack arrived at Getario's fifteen minutes early. Being punctual was an important quality that had been pounded into him early in life while in the military.

Getario's wasn't the finest Italian restaurant in Los Angeles, nonetheless, it was one of Jack's favorites. Its warm, cozy atmosphere lent a feeling of belonging, as if he and the business he had provided not only contributed to its success, but to its history as well.

As soon as Jack walked through the entrance, Ricardo spotted him and walked over to greet him with a smile. In black slacks and a crisp white shirt with its sleeves rolled up to his elbows, Ricardo blended in nicely with the restaurant's smooth but crisp Italian atmosphere. His short wavy hair was jet black without exception and slicked back neatly with the use of old-fashioned hair oil. In his early forties, he looked as though he had never wrestled a stressful day in his life. His calm, knowing essence showed the wisdom of his age, while his dark brown eyes still confronted life with a glimmer of youth's passion. Ricardo was not only the owner, but also the hardest working employee the restaurant had ever witnessed since he had opened it almost seven years ago. He was a well-respected man who took a great amount of pride in his restaurant and in giving his customers first class service.

"Hey Jack, it's nice to see you here today. How have you been?" He reached under the front counter in search of a menu.

"Never better. How's your family? Are they keeping you busy?"

Although Jack had never actually met any of them, he felt as though he personally knew every member of Ricardo's family. On several occasions throughout the last few years, he had sat through many conversations with the pleasantly mannered Italian fellow, listening to stories about his three children and his beautiful wife. Jack always enjoyed the time Ricardo spent at his table sharing stories about his family.

"Oh yes," he said with a smile followed by a forced sigh, "I have to come to work just to get a break from my boys. They're a handful."

Two years ago, after trying unsuccessfully to have their first child, Ricardo's wife had chosen to take fertility pills in a last and desperate attempt to conceive. Three months later she was pregnant with triplets, all of which were boys.

"You better grab two of those," Jack said referring to the menu Ricardo had taken from under the counter, "I'm going to be meeting a friend today."

Ricardo grabbed an extra menu and showed Jack to a cozy table in the corner of the restaurant. He poured two glasses of ice water and lit a small candle that had been sitting in the center of the table.

"Would you like anything while you wait for your friend?" Ricardo asked. He placed the burning candle back down on the table.

"No thanks, she ought to be here pretty soon," Jack replied looking at his watch.

The Watchful Eye

"She, huh?" Ricardo's thick black eyebrows raised inquisitively as he stood up straight and folded his arms in a resting position over his chest.

"Yes?"

"Attractive?"

"I suppose so."

"Suppose?" Ricardo replied mocking Jack.

"Yes, very attractive."

"Ah!" Ricardo smiled and showed even more interest in what he believed to be Jack's subtle guise.

"Been seeing her long?"

"No, we're just having lunch together."

"First date then?"

"No, just lunch. We're not dating."

"Interested?" Ricardo rearranged the neatly placed napkins and silverware.

Jack noticed a twinkle of amusement in Ricardo's eyes to go along with the slightly wayward curve at the edge of his smile. He shook his head in defeat and laughed at the Italian man's facetious prodding. "Is that garlic bread I smell burning in the kitchen?"

Smiling at Jack's effort for a distraction, Ricardo left well enough alone and asked if he could bring him something to drink other than the water.

"No thank you, I believe I'll wait."

"Good choice." Grinning, Ricardo walked off to take another customer's order.

Jack sipped the water.

Thinking about what had been said, Jack was relieved that he wasn't on a date. As few dates as he had been on in his life, he had never been able to tack down the whole dating etiquette thing. Besides, dating made him nervous. Most often, dates were less comfortable than a formal job interview. What do you do? Where do you live? What do you drive? On a few of his dates, he had half expected to be asked for a copy of his check stub. If so, his date would be able to study his potential earnings and verify his eligibility for round two.

He dried his sweaty hands on his napkin.

Jack enjoyed being in a woman's company and had plenty of female friends, but when it came to dating the rules between men and women seemed to change, brutally! He knew there were a lot of good women out there, but for some reason he hadn't been lucky enough to run across any of them.

Often, just being yourself wasn't good enough when it came to dating California women. Either you had to wear cologne that smelled exactly like money, drive nothing less than a beamer, or at least have produced a rock video or two. None of which Jack could say he had accomplished. He *was* successful in his own mind as well as happy, but he supposed that wasn't good enough for a dating resume. He made his living doing what he loved to do, and although most people would never know the extent of his role in protecting their way of life, he wouldn't change a thing even if he could. Throughout many years of service to his country he had acquired a great amount of pride in his accomplishments, regardless of the lack of public recognition. If he had made different choices throughout his life, the type that would have landed him his first million dollars, he would never date a woman that held him in that type of regard anyway.

He took another drink of water.

As he reached over to set the glass down, he looked toward the entrance and saw Sharon standing in the foyer. She was speaking with Ricardo and looked absolutely stunning. More so than he had remembered. He stood to meet her as Ricardo showed her to the table.

Upon noticing him, Sharon waved and smiled politely. With ease, she boasted more class and *"Je ne c'est quoi"* than a runway model. She was clad in a sophisticated ensemble that also managed to speak casual at the same

The Watchful Eye

time. She wore a crisp white, short sleeved, cotton V-neck blouse that accented an evergreen cotton, broomstick skirt. Matching green sandals revealed perfectly polished and manicured toes. Her silky blond hair was pinned back showing the delicate lines of her neck, while only a few select curls were allowed to cusp her beautifully sculptured face. Walking across the room, she carried herself with the grace of a lily as it slowly floated down a gentle summer stream.

"Good afternoon Jack, it's nice seeing you under more pleasant circumstances."

"It's good seeing you. You look lovely. How are you feeling?"

"I feel fine thanks to you"

Although Jack was a very confident man otherwise, he suddenly felt like a small child when looking into her eyes.

"Please, have a seat," he said as he stood and pulled out a chair for her.

"Thank you."

Sharon was flattered by his gesture. It had been a while since she'd been in the presence of a true gentleman.

After Sharon was comfortably seated, Jack walked back to his own chair and sat down.

"So, have you ever been here before?" he asked.

"No actually, I haven't. I've driven by several times but I never have stopped in. How's the food?"

"If you like Italian like I do, it doesn't get any better than this. Ricardo's the best cook in town."

For a moment, there was a slight, uncomfortable pause while Jack tried to think of what to say next. Sharon spoke first.

"Well Jack, what do you like to do for fun, besides run around town rescuing damsels in distress?" Even her voice was pleasant and naturally fit her polished demeanor.

"Actually, rescuing people is somewhat of a full time job. The pay isn't so great, but I get plenty of holidays while my cape and stockings are at the dry cleaners."

His joking reply, although he couldn't believe he had said it until after it had already passed his lips, was greeted with an ice breaking smile. Eyes included, Sharon's smile seemed warm enough to melt the entire North Pole and solve every water shortage in the history of the world. Jack, without exception, felt himself melting over the armrests and into the fabric of the very chair he was seated in.

Ricardo stepped over to their table. "Have you had a chance to look at the menu and decide what you'd like to eat yet Miss...?"

"Andrews," Sharon said smiling. She looked to Jack, "Do you have any suggestions?"

"Allow me," Ricardo said before Jack had a chance to reply. "Jack hasn't tried anything but our shrimp Alfredo since as long as I can remember, and it's not even our best dish."

"What is your best dish?" Sharon asked.

"In my opinion," he boasted, "it would start with a bowl of my famous Italian wedding soup, followed by veal parmigiana.

"That sounds wonderful." Sharon's reply was accompanied by another earth-warming smile.

Again, before Jack could say anything Ricardo added, "And one shrimp Alfredo!"

Jack laughed, "Sounds good to me."

"What would you two like to drink? Can I suggest a wine as well?"

"Actually, I think I'll have a beer," says Sharon declining the wine.

"I'll make that two," Ricardo cut in knowing that beer would be Jack's preference as well.

The Watchful Eye

With that, Ricardo walked away. Once he was well past Sharon's line of sight, however, he turned around and gave Jack his approval in the form of a thumbs up.

"You must come here often," she said after witnessing the way Ricardo had happily ordered his food and drink for him.

"Oh, at least a couple times a month. I love the food and Ricardo's a great guy. I guess he has me pegged, huh?"

The atmosphere was comforting, as were Sharon's warm beautiful eyes.

"So tell me Jack, what you do for a living?" She asked with genuine interest.

"I manage a fitness center. It's actually a nice place if you're into the health craze. If you ever feel like stopping in I could show you around. And you?" he added taking the focus off of himself, "What do you do? How do you like to spend your day?"

Ricardo returned bringing two frosted glasses filled to the rim with ice-cold beer. After he left, Sharon told Jack about her love of painting. Every since she could remember, she had loved to paint. Upon the completion of high school she had moved to Arizona where she enrolled at Arizona State University. Although her main interests were in art, she had majored in business. Nonetheless, by the time she graduated she had earned a few credits in art as well. After receiving her business degree, Sharon had somehow managed to end up working for a small struggling accounting firm. Accounting wasn't her dream job by any means, but it allowed her to spend a lot of time after work and on weekends painting. No matter where the rest of her life took her, she could always escape into a world of her own when she applied brushes and her imagination to canvas.

Three years ago, with a lot of coaxing from her father, Sharon had taken a few of her many pieces to an art show. Beyond her wildest dreams, one had sold and the other went to a gallery where it also sold a few months later. The first one was purchased by a local art collector who still has it on display in his personal gallery. Since then, her success had slowly built to the point that she had been able to quit her dead end accounting job and give her full attention to what she loved most.

"Really," Jack said with amazement, "it must be nice to be self employed?"

"I wouldn't say that. I mean it's nice, but I enjoy painting so much that I'm not sure I can call it work."

"What type of paintings do you do? Have I seen any of it?" Jack asked still fully entranced by her story of success and the oceanic swirl of her blue green eyes.

"Oil painting for the most part. Actually, two pieces of my work are at a gallery just two blocks from here. If you'd like, I can take you there after lunch. That is of course if you're interested?"

"I'd love to!"

Ricardo, with the help of one of his employee's, returned to the table carrying an enormous amount of food.

"Is there anything else I can get for the two of you, maybe another beer?" Ricardo asked referring to the two nearly empty glasses. They ordered another and Ricardo quickly returned with them.

While enjoying the delightful Italian meal, Jack and Sharon spent as much time talking as they did eating. Halfway through the meal, Jack excused himself from the table and left for the restroom. Sitting in the restaurant by herself, Sharon racked her mind trying to decide whether or not she had ever met Jack in her past. She couldn't get over that weird feeling of de'ja'vu.

While they were talking, sipping their drinks and waiting to be served, Sharon had paid very close attention to Jack's behavior. She had tried hard to determine what it was about this man that had caught her attention so drastically. As with hearing his voice on her answering machine, from the very minute she had seen him sitting at the table waiting for her arrival, she witnessed another unnaturally forceful feeling of having spent an important part of her past with him.

Even though she couldn't attach a time or place to the foggy memory, she was as sure of its past reality as she was about the fact that she goes to sleep every night and wakes up every morning.

She found him somewhat attractive, as well as extremely nice and polite, but she wasn't able to witness any key expressions or movements in his personality that might unlock her subconscious and allow the release of its blurred and detained memories. Although it was frustrating, she wasn't completely uncomfortable with these mysterious feelings. If anything she felt a strange sense of delectation in his presence.

She had also felt this way thinking about him while driving to the restaurant. It was like something a person might feel after spending large amounts of time with somebody they had, through time, learned to care a great deal about. In a way, it sort of felt like she was walking through her house in complete darkness. With one arm stretched out in front and the other stretched out to the side taking guidance from a wall, measured steps are taken slowly and carefully in an attempt to find, but avoid taking an open door face first. Whatever she was feeling, but not remembering from her past, was like her door in the dark. She wasn't frightened just because she couldn't see it, but she knew it was lurking in the dark somewhere and was eager, yet cautious, to find it. Whatever was nagging her subconscious, remained hidden.

By the time she saw Jack returning from the restroom, she had decided to try and explain the strange feelings she was having about him. Before he was halfway to the table, however, she quickly changed her mind for fear of sounding crazy.

Most likely, she was only feeling the way she was because he had risked his life for her. That was probably the best explanation. Jack was a true hero after all. He had risked his life to help her when most people would have fled in fear for their own lives and because of this, she was experiencing a new and different emotion. Without having ever experienced being rescued before, she might simply be mystified by the experience and not yet sure how to accept it.

The more Sharon thought about this new explanation, the more comfortable she felt with it. By the time Jack had sat back down at the table, she had managed to relax her mind and found that she felt very much at ease with her newest explanation.

The meal and conversation were both fabulous. As Jack had stated, Ricardo was a phenomenal Italian chef. However, before the meal was completely consumed, it lost its battle for interest to the power of conversation. Sharon and Jack both clicked well together and in no time at all, were enjoying each other's laughter and company like a couple of old friends.

Before long, Jack found himself asking about her shoulder and how she had been getting along after the attack. She simply denied any inconvenience, but remained on the same topic of conversation.

"What were those two guys after you for anyway?" she asked.

"I'm not sure"

"Do you know them?"

"No, I've never even seen them before."

"Well I sure hope they're in jail. People like that shouldn't be allowed to walk the streets."

"That's for sure," Jack said although he had not yet seen the report that Don had pulled from police records.

The Watchful Eye

"I picked up a police report after I was discharged from the hospital and according to it, they're going to be charged by the city."

Sharon seemed relieved that her presence wouldn't be necessary in a court room and that she wouldn't have to relive even one more moment of that situation.

"I'm glad that I don't have to testify. I spent eight days in the hospital trying my best to forget what had happened just so I could move on with my life without having to live in fear."

A splatter of confusion briefly struck Jack's face when he realized she had been in the hospital for seven days.

Noticing, Sharon asked, "Is something wrong?"

"Oh no," Jack said shaking his inward daze and focusing once again on Sharon. He thought about the day after the attack and how when trying to visit her at the hospital the very next morning, he was told that she had already been discharged.

"I'm sorry, I guess I was under the impression that you had only been in the hospital for a day?" he said thinking back to his short conversation with the nice old lady who wore thick bifocals and sat behind the receptionist's desk.

"Don't I wish! If that were the case, I wouldn't be so far behind on the piece I'm working on. I really wanted to have it finished and on display in the gallery last week."

Before long, the conversation shifted again and Jack had forgot all about his suspicion. The meal, atmosphere and company couldn't have been better. Jack wiped his hands on his napkin and asked one of the waiters for the bill.

"Wait a minute mister!" Sharon scolded. "This is supposed to be my treat, remember?"

"I'll tell you what, why don't you let me pay for lunch this time and maybe you can pick up the tab next time."

"Okay," Sharon said in response to the idea of a next time, "you have a deal. Are you still interested in a tour of the gallery?"

"If you're still up to it. I have to warn you though, I'm not very educated in the world of art so you might have to take a little extra time to explain what I'm looking at." With another one of her beautifully warm smiles Sharon replied, "I'd be honored."

After finishing their drinks, Jack paid the bill, left a gracious tip, thanked Ricardo for a wonderful meal and the two of them left the restaurant. Comfortable in each other's company, they walked over to the nearby gallery.

Cynicism; its commencement a seed undetectable by the naked eye. With roots as insidious and firmly planted as a willow tree embraces the earth with its knotted fingers. Cynicism ebbs and flows through the veins of its host growing steadily like a cancer changing forever the child its mother bore. An eccentric metamorphosis to fear and detest. A faltering in the human spirit resistant to celestial intervention and contagious to any porous and willing mind.

H.R.R.

Chapter Seven

At three o'clock in the morning, after only two hours of sleep, the charge nurse awakened Dr. Evans.

"Sorry to disturb you but I believe Mrs. Keens is finally ready."

"Okay, give me just five minutes," the doctor said wishing that his awakening was only a bad dream. Closing the door behind her, the charge nurse left the tiny break room.

This would be Dr. Evans' tenth delivery since twelve o'clock yesterday afternoon.

Somehow able to find the motivation, he peeled his saliva-crusted skin from the vinyl couch where he had been drooling during his short slumber, sat up, and slowly rubbed life back into his handsome young face. It had been a very long night.

Dr. Evans got up from the couch, straightened his scrubs and stepped into the small one-man bathroom adjoining the break room. A lone soda machine provided a soft steady hum accompanied by a small portion of light that hardly reached through the door of the restroom.

In his half-awakened stupor, he had to fumble for the light switch. When he finally found the switch and clicked on the bright overhead light, he was forced to squint. His tired green eyes fought to adjust and gain focus.

"Wow," he said admiring his reflection.

Looking in the mirror he saw exactly what he had expected to see looking back at him. Even while half-asleep, he was still great looking!

Twisting the handles, he turned on the faucet and waited for warm water. A few quick splashes were all it took to fully waken. Rubbing his whiskered face with wet hands, he wished he had enough time for a shave.

Again, he admired himself in the mirror while drying his face with a paper towel that he had pulled from the stainless steel dispenser mounted on the pale white wall. Strange, his five o' clock shadow seemed to enhance his looks making him somewhat alluring. Dr. Evans pointed to his reflection and winked at himself, "You, my man, are irresistible!"

Still ruffled, he combed his wet fingers through his sandy blond hair in an effort to smooth it out as best he could. Using the damp paper towel, he scrubbed the mild stench from his armpits. Unlike the great doctor himself, his deodorant had stopped working some time ago.

Without washing his hands, Dr. Evans headed over to delivery.

Screams could be heard from halfway down the hall. *Why did I have to go to medical school?* Dr. Evans thought to himself when he realized from behind which door the commotion was coming. *I should have been a plumber, maybe a mechanic. Electricians' don't have to take this kind of abuse! What is it about a full moon that fills the hospital to the rim with these crazy, screaming women?*

This night brought with it the havoc of a full moon. For some unknown reason, thought to be gravitational pull, a full moon encourages carrying women to go into labor. Tonight, the full moon's effects were most definitely apparent in the hospital, although it couldn't be seen through a window by many of its bed-ridden occupants.

Smiling, Dr. Evans entered the room with the skilled impression of a caring and concerned physician.

A nurse, Maggie Holsten, patted Mrs. Keens' forehead with a washcloth. Wet from the cloth and also from perspiration, strands of brown hair clung to Mrs. Keens' unusually large forehead making her appear even uglier to the doctor than he had previously determined. The nurse didn't look as though she was being driven half-mad by all the screaming and hollering. How could she stand it? As far as Dr. Evans was concerned, the patient was overacting due to some outrageous psychological disorder. Whatever she might have, it would definitely take the cake for best of show at the next hypochondriac convention. He wondered if there was such a gathering of idiotic people in this world somewhere? Probably!

Even if the screaming wasn't completely irritating, Mrs. Keens' deep and noisy exhalations stunk like a sulfur pit!

The nurse continued to pamper the patient, while the patient continued to scream. *Who would tire first?* he wondered. Most likely the nurse, after all, she wasn't as angelic as she appeared to be.

A few weeks ago, Dr. Evans had found Maggie extremely attractive. She had long wavy black hair with a clean silken luster, a smooth flawless complexion, straight white teeth that made her charming smile sparkle brilliantly and a body that most men would conquer worlds for. She was transcendently sensual, and without any effort, had seduced his heated desire to have her well past the boiling point, but that was a few weeks ago. Now, trying to find anything attractive about Maggie absolutely sickened him. Whenever it was possible, he found it best to completely avoid her, although lately she was making that harder and harder to do.

Lying in a bed of sweat soaked sheets, Dr. Evans imagined that Mrs. Keens looked very similar to that of a beached whale. Even though she was pregnant and fixing to deliver, the doctor couldn't see any reason why a woman would allow herself to get that big.

Nurse Maggie's soothing words and physical pampering seemed to go unnoticed. Dr. Evans looked at Mrs. Keens with a fraudulent smile. *Why can't you just shut up?* he thought to himself. He avoided making any eye contact with Maggie. As far as he was concerned she didn't deserve to be noticed.

Mrs. Keens, with all her ill-mannered screaming, easily lifted the fine hairs on the back of the doctor's neck. He imagined that her screams were probably similar to the squeals of a wild boar in heat.

Keeping a beautiful and perfect smile would have been hard work under these circumstances, if his smile weren't so beautiful and perfect.

"How are you doing Mrs. Keens? It looks like you're finally going to have this baby." *Baby wolverine I'm sure, considering the horribly pathetic sounds coming out of you!* he thought.

After hearing about as much of Mrs. Keens' ear shattering screams as he could stand, Dr. Evans occupied his mind by trying to determine what despising similarities both women had in common. With little time needed, he chuckled to himself as he came to a conclusion. The patient and the nurse both, although under completely different circumstances, scream like wild animals in bed; one in labor, and one during the throws of passion.

Still trying to avoid eye contact, he asked Maggie in the warmest, most affectionate voice he could muster, "How far is she dilated and how far apart are the contractions?"

The Watchful Eye

Maggie reported Mrs. Keens' condition while continuing her efforts to calm and relax the patient. He couldn't believe she spoke with self confidence like she actually believed her presence was appreciated and even worse, like he respected her out of ignorance for her self-degrading desires. *What a Slut!*

"Okay Mrs. Keens, we're going to make this as quick and painless as possible," he said with all the counterfeit concern he could muster. He did want it over as quick as possible, but could actually care less whether or not the procedure was painful.

"I just need you to relax and breathe. Don't push yet. I'll let you know when it's time." *Please lady just shut up!* he begged within his thoughts. *It's only childbirth. Don't get yourself pregnant if you can't handle it!*

Dr. Evans couldn't think of anything more pleasant than leaving the room and its occupants right this very minute. How he wished he could get away from this bellowing woman and her tarty little bald-faced nurse. Without crowning first however, pushing could possibly kink the infant's vertebrae and damage its spine. After less thought about the baby's safety than for his own desires, he quickly decided that it was a chance he was willing to take.

"Okay Mrs. Keens I see the crown," he lied, "take a deep breath and push." The lady's screams seemed to crescendo to the level of a would be holocaust. *Somebody gag her please!*

While trying to deliver the baby, Dr. Evans imagined that he could feel the nurse Maggie's hungry stare. Although he couldn't blame her for still wanting him as badly as he knew she did, it completely nauseated him. As hard as he tried, he couldn't recall what he had actually seen in her.

Dr Evans had been completely fascinated with Maggie shortly after she had started working at the hospital more than three weeks ago. She was quite professional at her job, and absolutely gorgeous. In his opinion, she had needed a man like him to appreciate her.

Now, after he had talked her into having dinner with him and then into his bed, she was no longer a thing of interest or beauty. She was nothing more than an old used sock. Just like the rest of them, she had tarnished herself with her desires. Glancing over at her, he couldn't find a single ounce of the beauty he had once seen.

"Keep pushing, you're almost there!"

With one final push the baby was delivered into the Dr. Evans' hands. *There are you happy? Somebody please take this stupid kid so I can wash this filth off of me!* "Mrs. Keens, you're the proud mother of a beautiful baby girl."

After starting the baby's respiratory system by smacking her bottom and back a little harder than was necessary and then using a cut and clamp kit to sever the umbilical cord, Dr. Evans gave the baby to the used up nurse for suctioning and routine APGAR testing. He was finally able to leave the room and did so without speaking another word to either the patient or the nurse.

★★★

Dr. Evans had graduated medical school with honors five years ago at the young age of twenty-nine. Since then he had grown to hate his job. Money and his heightened luck with women after becoming a doctor were the only reasons he continued his work in the grueling medical profession. He just didn't have the compassion for patients that was required to enjoy the job, and day by drawn out day it was becoming harder to fake.

After cleaning up and changing scrubs, Dr. Evans decided to pay a visit to the nursery. He put on his lab coat, reached into his pocket and pulled out a key to his desk.

The Watchful Eye

From the locked drawer he took out a small cooler that he carried to and from work as his lunch box. Inside, it contained twenty small inoculation pens and an ice pack.

Two years ago, Dr. Evans had been sued for a caesarian section that had resulted in the death of the infant. It had cost him two and a half million dollars to settle out of court. He didn't have the money to settle without claiming it on his malpractice insurance, but couldn't afford to proceed to court and chance losing his insurance along with his license to practice. At this point, only he was aware of what had actually caused the infants death and feared that the truth would be revealed if he couldn't settle the matter soon. He had needed to come up with the money somehow!

Shortly after, his prayers were answered when he received a call from his lawyer.

"I have a suggestion on how you can pay your new debt. Come into my office at one thirty and bring an open mind."

Any idea would have been worth listening to and Dr. Evans at that point had been desperate. He had arrived at the law firm at one-thirty as instructed. From there, he had been taken into a conference room where he was immediately uncomfortable in the company of its occupants.

Four men occupied the room including his lawyer. One of them, an older looking man with gray hair and bluish-gray eyes, was seated at a conference table. He carried a knowing look on his face, and at first glance, gave a strong impression that he was a man of importance, a man with great power. And those eyes, Dr. Evans would never forget those eyes as long as he lived. They overflowed with confidence and vaunted too much intelligence. He felt completely exposed under the glare of the confident stranger's almost ghost-like eyes.

The other two men stood at attention. They were directly behind the stranger and Dr. Evans' lawyer who was also seated at the table. They both wore black, military type uniforms. If not for the color of their hair and a few minor facial features, they could have been mistaken for twins. They were both dressed identically and also carried the same blank stare on their faces. The doctor felt his skin crawl every time he glanced over at them.

"Have a seat Mr. Evans," said the older man pointing to a chair across the table from where he himself was sitting. The lawyer, looking somewhat nervous had started to make introductions and was immediately cut short.

"There's no need to exchange names. Have a seat Mr. Evans." After the second recommendation to sit down, one of the men standing at attention behind the table gave the doctor a threatening look insinuating that the offer to sit was an *order* to be taken seriously. Dr. Evans quickly took a seat.

"I'll be frank with you Mr. Evans, I don't care anything about you. I do know however, that you're having some financial difficulties and I believe I can help you. Well, let's just say we can help each other."

"What do you know about my finances and why would you want to help me?" the doctor asked with skepticism. The elderly man stared intently at Dr. Evans for a few seconds.

"I work for the government Mr. Evans." He opened his wallet and flashed an ID that looked very official and was stamped "Department of the Surgeon General."

"I have a proposition to make. If you help us, the government of the United States will help you." Then he continued to inform the doctor of his expectations.

The Watchful Eye

After listening to the proposal Dr. Evans stated, "I can't agree to this! I would lose my license for sure if I did this for you!"

"If you don't feel like participating Mr. Evans, I would completely understand," the man said with contumelious intent. "However," his voice picked up a threatening tone, "very bad things would happen to you if you don't. You could very possibly end up bankrupt and ruined financially to the point of a begging, pathetic, vagrant. Or how do you think you might feel on Death Row? Can you see yourself convicted of a murder you didn't even commit?" He turned in his chair to look at one of the large men standing behind him. "How do you think he'd look in a straight jacket?"

"I believe he'd look rather nice Sir," the mechanical-minded man replied.

Staring deep into the doctor's eyes, as if he had found the most direct path to his fear infested soul, the gray-haired man continued, "How about spending the rest of your life drugged and in an asylum for the mentally insane. Tell me Mr. Evans, does that fit into your ten-year plan?"

"Are you crazy? You can't do this!" Dr. Evans looked to his lawyer, "Phil are you a part of this preposterous scheme?" With a glum look on his face and remaining silent, the lawyer lowered his eyes in shame and looked away.

"Not only can I do this, but I will. Your life means nothing to me and if you think I'm going to let you walk out of here with the information you've already been given, you really do belong with the insane...It's an easy choice to make Mr. Evans. We're willing to pay the remainder of all your debts, student loans, your house payment and your lawsuit, in exchange for your cooperation. It's either that or destroy you. I could care less either way."

Dr. Evans couldn't believe the trap in which he had walked into.

"I need an answer now Mr. Evans!" With that, the gray-haired man made a gesture to the two men standing behind him.

"Would you two please help him make up his mind, I'm in a hurry!"

Before the doctor could react, the two men grabbed a hold of him and slammed him on the table so hard that he was almost sure he wouldn't be able to walk out of the room on his own accord.

"I need an answer Mr. Evans!"

"Okay, okay, I'll do it!"

After receiving the answer he knew he would get, the stranger reached into his jacket and retrieved a small black inoculation pen.

"This is our little insurance policy. Don't screw with me Mr. Evans." He jammed the pen into the doctor's shoulder and squeezed the trigger.

"Click!"

Looking at the two men holding Dr. Evans, but talking to himself in satisfaction, he smiled an evil smile and said, "Gentlemen, we're now the proud owners of another new doctor."

Since that day, Dr. Evans had been taking care of business as assigned.

★★★

He removed ten black pens from the cooler and then made his way to the nursery.

"Hello Dr. Evans. How are you this morning?" a nurse said to welcome him as he walked into the large infant-populated room.

"It's been a very long night but I feel great. You look as lovely as ever. How are things coming along in here?"

"All the little cuties are asleep right now, can you believe it?"

The Watchful Eye

Lisa Hayes was an attractive young woman with a well-developed figure. Although the nursery demanded her constant attention, she always enjoyed her job and loved taking care of the infants. It was something she had wanted to do ever since graduating high school.

"Looks like you've been really busy lately. I imagine you're just exhausted after all of these deliveries."

Lisa had a beautifully seductive smile that was enhanced by the hungry gleam in her eyes. There was no doubt in his mind that she wanted him. Even though she was probably just far too classy or maybe even a little too naive to act on it, he didn't let her innocent act fool him for a minute.

Lisa was the girl for him. He imagined losing himself in all of her beauty.

"I could use a full day in bed, that's for sure. How about you?" He made sure there was a slightly provocative hint in his voice.

"Well, I'm sure all of these beautiful babies appreciate all of your hard work." Lisa said as though she didn't recognize his desires.

She was exactly what he needed even though she was obviously playing hard to get. If he didn't know any better, he would have thought she wasn't interested in him. The chase, however, would only make the catch more intense and the thought of that pleased him immensely.

Dr. Evans watched Lisa bend over to coo at one of the newborns and began to get aroused. He knew she found him attractive and wouldn't be able to resist his great looks and charm for long. All women found him attractive and she too would soon be one of his new play toys.

"Lisa, I need you to go down to the pharmacy with this prescription and pick up some antibiotics for the Keens' baby. It looks like she's getting an eye infection and I don't want to take any chances. I'll keep an eye on all of the little tykes for you while you're gone."

"Okay, make sure you take good care of all my little sweethearts."

"Oh of course, they are our future you know."

As soon as Lisa left and the door had closed behind her, Dr. Evans removed the pens from his lab coat and began inoculating the babies. He was very careful to use aseptic technique, knowing that he couldn't afford to leave any evidence behind in the form of irritation or infection.

"Welcome to your New World you little bastards!" he laughed to the now crying babies.

Dr. Evans quickly jotted down their mothers' names and social security numbers, then the inoculation number along with the infants' sex.

He looked at the Keens baby, and then at another little girl that had been delivered that same morning and chuckled with his new idea of entertainment. Within a few minutes he was able to switch the two babies along with their identification bands.

"If you ever get a chance to meet your real mother, tell her the good doctor says hi."

Dr. Evans had just finished the switch when the door opened and Lisa walked back into the nursery. Upon entering, she immediately began trying to comfort them.

"What happened? Why are they all crying?"

"I'm not sure," he lied. "Either it's close to feeding time or I said something offensive. Anyway, I'll leave you alone with them, maybe you can figure it out?"

"What about the Keens baby?"

"What about her?" Dr. Evans asked nervously.

"Can I get you to help me with the eye medication? It sure would make things easier."

"Sure, I have ten more minutes before I'm due to make my rounds." Dr. Evans replied with relief.

As Lisa focused on medicating the infant's eyes, Dr. Evans focused on her cleavage and thoughts of what she might be capable of doing to him.

The Watchful Eye

After the wrong baby was medicated, he left the nursery whistling contentedly.

Chapter Eight

Never really having taken time in the past to enjoy art, or even understand it for that matter, Jack was not in a position to be a critic. Regardless, he knew enough to understand that Sharon's work was good enough to be sought after. She was by no means struggling to swim her way up from beneath the starving cesspool of artists who were constantly striving to make a name for themselves.

"Wow! This is beautiful," he said looking at one of Sharon's paintings. He wasn't simply trying to be nice, as far as he could tell it was an exceptional piece of work.

The painting was labeled, "Wink." The portrait was of a man, woman, and a small child sitting at the grassy edge of a pond. Laughing, they were having a picnic under the warm midsummer sun while feeding a small group of waddling ducks.

Although the portrait was oil based and on canvas, its likeness to life was astounding. From a distance, it could very well have been mistaken for a professional photograph blown up to three times its size.

"This is amazing!" Jack stared at the portrait and then at Sharon. "How long have you been painting?"

"I've always enjoyed it. Every since I can remember I've had a brush in my hand with who knows what color on it. I love to paint the things I find interesting while trying to portray a feeling."

Jack studied Sharon's subtle movements, her smile, and her glimmer of pride as she looked at her own portrait hanging on the wall. Watching her, he witnessed an overpowering emotion glowing from within her soft, but dazzling green eyes.

As she looked at the portrait, Jack knew she was remembering its creation. Who else but the artist could actually understand the deep, heart felt feelings it must have taken to create it. Only the artist can understand those it was truly meant to portray.

"What about this one?" he asked referring to "Wink." "Do you know these people?"

"Actually," she said somewhat hesitantly, "it's how I remember my family from when I was a small child."

After a comfortable silence they walked slowly through the gallery together appreciating the art on display along with each other's company.

Before they had finished, a tall, slender man approached. Sharon introduced him as her dealer Sam. He appeared to be in his mid to late forties. Jack recognized the man's crisp dark toupee first thing while shaking his hand. At a glance Jack had determined that this man carried himself in high regards but would swoop down in an instant to kiss the feet of anyone who controlled large amounts of money or power. His eyes were dull blue in color as if they had lost their sharpness throughout many years of focusing on himself, rather than taking the time to see the beauty in the world around him.

When Sam realized that Jack was of no importance in the art industry, he quickly removed his hand, turned up his nose and then focused his attention on Sharon. He wasn't

The Watchful Eye

the least bit inconspicuous in his attempt at completely ignoring Jack thereafter.

"Where were you Sunday?" Sam asked referring to the art show that she had missed. "I looked for you all day and couldn't help but worry about you when you didn't show up."

"I'm sorry Sam. I should have at least called to let you know I wasn't going to make it. I had a few personal problems to deal with and was so wrapped up in them that I completely forgot."

"Really," Sam said with renewed interest. "What happened?"

"Oh just personal stuff, nothing I'd want to bore you with." Knowing he would insist, she quickly changed the subject. "By the way, do you have any paperwork for me?"

"As a matter of fact I do," Sam said with a half-hearted smile. Although he tried not to show it, he was obviously dissatisfied with her objection to telling him about her personal matters. He turned and walked away.

"He's a little strange," Jack claimed hoping his comment wasn't out of line.

"Yes, but he's a highly acclaimed dealer and he manages to sell a lot of my work." Sharon felt bad about brushing Sam off the way she did, but knew he would insist on hearing every gory detail of the attack. Then, he would probably make a big scene throughout the gallery. Sharon had learned a long time ago to keep things as short and sweet as possible when working with Sam.

In no time at all Sam rounded the corner with a hand full of paperwork and two envelopes.

"Today is a good day Ms. Andrews. I have extra paperwork to be signed, *and*, an extra envelope for you."

"Extra, what do you mean?"

"Well," he said handing her the paperwork. "I need you to sign for the prints we sold at the art show, and I'm also going to need a signature for the original we sold this morning."

Jack immediately felt Sharon's excitement level rise. She looked over at the wall where her second piece should have been hanging, and noticed that it had been replaced.

"That's wonderful news. Are you going to be able to take in another one?"

"Absolutely," Sam said. "If your work keeps selling like it has been, you'll be our best client. How soon will you have your next piece ready?"

"I'm almost done now. I can probably have it finished in a few more weeks." She looked at Jack and in her excitement, gave him a hug. "I can't believe I sold another piece so soon."

Sharon's hug caught Jack off guard. After signing and returning the papers, Sam handed her the two envelopes. Each one contained a check. One was for the sum of her percent of the prints that were sold, and the other was for the original.

"Thanks Sam. I appreciate all that you've done for me." Sam smiled and said the nicest, most genuine thing she had ever heard come out of his mouth; "Your work is good. You deserve this Ms. Andrews." With that, he turned to walk away. Jack stuck out his hand. "It was nice to meet you." Sam simply looked at Jack's outstretched hand and kept his own crossed in front of himself while holding on to the paperwork. "Likewise." He turned around headfirst and left.

"Wow," Jack said in astonishment. "I believe I've just met the rudest subspecies of human this planet has to offer."

"He's not so bad," Sharon replied.

"No?"

"No, not at all. If you want to escort me to an art show sometime in the future, I could introduce you to a few people that make him out to be rather sweet."

The Watchful Eye

"You've got to be kidding. There's people ruder than Sam?"

"Plenty of them. Didn't you know that the art business is crawling with them? What do you say, are you up for it?"

After she had already asked, Sharon began to wonder if she was being a little too forward. She wasn't in the practice of asking men to go out with her, and to top it off, an art show meant formal wear and probably dinner.

"I'm always up for something new and interesting, but there's conditions that apply."

"And those would be?" she asked smiling.

"Protection. I'm going to have to have your promise of protection from people like Sam and his mentors."

"You? Protection? I saw what you're capable of Mr. Fu Manchu. Don't tell me that you're frightened by someone like Sam. I'm not even scared of him."

"Yeah but that's you, I get a little frightened around those starched white collar guys."

"Oh quit Mr. tough guy," she said giving him a gentle nudge with her elbow.

Jack laughed, "Okay now, who am I? Mr. Manchu or Mr. Tough? Do I need to introduce myself again?"

The playfulness in the conversation was refreshing. Sharon couldn't remember the last time she had been in the company of an attractive man that had a great sense of humor as well.

There was that eerie feeling of being involved with him sometime in her far past, at least when she thought about how she had felt prior to formally meeting him anyway. Now, after spending time with him and getting a chance to know him, she was extremely comfortable in his presence, almost too comfortable. Maybe she *had* known him, or maybe he was what some people referred to when they talk about a soul mate.

That wasn't it. Sharon didn't believe in soul mates or destiny. Destiny was what you made of it, nothing more, nothing less. What would be the purpose of living if our lives had already been planned out? If all life on earth is predestined, then the beginning, middle, and end have already been accomplished. If so, what would be the point to living in the now. At least that was how she felt although she couldn't explain the de'ja'vu.

Whatever the reasons for her feelings, she decided to keep them to herself. First of all, she couldn't even explain how she was feeling to herself, much less to a man she had just met. Second, he'd probably think she had lost her mind. Whether she had lost her mind or not, being in Jack's company felt right and the best thing she could do for herself at the moment was to flow with it.

"Hey, where did you go?"

"Huh, what?" Sharon opened her eyes to find herself in Jack's arms.

"Are you okay? You looked like you were about to pass out."

"I'm not sure, what happened?" Sharon asked looking frightened. A minute ago she was walking through the gallery talking with him and laughing. She remembered nudging him in the ribs with her elbow and thinking about how much fun she was having with him. Then, like earlier today in her kitchen when she had been trying to call her father, a piece of time seemed as if it simply disappeared. How did she get into his arms? Jack helped Sharon over to a bench where she would be able to sit down.

"You were laughing and giving me a hard time and then all of a sudden your eyes glazed over and got,...I don't know,...kind of a blank look to them. Before I knew it you were headed for the floor so I caught you."

"Thanks." In her confusion, Sharon was at a loss for words.

"Why don't you sit down and I'll get you a glass of water or something cool to drink."

The Watchful Eye

Sharon looked around the gallery and noticed Sam watching them. He looked like he was about to come over and find out what all of the fuss was about. She really didn't feel like dealing with him at the moment.

"It's okay. I feel fine. I'm ready to go. Can we just leave?"

Jack noticed Sam as well and understood her desperation. With his arm around her, he walked her out of the gallery.

Outside, the air felt crisp and refreshing. On the short walk back to Getario's Italian restaurant, where Sharon had parked her car, the conversation was minimal.

Jack wanted to talk more about what had happened. He couldn't help but worry about Sharon. The way she had blanked out and became so expressionless was like nothing he had ever witnessed before. Something was wrong and he felt a need to know what it was. Knowing that she was embarrassed and not wanting to talk about it any further, he decided to let it alone.

As they approached Sharon's car, she stopped to face him.

"I really had a wonderful day Jack. Thank you."

"Are you going to be okay? Do you feel weak or dizzy?"

"No I'm fine. I think I need to go home and relax for a while. It's been a rough week."

"Are you sure? I can take you to the hospital if you want me to. I don't mind at all."

"Yeah I'm sure. I just left that place two days ago. If something else was wrong with me, I'm sure they would have told me. I think I need to go home and soak myself in a hot bath, and then get a good night's sleep. By tomorrow I'll be much better."

Jack pulled out a business card for the fitness center and wrote his cell and home phone numbers on the back.

"If you need me, don't hesitate to call."

"Thanks. By the way, did you hear me? I said I had a wonderful day."

Jack's reply was a little more serious than she had expected, but nice. He was still worried and she felt flattered.

"I had a really nice time too. You're going to call if you need anything right?" He handed her his business card.

"I already told you it's nothing that a bath and some sleep won't take care of, but I might call you just to talk."

"Well if you don't, I'll be calling you."

"You're sweet," she said and then leaned in and gave him a small kiss on his cheek.

Sharon reached into her purse and retrieved her keys.

"I don't think you should be driving. Why don't you let me drive you home?"

"That's awfully nice of you," Sharon said realizing his honest intentions, "but then how will you get home?"

Jack thought about it for a while trying to come up with the best solution. He would drive her home and then take a taxi back to the restaurant to pick up his car. When he explained the idea to Sharon she hesitated and then told him he was going through too much trouble for nothing.

"It wouldn't be any trouble at all. Besides, I'd have a much better day knowing that you made it home safely."

"Do you ever stop being the perfect gentleman Jack Kurts?"

"I really want to do this. Will you let me drive you home?"

Again she hesitated.

"Sure, but I don't see what you're so worried about. I feel fine."

Sharon handed Jack her keys and walked around to the passenger side. Actually, she was thankful that Jack had insisted on driving her home. Twice today she had lost what she thought to be a small piece of time. When she had blanked out at home on the phone, she had tried to blame it

The Watchful Eye

on residual side effects of the drugs that had been pumped into her at the hospital. If not, she might have been able explain it in the form of a hang over. Maybe she had a head rush from standing up too fast, although deep down inside she had known that not to be the case.

Now, after the incident at the gallery, she was quite positive that something was happening that she couldn't blame on medication, alcohol or gravity.

She still halfway wondered if she was going crazy, but now she also had to consider more extreme possibilities like a tumor, a stroke, or maybe even some form of seizures. Young and healthy, she knew there were probably more likely causes for what she was experiencing, however, she couldn't think of any at the moment. She was frightened.

What if she blanked out while driving home and happened to get into an accident? She would never be able to forgive herself for blatantly harming another human being, or even worse a small child.

Jack followed her around the car and opened her door. As he walked back around to the driver's side, she watched him through the windshield and was thankful for his pure and honest kindness.

After they had pulled out of the parking lot, Jack was about to call a cab company to make sure he would have a ride waiting for him at her house when his phone rang.

"Hello this is Jack." Don was waiting on the other end.

"Jack you're not going to believe this!"

"Believe what?"

"I shouldn't tell you over the phone. How soon can you get here?"

"It'll be a while. Can you meet me somewhere else instead?"

Jack asked Sharon for her address and then relayed it to Don. Without saying anything else Jack hung up.

When Jack and Sharon pulled into her driveway, Don was parked by the curb and waiting in his car. He looked impatient. Before Sharon got out of the car, Jack placed his hand on her arm to get her attention.

"I'm glad you had a wonderful day, so did I."

Sharon flashed her beautiful smile that spread itself across her face and then remained entrapped in her dazzling green eyes.

"You are a wonderful gentleman Jack. Thank you for taking care of me."

"You're welcome. Why don't you get some rest and then call me and let me know how you feel." Again she leaned over and gave him a kiss. Her soft lips lingered slightly on his before she pulled away.

Getting out of the car, they walked over to where Don was parked and still waiting in his. After introducing the two of them, Jack got into the passenger seat and they drove away.

Chapter Nine

Although the smile smeared across Don's face made him look like a young child that had just seen something he wasn't supposed to, he waited until Sharon's house had vanished from his rearview mirror before he spoke. Seeing his smile, Jack already knew what Don was thinking. It was obvious that he could hardly wait to express those thoughts.

"Just want to make sure she's all right, huh?"

Don couldn't wipe the smile off his face, and furthermore, was unable to resist the opportunity to harass Jack. Jack on the other hand, tried to remain as expressionless as he possibly could.

"I told you already. It's not like that. She offered to take me lunch and I accepted."

Don's grin broadened. "Well if it's not like that, how did you end up at her house with her lipstick all over you?"

Jack reached up and pulled down the visor so he could inspect his face in the mirror. There was nothing there. Don laughed. Trying not to fuel the fire, Jack changed the subject.

"Isn't there something else we need to be talking about?"

Even though Don had caught a glimpse of his boss smiling while thinking about Sharon and what had just happened, he let the whole thing slide.

Jack told Don where he had left his car and then listened as Don explained what he thought to be a huge stride for their agency.

According to Don, he had been doing his usual job sitting behind his massive computer system and scanning through anything that might be of interest to their organization. Without being able to find much, Don decided to take his lunch break. After warming his food in the microwave, he went back into his super high-tech office and decided to take care of some personal business.

"By the way, I hope you're not angry. I know I'm not supposed to have food and drink in there," Don said referring to the very expensive equipment that made up his office. "Ted already chewed my ass. I'm sure you'll hear all about it when we get back." Don shifted in his seat with the pretense of being lopsided.

For a few years now Don had been sponsoring a smile child from Kenya through one of the many children's relief programs. During lunch, he had decided to check for any new information that might have been posted. Sometimes the site contained news about improvements in his child's health and well being. That's when he saw it. A small glitch. Nothing about this glitch had anything to do with his job, but because of who he was and his love for computer programs, he took it upon himself to fix it. Then he realized it wasn't a glitch at all. It was actually a doorway to a high tech program called the Watchful Eye.

"What's that?" Jack asked.

"I'm not sure. It might be a legitimate military program, but then why would they hide it behind the facade of a children's relief fund?"

"What else did you find?"

The Watchful Eye

"That's it. I got out of the program as quickly as I could. I wanted to have your approval before I continued any further just in case it was legitimate. I don't want to chance blowing our unit out in the open by making a mistake and setting off a defense mechanism that would land the Delta Force on our front porch with bazookas pointed up our you know whats."

"Well, you did the right thing by talking to me first. If it is a military program, especially being hidden the way you say it is, I'm sure we would have been informed of it by now. What do you think, you're the computer genius?"

"I was hoping you would ask me that."

Don started explaining his thoughts. Although it seemed at a glance to be stacked with major security measures, he didn't believe it to be the military. Government yes, but not property of the U.S. Armed Forces.

The military wouldn't have any purpose in hiding a program where it could be accessed by outside lines. They would definitely use a closed system that could only be accessed by their own personnel. They do have weapon systems that are susceptible to outside interference, but in those instances there is always an extensive amount of research done to reduce the parameters down to the very bare minimum and still maintain a highly operational system.

This program was set up with the intention of being accessed by remote network. That's why it had a hidden doorway. The only reason behind that doorway, the one that appeared as a glitch in another program, was a security measure to the operator in order to prevent a lockout.

Don explained it to Jack as an entrance into the program that wasn't known by the employee's in charge of running it, whoever those employees might be. It was put there as a last resort, a means of overriding the program with the intentions of shutting it down or destroying it from an outside line if ever it fell into the wrong hands.

Don pulled into Getario's parking lot and parked beside Jack's car.

After thanking Don for picking him up at Sharon's house, which earned him a devilish smile accompanied by a few more teasing remarks, Jack got into his own car and followed Don back to the fitness center. There he could have a first hand look at this Watchful Eye.

Entering the center, Jack took a couple minutes to mingle with the regulars. Then, he rode the elevator down to the underground portion of the building where Don would be waiting for him.

When the doors opened, Jack noticed Ted sitting in the meeting room reading one of his romance novels. Ted looked up from his book in surprise. "What are you doing here? I didn't think we'd see you till sometime later on this evening."

"Something came up that need's my attention," Jack replied. He found it odd that Ted would question him as to when he entered and left the building.

"Is it something I can help you with?" Ted asked.

"No not really. I just need to look over some paperwork that Don received from Unit Eight," he lied, "nothing that would interest you I'm sure."

Jack felt that his employees were on a need to know basis and expected that both Don and Ted understood this. He also found it odd that Ted would ask to be involved in something that the two of them were working on, when normally he chose to keep completely to himself.

"I'm probably going to be going over those documents for quite some time. If you want, why don't you go up stairs and get a workout, or go out and get a bite to eat if you haven't already."

The Watchful Eye

"Are you sure you guys' don't want some help? I don't mind besides, I don't have anything better to do." Ted seemed insistent on helping.

Jack didn't want to discourage him from trying to be a team player, but couldn't ignore his work ethics either. Not only that, but this new program Don had found might be something of huge importance. If it was and he involved Ted, he would be breaking protocol even though they both worked for the same organization.

In the event it was important, Jack was to report his findings directly to the Director, Frank Thomas. From there, the Director would decide whether or not other members of the organization would require this information based on how helpful it would be to the organization as a whole.

"No we're fine. I appreciate your offer, but you'd probably be bored as hell. I know I'm going to be!"

"You're sure?" Ted insisted. Jack smiled. "If we need any help, I'll be sure and beep you." Ted didn't say anything else. He turned to the next page in his book and picked up where he had left off. With that, Jack walked down the hall to Don's office where he knew Don was already at work and let himself in.

There was an extra chair already in front of one of the many monitors next to Don. "Have you found anything yet?" Jack asked.

Don was staring at the screen in front of him and appeared as though he hadn't heard the question. Then he pointed to the monitor abruptly.

"There! Did you see that?" Jack only saw pictures of some poor malnourished children in what looked to be Somalia. "No, what am I supposed to be looking at?"

Don looked excited to be sharing his world and the knowledge he had of that world with Jack. Again he pointed to a spot on the monitor and looked at his stopwatch. "I wanted to start at the very beginning and show you the doorway in six...more...seconds...There! Did you see it that time?"

Jack still didn't see anything other than the pictures he was intended to see.

Don kept an eye on his stopwatch while he explained briefly how the glitch worked and that it wrapped around to repeat itself every sixty-three seconds.

"How could I have missed this? I check on my child at least once every couple of months. I mean it is small and hard to see after all, but I bet I've looked at this repeating doorway at least a hundred times. I should have noticed it a long time ago."

Jack couldn't help but laugh. "You've got to be kidding me, I've literally had it pointed out for me and I still haven't seen it!"

Don kept checking his stopwatch and talking to himself, "I can't believe it's been under my nose all this time and it's probably exactly what we've been looking for!"

Jack was about to ask how the doorway was used when Don's fingers came to life, and interrupted his thoughts with their frantic dance on the keyboard. The computer monitor blacked out briefly and then opened into a cryptic looking display with bright red text in which were displayed numerous numerical sequences. Don smiled, "Voila`!"

"How the hell did you do that?" Jack asked with amazement. Don just smiled and replied, "It's all in the wrist baby!"

Jack was stunned by what he had just seen. "Seriously, I don't even know what you did much less how you can manipulate this thing like that," he said referring to the computer. He looked at his friend and co-worker with a new and greater respect for his talents.

Jack had always known that Don was exceptional with computers, after all, he had been the one who looked through his portfolio along with a long list of other technicians the AFA was looking to recruit. Until now,

The Watchful Eye

however, Jack had only seen him hack into programs that were used occasionally by government agencies to perform illegal background checks or initiate semi-complicated tracking procedures, but those were all pretty much routine for Don.

Jack had no idea up until this point what Don was really capable of, although he was expecting that he would soon find out.

"Years of practice," Don said studying the rows and columns of numbers.

"Any idea what your looking at?" Jack asked.

"Not yet," Don replied. He directed his words more toward the program then toward Jack, "but I don't think it's encryption. Let's have a look around!"

Again Don's fingers awoke to create an unorthodox rhythm against the small keys. Jack leaned back against his chair to give his computer genius more space in which to work.

As he watched his talented technician flip through several different screens that made no more sense to Jack than the first, he had to keep reminding himself to stay out of the way.

Don finally stopped typing, slid his chair back from the monitor abruptly, and took in a deep breath with which he slowly and thoughtfully exhaled.

Seeing him do this out of habit plenty of times in the past when near the completion of a task, Jack asked excitedly, "Well? What is it?"

This time, for the first time since his recruitment, Don didn't have all the answers. "I'm not sure?"

Don continued to focus his attention on the screen as a General might concentrate diligently on a battle map in search of a foolproof strategy. Jack could hear the frustration trailing in his voice as he spoke. "I'm having a hard time getting around in this damn thing."

"What do you mean?" Jack asked. He could almost see the gears turning in Don's head.

"Its set up is weird. I've never seen anything like it. It's not the military's, that's for sure. I can work my way through any military set up with my eyes closed. This is...I don't know?"

"Is it something we should be concerned with?" Jack asked.

Don just stared at the monitor. He was deep in concentration with an almost hypnotic look on his face, "I'm...not...sure?"

Don continued to stare at the monitor while thinking through every possible solution he could. Jack on the other hand felt ignorant and useless.

Sitting next to Don who was in another world, one of his very own, he knew Don was talking to him from the back of his mind. He wasn't consciously registering Jack's questions, or even his own answers. Jack could have turned on some rock music videos with half naked women dancing around and probably wouldn't be able to elicit any more attention from Don than he was getting right now. He felt all but invisible.

Jack decided to get up and go out into the meeting room to make a fresh pot of coffee. Don could probably use a little time to himself with his computer. Without distractions, he might possibly be more efficient. If not, taking a few moments to enjoy a nice hot cup of coffee would do him good. A coffee break might be just what it takes to alter and refresh Don's train of thought. Jack was about to ask Don if he wanted cream and sugar when the technician's eyes lit up bringing him a little closer to the world in which he was sitting in.

"Unless maybe?" Don mumbled to himself and the program rather than to Jack. Rolling his chair back toward the keyboard, his fingers met it with an urgent desire for communication. As he typed, a greedy smile slowly

The Watchful Eye

appeared across his face and rapidly washed away his remaining smudge of frustration. Within seconds, Don appeared to be moving around within the program at his leisure.

Still talking to the program, but now aware of Jack's presence and including him in his victory, Don boasted, "That's right baby! Who's your daddy!"

Jack smiled in sharing Don's excitement, then took advantage of the triumph to leave the room and set out to conquer the coffee maker.

In the meeting room, Ted was still reading his novel. "How's it going in there?" he asked looking up from his book when Jack walked in.

"Oh, no different than usual. You know how paperwork can be," Jack said with as little enthusiasm as possible. "How's the book?" Ted didn't reply. He just flipped the page and continued reading his novel.

Jack made a thick pot of coffee and poured two cups. Then he grabbed a couple packets of cream and sugar for Don. He looked at Ted who was buried in his book. "Coffee's made if you want some." The offer wasn't even acknowledged. Jack spent the little time it took him to walk back to Don's office trying to figure that guy out.

Back in Don's office, he quickly forgot all about Ted and the mysterious things, whatever they were, that made him click. He walked up to Don with the two steaming cups and realized how thankful he was to be working on this project with him and his personality, rather than with Ted and his lack of.

Don looked up from his newest obsession and then rolled his chair away from the computer to accept the coffee.

"Thanks boss."

Jack handed him the cream and sugar, which he quickly discarded by means of the brutal paper shredder that lay in waiting underneath his desk.

Before Jack could ask, Don began telling him what he knew at this point. According to him, the program was a very sophisticated system that either monitored Satellite location or was an interactive interface used to control satellite function. He believed the first to be more likely as satellites were pre-programmed to function throughout an indefinite period of time before they were even sent into space, with the exception of a few basic commands on recently launched probes. However, he hadn't been able to open up the operation portion of the program to be able to fully make that judgement. While talking out loud, pondering through the information he was able to obtain, he reached up and strolled his fingers across the key board bringing the program back around to the first screen that had appeared when he first entered the program.

"This is odd," Don said. "No matter what I do, I can't have my way with this part of the program. It's more like lines of information rather than modes of operation. The whole thing is set up with unbelievable lockouts and security measures, except this piece." He referred to the rows of numbers that were displayed on the screen.

They both studied the rows of numbers for a while then Jack said, "Maybe it's just what it appears to be; numbers that have their own individual value. Don sighed, "I don't think it's that easy but maybe you're right."

He started inputting his thoughts through the keyboard as he tried to manipulate the numbers. By the look on Don's face, Jack knew he was beginning to make progress when out of nowhere the screen blacked out. It lit up again briefly to show an aerial view of the globe. Again it went black, and then opened back up with a closer look at the globe.

Don immediately realized what was happening when he recognized the land formation that shared a portion of the screen with what appeared to be an ocean. A satellite was

The Watchful Eye

zooming in on the state of California and it was searching for them!

Jack jumped out of the way when Don dropped his coffee and shoved himself over to another monitor that also had a keyboard at the ready.

He feverishly pounded on that keyboard, which in turn lit up a second monitor that displayed rows of numbers and symbols.

Jack looked back at the first monitor in time to see it black out again. This time when it opened, it showed real time satellite imagery of the city of angels. Don hammered away at the second keyboard oblivious to all else.

Jack watched both monitors closely as he felt bundles of nerves steadily growing and clenching in his stomach and chest. Without hearing it first from Don, he knew what was happening; they had been caught!

Looking at the first monitor, it appeared to be stuck in limbo as if the satellite image was threatening to burn a permanent imprint on the screen. The second monitor was rolling through sequences as fast as Don could manipulate the input keys. It was so fast, Jack had a hard time recognizing the symbols and numbers before they disappeared and were replaced.

The first monitor held fast and it appeared that Don was gaining control, he was also beginning to perspire.

Then, without warning, the first monitor went completely black. Don stopped typing and watched it as if he were expecting to see whether or not the world was going to come to end. A worried look on his face led Jack to believe that the battle had been lost. When the monitor finally came back to life, it contained the bright red text of the numbered columns and rows. They were once again back to where they had started. Don let out a sigh of relief.

Wanting to know for certain, Jack asked, "Is it over?" Don looked at him with dread showing in his eyes and said, "I'm not sure. The program itself was trying to track us, but

I managed to input our signal pulse into its data bank as non hostile."

"So it's over?" Jack asked again wanting some assurance from the only person that could give it to him.

"Well, we should be safe from activating another security watchdog."

Don didn't look or act relieved with what he was telling Jack and he was adamant about keeping an eye on the monitor as if he expected the whole process to start over again at any minute.

Jack looked incredulous. Don wasn't saying that they weren't safe, but at the same time he appeared to be putting more effort into answering without saying that they were. "What is it that you're not wanting to tell me?" Jack asked. "Is it over or not?" Don still watched the monitor, nothing was happening.

"I don't know for sure. The program isn't worried about us, as far as it's concerned, our signal is now nothing more than a part of the program. The only thing we have to worry about now is whether or not someone was operating the program and witnessed the security breach."

"And if that's the case?" Jack asked although he already knew the answer but wanted to know the details.

"Well, if that's the case they're probably looking for us."

"Who are they?" Jack asked.

"I don't know."

"Can they find us?"

"Not with the satellite anyway. Unless they locked onto our signal before I found one that was compatible, but I can almost assure you that they weren't able to do that while their program was running through its security file. The only other thing we have to worry about is, if there *was* an operator watching the whole process from another monitor, he could bring the satellite back to it's last tracking position and then zoom in and pinpoint our location down to about a

The Watchful Eye

hundred-mile radius." That was the most possible threat and also very probable.

Don was hesitant, but he rolled back over to the first keyboard and started looking for a way to call up the satellite that had tried to track them. If he could, he would then know if someone were calling it back into position.

In the next hour and a half, Don was able to locate a satellite-tracking driver, download it, and then recall the satellite's memory log. It confirmed that no one had been manning the program.

As soon as Don knew he was in the clear, he proceeded to the first screen that the door had led to. He had to know what it was before he could shut down. *It must be important!* he thought. After all, that's where the trap had been set that they had already fallen into. Jack left to get a couple more cups of coffee and by the time he returned Don had some answers.

"They're people!" Don said with excitement. "I still don't know what all the numbers stand for but the first nine numbers identify people through social security." He pointed a row out to Jack and then slid his chair over to an adjacent keyboard where he typed the first nine numbers into the Social Securities' central processing center. He had quickly hacked into it while Jack was using the restroom and bringing back the coffee. The computer pulled up a file for a Frederick Arthur Jones. Jack looked at the file and asked, "How does this tell us anything? If I picked out nine numbers at random and typed them into the computer, I'm sure it would make a match with somebody."

"Yeah," Don smiled with confidence, "but would the birthday match the next six numbers." Frederick Jones' birth date was identical to the following six numbers on the row that contained his social security number.

Don typed in nine numbers from the next row. It too brought up a person's file that also matched the six-digit birth date that followed. As did the next six rows of numbers that they checked.

Don printed three sheets worth of columns. Tomorrow, he would identify one hundred people from the list, run background checks, and then he and Jack could work on finding anything that they might all have in common.

Chapter Ten

Dr. Evans didn't hear the announcement right the first time because he was deep in thought. Then, he was snapped from his methodical daze when he realized his name was being broadcast over the intercom.

"Dr. Evans line four please, Dr. Evans line four."

Dr. Evans continued down the corridor to the nurses' station where he picked up the line.

"This is Dr. Evans, how may I help you?"

"I need to see you in my office right now Michael!"

"Okay,...Sure,...What is it that you need to see to me about?" Dr. Evans asked trying to ease his mind.

Richard Healt sounded a little upset, but than again he usually did. Dr. Healt was the Chief Medical Director and had played a big part in hiring Dr. Evans after he had graduated medical school and completed his internship.

"Dick" as Dr. Evans liked to refer to him when nobody was around to hear, didn't seem to have a whole lot of personality. Dr. Evans considered him to be nothing more than an overpaid ignoramus who sat in an office and ruled over the hospital's staff from a safe distance.

Even though Dr. Healt had given him his job, Dr. Evans had found it hard to muster any respect for the overweight, baldheaded, weeble-wobbly poor excuse for a doctor. Those inner feelings for his superior were always kept hidden. On the outside, however, he was always able to show "Dick," the utmost respect. This was a beneficial trait he had had to learn long ago in order to live and work successfully in a world full of idiots. Furthermore, he was positive that Dr. Healt looked to him with a great amount of pride. After all, he did hire him and there was no doubt that he was the best doctor the hospital had to offer. Like most of the staff at the hospital, Dr. Healt was obviously good at hiding his affection.

"We'll talk when you get here. Drop whatever you're doing. I want to see you in my office right away!"

"Okay, I'll head over there now. See you in a few minutes."

Without any further words being spoken the connection went dead. "Well," Dr. Evans said under his breath, "good bye to you too Dick!" He set the handset back down in the cradle.

On his way to "Chief Dick's" office, Dr. Evans began to feel as though other staff members, even those whom he didn't know very well, were staring at him. What the hell do they know that he doesn't!

Maybe he was overreacting. After all, it was possible to mistake Dr. Healt's tone of everyday voice for that of one with an accusatory, "what's wrong with you," chime.

That couldn't be it. Dr. Evans didn't make mistakes. He was fixing to be yelled at and it sickened him to think that he was going to have to stand in front of the "Dick" and be criticized. Even worse, he would have to act as though he was thankful for the wisdom and insight being showered upon him. That thought was more than he could stomach!

How dare "Dick" talk to him like that on the phone! Didn't he have better manners than to hang up without saying goodbye first? What kind of person did that make his mother for raising him to be so rude and disrespectful?

The Watchful Eye

Before he could sicken himself with the thought of a woman big enough, and ugly enough, to bear a fat, baldheaded, hairy bastard of a man doctor, one who has probably never once in his life pleased a woman, he desperately cleared his overactive mind.

Rounding the final corner to the corridor in which Chief Healt's office was located, he noticed Lisa Hayes stepping into the elevator. He had barely caught a glimpse of her before the automatic doors closed, occluding his line of vision.

Damn she looks good! he thought. Dr. Evans decided to go to the nursery and grant Lisa some of his precious time after ignoring the meaningless ass chewing he was fixing to endure.

When he stepped up to the Chief Medical Director's office, the door was open.

"Knock, knock!" he said announcing his arrival.

"Come in and have a seat. You're familiar with Mr. Dearis?" asked the Chief, referring to another man that was sitting in the corner of the room.

"Yes I am," says Dr. Evans while focusing on the C.E.O.

"How are you, sir? I haven't seen you in quite some time."

Without standing to shake Dr. Evans extended hand, Mr. Dearis simply replied, "Don't mind me, I'm just here to listen in. Why don't you take a seat so we can get started."

Something was definitely wrong. Mr. Dearis' forced smile and lack of welcome brought Dr. Evans to the conclusion that this was going to be more than a simple bite wound to his derriere.

Dr. Evans sat in one of the two chairs placed in front of Richard's desk. The cushion was still warm from its previous occupant. Turning his attention back to the "Dick" at the desk instead of the CEO, Dr. Evans forced a smile. "Seems a bit stuffy in here. What's the problem?"

"It would seem Michael, that some serious wrongdoings have been committed at this hospital against a few of our patients. Do you know anything about this?"

"Wrong doings? I guess I don't. Maybe you can fill me in a little."

"One of the employees has brought it to my attention that you were seen in the nursery,...There's no other way to say this so I'm just going to come out with it. You were seen switching babies."

"Those are some very strong accusations to make don't you think? Who would possibly say such a thing anyway?"

Dr. Evans could feel his temper lifting up into a fit of anger at the thought of facing such an accusation.

"There's no sense in trying to deny this Michael. We've already compared the foot and fingerprints on both of the baby's birth certificates and they didn't match up. My witness also claims that the babies had already been banded. When I looked at the bands, it was clear that they had been tampered with."

"And you think I did it?"

"Honestly, I find it hard to believe that anyone would do such a horrible thing! After seeing the evidence and hearing statements, however, I have no other choice than to believe that you did do it. And though I can't understand why, it appears that you did it on purpose."

"This is horse shit!" Dr. Evans yelled as he stood up from his chair. "Somebody's trying to set me up! Can't you see that? Surely you don't believe this crap!"

Dr. Healt stood to equal him. "Actually Michael I do. I've been hearing a lot of complaints lately concerning your ethics and professionalism. Pending further investigation you're hereby suspended from practicing any form of medicine. However, if you're cleared of these charges you'll be fully compensated for your lost time."

"Who do you think you are? You can't suspend me!" Dr. Evans stared deep into the Dr. Healts' eyes. "You're

The Watchful Eye

nothing without my skills. I'm the best damn doctor in this hospital! The best that's ever worked here!"

"Think what you may Dr. Evans, but you *are* suspended and if I have any say so in the matter, you'll never practice medicine again for as long as you live."

Furious, the doctor yelled. "Go to hell!" Turning to leave the room he glared at the C.E.O. "And why don't you go with him!" Halfway to the door, he noticed the two security guards that were waiting for him. The Chief Medical Director followed him across the room.

"Take this man to his office to collect his belongings and then escort him out of this hospital immediately!"

✯✯✯

In his office, with the two security bullies waiting for him on the other side of the closed door, Dr. Evans picked up the phone and dialed.

"This is Michael Evans. Get your boss on the phone right now!" A few seconds later Dr. Evans heard the phone being picked up. He also heard a voice on the other end ask whoever was in the room to please allow for some privacy. Then, the elderly man put the phone to his ear.

"Good afternoon Mr. Evans. There had better be a good reason as to why you're calling and demanding to speak to me."

Dr. Evans did know better but at the moment he didn't care. "Yes there's a reason, and if you'll shut up for a moment I might have the opportunity to tell you about it!" After hearing his own tone of voice Dr. Evans quickly contemplated whether or not he had made a mistake in calling. He was about to apologize for his actions when the elderly man spoke.

"You seem to be somewhat distressed Mr. Evans. Why don't you take a moment to calm down and then let me know what's wrong."

That's right! he thought. *I have the upper hand! I'm in control now!*

"I'm in a lot of trouble and I need your help! I've been doing what you've asked of me for years now, years of your inhumane sadistic work without causing you any problems. Now its time for you to return the favor!"

"What is it that you want Mr. Evans? We've already paid every cent of your debt, kept you from losing your license, and literally kept you from going to jail. What more do you want from me now?" Strange, his voice was extremely calm and also seemed to carry a tone of concern.

"I want the Chief Medical Director at this hospital fired! Not only that, but if I were you, I'd be thinking of a way to make sure I'm his replacement!"

"Slow down Mr. Evans. What makes you think I have the power to make something like that happen? And if I did, what leads you to believe that you're in any type of position to make that sort of demand?"

"I've got a whole box of your precious little injections left, that's what! Now I can either finish using them and turn all of my documentation in to your men as usual, or, I can take the whole lot of it and turn it over to the authorities. Do you think I sound like I'm in any position to make demands now? Well? Do you?"

"If you look at it that way I suppose you are, although it wouldn't at all be necessary. After all I've always thought that we had a good relationship. Don't you? I'd hate to see it destroyed by the use of threats."

"That's what I was thinking too. I just wanted to make sure we're both on the same page. When can you make it happen? Sometime today I hope?"

"These things take time Mr. Evans. It won't at all be impossible to grant your wishes, but we're going to have to hammer out some details. Tell you what, I'll have some of my men meet you outside the hospital to pick you up in

about...say thirty minutes. Then, we can discuss all of this in person."

"Okay, that sounds great!"

"Bring the remaining inoculations and the paperwork Mr. Evans. I'd hate for someone to find them and be able to connect you to what's been happening. We don't want any evidence left behind. Besides, then I'd never be able to put you on the top of that ladder."

"It's that easy? You're really going to help me get out of this mess?"

"You can count on it Mr. Evans. I'm going to see to it that you get everything you deserve."

"Wow. This is going to be great. I'll be out in front in thirty minutes. Make sure your guys aren't late."

"Oh they'll be there! Don't forget to bring the pens and the paperwork Mr. Evans."

After hanging up, Dr. Evans unlocked his desk and removed the cooler that contained the inoculation pens. All of the paper work he was asked to bring was lying in the bottom of the same drawer. He grabbed it and stuffed it into his briefcase. Then he picked up the cooler and opened the door.

One of the guards looked at the two items the doctor was carrying and then at all of the items that were being left behind. "You need to remove all of your property. Once you leave, you're not coming back in," he warned.

Although the security guard was actually four inches taller than Dr. Evans, the doctor looked down at him and smirked anyway. "Oh it's not over yet! I'll be coming back. And when I do, you can both count on being fired!"

Neither one of the security guards had a problem rough handling the doctor to the front entrance. After shoving him out the door, they both stood by it smiling.

Waiting for his ride to appear, Dr. Evans ignored the two buffoons watching him from the entrance. Although they now tried to remain expressionless, he could almost feel them laughing in disbelief of his threat. Let them have their laugh, he'd show them. Let's see if they're still laughing a few days from now!

For the next ten minutes, until a black SUV pulled up in front of the hospital to pick him up, Dr. Evans thought of all the fulfilling and numerous ways he could fire the two idiot guards for treating him with such disrespect.

★★★

Two men, dressed in military attire, were sitting in the front seat. Another man, also dressed in a black military uniform, sat in the rear. Dr. Evans sat down in the seat next to him and closed the door.

He was quick to feel puny and helpless in the presence of these three huge men. Looking for comfort through thought, he decided that his brain, the thing that mattered most in life, was larger and most likely worked better than all three of their brains put together. All three of theirs combined, he decided, were probably not much bigger or more complex than that of a small bird.

The man sitting to his left snatched the cooler from his grasp.

"I assume all the injections that were assigned to you are in here?" he asked while opening the cooler to inspect its contents. His voice was rough and indifferent.

"Yeah, they're all there," said the doctor suddenly feeling puny again.

"What about all the documents?"

"They're right here." Dr. Evans handed over the briefcase.

The case and the cooler were given to the passenger in the front seat. The large man sitting beside Dr. Evans waited for affirmation.

After carefully looking over the paper work and taking inventory of the cooler, the passenger turned to the driver.

"It's all here." Then he nodded back to his partner who was sitting next to Dr. Evans.

As the vehicle began to move, Dr. Evans felt a hard solid object smash against the base of the skull. That was the last thing his large brain processed before he slid out of consciousness.

Chapter Eleven

Dr. Evans vision began to clear as he struggled for focus. He was lying flat on a hard cold surface. Unfamiliar with his surroundings, he was unable to determine where he was. Although the objects around him were slowly coming into view, his thoughts were still a blur. The last thing he could remember was being whacked on the back of his head.

He was lying face down on a black ceramic tile floor. Amongst the silence he could hear something that sounded like a small waterfall off in the background. A dull thumping ache plagued the back of his head and neck. He lay motionless on the cold tile for a moment listening to the sound of flowing water. It was accompanied by a slight mechanical hum.

Where am I? How did I get here? he thought to himself. Then, he remembered sitting in the back of the SUV with the three steroid-crazed men. Suddenly he felt an urge to run.

As soon as the doctor tried to stand up, the dull ache residing in his head and neck flared into an unbearably hard thumping pain. Reaching back with a trembling hand, he felt thick clumps of dried blood matting his hair.

Underneath the matted hair lay a swollen knot of flesh toward the base of his skull.

"It's nice to see that you're finally awake Mr. Evans. How was your nap?"

The voice came from behind him and he recognized it immediately. Turning to look, another sharp pain shot bullet-like through his head and neck threatening to take back his vision.

Getting to his hands and knees, he saw the older, gray-haired man, sitting behind a very large and expensive looking stainless steel desk. His feet were propped up and he was stirring a glass of pink lemonade. The ice rattled noisily as it swirled against the glass.

The room was furnished boldly in black leather and touched awkwardly with a complete ensemble of stainless steel tables that matched the large desk. Black Venetian blinds hung over four enormous windows that looked out into the world beyond. The view they captured held rolling oceans of healthy, green grass sprinkled sparingly with cherry, plum and apple trees, all of which had been precisely pruned to an almost mirror like perfection.

Inside, the room's cold and sterile atmosphere seemed to be without personality. That, along with its warehouse type openness, gave the doctor an exaggerated sense of being completely exposed. Weak and afraid, he had been ripped away from any safety the outside world might provide.

The wall that stood behind the large desk was painted jet black to match the tile floor that was in conflict with the remaining three that were painted stark white. Centered behind the desk, about eight-foot long and almost four feet tall, stood a brightly lit three hundred and fifty-gallon saltwater aquarium. In recognition to the sound of a waterfall, he realized that he had been listening to its humming filtration accompanied by the sound of the exchanging water.

The Watchful Eye

Over the fish tank hung a lone piece of modern art. As far as Dr. Evans had noticed at this point, it was the only piece of art that was displayed in the entire room. On any other occasion he would have never paid much attention to the painting, however, this piece seemed to pull at his intellect as though it was begging for his attention. In cold dark colors that clashed in contrast with the rest of the room, two separate figures that were meant to represent one person, twisted wickedly amongst each and appeared to be crying out in pain. Staring at the painting, as though he was locked in a hypnotic gaze, Dr. Evans couldn't shake the feeling that the piece was somehow created to represent him in the here and now. The painting was truly morbid.

"Would you like some Mr. Evans?" the older man asked. The sound of his voice not only broke through the loneliness created by the room itself, but also shattered the painting's cabalistic appeal to his subconscious. From behind the desk, the gray-haired man raised his glass of lemonade.

Contemplating an answer, Dr. Evans caught a glimpse of movement from the corner of his eye. The large steroid-obsessed, tiny-brained man in uniform, the one that had knocked him senseless in the back of the SUV, had been sitting on one of the black pieces of furniture in the corner. Heretofore, his black uniform, along with the doctor's shaken vision, had blended him into his surroundings. Dr. Evans hadn't noticed him. He stood up and walked a few steps over to a wet-bar. From a small refrigerator located behind the bar, he removed a glass pitcher and proceeded to pour another glass of lemonade.

"Thank you so much Sgt. Stalls. By the way, have you two had the chance to formally meet each other yet?" Dr. Evans detected an inkling of sarcasm.

Stalls didn't say a word. His evil stare, full of hatred and directed at the doctor, spoke more than words could say. Dr. Evans, who was scared and already in an enormous amount of pain, didn't speak either for fear that any answer brought with it consequences. He remained silent.

Carrying the glass of lemonade, Stalls walked across the room and grabbed the doctor by his shirt-collar, skin and all, and lifted him up off the floor. With one hand holding the lemonade and the other holding Dr. Evans, he carried them across the room to a chair next to his boss' desk. The tips of the doctor's shoes barely had the chance to brush against the tile. Almost throwing him, Stalls shoved Dr. Evans down into the chair where he landed with enough force that it almost toppled over backwards. Sgt. Stalls grit his teeth. From between them grumbled, "If you spill this, I'll be using your head to mop it up!" Then, he handed over the glass of lemonade.

Upon hitting the chair, a tsunami of pain had crashed through Dr. Evans and nearly materialized in the form of tears. His pain-infested neck had hit the high back of the chair with a thud. Then, as if that wasn't enough, the teetering chair had threatened to topple over backwards and send him smack down into the ceramic floor contusion first. What was this overgrown, steroid-swollen asshole trying to do, kill him? Scared not to accept it, he reached for the glass of lemonade with the skill of a surgeon, being careful not to spill even the smallest of drops.

Laughing out loud, the elderly man said, "Don't get yourself all ruffled up Mr. Evans, and for God's sake don't take it personally, Sgt. Stalls has a hard time getting along with everybody. If anything, I'd have to say he likes you. That's the nicest I've seen him treat anyone in a long time." He looked at Stalls who was already sitting back down in the corner of the room.

"Are you getting soft Sgt.?"
"No Sir."
"Candy ass?"
"No Sir."

The Watchful Eye

"I don't want to have to replace you," he said with an overly friendly smile.

"Never Sir."

"Good. Now try and toughen up a little would you?"

"Yes, sir."

Turning his chair back toward the doctor, the elderly man slowly shook his head in an exaggerated effort to show his disappointment.

"You know Mr. Evans?" he took a deep breath and sighed. "I really have a hard time with the fact that you've breached the trust in our relationship." He took another moment to look deep into the doctor's eyes. "What are we going to do now? I'm not quite sure if I'll ever be able to think that this relationship can function properly again. Can you?"

"I don't think you understand," Dr. Evans said trying to explain his actions and at the same time steer himself from any further trouble. "It's not that I wanted to cause any problems. I had to call and ask for help!"

The gray-haired man stood up from behind the desk and pounded the fleshy underside of his fist down on its surface with an amazing amount of strength. Furious, he was now yelling at the doctor.

"Well Mr. Evans you did cause trouble!" He pounded his fist onto the desk again. "I trusted you to do a simple job! Nothing more, nothing less! Was that too much to ask Mr. Evans? After all the money I've paid to save your worthless ass, you have the nerve to call me with threats and demands? It doesn't work that way Mr. Evans! *I OWN YOU!*"

Standing behind the desk and trembling slightly in his anger, he stared at Dr. Evans. After the few moments it took to contain himself, he took his seat. His breathing was still faster and deeper than normal. In an effort to further gain composure, he picked up his glass of lemonade and took a drink.

Dr. Evans sat fearfully in silence not knowing what was next.

After a moment, the gray-haired man stood up and walked over to the fish tank.

"Well Mr. Evans," he said staring into the fish-tank with his back turned to the doctor. "Somehow I'm going to have to feel that you're still trustworthy in order for us to move forward with this relationship you've tried so hard to destroy."

"You can trust me," said Dr. Evans. "I don't know what got into me. I shouldn't have threatened you like that, but they're going to fire me! I couldn't help it! I just blew up! Anyway, I'm sorry. I shouldn't have taken it out on you."

"You should be sorry Mr. Evans, and I'm glad to hear you say so, but you don't think I can just take your word for it. You made some pretty big threats and that's something I can't ignore."

"Oh come on," Dr. Evans said realizing that the worst of it was yet to come. "They're going to fire me. I was stressed out that's all. I've had time to think about everything and I've calmed down. You've got to know that I wasn't serious. I'll find another job. I'm a damn good doctor. In a week or two I'll be delivering somewhere else, plus doing all the jobs you *need* me to do! Everything will be back to normal in no time at all. Come on, trust me. You have nothing to worry about."

"That all sounds great Mr. Evans. There's only one thing that bothers me?"

"What's that?" he asked. Maybe the worst was past. Things seemed to be going better.

"Somehow I have to know you've learned a lesson. I lost trust in you and we can't work together without that."

"Anything you need," says the doctor. "I'm your man!"

With a nod from his boss, Sgt. Stalls walked across the room and grabbed Dr. Evans by the wrist, put him in

The Watchful Eye

submission using joint manipulation and in the process somehow stretched his hand out flat on the big stainless steel desk. Making sure the manipulation was extreme and painful, Stalls smiled viciously when the doctor cried out in pain.

"AWE! What the hell are you doing!"

Stalls twisted a little harder causing the doctor to cry out again even louder. When Stalls finally eased off, Dr. Evans fought to remain quiet for fear of more punishment.

From in front of the large tank, the gray-haired man turned around to glare at the doctor with his penetrating bluish-gray eyes. "The only way I believe I can regain the trust I lost in you, is to know that you've lost something as well Mr. Evans." Before he had even finished talking, Stalls had removed his knife and began cutting a circular pattern around the last knuckle of the doctor's pinky finger.

Ice cold, but yet burning ferociously, the large black powdered knife easily sliced through the doctor's skin. Its edge was razor sharp. Trying to fight back his tears, Dr. Evans couldn't help but scream. Pain swirled through his finger, hand, and all the way up his arm into his elbow. He screamed at the top of his lungs.

Although the knife was extremely sharp, Stalls took his time carving through the skin, tendons, and muscle that made up the doctor's pinky finger. Then, he applied his weight and cut through the bone. Smiling wickedly, he removed the entire finger with the exception of a small sliver of skin that still attached it to the doctor's hand. Stalls enjoyed every minute of the grotesque process.

When he was finished whittling on the doctor's finger, Sgt. Stalls grabbed Dr. Evans by his shirt-collar once again and swiftly carried the whiney, pitiful excuse of a man over to where his boss was standing in front of the fish tank.

After removing the lid, Sgt. Stalls forced Dr. Evans hand into the cool salty water. The salt water entered the open wound with a vengeance.

Darkness crept in on Dr. Evans peripheral vision. In a temporary gift of God's good mercy, he was on the verge of passing out. Beginning to weaken, he looked at his shredded finger through the glass. Its refracted appearance magnified its size, showing a close up version of his bloody, butchered finger.

Sgt. Stall's evil delight was heightened when the three large triggerfish, which had been frightened by the commotion, came back out of hiding. Tasting blood in the water, they circled excitedly until they saw the dangling finger. In his excitement Stalls could almost taste the blood himself.

All three triggers shot across the aquarium in a race to reach the finger first. The largest of the three, a Sickle trigger, hit the hanging pinky with enough force to finish ripping it from the doctor's hand. Still in a frenzy, the fish then smashed it against the glass on the other side of the tank. The attack was so forceful, that the thud of impact sounded as though it should have been powerful enough to shatter the tank. That fish was followed by the second trigger, a Picasso, who was competing violently to consume as much of the food as possible. They shredded it to the bone in a matter of seconds.

Dr. Evans, full of disgust and fear induced adrenaline, managed to jerk free of Sgt. Stalls and the fish tank when he realized that the third trigger, also a Picasso, was devouring small pieces of flesh and muscle from the stubby end of his finger.

Dr. Evans held his throbbing hand as close to himself as possible, while applying pressure to the end of the stump in an effort to stop the blood.

He had never been so scared in his entire life. From the time Stalls had started cutting into his skin, he began living from second to second not knowing what was going to happen to him next. Until then, he hadn't truly felt the emotional power of his fright until he was completely consumed by it, whereupon he had managed to jerk himself free.

Now however, the struggle was temporarily over and again he felt helpless. What would he do if they decided that he hadn't had enough? Roll over, expose his belly and cry for mercy? Beg for forgiveness?

Physical conflict was something he had always been able to avoid. Not because of his beliefs, but because of fear. Never having been in a fight, not even in elementary school, he had never had an understanding of how brutal, degrading and cruel, people could actually be. These two were beyond anything he had ever comprehended.

Until now, he had believed them to have some morals and at least an ounce of understanding. He had expected nothing more than a few ugly threats and maybe a little pain, but nothing like this. Is this just a game to them? Anger and disgust began to swirl throughout his emotions until they finally boiled into a rage.

Don't they have a heart between the two of them that can understand the agony and hatred they've caused? How could one person be so animalistic toward another? He felt violated. These people had taken something from him he would never get back. Not just his finger, but his pride. How dare they look down on him like this! Treat him like this! Violate him like this!

Now that it's over, do they think everything will be normal again? That he'll act like a good little boy? That he'll be at their every beck and call?

"It looks like we're on even ground again Mr. Evans," said the older man. Dr. Evans said nothing more than what was revealed in his eyes.

"Cheer up. We can be friends again! Aren't you happy with that?"

Still, Dr. Evans said nothing.

The gray-haired man began to look perturbed. Dr. Evans knew it was because he found him to be weak and pathetic. Maybe he was? Maybe he always would be? Why was he afraid to fight? What more could they do to him? How much more pain could he possibly feel? A finger, an arm, a leg? How much worse could it hurt than the painful gash they had opened in his pride? How much longer was he willing to be a puppet?

"It's just a finger Mr. Evans, be thankful!" After giving Dr. Evans a disapproving look, the older man headed toward the door to leave the room.

"What would you like me to do with him?" Sgt. Stalls asked. The older man stopped and turned back around to look at Dr. Evans.

"Make him clean up his mess," he said referring to the blood on the floor and desk. "Then get him out of here and back to work." Still looking at the doctor he added, "This is the last time we'll have this problem right Mr. Evans?" The doctor only stared. Turning back toward the door and walking away, the older man added one last bit of advise. "If I ever see you again, I'll kill you!"

Dr. Evans refused to live any longer feeling so helpless and disappointed in himself. From the desk he grabbed a heavy marble paperweight with his good hand and ran for the gray-haired man. In his rage, he was finally ready to even the score even if it cost him his life.

Leaping, Dr. Evans swung the hefty paperweight as hard as he could with the full intention of knocking the man down, and then beating him repeatedly until he no longer felt the pain that they had inflicted.

Caught by surprise, Sgt. Stalls nearly detected the doctor's reaction too late to prevent him from hurtling himself onto his boss. Acting as quick as his body would allow, Stalls managed to throw himself at Dr. Evans and knock him off balance. Robbing the doctor's energy mid-swing, Stalls prevented him from accomplishing what he had set out to do.

The Watchful Eye

Hearing the commotion the older man turned back around in time to see Dr. Evans hit the floor face first. The massive paperweight hit the floor next to him, shattering two of the ceramic tiles. Stalls was immediately on his feet and standing over the doctor who now lay on the floor crying. His spirit shattered in as many pieces as the broken tile beside him. Without saying a word, Stalls commenced to kicking the broken man with all his might. Dr. Evans continued to cry. In his mental anguish, he was oblivious to the physical punishment.

Chapter Twelve

Jack sat in his car outside the fitness center thinking about the Watchful Eye program. So far, he didn't have a clue as to what it was capable of or what government agency might be responsible for running it.

As far as the thousands of rows of numbers that represented people, he considered the fact that they were probably nothing more than a list of employees working for that particular agency.

At this point, Jack knew that the rows contained social security numbers and birth dates for identification, but what did the rest of the numbers in each row represent? Maybe they stood for the department or location of employment for that individual employee. He was quite sure that he and Don would be able to figure it out eventually, if not tomorrow.

Jack started his car and headed home. Before he was out of the parking lot he had already put those thoughts to rest and was moving on to new ones. Driving away from the center, he recalled how much he had enjoyed spending time with Sharon earlier that day.

She was beautiful, intelligent, witty, and independent. In his mind, the list went on and on. As soon as he got home he would put dinner on, which meant nuking something from out of a box, and then give her a call. Hopefully she was feeling better. If not, he would try to talk her into going to the hospital.

Hospitals were always a place to avoid whenever possible, at least that was Jack's opinion. However, he couldn't stop worrying about how she had lost consciousness at the gallery. Most likely, she needed to see a doctor. If something were wrong with her, something that she wasn't already aware of, he would have to get her to one.

Seeing her fear at the time of her spell, and then her embarrassment, he hadn't had the heart to embarrass her further by telling her what he had seen. What had he seen actually? Had it been a flight of his imagination?

Right before she had lost consciousness the skin on her forehead, cheeks and around her eyes, sagged down if only for just an instant. It reminded him of the permanent scar that strokes usually left in the facial muscles of its victims. It had happened so fast and then had ended just as abruptly, that he didn't know or understand what he had seen.

Now, after all the countless hours he had just spent with Don in front of the computer, he could hardly recall the image her face had left in his memory when it had appeared to lose its substance.

What he didn't question however, and could still picture clearly, were her eyes. Throughout whatever was happening to her, her eyes had glazed over and transformed themselves from the most brilliant and beautiful eyes he had ever seen into what looked like a dull and foggy, lifeless stare. Driving down the freeway, he couldn't stop thinking of how blank they had appeared. There had to be a reasonable explanation for her condition.

Jack had never seen symptoms of epilepsy before, but had heard about it. Was she epileptic? If so, why would

The Watchful Eye

she be so embarrassed by it? We all have our ailments. Some of us simply don't show them.

After thinking about it some more, and then remembering again how frightened she had looked upon learning that she had fainted, he decided that epilepsy was probably not the case. Whatever it was, she probably didn't even know herself.

Jack had made it home and was about to pull into his driveway when his cell phone rang. It was Sharon and she sounded panicked.

"Yeah," Jack said. "I'll be there directly." He backed out of the driveway and drove to her house as fast as he could.

★★★

When Jack pulled up in front of Sharon's house, all of the inside lights were on. She was pacing in the living room up until the minute she saw him and then went immediately to the front door to let him in.

"What happened? Are you okay?" Jack asked with sympathy when he met her on the porch. Without saying anything she wrapped her arms around him and started to cry. Until she let go, he held her tight in the open doorway and did his best to comfort and sooth her.

When she was able to get a hold on her emotions and stop crying, they went inside and sat down on her couch where she started telling him about her latest spells.

She had had one an hour after he had left her house this afternoon and then another right before she called. She also told him about the one that she had experienced before talking to him this morning on the phone.

"What's wrong with me? Am I going crazy?" she asked reaching over and taking some tissue from the carton on the coffee table to dry her eyes.

"It's possible, after all you did hang around with me most of the day," Jack said jokingly in an effort to cheer her up.

Sharon let out a small muffled laugh, but it quickly crumbled under the trepidation displayed in her eyes.

"Hey don't worry about it so much," Jack said reassuringly while trying to ease her mind, "I'm sure it's something that can easily be explained."

Jack put his arm around her shoulder and pulled her close to sooth her.

"Have you eaten since lunch?" he asked easing the conversation and trying to somewhat down play what might very well be a serious reason for concern. Sharon shook her head while looking down at her fingers. They were fumbling relentlessly with the worn out tissue.

"Why don't you let me take you to the emergency room so we can get a professional opinion and then after their done prodding, and poking, and digging, and testing, and…"

Sharon cut in with the first smile he had seen since he had arrived, "Okay, that's enough. I get it."

"Anyway, after they do all that we'll stop and get something to eat."

Sharon turned to him and hugged him. Smiling with appreciation, she thanked him for taking the time to go through this with her. She also thanked him for being such a good friend on such short notice. Together, they drove to the emergency room.

Sharon and Jack waited in the front lobby for almost an hour before she was finally called back to one of the exam rooms. Jack went with her.

Cindy introduced herself as their nurse. She wore bright cheerful scrubs to match her upbeat attitude. Her

The Watchful Eye

brown hair was cropped short and she wore silver rimmed glasses that complimented her light brown, intelligence filled eyes. She was as physically healthy as her personality appeared to be mentally.

After introductions were made Sharon explained why they were there, while Cindy kept herself busy taking vital signs, charting, and asking questions. When the nurse was satisfied with her assessment, she left the room and returned shortly thereafter with a couple of blood tubes and a vacutainer.

As she was filling the rubber-stopped vials with Sharon's blood, she explained that it would be sent over to a nearby lab and the results would then be sent to St. Francis hospital. Sharon was to call the hospital in the morning and set up an appointment to go over the values. Depending on what those values were, they would then decide whether or not a CAT scan would be required for further investigation. Thirty minutes later, they were back in Jack's car looking for Chinese take out.

"I'm glad we went," Jack said.

"Yeah, me too. I hope they can figure out what's wrong with me."

"I thought we had already decided that you were crazy, but just needed to have it confirmed," Jack said with a laugh.

"That's what I'm afraid of." Sharon laughed too.

Back at Sharon's house, the two of them sat on her couch and ate the Chinese fast food as they talked about the day. It wasn't long at all before her spells were forgotten and they were laughing and sharing stories. Sharon talked about her college days and what a great experience it had been. She also listened with lively interest when Jack told her about his days as a Navy Seal. After a few hours, when the conversation had faded to a lull, Jack looked over and realized that Sharon had fallen asleep. Being careful not to wake her, he picked her up off the couch like a baby and carried her to her bed where he pulled the covers down, removed her shoes, and then tucked her in. Satisfied that she would be comfortable, he returned to the living room and stretched out on the couch. He fell sound asleep shortly after.

★★★

Three hours had past before Jack was awakened by the sound of Sharon's screams. Getting up quickly and finding his bearing, he made his way down the hallway and back to her bedroom.

"What's the matter?" he asked as he walked through the doorway and flipped on the light switch. Sharon was sitting up on the edge of her bed with both hands covering her face. Startled, she let out another frightful scream before she recognized Jack who was still standing in the doorway. She had forgotten that he was at her house.

Frightened and confused, she had woken in the middle of a nightmare to find herself in bed fully dressed. To make things even worse she couldn't recall how she had gotten there.

"Did I do it again?" she asked.

Acknowledging the question according to the look on her face, Jack couldn't help but smile at her confusion and in feeling relief in knowing that nothing bad had happened.

"No."

Jack walked over to the bed, sat down next to her and began massaging her shoulders. "You fell asleep on the couch while we were talking so I carried you here and put you to bed."

Thankful that she hadn't blacked out again, Sharon began to tell Jack about her dream.

The Watchful Eye

Brightly lit but cold, she was in a small room strapped by her wrists and ankles to the stainless steel rails of a hospital bed. Although the straps were snug and securely fastened, they were needless, for no matter how hard she tried she couldn't find the strength to move anyway. In a blurred and confused, drug-induced-haze, Sharon watched as four doctors strolled back and forth between her and the equipment that she was connected to. Ignoring her, they were busy jotting down notes and talking amongst themselves.

Against her will, they injected various syringes full of liquid into an IV port that was taped firmly to her wrist.

Throughout the process, she tried without success to scream and kick at one of the doctors that, while drugging her, came close enough to her bed.

Knowing she was incapable, he only laughed under his breath while watching her with his icy glare.

Impossibly, she felt the medications flowing through her veins and killing living cells as they went. Then, when the poison had finally breached her entire body, she rose up from her remains to the ceiling where she watched her body shrivel up and die. She couldn't leave.

Although she wanted to fly away and go to a better place, something evil prohibited it. In limbo, she didn't have a choice but to hang helplessly in midair above her dead body and watch the doctors as they continued to work. Then she realized it was them. They were the evil she felt. They were the reason she was unable to fly away. They weren't done with her yet.

Still ignoring her, she could somehow feel their attention as they focused in on her thoughts and feelings. They absorbed them like energy. Even though they hadn't appeared to fully acknowledge her as she floated defenselessly over the bed, they were somehow not only connected to, but were draining life from her through her thoughts.

Below her, one of the doctors injected even more liquids into her dead body. Then like a scene out of a horror flick, the eyes on the dead body flickered momentarily and then came to life with malicious desire. Her dead body wanted her back.

As the dead Sharon on the bed below struggled to free herself, she watched helplessly from the air above in terror. The dead woman's fingernails and hair fell out in her vicious struggle to break free of the straps. The doctors went about their business in oblivion, as if nothing were actually happening.

Still floating above herself, unable to move, she watched the struggle knowing that the dead Sharon would eventually escape her bonds. Below, the maddened body bit at the air toward her, and as it did, she watched her own teeth fall out. She could feel her own intentions struggling to be fulfilled and therefore knew that she wanted desperately to end her life. That's when she awoke with a scream.

Still massaging her shoulders, Jack wrapped his arms around her and gently rocked her from side to side while reminding her that she had been dreaming and that it hadn't actually happened.

"It was only a dream, and more importantly, you didn't have another one of those spells. I carried you here and tucked you in after you fell asleep on the couch," he reminded.

After holding her in his arms and rocking her for a few minutes to help ease her mind, Jack decided that it was time for him to leave the room so that she could get her rest. Sharon had a long day ahead of her tomorrow and would need as much sleep as she could possibly get.

Feeling his embrace begin to loosen, Sharon reached up and placed both of her hands on top of his arms with hopes of preventing his release.

"Hold me please."

The Watchful Eye

In reply, he wrapped his arms around her even tighter.

"Okay, for a little while," he stated, "but you need your rest for tomorrow. Don't worry, I won't go anywhere. If you need me, I'll be on the couch."

"No," she said. "What I mean is…I want you to hold me tonight."

Sitting on the bed behind her with his arms still around her, Jack couldn't see Sharon's eyes or the expression that might be revealed in them. Hearing a faint quiver in her voice, however, he was able to understand the question he had just been asked.

"Are you sure?" Jack whispered without loosening his embrace. Lacking a spoken answer, Sharon turned around to face him with a kiss. Then she kissed him again.

Expressing her steadily growing passion with a soft touch, she reached up with both of her hands and gently caressed his neck while running her fingers up the back of it and then into his hair. Holding him in her delicate embrace, she looked deep into his blue eyes with a calm and reassuring gaze that stated her desires unquestionably. Then pulling him closer, she softly kissed her way across the side of his neck and up to his lips.

Daring not to spoil the moment with any further conversation, Jack returned her passion with kisses of his own, and began to unbutton his shirt. Sharon helped him, and then proceeded to remove her own.

Half undressed, but not feeling in the least uncomfortably exposed in his presence, she leaned against him and pressed her soft bare breasts against his chest, followed by another barrage of warm tender kisses. Holding her close in his arms, Jack carefully lowered Sharon onto the bed where he gently kissed her firm beautiful body while taking time to remove the remainder of her garments. Passionately, and in perfect harmony, they made love.

★★★

In the morning Jack woke to the smell of bacon and coffee. Sitting up on the side of the bed, he looked for his clothing while reminiscing about what had happened the previous night. There wasn't a word he could think of to describe how good he was feeling now or how sensual and compassionate he had felt while in the throws of love. Sitting on the side of the bed, he felt satisfaction and happiness in knowing that she would be a part of his day and that he would also have the privilege of sharing hers. Getting dressed he also felt pride in being a shoulder for her to lean on throughout her hospital evaluation.

Once he was dressed, he followed the thick aroma of breakfast into the kitchen where Sharon had heard him coming and was already pouring him a cup of coffee.

"Good morning," she said handing him his coffee with a kiss. Jack set the cup on the counter next to him and pulled her into his arms where he held her close. "How are you feeling today?"

"Positive," She said accompanied by an honest smile, "I feel very positive."

While talking about the day ahead of them, Jack helped Sharon set the table and then the two of them sat down to eat. When breakfast was finished, they quickly cleared the few dishes and then Sharon called St. Francis where she set up an appointment for eleven o' clock. Her mood remained cheerful.

Talking him into taking a shower with her, Sharon was teased for being not only duplicitous, but mischievous in claiming that they would save time and water if they did, only to encourage him into another love making session which resulted in them accomplishing neither.

Having showered, they dressed for the day and then set out for the hospital. On the way, they stopped by Jack's house where he changed into a clean set of clothes.

The Watchful Eye

Walking through the hospital and then up to the second floor where the Radiology department was located, Jack didn't feel his usual discomfort. He could still think of at least a hundred places he'd rather be than in a hospital but his desire to be strong and reassuring for Sharon's sake outweighed his chagrin.

Sitting in the waiting room, they watched several other patients enter and leave with problems all their own until Sharon's name was called.

Following a technician down the hallway and into a private room filled sparingly with medical equipment, Jack noticed Sharon's positive attitude slightly begin to dwindle. The technician then left them alone in the room where they again waited, this time for the Radiologist. Soon after the technician had left, a doctor knocked on the door and let himself in.

"Hello, I'm Steve," he said looking at her chart, "you must be Sharon." He smiled and then leaned over with an outstretched hand. Jack did the same and introduced himself.

Steve Howden appeared to be very easygoing and genuinely concerned. Dressed comfortably in Khaki's and a crisp white button up accented with a black belt and soft black leather loafers, he was clean-shaven and well groomed. Steve was probably in his late forties, but looked and acted a healthy vivacious thirty.

Immediately at ease, Sharon didn't have any trouble explaining what was, or at least had been, happening to her since the attack and her hospital stay. Steve listened intently while also reading what the emergency room nurse had written in her chart. Then he went over her lab values and interpreted what each set of numbers meant.

According to her blood work, her chemical composition was normal, therefore, he had taken it upon himself prior to their arrival to set up a routine CAT scan.

"Your labs are normal, and that's good." He reassured her, "All we have to do now is make sure there aren't any physical abnormalities that could be causing these spells. It's a simple procedure that's painless. Hopefully we can rule out any physical implications and then go from there."

Eager to get started, Steve directed them to the CAT room where he would begin the procedure.

Jack waited outside in the lounge while Sharon was in radiology going through the process of having her brain scanned. He tried without success to interest himself in the many tattered magazines that were scattered amongst the small tables placed randomly between orange plastic chairs.

Feeling fidgety after what seemed to be hours of patient waiting, he put down the magazine that he couldn't quite concentrate on, and went in search of a soda machine.

★★★

Exam finished, Sharon walked out into the small lobby where Jack was waiting for her. He wasn't there. She was about to go in search of him when Dr. Clemens rounded the corner and spotted her.

"Mrs. Anderson, what are you doing here?" he asked looking somewhat uneasy.

Clemens had been the surgeon in charge of mending her shoulder after the attack at Venice Beach. As he listened attentively, she explained briefly what she had been going through the last couple of days. The more she explained, the more she noticed him fidgeting nervously. Not only did she find his actions somewhat strange, but he also appeared to be extremely interested in the symptoms she had been experiencing. His interest didn't reflect concern for her as a patient as much as it appeared to be for fear of what he was hearing.

Clemens was in the process of asking a multitude of detailed questions when Jack entered the small waiting

The Watchful Eye

room from behind him. Sharon looked at Jack with a smile and was preparing to introduce the two of them when Clemens turned around and saw him. As if he had seen a ghost, the doctor's eyes widened with fear and his jaw dropped. Before Sharon could begin to make the introduction, Clemens dropped the chart he was holding and ran out of the room.

"What was that all about?" Jack asked with interest regarding the doctor's unorthodox behavior.

"I don't know?" Sharon answered with a puzzled look as though she didn't believe what had just happened, "as soon as he saw you he acted like the sky was falling and ran away."

Jack's interest heightened considerably. "Who is he?"

When Sharon told him that he had been her surgeon after the attack, Jack ran out of the small lobby in pursuit.

In the hallway, Jack almost didn't see Clemens before he stepped into the elevator and the doors closed. He ran over and called for the next elevator but it was on the sixth floor, Clemens was headed to the first.

Jack raced to the stairwell and with both hands on the rails, took the steps four at a time down to the first floor. Entering the first floor hallway, he saw Clemens quickly exiting the hospital through a small receiving door. Running as fast as he could, Jack made it to the exit and then out into the fresh clean air. Clemens was nowhere in sight.

Jack walked in circles outside the small loading bay frantically trying to decide in what direction the doctor had disappeared. He was about to give up the search when he heard an engine revving much higher than normal and then saw the doctor racing through the adjacent parking lot like a madman. Turning onto the connecting street, Clemens glanced over at Jack with a look of disbelief and then sped away. Keeping his mind, Jack managed to get a close look at the car's license plate and then filed it to memory while reaching for his cell phone.

Walking back to the front entrance of the hospital, Jack called Don and recited the doctor's license plate number. He asked Don to do a complete background check and then call him back with the results.

As soon as Don was able to provide him with the information he had requested, he would pay the doctor a visit.

Chapter Thirteen

As the drugs began to wear off, Dr. Evans slowly woke from a long comfortable sleep. Lying in bed, eyes closed, he thought about how nice it was to finally be back at home and wrapped in the comfort and safety of his warm sheets, but most of all, how wonderful it was to still be alive.

He should have never involved himself with that evil, gray-haired man. Now it was too late. He didn't dare think again of trying to expose him and his organization for the awful things they were doing to humanity. Last time he considered that, it cost him a finger. He only had nine left and wanted desperately to keep each one of them.

Thinking back to yesterday; that horrible Sgt. Stalls and those nasty fish, and how they had consumed the devastating loss of his precious pinky finger, he began to feel his anger arise.

Quickly, he calmed himself back down. He couldn't afford to allow himself to feel anger and hostility again, not after what had happened the last time. From now on he would simply have to comply. After all, who knows what they might decide to cut off next time?

Nothing was wrong with complying, he thought. He could do it. Especially if it meant staying attached at the seams. As long as he did whatever he was asked and didn't make any more threats, he would always have a job that paid good money. Besides, he was worthless to them outside of a hospital setting. As long as he did their dirty work he would always be of valuable to them. When they didn't find him worth keeping any longer, someone else would probably find him dead.

Lying in bed with the comfort of the warm sheets holding him closely, quite snug actually, Dr. Evans thought about how this organization could change his life for the better. Of course he would always be at the mercy of the older, gray-haired man, but as long as he always did what was expected of him, the organization would take very good care of him. He provided a service that was of the utmost secret nature, not to mention deathly important. They needed him.

That's all I have to do! he confirmed with optimism. He would do his very best to please the wild-eyed, gray-haired man and whatever organization he worked for and life would be good. Damn good!

Maybe I can even take advantage of my situation. I'm not only going to do what they ask of me, but I'm going to enjoy it! If I do an outstanding job, I might even be able to get a bonus of some sort. After all, they do have access to a lot of money, he thought.

They had already paid off his lawsuit, house, and medical school. Who knows, maybe they would even be willing to part with a cash bonus for an outstanding job.

This was just what he needed, a positive attitude. Not just a positive attitude, but a confident outlook toward his new life altogether. Why couldn't he have thought of this while his pinky finger was still attached?

Thinking again about his missing finger, Dr. Evans again began to anger. Again he quickly thought of the consequences that had resulted from his anger and calmed himself down. *It's only a finger after all*, he thought.

The Watchful Eye

Besides, he still had nine more not to mention that the one he had lost was the smallest and most insignificant. He didn't need it to grasp anything. A pinky finger in the scheme of things is useless. Maybe it would be nice to have one for cosmetic purposes. Oh hell it was just a finger and he would be quite fine without it. Someday it would probably just get in the way anyway.

Gloves! he thought instantaneously. He could cover the ugly stump with a pair of fine leather racing gloves. That would look mysterious. Thinking about it, he was pleased with the idea. Women would probably beg for his attention if he constantly wore high fashion leather gloves. As great looking as he already was, women wouldn't be able to try and resist him with the alluring mystery behind a great pair of gloves!

Smiling on the inside, he was pleased with his decision to comply and his renewed purpose and hope for a fabulous new life.

In the distance, swirling amongst the background of his thoughts, he could have sworn that he heard a door handle swivel and then click, as though someone had released its metal catch. Listening more carefully now, he also thought he heard the soft-spoken but squeaky hinges of a door opening to confirm his thoughts.

As he had suspected, a door opened in the distance, and only briefly filled the room with chattering echoes from somewhere beyond. Silence swiftly regained control, when the room's ceiling and walls rapidly absorbed the echo of the brisk, heavy door's thud when it closed. Someone was in his house! Listening intently, he could hear footsteps.

Whoever had let themselves in, they weren't even trying to be the least bit quiet. That was rude. Who would be in his house and why?

The footsteps were coming closer, louder. Something seemed strange about it. Although he couldn't clearly identify his thoughts, he knew they didn't feel right.

WESS REED

He knew his bedroom was carpeted, but he could hear loud footsteps as clear as a bell. *Tile floor?* That's what he heard. Footsteps on a tile floor, two of them, getting closer.

With all of his effort, he couldn't open his eyes more than a slit. His struggle to see gained him little more than a brightly lit, out-of-focus view of what appeared to be the ceiling; it didn't look as it should. Wrestling his own body he tried to lift his head, but couldn't. *What's wrong with me?*

"Who's there? What do you want?" he tried to ask, but no sound issued from his motionless lips. He wasn't able to move at all.

Dr. Evans tried to sit up, nothing. *What the hell is happening to me?*

Through his slightly parted eyelids he was able to make out the fuzzy outlines of two bodies hovering over him. Brilliant white shapes. Almost like bright shadows, angels? Was he dead? Again he tried to talk to them, again nothing came out.

They were speaking. At first he hadn't heard them, then he realized that they were already in the middle of a conversation. Something about sports scores. He recognized the name of a professional basketball team amongst the cluttered words. Their voices were deep. *Male angels?*

Dr. Evans didn't know much about basketball or any other sport for that matter. People that enjoyed sports in his opinion, obviously enjoyed wasting their time. What was the purpose of following sports anyway? If you watch enough of them, you could waste away most of your life. *Why would angels want to watch sports? Why would a place like heaven even allow for sports?* Disappointed, he couldn't believe that heaven wasn't all that the brochures had made it out to be. Maybe sports were allowed because of the women they attracted. *Heavenly cheerleaders!* That was a nice thought.

The Watchful Eye

Vibrations, something started vibrating. He could feel it throughout his entire body. He was moving.

Bright lights passing by overhead. He was still in bed. The angels were still talking. They were moving him!

Trying, but not able to, Dr. Evans found that he couldn't even swallow. Drool ran down the side of his face. He could feel it on his cheek as it cooled in the passing air.

The angles were talking about a girl now. Steady light, slowing down. They stopped. Moving again momentarily, something rough rattled under the bed. Then they stopped again.

Woozy, there was churning in his head and stomach. He could hear a familiar mechanical whine. The angels still talked about the girl, she sounded nice.

"Ding!" another familiar sound. Moving slowly again, he felt the bed shake as it rolled over something rough. Why would angels roll a bed? Shouldn't angels be able to fly?

An elevator! He was just in an elevator, not in heaven.

Dr. Evans watched the blurred ceiling flow by light by shiny light as he was rolled down the corridor. Besides the two men guiding his bed who weren't angels by any means, he heard unfamiliar voices talking, murmuring, and occasionally screaming as they approached, past, and then faded away in the distance. Again he tried to move and again he couldn't. He longed to know where he was.

While being rolled down the murmur-filled hallway, Dr. Evans heard a loud echo rumble through the building that sounded awfully familiar. Then, like waking from a dream, he realized he was in a hospital. The boisterous cry of an intercom searching for an employee was music to his ears.

He didn't remember going to a hospital. He might have gone to get his finger checked out, but he couldn't recall when that would have been.

Then he remembered being kicked repeatedly by Sgt. Stalls. It seemed to him as if it hadn't really happened, like it was more of a thought than a memory, but somehow he knew it had. There wasn't any pain now, at least none that he could feel anyway. He somehow knew that there had been, a prodigious amount of it at that, but now it was all gone.

That must be why he's at the hospital? That gorilla Stalls must have broken one of his ribs or damaged an internal organ. Because of the pain, he must have passed out during the beating. That would explain why he didn't remember checking into the hospital. Stalls and the old man must care about him after all? If not, why would they have brought him here? They must feel terrible for what they've done? Feeling somewhat vindicated in knowing that Stalls and the older man had cared enough to get him medical attention, Dr. Evans decided to forgive them. When he got to his room, he hoped to find a gift basket or maybe even flowers. He couldn't wait to read the card.

Being a doctor himself, he knew the hospital staff would take good care of him. If not, he would know exactly what roads to take to have them suspended or even fired. It was comforting to know he was in a hospital and in good hands.

The two men pushing him down the hall must be Certified Nurse's Assistants, not angels. He wished he could meet the girl they had talked about. She sounded like a real looker. Oh well, she'd only fall in love with him and then be left brokenhearted like the rest of them. Too bad he wasn't going to get to spend time with angelic cheerleaders. Heaven must be a great place.

A chuckle caused by his ignorance rolled through his mind, however, he still lacked the ability to convert it into sound and expression. Now that he realized that he was at the hospital, he felt comfort in knowing that as soon as he got to where they were going, someone would talk to him. Hopefully, they would take the time needed to thoroughly

The Watchful Eye

explain what had happened, what was now wrong with him, and what his prognosis would be.

Doctor Evans felt the bed slow and then come to a complete stop. He couldn't see them clearly through the small slit between his eyelids, but he was almost certain that the two CNA's were looking him over carefully. No doubt they were eyeing him with respect. They had probably been told what a prestigious doctor he was, and hoped to be like him someday; without all of the abrasions and contusions of course.

At the time, he wished he was capable of telling them stories about medical school and his internship. They would love to listen to him and have the chance to learn something from a phenomenal man such as himself. He might have even enlightened them with stories of all the many women he had had in his lifetime. Then again, if he were capable of talking and sharing stories, he certainly wouldn't waste his time on two idiot CNA's. Before they left, he felt the bed tremor as the wheels were locked in place. Then he heard one of the men ask the other, "Do you think his restraints are tight enough?"

"Are you kidding?" the other answered, "Harry Houdini couldn't even get out of that! Besides, he's so doped up he doesn't even need restraints." Laughing, the two of them walked away.

For the next thirty minutes Dr. Evans tried without success to contemplate why those two idiots would say such a thing. Why would anyone feel the need to restrain him? He couldn't feel any restraints.

He was still trying to find logic in what they had said, when the door opened and another set of footsteps came closer. *Thank God!* he thought. Someone was in the room that would finally tell him what was going on!

Breaking the silence, he heard the clattering of what sounded like utensils on a bare metal table. It sounded like something that might be heard on the surgical floor. Then he saw a face, although he couldn't make it out clearly, leaning over him and up close. From his view the face was upside down. Didn't whoever was in the room with him have the decency to stand beside him rather than above him to talk?

"Good afternoon Dr. Evans."

The voice came from whoever was rudely leaning over him. In the background he heard a quick mechanical buzz. It sounded similar to what one might hear while reclining in a dentist's chair waiting to have cavities drilled. Directly above him, the man spoke again in a very calm, self-satisfying tone.

"I know you can't respond to what I'm saying, so I won't ask you to. Oh yeah," the voice said as if something had been forgotten. "Before we get started, I'm supposed to inform you that," again he heard the quick sharp buzz as the tool was throttled repeatedly, "a couple of your most recent acquaintances wanted to be sure that I extended their compliments."

Although it couldn't be seen on the outside, Dr. Evans smiled on the inside. He knew Stalls and the older man felt awful. The unseen doctor continued.

"What's about to happen should be considered a special gift from them. I assured your friends that I would perform one of the older, more barbaric lobotomy procedures, and that you wouldn't care after it was over anyway, but nonetheless they still insisted that you know. They truly sound like they care about you, don't you think?" The voice laughed with pleasure.

With all of his heart, Dr. Evans tried to scream for help but couldn't. The Succinylcholine Chloride prevented it. In small doses, Succinylchloline Chloride blocks neuro-muscular transmissions, which in turn temporarily paralyzed Dr. Evans and prevented him from having voluntary muscle control. However, it still allowed his body to function autonomically thus permitting his mind to

The Watchful Eye

fill with fear and confusion as he realized what was happening. In Dr. Evans case, the drug was dangerously hooked to an IV drip because of its rapid metabolism.

As the man above him went to work, Dr. Evans heard the speedy buzz of the small drill followed by a whining vibration that spread out across his forehead. Soon after, he caught the vitriolic smell of his own burning skin.

Although he lived out the rest of his natural life, that was the last thing that would ever enter Dr. Evans' mind.

Chapter Fourteen

Jack and Sharon drove past Dr. Clemens' house at nine o' clock that evening, and then parked half a block away. Clemens' house stood on the corner of a ritzy neighborhood that boasted at least a dozen beautiful homes ranging anywhere from Santa Fe and Mediterranean-styled Architecture to the modern day three-story mansions.

Jack had planned on confronting Clemens alone, but Sharon, remembering how restless and edgy he had acted when discovering she had just received a CAT scan, had insisted that she accompany him.

With the exception of sparse illumination scattered throughout the neighborhood, compliments of the few soft glowing windows, whose curtains and sheers hid their occupant's activities, the streets were dark, quiet, and empty. Getting out of the car, the two of them walked to the edge of the doctor's property.

The large front yard was enclosed with thick sections of Redwood lattice that wearily, after years of neglect, supported a blanket of fractiously overgrown honeysuckle vines. At the front gate Jack noticed a small portion of soft, muted light creeping steadily from behind a dark curtained window.

Opening the gate, they followed a cement walkway through tall dense patches of water-thirsty grass. At the house, the sidewalk disappeared under a long over-stretched porch that like the yard, was enclosed with lattice and honeysuckle to match the perimeter fence. The door was far off to their right, and nearly imperceptible under the dark unlit shelter of its wood, plant, and gray stuccoed dungeon.

"Do you think he's home?" Sharon whispered. He could feel the tension she unconsciously transferred through her grip on his arm as she followed him, in the dark, to the door. "There's only one way to find out," Jack said while running his hand alongside the doorframe in search of a doorbell.

After the second ring, the porch light flicked on brightly allowing the enclosed walkway to bloom from out of its depression in to a welcoming, wholesomely decorated entrance. The door's handle jiggled slightly before it was opened as wide as the short security chain would permit. Dr. Clemens peered out at them from within, and then swiftly shut it again. Jack was just about to reach for the handle and try the door, when he heard the security chain clatter as it was being disengaged from the other side. Then, the door opened again. This time Dr. Clemens opened it completely. With fear and anxiety displayed in his eyes, he quickly ushered them in and immediately closed the door behind them.

"I knew you'd come looking for me sooner or later after I saw the two of you together at the hospital." Clemens led them through the living room and into the kitchen. Without unnecessary introductions being made, he offered them both a chair in which to sit at the large wooden table. Jack had sensed distress quivering in the doctor's voice.

"That's what you're going to explain," Jack demanded, adding, "Why did you run from me today?"

The Watchful Eye

Clemens fumbled around in the cupboards without answering the question. Looking for glasses, he offered them something to drink while pouring himself a shot of vodka, "I don't usually drink this stuff, but tonight I'll make an exception. Would you care for some?" Jack and Sharon both declined but accepted water instead.

After downing the shot, Clemens filled the glass with ice, added another healthy measure of vodka, and then topped off the ensemble with orange juice. Taking the half-empty bottle of vodka with him, the doctor sat down at the table next to his guests and searched his mind for a comfortable place to begin.

Sharon and Jack watched and listened silently as Clemens began to tell his story. Looking to find the easiest path for his own conscience, he began to talk in circles without making much sense. Finally, he got himself on the right path and started his story from the very beginning.

Telling his story, he often sank momentarily into a weary depression. From the other side of the table, Sharon thought she saw a man who was teetering on the brink of destruction. One that would probably give up looking for a possible means of escape from whatever problems plagued him.

Five years ago, as Dr. Clemens described, his wife had been diagnosed with lung Cancer. Luckily, there had only been only one small tumor growing in the lower lobe of her left lung. Without having to treat her chemically, or with radiology, the oncologist, along with the hospital's best surgeon, decided the best possible solution would be to remove the lower portion of that lung, taking the cancer with it. The surgery had been a complete success and his wife was given a clean bill of health. One year later, however, she was back in the hospital with numerous tumors attacking the remaining half of her lung as well as her spinal column.

"The pain is horrible for her. She can't even sleep throughout the night without a massive dose of drugs." Clemens eyes started to tear up but he quickly got a hold of himself.

The following year Clemens had lightened his patient load in order to spend more time taking care of his wife and her many needs. Both of their boys who were off at University, one studying criminal law, and the other in his second year of medical school, had offered to quit their studies to come back home and help take care of their mother. Proud of his sons and their intentions, but focusing on their best interests, Clemens wouldn't stand for it. Both had worked pragmatically to earn their scholarships, and both were wonderful and intelligent boys who deserved the best for the future. He demanded that they stay in school.

As the medical bills were slowly piling up, Clemens decided on selling the house. Without a huge mortgage he would have the means to catch up financially, and possibly lighten his patient load even further. If he invested his equity wisely, he would have plenty of cash to pay for her treatments, and still have enough left over to purchase a small cozy home.

That's when his problems began. Two weeks after he had put his house on the market, he was informed that the government had put a lein on his property for its full worth. Further investigation showed that he was in to the IRS for eight hundred and sixty-three thousand dollars. This was preposterous.

Dr. Clemens hired a lawyer, but that didn't get him anywhere. Three had taken his case with incontrovertible reassurance to its outcome, only to return his retainer and drop him like a hot potato shortly thereafter. Clemens had no other choice but to increase his patient load and put his wife in a care home where someone would be available to take care of her every need on a twenty-four-hour basis.

The Watchful Eye

Then, as if his troubles weren't deep enough, things only got worse. Scott, his oldest son, received a letter from his University's financial department regarding his scholarship. He was being dropped. According to the letter, Scott had been convicted of drug trafficking prior to his acceptance. Stating that he had lied on his application, they were left with no other choice but to revoke his scholarship. Clemens knew without having to ask that his son was completely innocent. He had never touched drugs in his life, and Clemens would bet his own if he could.

That same week his younger son Brad was arrested while walking home to his apartment on two separate counts of rape and aggravated assault. Crying, he had called his father from jail where he was being held on a three hundred thousand-dollar bond.

In a two-week time period Clemens life had gone from one of hope-filled desperation to a measure of pure living hell, where he was utterly surrounded by maddening defeat.

Jack and Sharon were in complete awe. Listening to Clemens story, they had all but forgotten why they were there. Sharon watched Clemens as he slowly swirled the small primarily melted slivers of ice in the bottom of his glass. No wonder he looked so impoverished and mentally beaten. She wanted so badly to console him, but knew that there was still more to the story. Whatever it was, it somehow involved her and Jack.

"I tried everything I could think of but there was nothing I could do. Both of my boys needed me, and I couldn't help either one. My wife needed me, but my hands were tied there too. The whole world seemed to turn against my family and I couldn't do a damn thing to change it." Clemens eyes sunk deeper into sadness as he continued to tell the story.

Two days after he had received the heartbreaking phone call from Brad, he had returned home from work to find an older looking man comfortably lounging in his living room while awaiting his arrival. Had he known he were there before he had opened the door and walked in, he would have notified the police, but by the time he saw him, the door was slammed shut by a large man in a black uniform.

Clemens was trapped. At first he was in shock and thought that he had entered the wrong house, but a quick look around at his furnishings proved that thought to be wrong. Before he could ask who they were and what they were doing in his house, he was grabbed from behind by the man in uniform and shoved over to his couch where he was forced to sit down in front of the older, distinguished looking, gray-haired man. Flashing credentials, he had explained that they worked for the government. Not being able to make out the names or organization on the IDs', Clemens had demanded to see them again. He wanted to be able to confirm their employment, followed by a serious complaint to their superior. Breaking and entering was illegal no matter what overzealous arm of the government they worked for, not to mention the way they had forced him to sit down like a dog in his own living room. Clemens quickly learned that demanding any information only roughened his treatment. His questions were ignored, and only resulted in him getting punched in the gut by the bulky uniformed man. When he was finally able to catch his breath and sit up, he was told by the man in the suit that he was to listen and speak only when asked to. Then the elder man asked him if his son Scott would be able to clear his record in order to complete his medical school; how his wife was coping in a nursing home, and if the cancer looked like it might go into remission. He had even memorized information from her medical charts, details that weren't normally permitted for viewing by family members. They knew about the lein on his house and his finances, all the way down to the last penny. They knew everything.

At first, they had almost acted like they felt sympathy for what the doctor and his family were going through, but eventually, it became clear that all of his recent hardships, with the exception of his wife's cancer, were of their doing. It wasn't long after that they began making demands.

"I couldn't believe what was happening to me!" Clemens stated. "It was obvious at that point that they didn't work for the government, but how else would they know every breath my family took and when? They knew every medication my wife was on and what time it would be administered. They even knew every test score my boys had received in school and could account for every minute of their day. Lord only knows what they know about me. Hell, they probably even know what color my urine was this morning before I went to work."

As Clemens was telling his story, Jack became more certain that Clemens *was* in fact, dealing with the government. While in the CIA, he had learned all of their many predatory tactics for finding a target's weakness, and then magnifying that weakness until the target is overcome into mental submission, without any use of force. Once backed into a corner, it was amazing what people would give, or give up, to bring order back into their lives.

Thinking along those lines, Jack couldn't see any reason for the CIA's interest in Clemens. Before coming, he had looked at a thorough background check of the doctor himself, besides, laws prevented agencies from disrupting its own citizens privacy. Use of predatory tactics would only fault the agency in question if ever their findings were called upon for legal purposes. What had this guy done that Don hadn't been able to pull up on his computer? Confident in his assumption, Jack continued to listened inquisitively as Clemens continued to tell his story.

Clemens stated that he had been asked to give three injections at the hospital to three unnamed people in order to get his life back. With the state his life was already in, these were interpreted as serious demands with heavy consequences for failure. According to the man sitting in his living room, after all three were given, his life would return to normal and he would no longer have a need to sell his house. His two sons would be given sincere apologies for the awful mistakes that were bestowed upon them by the authorities in question. They would also be honored back into their Universities with every effort made to see that they were given a fair chance to resume their academic standing at the time of the mishap. The lein would be released from his property and his house would be paid in full as well. The only thing they weren't able to arrange was his wife's freedom from cancer, unless he chose not to comply.

"If you're not willing," the man had said nodding to the bulky man in uniform, "Sgt. Stalls knows how to take care of cancer. Don't you Sgt.?"

The large man dressed in black fatigues placed his hand over an enormous gun that was strapped to his waist. Saying nothing, but glaring hatefully at Clemens, he conveyed a look of pleasure with the thought of delivering death's ultimate passion to Clemens' helpless wife. Looking into Sgt. Stalls' eyes, Clemens had seen evil in its purest, most hateful state. Thinking of the suggestion and how it was made, Clemens had almost thrown up.

"What are the injections for, and who were you supposed to give them to?" Jack asked.

"I'm not sure what they are. They never said, and I was too afraid to ask." Clemens stood up and walked over to the refrigerator where he removed a small bag that contained all three of the inoculation pens. He sat back down at the table and handed one of them to Jack.

"Do you know what they are?"

Jack was confused by the question. "No, why would I know?"

Clemens hesitated. "Because that one was for you," he said referring to the empty pen that Jack was rolling between his fingers.

The Watchful Eye

Dumbfounded, and in complete silence, Jack studied the pen even closer. It was about half the girth of an ordinary pencil, and almost four inches long. There was a seven-digit number stamped across the length of it. "What does it do?" Jack finally asked.

"I don't know. I was hoping you would. I was only told to administer it."

"Did you?" Jack asked looking straight into the doctor's eyes. For a long drawn out moment, silence filled the kitchen and provoked Jack's impatience with its ignorance. Avidly hoping to bridle his fear, as well as fill the agonizing void of rejoinder, Jack lent his hunger to the question and asked again with vigilance, "Well, did you?" His probing stare narrowed in on Clemens vacuous expression.

"Not to you," the doctor said so quietly that he could have been mistaken for speaking to himself. Jack almost felt a flutter of relief before he realized the doctor's saddened eyes were regrettably focusing on Sharon. Following the doctor's penitent stare, he could almost feel remorse as though it were flowing from Clemens every pore and slowly filling the room. He looked at Sharon and felt the hands of pain twisting and tearing at his heart.

Sharon's eyes were frozen in disbelief. Watching the doctor's expression sink deeper into despair, she had already determined what Clemens had avoided saying. The inoculation had been given to her.

Chapter Fifteen

Forty-five minutes had passed since Sgt. Stalls received the glorious phone call informing him that his services would once again be requested. Since then he had been kneeling on the floor in the middle of the small bedroom with his eyes closed in an attempt to disconnect himself from his surroundings. Darkness held every explanation for life that he could possibly search for in the palm of its quiet, soothing hand. In this darkness, he was able to escape the confinement of an inchoate world into which he was so crudely born.

Had he another chance, he would kill his mother all over again for having brought him into this world without his permission. She had been a cruel woman. One that had needed to be punished for her mistakes. Every day that he lived, Stalls reminded himself of the extent in which he despised the witch for what she had done to him by giving him birth. Birth was not a gift, it was a cruel form of punishment that he was unable to give back.

Eyes closed to the world around him, the beautifully deep and darkened silence flowed through his soul and slowly washed away his restless anxiety, leaving behind a much stronger regenerated sense of self-being.

While in the depths of meditation, Stalls was not only in tune with, but *was*, in his mind, each and every cell of his body. He was his heart, his soul, and his mind in the most intimate of senses. As his soul, he glided gracefully through his body controlling any and all of his internal organs and their respective functions.

Although this was not actually the case, while in meditation, Stalls believed that he was the very tissue of each individual organ in his body. Every neurological impulse that shot across his brain was felt in a personal sense, as if he himself were a single or any combination of the millions of neurons of which it were composed.

With the use of his powerfully meditative and enlightened mind, he believed he could crush his own heart with the very muscles that kept it alive, rendering himself lifeless and allowing his soul to be freed from the clutches of its organic prison, the prison his wicked mother had unjustly put him in.

Many times while meditating, Stalls had considered doing just that and would have had it not been for his fear of sinking permanently into the unknown. Death wasn't a gift that a person could bestow upon himself, but a gift that had to be given with honor. Stalls had given death's gift repeatedly throughout his life and had patiently waited for its return every since he could remember.

Stalls didn't believe in God, therefore, he wasn't afraid of leaving this world to be trapped in the next. If there were a God, Stalls' biggest fear would have been imprisonment in that hopeless *God-made* afterlife. One in which millions of people in this fatuous world struggled for throughout their severely deranged and pathetic lives. What for? Hopes of living on after death in a make believe heaven?

Death most surely is permanent for the weak and inattentive. Afterlife is only a feeble idea created by cowardly men who didn't have the guts to take what they wanted in this life. Punishment for sin was nothing more

The Watchful Eye

than an excuse created by those cowards with hopes of being able to live comfortably under the scrutiny of their fellow man without the burden of having to fight for right or reason to live as one chooses.

Turbulent in his thoughts, Stalls felt a rush of anger and hatred for these insanely sanctimonious men who created the idea of sin and order, and their hellish guidelines. Hopeless and pathetic, society has used the fear of God's punishment as a weapon against stronger more versatile men like himself. Men who live by taking brutally, if necessary, one's desires and wishes. Only the strong survive was Stalls' motto. Weak, pathetically intimidated men use politics and democracy as a means to fight for their freedom and preach Christianity in hopes for survival against men like himself. Men they most certainly should fear.

Throughout time, fear of this so-called God and his punishment, along with government and its laws, has brought a once barbaric society slowly to its knees before appointed leaders. Conforming as puppets to this ever-changing society of cowards who call themselves lawmakers, the strong had renounced a power once held proudly. The thought of it sickened him. Eventually, Stalls would get that power back. Eventually, the world would bow down to him!

Stalls didn't believe in Satan either, although he sometimes wished a demon of great power and a love for destruction actually existed. If so, he would proudly serve this fairytale devil to the ends of this coward-infested earth, gladly witnessing its painful destruction.

Nonetheless, had he killed himself during meditation instead of being killed, he might possibly be lost forever without honor. Even though he could feel the power of his soul through meditation and was certain that it would remain as powerful after death, godlike in its own right and devastatingly formidable without its body-like prison, he couldn't bring himself to risk being wrong. Honor and death went together hand and hand. Stalls knew that separately, both were worthless. Death was what he aspired to but in order to die with honor, he would have to be killed by the hand of another. Smiling at the thought of one day having that honor, Stalls desired that his death be painfully brutal. He wished to die the most honorable death possible. Then, he could leave this world with power, not as a helpless soul condemned to heaven or hell, but as a free spirit with honor.

Slowly he brought himself back from the darkness that surrounded him. Deep in meditation, he had lowered his heart rate and respirations to a pace that was very near death. Drawing nearer to a full state of consciousness, he began to feel a dull throbbing ache in his knees and ankles brought on by being tucked under the full weight of his body. More aware of his physical being as a whole, he began to see unrecognizable patterns floating across his retina as his eyes attempted to focus under his still closed eyelids. Sitting as still as he had been, he opened his eyes and looked straightforward.

Seeing nothing more than his inner thoughts, as if he were still in a trance, Stalls basked in the fresh new feeling that always accompanied time away from himself and his physical surroundings. Then, as if someone had abruptly snapped their fingers, he broke through his mental barrier and came back to where he had always been.

The small room was mostly dark with the exception of three burning candles that he had lit and placed single file on the top of the cheap wooden table prior to meditation.

With the exception of his calm, steady breathing, not a sound moved through the room, and none seeped in from outside beyond the window. The night was exceptionally silent.

The Watchful Eye

Shadows danced slowly and seductively in all four corners of the tiny room, relentlessly trying to overcome the minimal amount of light cast by the tiny, flickering flames.

Something small moved high up in the corner by the ceiling catching Stalls' attention. He noticed a small dark shadow maneuvered carelessly from within the pitch-black corner. Steadily moving, it transformed into a cockroach as it continued across the wall, its features uncovered by the candles' flickering flames. From out of the darkness it progressed across the wall until it was directly in front of him. From there it headed down toward the baseboard.

Stopping occasionally, and then scurrying again, the cockroach slowly made its way to the carpet and began crawling across the fibrous blue hills and valleys. It appeared as though it was on a collision course with the Sgt. himself who was still kneeling in the center of the room. Stalls remained perfectly still as he watched the small dark insect make his way curiously across the carpet and over to his left.

Candlelight flickered across the top of the cockroach showing a brownish-red tint between the smooth, moving, soft segments of its abdomen. Its head and hardened forewings were midnight black. Stopping sporadically along the way, it finally reached Stalls and began to crawl up the side of his bare leg.

Stalls focused all of his attention on feeling each one of the insects hairy little legs as it crawled across his skin. He continued to watch as the filthy little bug stopped halfway up his calf to wave its long, thin antennae from side to side. Stalls wondered what unessential thoughts a bug could possibly have. Moving again, the cockroach crawled up from his calf onto his thigh. From there it made its way up and across the back of Stalls' left hand that was still resting atop his knee.

Stalls lifted his arm in an effort to eliminate the roach's quickest means of escape should it choose to scurry off.

With the exception of waving antennae, the bug remained perfectly still. Stalls brought his hand toward his face in order to closely study the cockroach.

"So you're the only thing on this earth that would survive a nuclear holocaust, huh?"

He rotated his wrist to look at the roach from all angles, then in the blink of an eye, snatched up the roach with his right hand.

"What makes you so special?" he said, now holding the squirming bug between thumb and forefinger. Stall's squeezed it in hopes that it might make a noise, a squeal, or maybe some sort of bug scream. Nothing.

Being creatures of survival, Stalls decided to put the odious little bug to the test. He brought it to his mouth and bit off its head. He chewed on the crunchy segment of insect until there was nothing left to chew, then swallowed. It didn't taste as bad as he had expected, somewhat bitter if anything. He discarded the roach's body into the waste can.

"Let's see if you can survive that!"

Stalls got up from the floor and walked over to the little tattered table, thinking that somewhere he had heard a cockroach could survive for a week without the use of its head.

He blew out the candles, turned on the overhead light, and then picked out a fresh black uniform. After showering and dressing, he would drive over to the hanger and then fly out to a temporary command post that would be set up for Operation Nighthawk. The mission had finally been placed back on the active roster and he was ecstatic at the thought of being unleashed.

Chapter Sixteen

For a moment Sharon was speechless. Then, as if she didn't believe that it was actually of any consequence to her, she calmly asked Clemens to tell them exactly what had happened.

Feeling nothing but remorse for what he had done, Clemens poured another shot of vodka with unsteady hands and answered the question without any expectation of forgiveness.

"I administered the injection to you while you were at the hospital having your shoulder sewn back up the same day that you had been brought into the emergency room. Before I was told to give it to you, I had been paid a visit by another so-called government man. He had given me a manila folder that contained several snapshots of you," he said alluding to Jack, "and told me to prepare for your arrival. According to him you're a very dangerous man, Jack. He also said that their organization has been keeping tabs on you for quite some time and that if I messed this up I wouldn't be given another chance. That's why I ran from you today. I couldn't believe it when I saw you in the hospital and realized that the two of you were together. I thought you knew what I had agreed to do and were at the hospital looking to beat me to death."

"I wasn't," Jack stated, "but the thought *has* crossed my mind since." Although Jack's comment wasn't meant to be a solemn vow, Clemens knew by the look in Jack's eyes that it wasn't meant as a friendly joke by any means.

"So why did you infect me, or whatever the hell it is that *that* thing does?" Sharon asked in reference to the empty inoculation pen that was now laying on the table in front of Jack.

Even though she had already been contaminated and was now carrying whatever substance it had contained around inside of her in a possibly lethal mix with her own life fluids, she couldn't bring herself to pick it up, not even in the name of morbid curiosity. That would only lend to an acceptance of violation and the thought already sickened her.

"For some reason they changed their mind. I don't know why and didn't ask. All I know is that I received a phone call about five minutes before you were brought in. They told me that their plans had changed and that I was to inoculate you instead. I wished afterwards with all I was worth that I hadn't, but I did."

Looking back at what he had done, Clemens resented himself for being too cowardly to find a different solution.

"These men are ruthless and I was afraid of what would happen to my family if I didn't do as they asked. At the time, I felt like I was doing what I had to do in order to survive. You've got to understand. I couldn't see that I had any other choice."

While he was talking Clemens half-expected Sharon to reach across the table and grab for his throat, but she remained remarkably calm. She was a beautiful lady who deserved much better than what he had dealt her, whatever that was. He thought about his two boys and the horribly destructive situation they had been placed in. How could he

The Watchful Eye

have allowed himself to do the same to her? What was going to happen to Sharon? What had he done?

As terrible as the men were who were controlling him, he now felt that he was just as bad. Looking at Sharon, he was profoundly ashamed of the part he had played in transferring his own hellish struggles on to her in a desperate attempt to release his own family from intended harm. Overwhelmed by his many troubles, along with the sacrifice he had made to his morals and self-respect, Clemens held his face in the palm of his hands and cried.

Lacking an ability to feel forgiveness, which would allow absolution of Clemens' actions, yet able to understand his predicament, Sharon slid over into the chair next to Clemens and placed a comforting hand on his shoulder.

Jack was unable to share her sympathy. Instead, he reached for the vodka and poured himself a shot. The burning sensation provided by the alcohol only complimented his fiery desire to reach across the table and add another threat to the doctor's long list. This one, however, would be fulfilled only a split second after it was made. Realizing that he wouldn't accomplish anything by releasing his anger physically, Jack redirected his indignation toward the problem at hand. Whoever these men were, they seemed to know something about him. Was it possible that they knew about the AFA? He spent some time thinking about all of the unit's recent findings and tried to determine whether his team had been discovered. If so, what had they found that might have been considered a threat to whatever they were trying to accomplish. Looking at Sharon, he only drew a blank. What could she possibly have to do with anything that would interest the government or this seemingly malicious organization? He couldn't think of anything they might know about him that could possibly be related to her. He hadn't even met her until the day she had been attacked, and even then, she had only been an innocent bystander. No matter how hard he tried, he couldn't come up with any ideas that might connect her to him or his line of work.

What was the purpose of the injection and why had it been intended for him in the first place? Jack was already creating a plan of action. As soon as he was back at the unit, he would look over Don's report from the police department's computer files. Maybe it would give him an understanding of who those two guys were that had attacked him at the beach. If not, he would at least have a lead on how to find them. As the intended target for this injection, he had also been expected to arrive at the hospital that day. If so, that means that those two punks were somehow involved. They weren't just a couple of trouble making idiots, they had a hidden agenda that ran much deeper than a meaningless little brawl on the beach. This led him to think about Ted and how different he had always seemed. Now, considering the idea of using his sadistic talents for interrogation as a means to squeeze a few answers from those two intellectually deprived lunatics, he was almost able to consider Ted a friend.

"Is there anything you can think of that you might have left out?" he asked the doctor who was now wiping his face with a tissue. "Something that might explain what the injection does or why you were told to give it to her instead? Anything at all?"

"No, nothing," Clemens said searching his brain for memories of anything that had been said, "I've told you everything."

Jack took a pen and a small piece of paper from his breast pocket and wrote down the numbers that were imprinted on both of the two remaining pens. On a different piece of paper he wrote down the number to a secured line that would connect Clemens to the gym's underground unit. Then he wrote down his cell phone number. Jack picked up the empty inoculation pen and placed it back in the pouch with the two that had remained unused. He asked Clemens

The Watchful Eye

for a zip lock bag and the doctor complied. After placing the pouch inside the zip lock, he filled the larger bag with ice from the freezer and sealed it.

"What are you going to do?" Clemens asked.

"I'm not sure yet," he lied, "but it involves finding some answers."

"What do you want me to do?"

"I want your help in finding those answers."

"How can I do that? I've already told you everything I know."

Jack handed him the two separate pieces of paper with an explanation.

"Whatever you do, don't repeat anything you've told us to anyone else. Go back to the hospital tomorrow morning and do whatever it is you do as if none of this had ever happened. If you're asked to give another one of those injections, agree to do it and then give them one of those pen numbers I wrote down as if you had. Finish your shift as you normally would and then call my cell number from a pay phone after you've left the hospital. Don't leave your name, your number, or any sort of message that can be overheard by an outside source. Leave a call back time so I'll know it's you."

"What do you mean?"

"That second number will put you through to a secured phone line and I'll be waiting for your call at whatever time you've specified. It's very important that you only call from a pay phone, preferably a different one each time. From there we can determine a safe place to meet. I'll want you to bring me the full name of whomever you were asked to inject along with anything else that you know about that person. This is very important. You have a chance to do the right thing. Can you do that?"

"Yes of course."

Jack, full of confidence and calculation appeared to know exactly what he was doing.

"Are you a cop or something?" Clemens asked.

"The less I tell you, the safer you are. Just know that I'm someone you can trust and that I want to help."

Clemens looked at Sharon hoping to find the answer in her eyes, but she was also looking to Jack with awed confusion. Recognizing her to be as innocent a victim as he himself was, he decided that he was willing to do whatever it took to make up for what he had done to her. He felt confident that Jack knew what to do. With a chance to right his wrong, he also felt a sliver of hope toward restitution for his treachery. After all, whoever these horrible men were, they had expressed a fear of Jack as if they considered him an enemy. Jack seemed to have an understanding of them as well. With confidence in Jack's calm-and-collected approach, and lack of any better solutions thereafter, Clemens smiled for the first time in months. Relieved, he agreed to do whatever Jack desired as long as it meant keeping harm from coming to even one more person.

Feeling comfortable that Clemens had turned a new leaf and that there was nothing left to discuss, Jack picked up the zip lock full of ice-cold mystery and walked Sharon out to his car.

Parked at the curb on the side of the nearly vacant street, Jack hadn't a chance to turn over the engine before Sharon started in with questions of her own.

"Who are you and what just happened in there?"

"Can this wait a minute so I can think?"

"Absolutely not! You seem to know what's happening and I think it's time you shed some light pal."

"Look, I'll tell you the same thing I just told him. Less is more. The less you know the safer you are."

"Listen Mr. Policeman, or Detective Kurts, or whoever you think you are. Whatever you're carrying around in that little bag, I'm carrying around in my body. If anyone has the right to know what's going on, it's me. What can't you

The Watchful Eye

tell me that's going to hurt me more than whatever *was* in that pen thing?"

"Okay, you have a point," Jack agreed, "but what I'm going to tell you has to stay strictly between you and me, agreed?"

"Agreed. Now start talking!"

Jack explained everything he knew to Sharon, which wasn't much. He told her about the AFA and its objective, but little more. As far as the inoculations, he didn't even have a clue yet as to what their purpose might be, but he assured her that he had a friend that could possibly help him find out. He also told her about how Don had checked department records on the two guys that had attacked them at Venice Beach. Other than that, he was unable to provide the answers she was looking for.

Bewildered by what she had just heard. Sharon didn't say much. For the most part, she sat in silence while Jack started the engine and flipped the car around in order to head back the way they had come. Nearing the end of the street Jack noticed a black SUV parked along side the curb. What he didn't notice through the darkly tinted SUV's windows were the two heavily armed men in uniform, one whose left ear was adorned by a small one-way listening device. He turned right and drove away without giving it much concern.

"So you're a spy?" Sharon asked.

"No."

"Sounds like it to me."

"No, it's nothing like that. If you had to classify what I do, it would be a little more like law enforcement. You know, to protect and to serve."

"So why did you lie to me?" Sharon asked angrily.

"Lie?"

"Yeah, you know, telling me you run a fitness center. Is your name even Jack, or is that just a name you use when you're deep undercover?"

"Look," Jack explained. "What I do for a living is kept secret for very important reasons. I didn't lie to you, I was just doing my job."

"You did lie to me and if that's part of your job, somebody needs to give you a raise because you're doing a great job!"

"Obviously you're upset and I can understand that but you have to realize that I'm not the enemy. If I went around telling everyone I meet for the first time that I work for a secret government agency, it wouldn't remain a secret for very long. I'm sorry this has happened to you and I'll do anything I possibly can to change it. I want to be your friend and right now you could use one. What do you say?"

"What kind of name is Kurts anyway?" Sharon asked, smiling and trying to change the subject.

"I don't know. Probably English, why?" Jack replied furrowing his brow.

"Wasn't James Bond English?"

"James Bond? What does he have to do with anything?"

"He's a spy."

"I told you already, I'm not a spy!" Jack laughed.

Sharon opened the glove box and began shuffling through his belongings. Curious and a little concerned, he asked what she was doing.

"Looking for buttons," she exclaimed still shuffling through its contents.

"Huh? What buttons?"

"You know, the one that controls the machine guns. There has to be more to this car of yours than meets the eye." Sharon couldn't help but laugh when she saw a disbelieving look on Jack's face. Facetiously she began humming the theme song from mission impossible.

Chuckling to himself, Jack realized that he had been duped from the start. Continuing her antics, Jack watched and laughed as Sharon started bobbing her head and slapping a beat on her knees in unison with the spy music she was happily humming. Defeated, he merely shook his head and returned his focus to the road in front of him.

Once out of the neighborhood and back onto the main roads Jack decided to pull over at a restaurant so they could grab a bite to eat. He called Don as he was pulling into the parking lot and set up a time to meet at the center after he and Sharon ate a late dinner. He then hung up.

"Spy stuff?"

"Huh?" Jack asked although he knew exactly where she was going.

"You're meeting with spy guy Don. Spy stuff right?"

"If I told you, I'd have to kill you. You don't want that do you?"

Sharon laughed playfully and then with exaggerated helplessness stated, "That's a big double no seven."

During the meal, Jack noticed Sharon's mood decline as she thought about what had been done to her. He had already determined that her playfulness in the car earlier had been nothing more than a protective strategy she had used to cover up her fear and denial. Putting himself in her shoes, he couldn't blame her at all.

With everything to say, but not sure how to say it, they ate together in an agreeable silence. Trying to lift her spirits, he promised that he would do everything in his power to help her and she believed him.

After dinner, he dropped her off at her house where he held her close for a while and offered her more reassurance.

After seeing her safely inside her house, he left for the center where he would meet with Don.

Chapter Seventeen

Impatiently, Jack rode the elevator down to the underground portion of the fitness center where Don was already in the meeting room making coffee. Even as late as it was, Don looked cheery as usual.

"How's the coffee?" Jack asked as he stepped from out of the elevator.

"I made it strong just like you like. The way you sounded on the phone, I figured it was going to be a late night. What's up?"

"We'll talk about it in your office," Jack said while taking a quick glance around the room. "Where's Ted?" he asked when he didn't find what he was looking for. While walking through the center, Jack realized that he hadn't seen him on any of the equipment upstairs.

Usually, Ted spent a lot of late evenings at the center when he wasn't being pulled from the area and sent off on assignment elsewhere. When he was at the center and off duty however, he simply hung around with his face buried in one of his newest books. Other times, he spent those long late hours making full use of the many exercise machines that were scattered throughout the floor above.

WESS REED

To Jack, Ted seemed obsessive when it came to his workouts. Frequently out of town, he claimed a need to put extra effort into his workout to make up for the lost time when he had to miss a session or two. Ted's idea of extra effort, however, was more like a valiant attempt at anger management that most often ended in failure. Jack often wondered how Ted's favorite pieces of equipment managed to survive those long and vigorous punishment sessions. If the machines had been capable of spirit, Ted had surely shattered them long ago.

"He was called out about three hours ago. Too bad he always comes back, huh?"

"What do you mean?" Jack asked. Don wasn't the type to complain, so his statement managed to catch Jack's full attention. If Don didn't like a certain person, or the way something was going, he simply tried a different approach guided by a positive attitude. This seemed to be out of character for him.

"That guy really gives me the creeps. He never talks to anybody. He never tries to be a part of what's going on. He just hangs around reading those stupid books like he's on vacation. When he finally does look up, he always has that mean look on his face. You know the one, like he's way too busy to concentrate on what was said because he's hard at work trying to determine how many different ways he could stomp your ass. What's with that guy anyway? Does he have a purpose here other than being our freakishly overgrown hall monitor?"

"Oh come on, he's not that bad," Jack said with a laugh, "just give him a chance. He'll come around eventually. Before you know it, you'll be spending your weekends over at his house having cookouts and telling each other stories on the back porch."

Don's face, like a child who just experienced his first taste of lemon, shriveled with disgust in an attempt to display his outright disagreement. Jack laughed again at

The Watchful Eye

Don's over exaggerated expression. Obviously, he had taken the remark for being downright offensive.

"Yeah right. I can already imagine the different ways we could get along. He could use my head as a door stop, or a book end, or a medicine ball, or a..."

"Okay, that's enough. We've got some work to do." Jack poured his coffee and headed for the offices down the hall. Don followed him while still mumbling under his breath, "maybe a basketball, or a shot put, or a bowling ball..."

Jack stepped into Don's office and sat his coffee cup on a small corner table that, unlike the rest of the tables in the room, wasn't under the burden of holding up some form of electronic hardware. He pulled out the zip lock and set it down as well. Watching, Don asked, "What's in the bag?"

"That's what we're going to work on tonight," Jack replied. Then he repeated a much briefer version of the story Dr. Clemens had told him and Sharon earlier that evening.

"What do you think was in it?" Don asked studying the empty pen that Jack had removed from the pouch.

"I'm not sure yet. I'm gonna get Avery on the line and see if he can come down and have a look."

Avery Harris was a scientist that Jack had met during the time he had spent working for the CIA. They had both been assigned to work on a highly classified atomic weapons detection project overseas. Together, along with a handful of other men, they had worked on the assignment for three weeks before enough intelligence had been gathered to uncover the plant and have it shut down permanently. During that time, they had plenty of opportunity to get to know each other and had eventually become good friends. They had remained friends since. Jack carried no doubts that Avery was a man he could count on and trust.

"While I'm talking to him," Jack continued, "I was hoping you could gather up everything you had found on those two guys from the beach a couple days ago."

"Is she okay?" Don asked.

"I hope so, but until we can find out what was in that thing we can't be sure. Could be some kind of medical experiment. If that's the case, we'll have a hard time finding out anything."

The concern shown in Jack's eyes pulled at Don's heart. After all, Jack was by far the best boss, and probably one of the better friends Don had ever had. But, because they had only spent time together at work, he couldn't state his thoughts on their friendship factually like people that hung out together could.

Outside of work Jack liked to keep distance between himself and his employees, however, there was no doubt in Don's mind concerning what type of person Jack was. Don had worked with Jack long enough to consider him a true friend, and knew that if they had been friends outside the office, Jack would be the kind of friend you could count on through thick and thin.

As soon as Jack had finished telling Don the story about the mysterious pens, he placed them back in the pouch and then carried them over to the small refrigerator in the meeting room. From there he went into his own office where he called Avery on a secure line. Thirty minutes later he had finished setting up a time and place to make the transfer, then hung up.

Don knocked on the door shortly after and stepped into the room looking distraught. He had a hand full of paperwork that he spread out on the big desk.

"You're not going to believe this," he said handing Jack a printout from the police records that he had broken into a few days earlier. "This is everything the police department had on file for those two thugs that jumped you. While you were on the phone, I used this information to cross reference phone bills, bank records, utility services, anything I could do or think of to find a correct physical address for them. It appears that the police department doesn't have one."

"And?" Jack asked examining the printed version of the few negative impacts Scott and Preston had left on society.

"Well, they either lived in a cardboard box, or they both lived with their parents. Neither one of them popped up when I looked for a credit trail."

"So there's no way of finding them?" Jack questioned with disbelief.

"That's the thing. After doing an automatic search through public records, I did find them," he handed Jack two more sheets of printed paper, "but, they're both dead."

Jack let out a heavy sigh while reading the printout. According to Don's latest find, Preston Felder and Scott Smith were both found dead, floating upside down in a half sunken fishing boat off the coast of San Diego three days after they had attacked Jack and Sharon at the beach. Both had been shot in the back of the head execution style.

"How could this have happened?" Jack demanded in frustration. "Those two idiots were the only lead I had."

Jack flung the papers he was holding onto the desk as he leaned back into his chair. With hopes to shun this new disappointment, he closed his eyes and struggled to contain his emotions. Somehow, he had to find another lead. He had to know who was responsible for these injections and their intended purpose if he were going to find any possible solution. From within his eyelid-induced darkness, nothing came to light.

Feeling defeated, Don went back into the computer room to close up shop and go home. He had offered to stay and keep Jack company until he was ready to go make the drop with that lab guy, but Jack requested some time alone to think things through. He looked very discouraged and Don couldn't say that he blamed him.

Don closed all of the open files that he had been looking into, and then programmed a few random night scans of his system. After shutting down a number of humming and blinking devices, he walked over to the door and reached for the light switch. Instead of turning out the lights, however, he walked back over to his chair and took a seat.

Not the least bit tired or hungry, Don decided that he'd rather stick around for a while. He had plenty of work to do, besides, if Jack thought of something that would require his assistance, he'd be here and on the ready.

Don noticed the list of people that he had looked up from the Watchful Eye program, and their background information that he had spent tedious hours obtaining. The process of looking through paperwork didn't excite him in the least, but he had nothing better to do. Picking up the list, he swiveled his chair around backwards and over to the little corner table where he would have more room to work. Before digging any further, however, he got up from his chair and decided to take a trip to the coffee machine. Without coffee, shuffling through paperwork would coerce his mind into a boredom-induced stupor in less than an hour, whether he was tired or not.

Staring at print on a computer screen didn't effect Don like paperwork did. Maybe it was because the computer allowed him to change and manipulate whatever he happened to be looking at, at any time he wished, and with an unending variety of options. With paperwork, his skills were pretty much limited to a simple flipping of the page.

In the meeting room Don poured a hot, steamy, mind-refreshing cup of coffee and returned to his office.

Previously, Don had scanned quickly through the first thirty people looking for things like employment, age, religion, location, income and anything else that would possibly be a link. So far he had found nothing. After scanning through another thirty he had decided that the only thing these people had in common was that they were all on

The Watchful Eye

the list, and furthermore, that he had invaded their privacy illegally. Other than that and the fact that most were female...*Female?*

Don scanned the rest of the list looking only at first names. Most of which *were* female. Then he looked for similarities that females might share and found that ninety two percent of these women had given birth within the last two years. Don picked up the three pages that he had printed the previous day. They were the ones that were filled with the rows of numbers from the Watchful Eye program, the ones in which he had randomly selected one hundred people whose privacy he would soon be violating. That's when he noticed it.

Don ran out of his office, down the hall, and into the meeting room where he removed the small pouch of pens from the refrigerator. He yelled for Jack who came out of his office just in time to see Don scurrying back into the computer room.

By the time Jack walked through the door, Don was already busy pushing buttons and flipping power switches on every electronic module the room contained. The empty inoculation pen, and the two that were still in the pouch, was laying next to a pile of papers on the small corner desk.

"What's going on?" Jack asked wondering what all the commotion was about.

"I'm not positive yet but I think the correct answer would be, I'm absolutely brilliant!"

While doing what he had to do to get his massive computer system ready to rumble, Don explained what he had discovered while going over the list. Looking over the first three pages and wondering how many were women, he had seen a number that looked familiar. It wasn't the social security number or the birth date, but the last group. On the last of the three pages, about half way down and on the right, one of the mysterious set of numbers following the birth date and social security seemed awfully familiar. It took a while, but then it finally hit him. It appeared to be the same number imprinted on the side of the inoculation pen that had been used on Sharon. Curious, he had ran into the meeting room and returned with the pouch to verify his discovery. They were identical!

Now in the social security department's data bank, he typed in Sharon Andrews and was rewarded with forty-three different listings. Don swiveled around and grabbed the piece of paper whose mysterious number group had matched the used inoculation pen number, and compared that social security number with the forty-three listings for Sharon Andrews on his computer screen. Halfway down the screen there was a match.

Don was astounded at the thought of being correct. If the social security number for this Andrews lady was the same Sharon that he and Jack knew, then all of the people who were represented by numbers on those three pages, had also been inoculated.

All three pages that he had printed contained a combined number of at least three hundred and fifty people. Had he printed the entire list, it would have required well over a hundred or so more pages. Don couldn't bring himself to imagine how many millions of people had been injected with some sort of virus or whatever those pens contained, and then placed on file in some sort of top-secret computer program.

He disconnected from social security, and in no time at all was into the Motor Vehicle Department's computer network. After typing in the matching social security number, he initiated a file search. Shortly after, he and Jack were looking at Sharon's photo ID. Don was right. It was her!

Jack stared at the screen in silence. Don's excitement quickly dwindled as well. Although they had determined that the inoculation was a part of the program, and that Sharon was now somehow tied to it, they were still just as

The Watchful Eye

full of unanswered questions as they had been. Jack pulled up a chair and sat down.

"What do you think it means?" Don asked.

"I don't know."

"Should we call her and let her know?"

"No, I don't think we have anything to tell her that'll make her feel any better. I'd rather wait until we know exactly what's happened to her. I mean, after all, we still don't know what this whole thing is about. Could be a life threatening virus or something as simple as a routine flu vaccination, who knows?"

Don thought about it for a minute in silence then asked, "Do you think it's because she's a woman? We could start looking into that."

"I don't think so. Before it was given to her, it was intended for me."

Trying to cheer up the atmosphere a little, Don said, "Maybe they realized at the last minute that you weren't a woman. I know you had me fooled for a while!"

Don was able to elicit a weak smile, but it quickly faded. He reached over and turned off the monitor that was still beaming Sharon's picture, and then shut the entire system down at Jack's request. It was nearing time for him to meet Avery, so Jack called it a night. Don had wanted to stay and work a while longer, but Jack ordered him to go home and get some rest.

"I want to see you back here tomorrow morning and I don't want you to work on anything else until you know that Watchful Eye program inside out. I want to know exactly what we're up against."

"You can count on it boss," Don said with reassurance. He patted Jack on the shoulder, "Don't worry, Sharon's in good hands."

Don stepped into the elevator to leave as Jack was closing up his office. Before the elevator doors shut, Don told Jack to be careful. He wasn't sure why.

After packing the zip lock full of fresh ice, Jack took the elevator up to the first level and then left the building. As he was pulling out of High Velocity's parking lot, he noticed another black SUV parked across the street from the center. It was identical to the one he had seen not far from Dr. Clemens' house earlier that same evening. Driving to the location in which he made the exchange, and then to his own house afterwards, he watched closely to be sure he wasn't followed.

He wasn't.

Chapter Eighteen

Roy Williams was considered by many to be tough as nails. Tall and burly, he had a full head of shoulder length hair and a bushy brown beard to match. Usually, Roy could be found clad in a pair of denim overalls strapped over a plaid-patterned flannel shirt.

Those that didn't know him were quick to step out of his way while making as little eye contact as possible. At first glance, he looked comparable to a two foot taller, fifty-pound heavier, pissed off version of Grizzly Adams on Ritalin. Those that did know him, however, were quick to shake his hand and spend some time in his company. Although he didn't smile much, he was a good man with a heart of gold and the temperament of a teddy bear, which was shone clearly through his soft brown eyes.

Roy was born and raised in Montana, where he now owned a ranch on one hundred and fifty acres just five miles northeast of Billings. Leaving the state where he had been raised, other than short family visits to his in-laws during holidays, had never been a desire. Montana's rugged beauty, along with its abundance of wildlife, was as deep down in his soul as was the love for his family.

Two years after graduating from high school, Roy had married his best friend, Cathy. Other than his mother, Cathy was the only woman he had ever truly loved. Eventually, after years of hard work and planning to provide a stable lifestyle, they had been blessed with the two children they had always hoped of having. Roy happily played the role of family man, a role that he took very seriously.

His two children, a thirteen-year-old boy, Joshua, and a ten-year-old daughter, Stacey, along with his wife, Cathy, where all it took to make his world turn. Without them he knew he could never continue in this otherwise hollow world. Just the thought of having to live without his family was enough to make him shutter in his tightly laced, scuffed to perfection, leather boots.

Employed by the Department of Agriculture, Roy had worked hard as a soil conservationist every since graduating from high school. His wife, Cathy, who, in his opinion, was still just as beautiful as the day they first met, worked as a hairdresser in Billings, during the winter months, while their children attended public school. During the summer she always took a leave of absence in order to spend the warm summer days taking care of her children while they were out of school. Even though Roy made a descent living and they didn't need the money, she always went back to work when the new school year started. Cathy enjoyed feeling as though she played her part in financially supporting her family.

Cathy was half Roy's size and appeared to be as delicate as a butterfly fluttering against a warm summer breeze, however, when her serene winsome face became the same color as her fiery-hot hair, Roy knew she was capable of dishing out one complete, full size butt-stomping! He carried a lot of pride in knowing what she was capable of without ever having learned the hard way. Ninety-nine percent of the time, however, she was very down to earth, as

The Watchful Eye

free and easy as the wind, compassionate in every sense of the word and often as amusing as a bagful of laughs. She had a full-size heart, packed with enough love for her husband and children to fill all the oceans of the world.

Even though Roy's parents had never forced religion on to him or his two brothers, he must have put holes in the knees of a hundred different pairs of overalls in the process of thanking the Lord each day for making him complete by first giving him his wife and then his two children.

Cathy, like her husband, also had Montana running deep in her blood. On hot summer days, they could usually be found hiking, fishing, canoeing, or rafting down the Little Bighorn. Anything they could do together they did, with one exception to the rule, Cathy didn't like to hunt. Eating venison didn't bother her, but she had never had a desire to kill big game or any other creature for that matter.

Roy, on the other hand, loved to hunt! The thrill of the hunt, not to mention filling his family's freezer with food, was something he looked forward to every year.

Along with hunting, he also had a great love and respect for guns. Shotguns, rifles, pistols, single fire, semiautomatics, he had at least a dozen of each, fifty-nine guns in all to be exact. He even had an automatic assault rifle, although he didn't have a license to own it. Never having used it, he had bought it only to own it. It was a fine piece of metal that had been crafted into a beautiful and well-made tool that he might have never had the chance to come in contact with again.

With the exception of the fully automatic M-16, which he had purchased on the black market when he was only twenty years old, all of Roy's guns were registered and locked securely in safes. Roy considered himself a responsible gun owner. Only one gun stayed in his house, a Glock 9mm, which he kept unloaded with a trigger guard in his nightstand. He would never in a million years be able to forgive himself if something bad were to happen to one of his children as a result of his irresponsible gun ownership.

Shortly after returning home from work this evening, Roy and Cathy had decided to have a nice family dinner outside on a picnic table that Roy and Joshua had built years ago as a father-and-son project. Although it was flimsy, and ugly in appearance to anyone other than Roy, Joshua, and perhaps Cathy, the rickety little picnic table stood for something very strong in the heart of the man who had helped his son to build it.

Cathy was in the kitchen putting together a salad while several ears of freshly plucked corn boiled eagerly on the stove. Their two children, Joshua and Stacey, were sprawled out on the living room floor playing "crazy eight" with a colorful deck of Mickey Mouse playing cards. Roy watched the laughter from outside one of the windows while cleaning the barbecue grill on the back porch.

Chore complete, he entered the kitchen and began dousing four steaks with a handful of seasonings that he had pulled from the spice rack before heading outside to warm up the grill.

He and Cathy, along with their outdoor hobbies, shared the daily chore of cooking and cleaning. When done as a couple, they both agreed that it wasn't so much a chore as it was a family event.

The evening was beautiful. Although not yet close enough to reveal its stars, the approaching night was crystal clear.

Glowing radiantly, while encompassed by a silver halo sent down from the heavens, the harvest moon boldly lit the sweet Montana sky.

After cooking the steaks and helping Cathy set the food out on the picnic table, Roy and his family sat down under the remaining day's light and bowed in silence as Josh started the meal with a blessing.

The Watchful Eye

Filled with rhythmic chirps from a nearby cricket, a warm country breeze gently floated by.

Prayer said, Joshua started talking about ideas he had been investigating for his school's science fair project. Fueled by a need for challenges, he was a very creative child with a tireless imagination. *Joshua will thrive at anything he sets his mind to*, Roy thought with twinkles of pride as bright as the Northern Stars in his eyes.

Stacey had a lot to talk about as well, although her topic of conversation wasn't as promising as her brother's. Hers pertained to a game of "Kiss and Chase" that had taken place during recess on the school playground.

"It was really gross mom! I never want a boy to kiss me again as long as I live!" Seeing the opportunity and not being able to let it pass, Joshua began chanting immediately. "Stacey's got a boyfriend. Stacey's got a boyfriend." Any time was a great time to taunt his little sister.

"That's enough young man," warned Cathy, although his teasing was of playful intention. After gladly listening to her brother's reprimand, Stacy finished the rest of her story without further hindrance. She couldn't believe she had actually been kissed. By the look on her face, she would have rather been kissed by a frog, snake, or lizard. Anything other than a boy.

After dinner was finished Cathy began to gather up the empty serving dishes. "As soon as you're done eating, bring in your plates and rinse them please." She picked up as much stuff as she could carry and took it inside the house with her.

Roy and Cathy worked together to wash the dishes and clean the kitchen before sitting down at the dining room table where the whole family played a couple of card games together. Joshua won both. Afterwards, it was time for Josh and Stacey to go to bed. School would come early and they needed their sleep. Each one received a goodnight hug from their mother and father. Roy followed his hugs with wiry beard-brushing to the ticklish nooks on the side of their necks.

Listening to the uncontrollable giggling, Roy thought back to the time when he was a small child and when his father had beard-brushed him and his two brothers. Raising his own children, he hoped to be at least half the father that his dad had been to him.

"Hey, I really love you two a whole bunch!" he said after the laughter inducing, beard-brushing hugs were over. "Now go to bed and get some shut-eye!"

Watching them as they trotted down the hallway, Roy felt a small but significant ache in his heart.

Josh was already thirteen years old. He was more than halfway old enough to face the world on his own and Stacey wasn't far behind. It just didn't seem right that they had to grow up so fast. Cathy recognized his thoughts and sat down on the couch next to him.

"What are you thinking so hard about?" she asked while putting her arm around his neck.

"Oh, not much, I'm just going to miss them when they're gone," he said with a saddened smile.

"Don't you worry, not only will they come back to visit more often than we'd like, but they're gonna end up bringing back children of their own. Well maybe not Stacey," she reconsidered with a smile, "After all, she doesn't ever want to kiss a boy!"

Roy's smile was accompanied by an infectious laugh that immediately followed the thought of his daughters little face squinting in disgust while proclaiming her disinterest in boys. "They're gross!"

"I'm going to bed. Are you coming?" asked Cathy as she got up from the couch.

"Yeah, let's go."

After turning off the lights and checking to make sure both Josh and Stacey had brushed their teeth and were in bed, Roy followed Cathy into their bedroom where they both turned in for the night.

Chapter Nineteen

Shortly after touching down and supervising the set up of a temporary base camp five hundred and eighty-three miles East of Billings, Sgt. Stalls stood before seven of his finest soldiers. As with Sgt. Stalls himself, all of his men had been recruited into a secret military project referred to as the "Ghost Army."

Throughout the years, thousands of men had served the army with honor before them, and each one of Stalls' men had the intentions to do the same. On active duty in one of the four branches of the armed forces, they had all been called upon to better serve their country. Every one of them had been declared as either a war hero who had perished in battle or had been given medals of honor and declared missing in action. Whatever the case may be for each individual, all of their families had mourned over a letter of regret after being informed that their loved ones had been lost forever.

Soon after being declared dead and stripped of any remaining identity, they began the hellish training program that would prepare them for the unseen army. Anytime the United States government felt it necessary to engage in dirty work, gorilla-type warfare, antiterrorist offensives, or manipulating neighboring countries into war and destruction, they called on the might of their own ghost army. Because the army didn't actually exist, at least as far as any claim of or lack of existing documents could prove, there wasn't the slightest chance that the U.S. government could be held responsible for the army's actions. With the use of these well-trained and unforgiving men, the country could engage in the dirtiest, most inhumane acts of large scale violence and still carry the illusion of innocence with sparkling clean hands.

With the briefing session coming to a conclusion, Stalls asked his men if there were any questions pertaining to the mission at hand. As he had expected, there was none. He might have thought less of his soldiers for not asking, but only if he weren't completely satisfied with his own abilities to lead them through the vigorous planning session, from start to finish, with complete attention to even the smallest of details.

Sgt. Stalls had been given the privilege of hand picking seven of his finest soldiers to construct this small but extremely lethal group that would be accompanying him tonight.

The operation was scheduled to commence at zero-two hundred hours. The object was to infiltrate a residence and remove a list of firearms that had been scheduled for destruction, along with any ammunition or explosives.

The target was a small ranch house five miles Southwest of Billings Montana. It had been picked at random from a long list of potential targets that had been red flagged for firearms two years prior by the FBI. Because of illegalities, as with most missions assigned to Sgt. Stalls and his elite team, the whole operation had been planned with the utmost precision.

Within six additional years of warring terrorism, both real threats and those concocted by the U.S. government itself, the majority of its citizens will have been slowly frightened into believing that terrorist threat is rampant within its own ranks. Laws would then be signed, allowing the United States Government the right to target multiple gun and handgun owners as a terrorist threat to its own citizens. At that time, following a fourteen-month voluntary firearm forfeit provision, U.S. branches of a One World task force would be assigned the task of infiltrating property and destroying weapons taken from those who do not comply. When that time comes, the ghost army would be selected to head up the task force. After removing the physical threat posed by multiple gun owners, the American citizen in question would be labeled a terrorist "by law" and would then face immediate imprisonment without the right to a trial by jury.

Satellite imagery of the ranch house had been provided to Stalls' team along with seismic photography of the surrounding property. This gave Sgt. Stalls and his men time to perfect their attack and construct a detailed mental map that they would then augment with the use of night vision equipment.

According to the photographs there wasn't any ammunition buried on the property, as there had been on seven of thirteen similar missions carried out by the team. This was good and would allow for a quick "in and out."

Until today, the operation had been put on hold for reasons that Stalls wasn't privy to. Either it was being considered for the scrap heap for financial reasons or deemed potentially unsuccessful. He had been almost devastated when it had been temporarily shut down.

Stalls found great satisfaction in raiding the homes of innocent victims. At the moment, the operation had been put back into action but was still considered a training exercise. He and his men had been instructed to avoid all physical contact with residents, but Stalls knew that things would eventually change. In the short years to come his team would be given full authority to engage the targets as hostile. When that glorious day arrived, they would be able to subdue and secure the resident location by any means necessary. Stalls shivered with excitement just by the thought of it.

Computer printouts previously reviewed, now laying on a table, listed makes and models of firearms and riot control weaponry used by the targets state and local law enforcement. Although it would be completely unacceptable to fail, the team would have the option of blanketing their mission by placing blame on the local authorities if the situation were to get out of hand.

"Are there any final questions?" Sgt. Stalls asked again while looking into the hardened eyes of each and every one of his finely tuned soldiers. Slowly, he paced the floor in search of a weak link. He quickly decided that none existed.

"We'll commence at zero one hundred hours. I expect all gear to be checked and then checked again. You have four hours. I want to see each and every one of you fully rested and on the ready. That's all. You're dismissed!"

Death is life's formidable opponent. A jester mocking, waiting, seething around the ticking of every moment, reaching purposely for the weak and inattentive. A lethal surprise even in the throws of a waning tenuous spirit before a last faltering breath. Death is the great equalizer. Its mirth steely cold and lasting especially for the unjust of souls.

H.R.R.

Chapter Twenty

With the exception of small ripples caused by movement inside the four-man raft, the lackadaisical river was profoundly tranquil. Trees and clouds, although slightly distorted, could be seen reflecting off its calm serene surface. A pair of metallic-blue dragonflies, connected front to aft, pleasantly hummed across the bow of the family's raft, looking for a temporary place to rest. The sun shone bright and the calm, cool breeze smelled fresh and pure after shedding its impurities through the filtering stream.

Looking down past the surface of the water through a shadow cast by the raft itself, Roy noticed a large school of fish slowly swimming along the river's rocky bottom.

His son, Joshua, with his mother's help, was sitting cross-legged in the middle of the raft while putting together a science fair project. He looked as happy and intrigued as any young man would in a quest to conquer the knowledge of physics.

Stacey, so young and innocent, was dressed in her finest Sunday clothes. White shoes accented her dark blue velvet dress. Roy remembered the day he and Cathy had bought it for her. She sat on the floor of the raft with her back to the air filled rubber bulkhead. She had a large, beautiful, almost iridescent Blue Jay perched upon her lap. Giggling delightfully, they appeared to be sharing secrets with one another.

Roy himself leaned upon the rear of the small rubber raft enjoying each and every breath of this naturally hypnotic day. Sun shining, cool breeze melodiously blowing, slowly rocking, children laughing, birds singing, wife smiling, leaves softly stirring, this could be nothing less than a little piece of heaven.

Looking again at the rocky bed of the river below, a sudden pang of terror ripped through his gut as he saw the last few fish darting quickly out of sight. Somehow, he had known they were fleeing in fear. Either he felt their fear, or they mysteriously felt his, he wasn't sure. Then again, he wasn't sure of what he was supposed to be afraid of or why, he just knew he was. Without looking up, he realized that the sky had grown dark under a heavy black legion of clouds. He could almost feel their weight. On the river's banks, the trees appeared to be groaning with pain, although he couldn't hear them over the new wind's restless blustering. Looking up, he again saw Stacey. This time, he recognized the bird for what it actually was.

Large interwoven feathers, tucked tightly against its body, gave the flying rodent an evil glimmer as black as the depths of hell. The raven stared intently at the giggling girl through radiant red, diamond slit eyes. Its beak, sharpened to a fine point, was mere inches from the oblivious child's face. She didn't recognize the pain caused by its razor sharp talons. They were buried deep within her bleeding thighs.

Yelling, Roy swung at the feathered demon with all his might, but nothing happened. He swung again, but again nothing happened. Although he could have sworn he had hit the evil bird both times, his efforts appeared to go unnoticed. The child continued to giggle still unaware of the crow's evil intent.

His wife and son now worked furiously on their project as if "life itself" depended upon its completion. They were too entranced with the job at hand to notice Roy's desperate screams for help. Again he swung at the bird. Stacey continued to giggle.

Releasing a putrid stench of sulfur, the river began to boil. Roy grabbed an oar and started paddling toward the riverbank. The small raft didn't move beyond the steadily increasing pull of the river. He paddled with all his might, but his feeble attempts were easily swallowed by the churning water's fury.

Boiling rampantly and emitting its angry sulfur stench, the river grew more violent by the minute. Moving faster and faster, the raft was thrown mercilessly by the water's steadily growing, swift and powerful currents. The mighty river raged out of control.

Stacey continued to giggle.

Twenty feet ahead, from out of nowhere, the seething water dropped off into the unknown. Somehow, Roy had to get his family to shore.

His paddle was gone.

Ten feet,...Five,...Two,...

Roy woke in damp and twisted sheets. Never before had he experienced such an awful gut twisting nightmare. His heart pounded like a sledge against his anvil ribs. He could feel the powerful beating from head to toe. Taking several long deep breaths, he tried to relax his racing heart. Cathy was still asleep. Careful not to wake her, he reached over and gently placed his hand on her back. Although he realized it was no more than a dream, he needed reassurance; he had to feel her breath. When he was satisfied with her well being, he leaned over and kissed her cheek. She fidgeted slightly which only helped to comfort his nightmare-induced anxiety.

WESS REED

Mouth dry and sour, Roy got up out of bed, put on a robe and slowly made his way into the kitchen. The master bedroom was on one side of the house while the children's rooms were on the other. Both hallways attached to the den, which also connected to the family room and from there the kitchen. Joshua's room was at the far end of the hall, where he usually left his bedroom door open. For this reason, Roy chose not to turn on any lights.

In the kitchen, Roy stood at the counter next to the running faucet while finishing off his first glass of water. Through a window above the sink he observed the brilliance of the full moon. He filled his glass a second time and shut off the faucet.

While drowning his remaining thirst, Roy studied the moon's different shades of white and gray. This was as close as he would ever get. He would never have the opportunity to probe its layers, walk on its surface, or even rub a small portion of its composition between his fingers. How would it feel to experience its texture? Even if he were given the opportunity, he would never forget how beautiful it looked right now, tonight. If he had a chance to walk across its surface a hundred times, he would still be able to enjoy the moon's mystic beauty as if he were looking at it for the first time.

While setting his empty glass down on the counter, Roy thought he saw some movement in his back yard. He watched closely, curious as to what type of wildlife was out and about, possibly stirring up trouble.

Last summer, Roy had caught Joshua leaving table scraps on the lawn. Like his father, Josh loved wildlife. Wanting to see the animals up close and hoping to eventually catch one for a pet, he had been leaving food to attract raccoons. His intentions were noble in Roy's eyes, however, he didn't understand that the animals could not only be destructive, but eventually turn to aggression after losing fear of humans. Roy also explained the possibility of attracting bears. If so, they would become expectant of the easy meal as well as terrorize livestock.

After studying the dark night beyond the window for a moment, Roy decided that what he had seen was nothing more than a figment of his imagination. Then, he saw it again. On a slightly higher level of alert this time, he was able to determine the type of species prowling through his back yard. It was man.

Angry with violation, he quickly made his way to the back door, opened it and flicked on the porch light.

"Who's out there?" he yelled looking in the general direction in which he had noticed the movement. Nobody answered.

"You have about five seconds to show your face before I start shooting!"

As Roy was securing the door to quickly retrieve his 9mm from the nightstand in his bedroom, a sharp blue flicker of light erupted from about fifteen feet away on the opposite side of the yard.

"Fwack!"

A small ballistic object, attached to a thin length of cable, ricocheted off the edge of the door missing Roy, its intended target, by only a fraction of an inch.

Taking less than a second to process what had happened, Roy slammed the door shut. *What the hell's going on?* he thought.

With his love for firearms, it didn't take long for him to realize that he had been shot at with an air cartridge tazer.

Law enforcement officials use these to immobilize perpetrators without inflicting much harm or causing death. Although similar to a stun gun, a tazer was a weapon designed to be effective from a distance.

This was some sort of mistake. Why would the police be on his property in the middle of the night? Why would they use aggressive tactics without warning? When he had called out to them, they should have at least identified themselves and stated their intentions. Roy quickly thought about what he could have done to place himself in this type of situation. He couldn't think of anything. Being a law-abiding citizen, he hadn't broken any laws. They must have him confused for someone else.

Maybe, Roy thought, they weren't police after all, but thugs trying to rob his house. He immediately went to the living room window and looked out to the front yard. If they were the police, there would be patrol cars in front of the property. There were none.

Running to the bedroom he grabbed his 9mm from the nightstand.

"Honey, what's happening?" Cathy was sitting up in bed awake, looking scared and confused.

"I'm not sure," Roy said. "Stay here and lock the bedroom door! I'll let you know when it's safe to come out!"

After loading the gun and removing the trigger guard, Roy stepped into the hall and waited until he heard Cathy lock the door behind him. After he felt that she would be secure, he hurried down the hallway and back toward the middle of the house in the dark.

In the den, he walked over to the edge of a window to peer into the back yard again.

"Daddy, who were you talking to?" The small innocent voice could only come from one person, *Stacey!*

Wondering who her father had been yelling at, Stacey stood at the end of the second hall rubbing her eyes. She had gotten out of bed to see what all the commotion was about. Until hearing her soft little voice, he hadn't noticed her presence or the fact that the hall light was on at the other end of the house.

"Come here sweetie," he said already rushing toward her. "I want you to go back to bed and it's really important that you stay there."

The Watchful Eye

With the pistol in one hand, he scooped her up into his arms and carried her back down the hallway toward her room. "I think there might be some bad guys outside so I want you to keep your door locked okay?"

"Okay."

Back in her room, he set Stacey back down on her bed and then got as far as the door when she said, "I love you daddy!"

"I love you too sweetheart. Now stay in here till I come back!"

"I'm scared daddy. Are the bad guys gonna get me?"

"No, I'm going to get them first so don't you worry, okay?"

"Okay."

"Don't forget, I want you to stay in your room until I come back."

Stacey didn't say anything but only shook her head. Roy pushed in the doorknob and then twisted it into the locked position before he stepped back into the hall. Door closed and locked, daughter safe inside, Roy started back down the hall toward the den. Halfway to the living room a window shattered. Quickly but with caution, Roy slid down the hall along the wall. At the end of the hall, gun at the ready, he peered around the corner and into the living room. The only thing he saw was an intense orange flash of light accompanied by a fierce explosion.

Roy's face, neck, chest and right hand, the one in which he held the 9mm out in front of him, was numbed in an instant. His chest fell prey to the drastic change in pressure caused by the explosion. Briefly, his lungs were sucked clean of the air they had been carrying. Then the pressure returned to normal as quickly as it had been vanquished. This caused his lungs to inflate painfully as though they had been ripped free of the plural cavity in which they were contained. Roy fell to the ground.

Sharp horrendous pains began to burn frantically throughout his body. His exposed skin, if there were any left, felt as though it had been instantly charred and then peeled away by the explosion. The pain shooting across his nerves was so intense it racked his gut, or what may still remain of it, and was trying to remove its contents. Roy looked to where he thought his right hand should be, desperate to know if it was still there. He couldn't see it. His vision was gone and all that his optical receptors were able to process was black. He was unable to see anything.

The grenade, a compressed plastic M25A2 riot control fragment type, was designed with the intentions of temporarily disabling all persons within a 20-foot radius.

On the floor in a fetal position, Roy felt for his face with his good hand. The skin covering his face was still intact, however, he couldn't feel his own touch. It was like he was feeling someone else's face in the dark although he knew that the face he was touching, was in fact his own. His hearing was temporarily damaged by the blast as well. His ears rang painfully, oblivious to any and all surrounding sounds. He reached over with his left hand to feel for his right; it was still there. He couldn't tell if he was covered in blood or not and his right hand felt dead to the touch but at least it was still attached.

He thought of his family. He had to protect them. Not knowing which way to go, he began to crawl as best he could toward what he believed to be the den. Before he got far, he bumped into a hard vertical object. Feeling with his left hand, he realized that he was against a wall. He wasn't sure which way he needed to go. Somehow, he had to make it to Cathy. In the shape he was in, whatever that might be, he knew his wife would be better able to protect herself and their children. If he could just make it to the back bedroom, Cathy could take the gun and get herself, Josh, and Stacey out of the house and to safety.

The Watchful Eye

Not knowing for sure, but knowing he needed to act, he started to crawl in the direction of what he believed to be the back bedroom where he could reach Cathy. Before he got very far, however, he realized that he didn't have the gun anymore. He crawled back to where he thought he had dropped it and felt the carpet frantically all around him trying to locate the 9mm.

When did he drop it? He couldn't remember whether or not he had been crawling with it, or if it had been lost in the hallway at the time of the explosion.

Finding the gun with only one blind hand would be nearly impossible. Even if it were only five feet away he might never find it.

He thought about yelling out for Cathy but didn't. He would only give away his position, and even worse, he would give away hers if she yelled back or came looking for him. His only option was to find the pistol, and then find her before someone else did. Then he thought about the rest of his guns. As long as he made it to her first, there was still a chance.

His face and chest were starting to tingle slightly. The pain was still sickening, but his normal sensations seemed to be returning.

Roy turned again to what he believed was the right direction and managed to stand up. After only three awkward steps, he heard a loud crash. Although part of his hearing was returning, he wasn't able to make out the sound. It almost sounded like one of the doors had been smashed open. He heard some commotion. Whoever had been out in his yard, was now in the house. He had to hurry.

Leaning into the wall for support, he moved as fast as he could. He heard more commotion. Halfway across the room he ran into something solid. Feeling with his left hand, he recognized the corner of the couch that was pressed back against the dividing wall. Roy now knew where he was and in what direction he needed to go.

Taking bigger steps and with more confidence, he left the guidance of the wall and headed across the middle of the room to the second hall entrance. From behind, someone shoved him face first onto the floor. "Stay down and don't move!"

Both of his arms were grabbed and cuffed behind his back while a second person shackled his feet together. As soon as he heard the shackles click into the tightest position, he felt a boot smash into his exposed ribs. A couple of them were fractured under the impact of the sledge-like kick. Roy fought for his breath but didn't allow himself to cry out in pain. Before his spasm-inflicted diaphragm allowed him to ask who these people were and what they were doing in his house, he was rocked by the sound of a single gunshot. The lone report was quickly answered with an abundance of commotion followed by three more shots. Silence filled the room momentarily.

"Status!" The voice was rough and demanding.

"Secure. It was the boy sir."

Roy died inside. The weight of grief in realizing he had just lost his son bore down on him with its great strength and crushed his heart. He felt paralyzed.

"I want the other two in here immediately!"

"Yes, sir!"

Grieving his loss along with the fear of losing the rest of his family, Roy's emotions converted into an uncontrollable anger. Releasing his fury, Roy screamed and struggled with all of his strength as he tried to break free of his bonds. Again, his side was pummeled with a boot as he struggled. Half maddened with rage, Roy continued his furious struggle oblivious to the punishment he was receiving. Then he heard doors being crashed on both sides of the house. Soon after, more voices yelled out in confirmation

The Watchful Eye

of the capture of his wife and daughter. Again he struggled to break free and again his body was punished for its efforts.

Roy heard his wife Cathy cry out in a struggle to free herself. Listening to her screams, he knew that they were dragging her down the hallway and into the living room.

As soon as Cathy saw her husband, she broke free of the grip the large man had on her arm. Crying, she ran over and dropped to the floor beside him where she managed to put both her arms around him before she was grabbed by the hair and pulled away from her husband. That's when she saw Josh.

Sweet and innocent, Josh was laying face up in a pool of blood soaked carpet. There were three bullet holes ripped through his chest. In his grasp was his father's 9mm handgun. He must have found it where it had been dropped and then fired it at the intruders in an effort to save his father.

Seeing her son, Cathy began to scream and struggle hysterically. Still dragging her by her hair, the large man in uniform swung his weapon against the side of her head knocking her unconscious.

Another man grabbed Roy by his arms and drug him across the floor as well. On the other side of the room, Roy was rolled onto his back and sat in a corner. Then the lights were turned on.

Roy saw two large men in his living room and one walking down the hall. They were all wearing black military uniforms. Their facial features were smeared over with thick, black polish that made them darker and more mysterious than the night outside. Cathy was propped up against the wall next to him. A small stream of fresh blood ran down the side of her face.

Roy's right eye was swollen shut from the blast, however, his vision was returning in his left. The man in the hallway had Stacey in his arms. Other than the redness and swelling around her eyes and down her cheeks from crying, she appeared to be unharmed. Her stare was blank and she looked as though she was mentally cut off from her surroundings. That's when Roy realized that she must have seen her brother. Roy looked around the room, but was unable to find him. A love seat, shredded by the plastic pellets of the grenade, blocked his view of the floor at the entrance to the hallway. That was most likely where he lay. Bringing Stacey over and setting her down next to her unconscious mother, the man had probably no other choice than to step over her brother's body. Stacy had received a bird's eye view of her dead brother.

"Are you okay sweetheart?" She didn't respond, but only stared into space with a blank, tear distorted expression. He wished more than anything that he could reach out to her and hold her in his arms close to his heart.

"I want Stanton in here on the double!"

"Yes, sir!"

"Tell him to bring the VS!"

"Yes, sir!"

As ordered, one of the men hurried out of the room. The larger of the remaining two seemed to be the one in charge. Roy glared at him with hatred.

"Henley!"

"Sir?"

"The perimeter should be secured, get the remaining men and start an evacuation sweep. I'm aborting the mission. Bring me another grenade and the kid's pistol."

"Yes, sir!"

As that soldier left the room, the one that he had requested earlier entered. He was carrying an electronic device that was about the size of a briefcase.

"Sir?" he asked waiting for his orders.

"Get the VS set up and wake the woman."

The man set the electronic device down on the coffee table and then hurried over to where Cathy was propped against the wall. After cuffing her hands together, he removed something from one of his pockets. He broke the small object between his fingers and then waved it under her nose. Cathy woke with a moan. Before she could react to the sight of her husband or daughter, the larger man in charge withdrew a .50 cal desert eagle handgun and pressed the barrel against Stacey's tiny expressionless face.

"Anything stupid lady and she's gone, understand?"

Cathy's heart pounded harder than her throbbing head. Her yearning to lash out shriveled at the sight of a gun pointed at her daughter in a threat to end her life.

"Do you understand!" he yelled forcefully.

"Yes, yes I understand. Please don't hurt her." He nodded to Stanton who was connecting the remaining wires to the VS device.

"Ma'am if you would please, I'm going to need you to come over here." She looked to Roy who nodded in approval and then back to Stacey. Trembling, with tears running down her face, Cathy slowly made her way to where Stanton was standing in front of the device wearing a set of earphones. They were attached to the VS.

"Now ma'am, what I'm going to need you to do is state your full name."

"What?"

"Your name please, now." He pushed a button on the device, which illuminated a red light.

"Catherine Angeline Williams." He pressed another button and then began typing on a small keyboard. The light turned yellow.

"Grateful, purple, spider. Could you repeat that for me please?" She looked at her daughter who was still emotionally gone.

"Please Ma'am?"

"Grateful, purple, spider."

Stanton pressed the button and began typing again. The light began to flash green. Stanton nodded to the big guy that had the gun to Stacey's head and smiled. "Got it sir."

He carried the device into the kitchen and set it down on the counter. Stanton unplugged the handset from the phone line and then plugged the line into the VS.

The first soldier returned with Roy's nine millimeter that he had retrieved from the dead boy along with another M25A2 grenade.

"We're clean sir and awaiting your orders."

"Good, have the men clear the area. Stanton, will clear out as soon as he's finished. After he's done, I want you to stay behind so we can finish cleaning up this mess."

"Yes, sir." Henley said.

"When we're done, we'll all rendezvous at the base camp."

After Henley left to deliver the orders, the man in charge took the gun and the grenade into the kitchen where he searched for cleaner and a paper towel with which he could thoroughly wipe down the 9mm. Then he walked back into the living room carrying the gun with the paper towel after he had placed the grenade on the kitchen sink.

"Sir, I'm all set and ready to roll," Stanton said.

"Good work, make it happen."

Stanton removed his headphones and began typing. Through an external speaker on the Voice Simulator, dialing could be heard followed by the line being answered.

"911 Emergency, can I help you?"

As Stanton typed, Cathy's voice could be heard talking to the operator over the VS's loud speaker. *"My husband has a gun and he's out of control. I need help."*

"What's your husbands name Ma'am?"

"Roy," Stanton typed.

"I need your name and address please."

"Cathy Williams, 5437 County Road 62. Please hurry."

"A patrol car is already on its way. I'll need you to stay on the phone."

Stanton disconnected the line, plugged the phone back in, and left the house with the VS. Outside, he heard three blasts from the nine-millimeter. Stalls was finishing the job. Stanton placed the VS in his gear bag and headed for the choppers. Henley and Sgt. Stalls would hide in waiting for the local authorities. The following morning, the Billings newspaper read.

Police arrived on scene where local man, thirty eight-year-old, Roy Williams, had murdered his wife and two children. While involved in a shootout with the crazed gunman, the two officers were immobilized with a riot control type grenade. After shooting and killing the officers, the gunman then took his own life.

Chapter Twenty One

The following morning, Jack woke early and began the day with a three mile run across the unforgiving sands of Venice Beach. Unlike his last visit to the beach, this workout was complete without the help of a violent confrontation. After clearing his mind of built up mental debris, as was usually the result of a nice quiet run, he hopped into his car and drove to the fitness center.

At the center, Jack rode the elevator up to the manager's office on the third floor. Large, open, and receiving plenty of sunlight, the nicely furnished room was built for a king. Jack stood for a moment at one of the three large windows and admired the growing city around him. Sometimes, he wished he *were* only a manager for the fitness center. Life would be so simple.

Sitting down at the large desk, he looked over a few financial documents pertaining to the center's current cash flow. After spending less time than he should have, he quickly completed the majority of his minor managerial duties and then walked back over to the large window.

Looking out at the city, and the few pedestrians on the street below, his mind wandered restlessly. Who was he trying to fool? If running a fitness center were his only source of satisfaction in life, he'd be driven completely out of his mind with boredom in a month flat.

Seeing the office space through a different perspective, Jack called down to the lobby and informed Nancy that he would be unavailable for a few hours. Then, he took the elevator down to where the worlds many troubles lent him a chance to feel truly successful.

The doors opened and Jack walked across the meeting room to the office that meant most. Flipping on the light, he looked over his real desk for anything that might be labeled urgent. Finding nothing, he walked down the hall to where Don would be in the computer room probing through the Watchful Eye program.

From the minute Jack rolled out of bed this morning, he had wanted to make a beeline straight to Don's office. Instead, he chose to stretch the morning and take time to wrap up some of the simple tasks first. If he had come straight away, he had been positive that finding any answers to Sharon's predicament might be jinxed due to his impatience. Chances are, Don showed early this morning and has been plugging away at his computer ever since. Trying to avoid any bad news, Jack had decided to give Don plenty of time to work through the program without added pressure. Now that he was here however, he felt he had waited as long as he could stand.

As Jack approached the door to Don's office and was raising his fist to knock; the secure line in his office began to ring. Jack returned to his office and answered the phone, "Jack speaking."

"Hi Jack. This is Avery. How are you?"

"I'm not sure yet, but I'll bet you're fixin' to tell me. What do you know?"

"Not a whole lot I'm afraid. I looked one of those inoculations over and managed to do more damage than I did good. I'm gonna have to take them with me to another

The Watchful Eye

facility where I can get a better look at them. I'm at the airport now, my plane leaves in an hour."

"What do you want me to do?"

"Well, I need some time to get set up, and then probably a day to analyze these things. Can you meet me in Charleston by tomorrow or the next day?"

"Whatever it takes. Just tell me what you want." Avery gave Jack some instructions and then hung up. Jack thought about what the scientist had said, *managed to do more damage than I did good.* He wondered what that meant?

Jack was walking out the door to his office when the secure line rang again. Picking it up, he expected that Avery had forgotten to mention something, "Jack speaking."

"They killed her!"

For a moment Jack didn't recognize the voice. Then, it became clear who it was, Clemens. He was half hysterical and crying into the phone.

"What? Who are you talking about?"

"I can't believe she's dead! I'm scared Jack! You have to help me!" Through the sobs, the doctor's voice shook with fear.

"You're gonna need to calm down so I can hear you. Who's dead? Who are you talking about?"

"Janice, she's dead! They killed her Jack! They killed my wife!"

"Where are you?"

Hyperventilating, Clemens had to give directions three times before Jack could understand them.

"Stay where you are. I'm on my way."

Jack hung up and hurried down the hall to the computer room where he entered without knocking.

"Hey Don, how are you coming along?"

Deep in his own world, Don looked up in surprise. He was startled by the interruption. "Not as good as I should be, but I'm making ground slowly."

"I've got an emergency that I need to attend to. Will you be okay while I'm gone?"

Thinking in his own terms, Don smiled as usual. "Sure I will, but I'm gonna miss you. Will you be home in time for dinner?" Although he continued to taunt Jack, Don was already focused again on the screen in front of him.

Jack turned and walked off. In the background, he heard Don bidding him a healthy good morning and promising to get the kids to the bus stop in time for school. Even when he had covered enough distance to drown out the majority of the words, he could still hear the computer genius rambling sentimentally while working on the program. As the elevator doors closed, Jack tried to ignore his specialist's loitering chants. Unsuccessfully, he was overcome by the desire to laugh. Quietly, he indulged.

When Jack pulled over at the convenience store, Clemens was nowhere in sight. Two pay phones stood empty against the side of the building. Surveying the area, he was unable to locate the doctor's car parked amongst the few vehicles that sat in front of the building or those that were parked beside the fuel pumps. Not sure exactly where to look, Jack slowly made a U-turn and headed back toward the street. Then he saw him.

Clemens had parked at a liquor store on the other side of the street a half block down. Already having seen Jack, he was waiting for a clearing in traffic so he could safely cross. As Clemens found his opening and began to cross the street, Jack noticed the black SUV.

Identical to the two he had seen previously, or possibly the same one, it was picking up speed and heading straight for the doctor.

Deep in depression, one he had been trying to drown out with alcohol, Clemens continued haphazardly across the asphalt oblivious to the quickly approaching vehicle. Jack yelled from the window as he launched his car onto the street, but Clemens didn't hear him.

In a race for the doctor, Jack held the accelerator to the floorboard spurring the already thundering engine. Shifting into position, the SUV began swallowing the street's white center lane markings as it angled toward the doctor. It was closing ground quickly.

Already flying, Jack nosed over as well prompting his vehicle into a head on collision with the SUV. Clemens eyes widened and his face contorted with confusion when he finally noticed the two vehicles approaching at breakneck speed.

As he had prayed for, Jack reached the doctor first. Missing Clemens by mere inches, he jerked on the steering wheel and stomped the brake pedal with all his might.

As the doctor passed by his window, Jack's car began to spin counterclockwise in a smoke-filled scream of smoldering tires. Jack gave the car's broadside to the SUV as a mandatory target while hoping to shield the drunken doctor. With thick gray smoke boiling off the tires, the vehicle swung into final position and Jack prepared for impact.

At the last second, the SUV swung to the right to avoid the collision. As it sped away, however, the passenger leaned out his window and unloaded three rounds from a semiautomatic rifle. Intended for the doctor, all three missed their mark and shredded the front fender of Jack's Mustang.

"Get in!" Jack yelled. Clemens stood in shock.

"Get in the car now!"

Clemens dropped the paper bag-covered bottle he was carrying and ran around to the passenger side where Jack had already flung the door open in waiting. When he sat down and slammed the door shut, Jack tromped on the accelerator again and found an open lane. He hoped it wasn't already too late to catch up with the SUV. Clemens reeked of whiskey.

"What are you doing?" Clemens asked. Quickly sobered by the near death experience, he was in total disbelief that Jack would even attempt to give chase.

"We're going to find out who those guys are and put an end to this mess."

"What?" The doctor looked astounded.

"If you have a better suggestion, I'm all ears," Jack said while weaving through the slow-moving traffic.

"They have guns! They were shooting at us!"

"Yeah?"

"Yeah?" Clemens couldn't believe what he was hearing. "What do you mean, *Yeah*?"

"So, they have guns. What would you rather do, let them get away?"

"That sounds like a good plan. It sure beats giving them another chance to shoot at me! Next time they try to shoot you they might not miss!"

Jack shot the car through an intersection narrowly missing another car that was turning left into their path. Clemens reached for the seatbelt and buckled himself in. He looked as ridged as a fence post.

"If we don't catch them now, the next time you won't see it coming. At least now we're prepared for it."

"We're not prepared for it! Maybe you are, but that's a far cry from we!"

Jack sped his mustang down the street while trying to catch a glimpse of the SUV. It was nowhere in sight.

"Look! Just because they didn't finish the job today doesn't mean they'll quit trying. If they want you dead, they'll just find another way to accomplish it. Later today, maybe tomorrow, sometime next week, who knows for sure? The way I see it, the best chance we…better yet, *you* have, is for us to catch these guys right now and put a stop to this."

The Watchful Eye

Clemens didn't say anything. He knew Jack was right. Shortly after, the chase ended anyway when Jack slowed down to the speed limit. Spending too much time waiting for the doctor to get into the car, he had lost the SUV before the pursuit had even started. Jack pulled over into a fast food parking lot and cut off the engine. It pinged, clinked, and crackled as it slowly cooled in resting for the next race.

"What now?" Clemens asked.

"I don't know yet. I'm gonna need a little time to think. Why don't you tell me what happened to your wife."

Although he tried not to, Jack's voice lacked sympathy for the doctor's feelings. After all, it was his own cowardly lack of compassion that put him in the predicament he was now facing. Deep down inside Jack knew this to be untrue, but he still couldn't help but despise the man for what he had done to Sharon. He sat in the car listening while Clemens told the story.

Last night after Jack and Sharon had left his house, two men in black uniforms broke in and roughed him up. After knocking him around, more as a threat than as punishment, they demanded to know what information he had shared.

"What did you tell them?"

"Nothing, I didn't tell them anything at all. At first I was going to, but then I decided not to. If they didn't already know, they didn't need to. If they did know, then they wouldn't have been asking, right?"

"Right, you did the right thing. What else happened?"

"After they got tired of pushing their weight around and threatening to kill me if I weren't telling the truth, they left. That's when they told me that I had already made a mistake and was going to pay for it. I wasn't sure what they were talking about until three o' clock this morning when the phone rang." Clemens eyes began to tear up. "When I answered the phone I was told that my wife had passed away during the night. Then, whoever had called simply hung up."

"Was it the care home?"

"I wasn't sure, so I called down there and a nurse that used to work at the hospital answered. She didn't know what I was talking about so she went to my wife's room to check on her. When she picked the phone back up, she assured me that Janice was sleeping comfortably. She even checked her vital signs and read them off to me over the phone."

"So what happened?"

"Well I thought it was strange that someone would call me and tell me something like that, so I got dressed and drove down there. By the time I got there she was dead. I know they killed her Jack. There's no other explanation."

"What are you going to do now?"

"According to the staff on duty, she died peacefully in her sleep. There's no reason to perform an autopsy, and I don't have the heart to push for one. She was a wonderful woman and now that she is gone and free from suffering, I think she should be left alone. She deserves the dignity to be laid to rest without being carved on first." Without voicing his opinion, Jack agreed.

"Do you like to fish?"

"What?" Clemens asked in light of the previous conversation.

"Do you like to fish?"

"I guess so why?"

"I think it's time you took your boys on a little fishing trip."

Jack started the car and pulled out onto the street. Clemens wasn't sure what to think. He didn't look the part, but maybe Jack had lost his mind. Now wasn't the appropriate time to venture out on a vacation of any kind.

Driving to the fitness center, Jack dialed Don from his cell phone. When he answered, Jack asked him to pick up Sharon immediately, and then meet him back at the center.

The Watchful Eye

After what had just happened, he was concerned for her safety.

On the drive, Jack watched in every direction for black SUV's. He had seen none. Once they made it to High Velocity, Jack took Clemens up to the oversized manager's office on the third floor. He gave him a pen and paper and instructed him to write down his and his son's, birth date and social security number while they waited for Don and Sharon. Although Clemens asked, Jack didn't inform him as to why.

When Don and Sharon arrived, Jack and Clemens described the events in which they had participated an hour earlier. Don wore a look of excitement and acted as though he were disappointed in not having been invited to the would be smash up derby. Sharon carried a look of shock.

After the story ended, Jack ordered lunch for four to be delivered to the center and then excused himself to take Don into an adjoining office.

"Wow!" Don said. "How come you get to do all of the fun stuff? You're like a real life action hero."

"What? Any time you want to trade places just let me know. After I realized what I had done," Jack said referring to the car stunt that had prevented the doctor from becoming road-kill but could have very well ended in the death of both of them, "I almost pissed myself."

Don's face shriveled in disgust as he looked down at the front of Jack's pants with hopes of not finding a wet spot.

"Anyway," Jack said handing him the paper that the doctor had written on, "I want you to run these through your computer. If they're logged into that program you're working on, I want to know about it."

"Then what?"

"Then, I want Canadian passports and ID cards for all three of them along with flight reservations that leave tonight. Give them new names too."

"What names?"

"I don't know. Be creative."

Don smiled.

Jack added, "Not too creative."

Don turned away to go back underground and work on the task he had been assigned. Jack followed him out of the office. Knowing that his boss was close behind him, Don stepped into the elevator and teased, "Spider-man never pissed himself. At least not when he was in his prime." The doors closed and the elevator made its descent.

While Don was busy working in his basement office, Jack explained his intentions to Dr. Clemens. He wanted him out of town and somewhere safe until he could find out exactly what they were up against.

Over the intercom Nancy called Jack down to the lobby. He rode the elevator to the first floor where he paid the delivery boy cash, and then returned to the office with their lunch. Then he took Don's portion down to the computer room where he checked on his progress.

Nothing had come up when Don ran the Social Security numbers through the Watchful Eye program. He was now finishing up the phony passports and ID cards. The flights, along with Brad's release had already been arranged.

Jack returned to the third floor and sat down to eat with Sharon and Dr. Clemens. About the time they were finishing, Don came back into the room.

On the table in front of Clemens, he spread out the three Canadian passports along with their corresponding driver's licenses. Clemens and Sharon looked up at Don in amazement.

"How did you do this?" Clemens asked holding the license that he had never even applied for. Don's proud smile broke free, but before he could say anything, Jack let Clemens know that how it was done was of no importance. Then he left the room.

The Watchful Eye

Don watched proudly as Sharon and Dr. Clemens studied the ID's closely and with wonder. Jack returned a few minutes later and handed an envelope to the doctor.

"There's enough money in here for you and you're boys to get away for a while. As soon as you leave here, go straight to the airport and take your boys with you."

"Where am I going?" Clemens asked.

"I booked three e-tickets to Toronto," Don said. "From there you'll be boarding a plane to a small town called Sudbury. It's in northern Ontario. Once you get there rent a car, a Skidoo, a snow plow, or whatever they use for transportation, and find a nice quiet lodge."

Listening to Don's instructions, Clemens got a look of distress on his face. "What about Brad? I can't leave him here and there's no way I can get him out of Jail. What if they take their anger toward me out on him?" Don put a hand on the doctor's shoulder and then looked at his watch.

"In about forty-five minutes you'll be able to pick him up. I've already scheduled for his release. All you have to do is get him out of town before somebody realizes what I've done."

Clemens stood and put his arms around Don and then hugged Jack and Sharon as well. Don gathered the passports and ID's and handed them to the doctor.

"Are these going to work?" Clemens asked. "Will they get me across the border?"

"They're as good as it gets," Don smiled. "The Department of Immigration couldn't make one of those that would work any better."

After another round of hugs, Clemens phoned Scott and made arrangements to be picked up in front of the center. From there, the two of them would wait for Brad outside the correctional facility and then all three would catch their plane at the airport.

When Clemens had gone, and Don had returned to his computer room, Sharon wrapped her arms around Jack's neck.

"You're a wonderful man Mr. Kurts." She gave him a kiss.

"Don't thank me yet, I still have to figure out what I'm going to do with you," he said returning her hug.

Together, they held onto each other while staring into the eyes of adversity.

Tonight she would stay at his house where he could offer her his own personal protection.

Chapter Twenty Two

Sgt. Stalls had supervised the tear down of the temporary base camp after a short debriefing of his men. From there, he loaded his personal gear onto the waiting helicopter and climbed aboard. He wasn't looking forward to the long flight ahead of him. Tired, he felt his mind was much too restless to allow for sleep. The mission had been a complete failure and now he was going to have to prepare an explanation. Trying to determine what he would say, he sat in anger as the rotor blades sliced furiously through their surroundings in an effort to carry the load up into the night and away from Montana. Stalls grew impatient as he waited for the helicopter to lift itself from the ground and gain altitude.

After takeoff, he watched out the window as the earth below faded away until it was completely swallowed by darkness. Thankful to be leaving, he wished to never see Montana again.

How was he going to explain what had happened? There was no explanation for incompetence. Returning home, he knew he would be looked down upon by his superiors for Henley's uncontrolled stupidity. That was unacceptable. Because of this, Henley had paid the price.

Closing his eyes, Stalls relived the events as they had unfolded. From the moment he had heard the tazer being fired, he knew that his only option was to recall the objective and begin a clean up operation. Of course he could have signaled for his men to retreat completely, but then for Stalls that wasn't an option. He only believed in moving forward.

Again, he thought about Henley. It was his own fault he was dead. If only he would have considered the consequences of his actions. Henley had served in the Ghost Army under Stalls' command for more than two years. How could he have made such a stupid mistake? Stalls was going to miss him.

Eventually, and sooner than expected, he fell asleep.

Immediately upon returning home, Stalls removed the bloodstained uniform and discarded it into the laundry. Then he stepped into the shower and washed himself of the remaining Montana filth. With a hand brush made for scrubbing floors, he worked on his skin until he was positive that every splatter of blood had been thoroughly removed. Then, he washed again. Then again. By the time he considered himself to be clean, his skin was raised with brush-welts and bright red with irritation.

Feeling clean and rested, he still couldn't clear the angry frustration that was infesting his mind. He dried himself with his only hand towel and then dressed in an old uniform that he once wore while serving in the Marine Corp.

Back in the bathroom, Stalls fumbled through the medicine cabinet looking for supplies. Of its contents, he removed a handful of cotton swabs and a bottle of rubbing alcohol that he carried, along with the soaked hand towel,

The Watchful Eye

into the small near empty room where he often sat for hours in meditation. Stalls placed them in the middle of the floor.

Thinking about Henley, anger, betrayal, and pity surged through his veins. He was proud to have been the one to kill his soldier and deliver the great honor that came with dying, but felt remorse for having to let him go.

Killing his soldier was nothing like killing the Williams family. He had shot all three and only regretted not getting the chance to kill the boy before one of his men had. Killing an entire family would have been something to be proud of for years to come. Although there was no honor in dying a pleading death as the three Williams people had, it would have been delightful nonetheless to have delivered each one of them their last rights. The right to die.

From the small closet, Stalls removed a large wooden trunk and gently placed it on the floor near the center of the room. Inside were his most sacred memoirs. Carefully, he shuffled through its contents and removed a beautifully crafted bamboo box. After studying its intricate design, he set it down next to the damp towel. From the trunk, he also removed an item wrapped in silk. It was about eight inches long and over an inch and a half wide, he placed it on the floor next to the small bamboo box and then closed the trunk's lid. Missing only one item, Stalls placed the trunk back in the closet and left the room.

From a large black government issued ditty bag, Stalls removed Henley's dog tags and attached them around his neck. They were similar to military issue, however, they lacked any information other than Henley's five digit ID number. Holding his never to be forgotten soldier's belongings close to his heart, he then returned to the small room and his sacred treasures.

Back in the room, Stalls walked over to the small table and lit the three candles. He turned out the lights.

Having all of the items he needed, Stalls knelt down in the center of the room and opened the bamboo box. From inside it, he retrieved a smaller felt box and placed it on the floor. Then, he removed a photograph. It was a picture of a young man named Jake Watson. He was dressed in a Marine Corp. uniform also. At the time the photograph was taken, Jake had only been 20 years old. He was a good soldier, and Stalls would always miss him.

In the Marine Corp, during Desert Storm, Watson had been one of the men under Stalls' command. Allowing his memory to drift back through time, Stalls recalled the last time he had seen Jake alive.

One dark night, after a long tiresome day in the desert, Stalls had assigned Watson to recon. According to intelligence, an Iraqi tank battalion was spotted six miles off to their east and they were being given orders to engage. After studying the intelligence report along with some imagery, Stalls had sent Watson out ahead of the platoon. Forty-five minutes later, Watson was dead. According to the report, Stalls had sent him directly into the middle of a minefield.

Amidst the confusion and excitement of the battle yet to come, Stalls had made a terrible mistake. A soldier had died due to his lack of attention and faulty calculations. He placed the picture on the floor next to the silk bundled object.

Stalls removed Henley's dog tags and gently placed them on the floor next to the picture of Watson. Picking up the silk bundle, he unwrapped it to reveal a razor sharp, black powdered pack knife that his father had given him when he was a young teen. Issued during the Second World War, it had been passed down from his grandfather. Built out of stainless steel, it was a beautiful instrument with a wickedly sharp blade.

Looking at the knife, Stall had a vision of the screaming baby doctor that had wriggled in pain as it was used to cut off his pinky finger. Thinking about the poor, whiney doctor, he tried not to smile.

The Watchful Eye

Spreading the silk cloth on the floor in front of him, he smoothed out the wrinkles. Then he set the knife down on top of it.

Removing his right sock, Stalls revealed only four toes. The nub where his pinky should have been helped serve as a reminder. After unscrewing the lid, he dunked two swabs in the rubbing alcohol and began the disinfection process.

Henley was a good man and Stalls couldn't find an explanation for his ignorance in firing the tazer. Henley had known better. Stalls had reviewed his strategy with his men to the point of exhaustion before they had set out for the ranch house. Although his planning and review had seemed to be flawless, he had somehow let Henley down. There was no other explanation. Now, because of this, Stalls would have to explain why his mission had ended in a complete catastrophe. Because Stalls had failed Henley somehow, his record would again be blemished due to ignorance. Knowing that, Stalls grew furious. Why should he have to explain his, or his men's actions to anyone? The thought of being labeled a failure for another man's incompetence infuriated him. Angry at himself and at Henley, he had to struggle to fight back hatred for the so-called system he had sworn to uphold. The only tool he had to ease his mind was knowing that he alone had killed the man that had brought him shame.

After killing the Williams family, and then the two policemen, Stalls had retrieved one of the dead officer's weapons and then used it to kill his own soldier. He remembered the look of surprise on Henley's face. He was a good soldier, but he had made a mistake and watching him die felt good. Stalls didn't allow for his own mistakes, or those of his men.

Mistakes deserved punishment, and in Henley's case that punishment meant death. If he were still alive to show his gratitude, however, Stalls felt assured that Henley would thank him for the killing and even show pride in having received his necessary punishment.

Death from this world was an honor. Stalls yearned for that same honor that he too would one day receive. Until that glorious day, he had no choice but to proudly execute punishment for his own mistakes. He had punished himself for the death of Watson, and now he would punish himself for the death of Henley. Until he could honor them with his own death, he would miss them.

After thoroughly cleaning his toes, Stalls discarded the swabs and held up the knife. He studied its contours as the cutting edge glimmered with reflections of candlelight. It was an instrument of honor and beauty. He placed the lid on top of the bamboo box and then covered it with the small damp towel. Then he placed his foot atop that.

With a swift precise slash of the blade, Stalls buried the knife halfway into his third and fourth toes. For his second mistake in the line of duty, he felt he deserved twice the consequences. The pain was excruciating and at the same time exalting. Fighting the urge to cry out, Stalls began chewing on the soft inner portion of his lower lip.

Blood didn't begin to flow from between his toes until after he applied pressure to the back edge of the knife and began sawing violently. In time, he managed to work the blade through the remaining flesh and bone.

Trembling with pain, Stalls carefully removed the lid from the small felt box. Inside, the only thing that remained of the pinky toe he had removed in honor of Watson, were the two rotting segments of bone. Shaking uncontrollably, he picked up the two fresh toes for Henley, and carefully placed them in the box. Picking up the picture of Jake along with Henley's dog tags, he held them close in his bloody hands and vowed to never fail again.

Free of his guilt, innocence and competence renewed, Stalls dressed his honorable wounds.

Tomorrow would be a brand-new day.

Chapter Twenty Three

The following morning, Sharon woke to an empty bed. Getting up, she went to the small adjoining bathroom where she washed her face and brushed her teeth. Sparsely decorated, the bathroom boasted no more than the necessities required for Jack to begin his day.

While involved in her morning routine, she contemplated the events that had taken place the day before.

Sitting in the upstairs office listening to what had happened to Clemens, she had agreed to stay at Jack's house until he could assure that she would be safe. Before they left, however, Jack had taken her down into the underground portion of the center where Don was hard at work trying to unravel the Watchful Eye program.

When they had stepped into Don's office and she had seen the enormous amount of computer components he was sitting in front of, she couldn't believe her eyes. The under ground unit was like nothing she had ever seen before. Of course they had stuff like that in movies, but she had never expected organizations like the AFA to actually exist. Upon realizing where she was, and that the unit had been right under her nose the whole time, she couldn't imagine the types of complications the unit dealt with on a daily basis; complications that she was now involved in herself.

Although it wasn't much, Don had explained to her what he knew about the program at that point. After more than two days of investigation, he seemed frustrated in having little more to talk about than speculation. What he did tell her, however, was more than enough to have rattled her nerves.

The idea of being a guinea pig to whatever experiment she had been included in, completely repulsed her. Then, after seeing the long list of others who were possibly going through the same process, she had been infuriated.

Drying her cleansed face, she also thought about the pages of numbers Don had shown her and wondered who those people might be, and like her, what they had done to deserve a possibly life altering injection.

Standing in a secret underground unit, listening to Don talk about things unimaginable, knowing that she had been injected with a foreign fluid of some sort, realizing that the world was nothing like she had always perceived, Sharon had felt utterly lost in her new reality. How was it that she had gone from being a self supporting artist that lived a peaceful life with few complications, to being an experimental test subject for the government. To make matters worse, she was now being sought after by crazed gunmen that work for the government, yet standing in a secret government installation while under the protection of secret government agents? It was almost too much to comprehend. How could this be possible?

Trying to process more than she could understand, more than she wanted to understand, Sharon had asked Jack to take her away from the center and back into the world that she knew and loved. Wanting to get away, she had received too much unwanted information for one day.

After leaving the center, Jack had driven Sharon to her house where she took some much-needed time to pack a

The Watchful Eye

suitcase full of clothes and some toiletries. While packing those items, she had realized that she couldn't run away from the problems in her mind. Regardless of how awful the world seemed at the moment, it was still the world in which she had to live.

Once she finished packing her suitcase, she had walked through her house checking windows and locking doors. It had felt ridiculous. If the people that had tried to run down Clemens wanted to break in and kill her, she was sure they wouldn't give up over a few locked windows. Nevertheless she had finished her task and then left her own house thankful that she would be unavailable to question their ethics if ever they did come calling. Sharon turned off the faucet and placed her toothbrush back in her overnight bag.

Leaving the bathroom, she was confronted by a wonderful aroma. Not having experienced it before, she followed the delightful smell into the kitchen where Jack was busy dicing roasted green chili. On the stove, along side a pot of seasoned meat, a pressure cooker chattered in time as it released its steamy fragrance of breakfast to come. Upon noticing her, Jack welcomed her with a smile.

"Good morning, how did you sleep last night?"

"Like a baby, and you?"

Sharon walked up from behind and wrapped her arms around him. Along with all the wonderful smells boiling throughout the kitchen, she could also smell a hint of Jack's cologne. It was nice.

"Not too bad, when you weren't snoring that is."

"Unh uh! I don't snore."

"Like a locomotive," he teased.

"What time did you get up this morning? I didn't even hear you," she asked noticing that he had already showered and was dressed for the day.

"About an hour ago. I'm usually awake by six o' clock whether I want to be or not. You were sawing logs and looking comfortable so I showered in the guest bathroom. I hope I didn't bother you."

"Not at all," she replied feeling spoiled in knowing that he would go through that much trouble for her. "It did feel good to sleep in this morning, but you should have woke me so that I could help you with breakfast."

"You needed the rest, besides, what kind of host would I be if I rousted my guests out of bed and made them cook their own meals?"

"The kind that's already done too much as it is. By the way, I want you to know that I really appreciate everything you're doing for me. I don't know what I'd do without you," Sharon said in a serious attempt to show her gratitude.

If it wouldn't have been for Jack and the feeling of safety he was providing, she would have probably witnessed her own mental breakdown by now. As bad as things actually were, his confidence in handling adversity seemed to smother her fears while bringing her closer to the peaceful life she was so used to.

"Not a problem," Jack said with a smile, "If things were the other way around I'm sure you'd do the same for me."

"Absolutely," she agreed.

"There's coffee made if you want some."

"Sounds great. What are you cooking? It smells terrific."

"Huevos Rancheros. Are you hungry?" he asked reaching into the cupboard to get her a mug.

"Starved. What do you want me to do?"

"I've got it all under control here," he said handing her the mug. "Here's a cup. The cream and sugar is on the counter. All I need you to do is keep me company."

While Sharon helped herself, Jack added the sliced chilli to the pot of meat on the stove and then refilled his own cup. Then, he sat at the kitchen table next to her and made plans for the day while breakfast finished cooking.

The Watchful Eye

After eating and cleaning the morning dishes together, Jack gathered an extra towel and wash cloth from the linen closet for Sharon. Then, when she had everything she needed and had stepped into the shower, he called Don at the center.

"I was just about to call you. Your scientist friend Avery just called and he sounded pretty excited. He wouldn't tell me what was going on, but wanted you to call him back as soon as possible. I told him I'd have you call the minute you got here."

"How's your work coming? Learn anything new yet?"

"No, not really. I had just walked in and sat down when your friend called. Haven't had a chance to get started yet. By the way, Ted's back."

"Tell him not to leave. I want to talk to both of you. As soon as I can, I'll be on my way."

"We'll be here." Jack hung up and sat on the edge of his bed while trying to think of all the different conclusions the scientist might have come to.

As soon as Sharon was dressed she opened the bathroom door to find Jack sitting on the bed in thought. While she got herself ready to leave, he told her about his phone call and of his new excitement in what the future talk with Avery might hold. Hopefully, they were about to receive a rather large piece to the puzzle. Once they knew what the injection was and where it came from, Jack could notify the Director, Frank Thomas, and bring in authorities that would be capable of dealing with the situation properly.

Listening to what Jack had to say, Sharon shared in his excitement but also felt restlessness in the fear of finally knowing what could very well be the worst news of her life. Trying not to let her mood get shaken, she clicked on her hair dryer and proceeded to ready herself.

From the bed, Jack watched as Sharon got ready through a view provided by the bathroom mirror. She was so beautiful and innocent. Watching her comb through her hair, he couldn't help but feel guilty in knowing that he was the reason she had been involved in the attack and therefore the reason her life was turned upside down. How could he ever make it up to her?

Not only was she beautiful in appearance, but she was every bit as lovely on the inside as she was on the outside. Watching her fling her hair this way and that, while running her fingers and the hair dryer's warm air through it, Jack couldn't believe how lucky he was to have met and spent so much time with a woman of her class and style.

Whatever it took, he would see to it that she would gain her life back and that whomever was responsible for those injections would not only reverse what they had done but would spend a lonely life behind bars as well. Maybe then he could truly appreciate her without the burden of guilt that he constantly felt in her presence.

Unaware that he was gazing at her reflection, Sharon finished as quickly as she could and left her hair slightly damp. After running a brush through a few minor tangles, she removed her belongings from the counter top and put them back in her overnight bag. Then, she unplugged the cord to her hair dryer and was rolling it up when it happened.

Cord and all, the hair dryer fell into the sink as her hand went limp. In the mirror, Jack recognized the before-seen blank stare that had now taken control of her eyes. Sharon was experiencing another black out. Leaping from the bed, he made it to her side and had a hold of her before she had a chance to fall. Instead of losing her balance though, her eyes filled again with life as quickly as they had faded.

Coming to, even though she had only lost consciousness for less than a second, Sharon was startled to find herself in Jack's arms again. That, along with seeing the blow dryer in the sink, she instantly realized what had happened.

"Did it happen again?" she asked in fear although she already knew what the answer would be.

"Yeah, are you okay?"

"I think so. I don't feel dizzy or weak like the last time. Maybe I'm getting better," she said fumbling to sound positive for herself as much as for Jack.

"Are you sure?" he asked walking her into the bedroom where she could sit down on the edge of the bed. Heartbroken at what was happening to her, he kneeled down on the floor in front of her.

"What's happening to me Jack?" Her voice was full of fear and slightly quivering. Looking into her beautiful blue-green eyes Jack felt a crushing weight brought on by their swarm of confusion. He took hold of her trembling hands and held them tight.

"I don't know yet, but I promise you that we're going to find out."

"And then?" she asked as though there was no hope in knowing.

"And then everything will be normal again. Whatever that injection contained, there has to be a cure for it and no matter what it takes, we're going to find it."

Full of despair, Sharon leaned into Jack's shoulder and started to cry. He held her tight and offered comfort, but was unable to reassure her any further. Without being able to offer her explanations, along with his own fears for her safety and well being, Jack's emotions began to grow heavy with anger. He *would* find out what the injections were, and he *would* find a cure. In desperation, he closed his eyes and prayed to God that there was in fact a cure.

In the car, Jack reached across Sharon's shoulder and pulled her close. With eyes full of warmth and concern, along with a hidden glint of uncertainty, he gently placed his forehead against hers.

"Don't worry, everything's gonna be fine," he said.

"How can you be so sure?"

"Because my heart tells me so."

"Yeah?"

"Yeah, besides, have you ever seen James Bond lose to the bad guys?"

"No."

"Well, there you go. If he can win, so can we." Jack forced a smile and backed out of the driveway. Leaving his house, they drove to the center.

Without stopping to talk to Nancy or any of the regulars as he usually did, Jack walked Sharon straight to the elevator where they rode down to the meeting room. Ted was standing by the elevator doors waiting when they opened. His look was disapproving.

Having looked to the security monitor when the three burst warning had sounded, he couldn't believe that Jack would breach the unit's security by allowing access to a civilian. This was completely unacceptable.

"What are you doing Jack?" he asked in a gruff and sturdy voice before they even had a chance to step from the elevator and into the room. His words were meant to sound more like a threat than the question in which he had formed them. "You know it's strictly against policy to even mention what happens down here, much less bringing someone by for a tour. Have you lost your mind? What is she doing here?" he demanded.

Jack quickly introduced the two.

"She's part of a big project Don and I have been working on and I'm fixing to clue you in as well. Why don't you go and get Don while I make a phone call. Then, we'll all have a seat at the table where we can talk about everything."

"I want her out of here now Jack!" Ted stood his ground.

"Look Ted, you're going to have to trust me on this. I think we're on to something really big here. Why don't you sit down and listen to what I have to say. Then, if you're not satisfied with what you hear we can discuss this a little higher up the chain of command."

Ted didn't exercise the conversation any further. He didn't look happy with the idea, but he directed Sharon as to where she was to sit, then headed down the hall toward the computer room. Jack stepped into his office where he would have access to the secure phone line and closed the door.

A few minutes later, Don walked into the meeting room followed by the angry looking man named Ted. As soon as he saw Sharon, he greeted her with a friendly hug.

"How are you?" he asked with his usual cheerful smile. His presence along with his happy attitude helped to ease the discomfort that Ted had instilled in her.

"I've been better." she answered in a quieted, uncertain voice.

Not liking the idea of the two of them being friends already, Ted gave them both a scouring look and then continued to watch closely with a blatant look of distrust.

Under the big man's hateful stare, Sharon began to feel uneasy again and noticed by the look on Don's face, that he was feeling the same way. *Who did this man think he was, and what childhood malady had caused him to act the way he did?* Sharon thought.

By the time Jack stepped out of his office and had come back into the room, both Don and Sharon were sitting at the table minding their own business as if they were kindergartners and Ted were the teacher in charge of detention. He sat down at the table and began to inform Ted of all the recent days' events.

"So what should we do now? Are you going to call in and make a report?" Ted asked insistently.

"No not yet. I don't want to make that call until I've met with Avery and have all the information I can get.

Besides, until we actually know what's happening, we have nothing to report."

"When are you supposed to meet with the scientist?" Don asked.

"First thing in the morning. By the way, I'm going to need a phony ID and a flight to South Carolina. While I'm gone I want the two of you to look after her," he said referring to Sharon.

Upon hearing his plans for her, Sharon shot Jack a look of discomfort and asked to speak to him in private. As the two of them got up from the table and walked into Jack's office, Don found himself smiling at the thought of finally getting in on the real action.

Don had never been put in charge of protecting anyone before, unless it was by way of keyboard of course. The idea enthralled him. Glancing over at Ted who was still glaring at him with that "I only want to beat you up look," he quickly wiped the hero smile from his face. How was that going to work? He could hardly stand to be in the same building with the ape, and that was when they were in separate rooms. Now were they going to have to be bodyguard buddies the whole time Jack was gone? No way!

When Jack closed the door to his office, Sharon immediately confronted him.

"Are you kidding me? You can't leave me with that guy. I don't even know him!"

"What's to know? He's quiet, minds his own business, besides, he's as strong as an ox. If anyone can protect you it would be Ted. I'll bet that guy could take on four full-grown men and not even break a sweat. You'll be alright with him."

"Yeah I bet. From the moment he saw me he looked like he wanted to break my neck himself. If I need protection from anyone it would be from him."

The Watchful Eye

"Don't worry, he always acts like that. That's just Ted. The whole time I've known him he's only smiled twice and I had to use a magnifying glass to notice it both times. Listen, he was upset because I brought you here and in honesty, he has a right to be. Just because I run this unit, it doesn't mean I can chance giving it away by letting outside influences know of its existence."

"I don't care if he has a right to be angry. I'm not staying with him!"

"Don will be with you," Jack said trying to sway her decision.

"Don?" she questioned through a boggled expression. "Don't get me wrong, Don's a real good guy and I don't mind hanging out with him, but even I can protect myself from that scary Ted guy better than he can. I'll end up having to protect Don too."

"Listen," Jack said changing his approach. "I can understand where you're coming from because Ted actually makes me uncomfortable too," he admitted, "but I don't have any other options. It's either leave you here in their protection or take you with me and I can't do that."

"Why not?" she asked stubbornly.

"If you go with me there's no way I'll be able to get you inside the lab and if you're not in the lab with me, then you're going to have to take care of yourself. Not that I don't think you can, but these aren't normal circumstances. I don't want to feel like I'm leaving you by yourself to fend off people that carry guns. You're beautiful, charming, and probably throw a pretty mean punch, but I don't think all of that will be enough to stop those men."

"I don't want to do it Jack," she disagreed. "Something doesn't feel right. I don't trust him."

"Look, those guys were dead set on killing Dr. Clemens and chances are, they're going to be coming after you next. I know you don't want to stay here with them, but I'm begging you to. If we're going to get to the bottom of this, I have to go on this trip, and the only way I'm going to feel comfortable doing that is if I know you're going to be protected."

Jack reached down and collected Sharon's hands into his. "I'm not sure where all of this is going, but I am sure that I'd be devastated if something were to happen to you while I'm gone. I'm falling in love with you Sharon and I don't want to see you get hurt. Could you please do this for me."

Half dazed by what he had said, Sharon looked deep into Jack's blue eyes and found her guidance.

"How long will you be gone?" she asked.

"One day, two tops."

"Okay, but not a minute longer," she demanded.

"Not a minute longer," Jack agreed.

With Jack still holding her hands, Sharon smiled a feeble smile and then kissed him. "I feel the same way Jack. Even though my world seems to be falling apart and I find myself scared of what each day is going to bring next, I can't help but feel that these last few days have been the best days of my life and it's because of you. I don't want this to end."

"That's why I have to know you're in good hands while I'm gone."

"Promise you'll come back to me?"

"I promise."

After a long embrace, Jack and Sharon walked back to the meeting room where Don was still sitting at the table with Ted. He looked thankful to finally be seeing them.

"Any questions?" Jack asked as he sat back down at the table.

"Yeah," Ted said. "Who's this scientist guy Avery? I've never heard of him."

"That's because he doesn't work for us. He's an old friend that I felt I could trust." Hearing Jack's explanation Ted looked irate.

The Watchful Eye

"Don't we have our own guys for stuff like that. First you send those injections to an outside scientist, and then you bring a civilian into the unit? If I didn't know better Jack, I'd think you were trying to destroy this agency." Ted stared at Jack in anger as though he were accusing him of treason.

"I'm trying to protect this unit," Jack shouted in rebuttal, "If that injection was intended for me the way Clemens said it was, then I have to take into consideration that this unit has already been discovered. The last thing I want to do is use our own guys. If they know who I am, chances are they know who all of us are and if that's the case, I be pissing in the wind by using our own scientists. The end result would be the same, don't you think?"

Ted didn't answer Jack's fiery return. Instead, he sat angrily in his chair at the table and glared across it with a look of disapproval.

Seeing the two men locked in a confrontational bout of eye contact while trying to prove who had the highest testosterone level, Don stood up and quietly excused himself. Not wanting to be involved in a brawl, he decided to leave before the conversation really got heated.

"I'm just going to go and arrange a flight and make your new ID," he said as he left.

"If it's not a problem, I think I'll go with him," Sharon added as she stood up to follow Don.

Jack and Ted sat in silence looking like two children engaged in an aversive staring contest while Don and Sharon quickly disappeared down the hall and into the computer room.

"Look Ted," Jack said when they were finally alone, "I really feel like I'm doing the right thing here. Can I trust you to work with me?"

Ted leaned back in his chair and folded his massive arms against his brick wall chest.

"Sure Jack, everything's gonna work out just as it should." His answer boasted confidence tinged with sarcasm.

After producing an ID card and arranging a flight to Charleston for early the next morning, Don, Sharon, and Jack, left the center in search of a good meal. Choosing to stay behind, Ted claimed a desire to finish the novel he had been reading and then hit the machines upstairs.

After dinner, Jack dropped Don back at the center where he had left his car. It was late afternoon and he still wanted to spend some time with the program. He felt as though he were getting close to breaking it completely and would if he could work on it a few hours longer. Jack took Sharon back to his house. Early the next morning, he would drop her off at the center where Don, and hopefully Ted, would be waiting for her. Shortly after, he would then catch his flight to the East Coast to meet the scientist. Tomorrow was going to be a long day.

Chapter Twenty Four

Golden rays of hope shone through small windows on the east side of the aircraft as it approached the South Carolina runway. With all that was at stake, the wheels couldn't touch the tarmac soon enough. Jack sat in the aircraft's small encompassing seat feeling like a prisoner to his own impatience. It would be more than two hours before he met with Avery and then at least another eight before he could be on another flight back home. Fearing for Sharon's safety, he was unable to smother the desperation in his heart.

Jack had never felt so desperate to find a solution in his life. Up until this point, however, nothing had ever been as important as his career and what that career stood for, but then he had never been in love. Until meeting Sharon, he had never even truly considered it a possibility.

Sharon was the kind of woman that he could easily see spending the rest of his life with. The woman that until recently, he had never thought existed. Thinking of how he felt for her, about the inoculation, along with her mysterious blackouts, and now the fear in losing her to a gunman, anger wrenched hard throughout his gut. He had to discover the purpose of the injections along with the identity of the people who were responsible for them. Jack already knew that the men they were up against were ruthless and destructive to the human race, but until he could identify who they were, he would never stand a chance of protecting her against them.

Even though he had believed that he would never experience the love of another human being, he had always possessed a great love for the human race and the wonders of life that surrounded it. How could these men not care for the people's lives that they were affecting? Whoever they were, and whatever branch of the government they worked for, they were obviously incapable of feelings all together. Without love and compassion for the world they lived in, how could that world ever make sense?

With that, Jack felt a strange sense of pity for the men in question. Those feelings of pity, however, were lost shortly thereafter, somewhere over the beautiful Southern shores.

When the plane touched down in Charleston, the only emotion for these men that shared space with his desperation to find them was that of detest.

The actions of these people had affected someone closer to his heart than even he had imagined possible. Long ago, Jack had prepped himself for a life of solitude. Protecting his country and the great ideas that it stood for had seemed to be enough, at the time, to feel a great sense of self worth and happiness. Now that he had found someone he wished to share it with, however, life and its fulfillment had taken on a whole new meaning. All that mattered now was protecting Sharon. No matter what the price, he would not let her down. Losing Sharon was not an option.

Jack checked out a rental car that he had purchased with cash under the phony identity, and then drove to the designated meeting place. During the drive he watched the rearview mirror carefully to be sure he wasn't followed. As he had hoped, the drive was uneventful.

Arriving at the Saltiss Motel right on schedule, Jack walked into the front lobby and paid cash for a room. In the room, he immediately closed the drapes and then waited for the scientist. Shortly thereafter, there was a knock at the door.

Glancing through the peephole, Jack saw Avery and opened the door. From the neck up, Avery looked like a reject that was still lost somewhere in the sixties. For a man in his early forties, his long and thinning brown hair seemed a little out of place even though it was nicely kept. That along with his mustache and goatee, he could have also passed for someone who had sat at the table with Christ and shared in the Last Supper. He wore thin silver rimmed glasses over his light brown eyes that complimented his narrow jawline. From the neck down, he looked very professional and fit the scientific dress code to a tee. He was dressed in a white button up shirt that was tucked and belted at the waist of his light brown khakis. Over it, he was covered by a large white lab coat that he wore unbuttoned while his light tan Rockports easily carried his zest for style and comfort. In his right hand, he carried a duffle bag.

"It's good to see you. How have you been?" Jack said welcoming his old friend.

"Wow, it's good seeing you too. It's been a long time Jack." The two old friends shook hands.

"No tails?" Jack asked as he let the scientist into the room.

"Not as far as I could tell," he answered.

Avery took one last glance at the surrounding area before entering the room. As far as he knew he hadn't been followed.

"Thanks for doing this for me," Jack said with the utmost sincerity. "I don't know what I would have done without your help."

"Hey, no bother. That's what friends are for isn't it?"

The scientist spoke through a genuine smile. "So what kind of mess are you in Jack? Are you still with the CIA?" the scientist asked as Jack shut the door behind him.

"Something like that." Jack replied. Finding himself to be impatient, Jack cut to the chase. "Well, tell me about the inoculations. What are they?"

"There's a lot more to it than you realize Jack." Avery reached into the duffle bag and retrieved a manila folder that he handed to Jack. "I think you're going to want to come down to the lab and see this thing for yourself."

The massive laboratory was at one time, one of the military's top weapons system research facilities. Although not as populated as it had been in the late seventies during the cold war between the U.S. and the Soviet Union, the laboratory was still used primarily for weapon system upgrades.

"Why? What is it you're not telling me?"

"Just trust me Jack. There's too much to talk about here. I don't know what you've gotten yourself into, but it's big."

"Well?" Jack waited.

"It's some sort of transmitter, but there's more to it. I think you need to go down to the lab with me so you can see this thing first hand."

"I can't go to the lab. I'd have to sign my life away to get in that place, and leaving my signature would only be asking for trouble. Before we could get through the front doors, the parking lot would be crawling with men in black SUV's waiting to greet me."

"I'm already one step ahead of you." Avery said nodding to the folder that Jack was still holding. Jack curiously opened the folder and began flipping through the paperwork.

"Are you sure this is going to work?"

"Oh yeah, I had to make a deal with the devil to get those. You couldn't have done any better yourself. Besides, we're going through a back entrance that's used mainly by military personnel."

Avery handed him the bag. Hesitantly, Jack looked over the outfit that Avery had brought him, and then went into the small bathroom where he could change.

When the door opened again, Jack walked out wearing a Navy uniform with a name tag that read "Lt. Chris Heisen." The fit was good. According to the orders that were in the folder, he was a Naval Weapons Specialist.

"Okay Jack, this allows you access to level two security only. It's the best I could do. Once you're inside though, we shouldn't have too much trouble getting around."

This seemed ridiculous. Because of his connections with the CIA, and the fact that he worked under the Director himself, Jack knew that he could have full access to the facility, or any other in the United States for that matter, shortly after placing a phone call. That not being the better choice this time however, he decided to place his trust in Avery even though it involved more risk then he was comfortable taking.

Thinking about what he was being asked to do, Jack shuddered with the idea of getting caught. If he *were* caught and found to be an imposter, it would take to a great deal of valuable time to clear up the mess, not to mention having to explain his actions to his superior.

Without contemplating the risks any further, Jack gathered up his belongings and followed Avery out the door. In the parking lot, the two men climbed into Avery's car.

"Once I realized what I was working with, I had to move my research materials into a small room off of the computer science department," Avery said as he guided the car onto the highway.

Picking up speed he continued, "Your little bug is a hell of a lot more complex than you could have ever imagined, it's quite ingenious actually."

"Bug?" Jack asked looking confused.

"Maybe you should tell me what's going on Jack. This whole thing is pretty serious isn't it?"

During the drive, Jack explained the recent events to Avery.

Upon arrival at the naval weapon station, Jack was allowed entrance into the compound without any problem. After his paperwork was examined, one of the guards escorted the two of them to an underground storage bunker.

From the outside, the bunker looked like nothing more than a large earthen mound with the exception of a heavy steel door. Getting out of the car, they had to walk fifty feet from the parking area to the bunker's entrance.

A couple hundred yards away stood the massive research facility. According to Avery, when the facility was built, it was connected by underground tunnels to three of the surrounding storage bunkers. If ever the facility needed, the bunkers could be used as an escape route in an emergency.

The thick metal blast door slid sideways with a low hydraulic grumble after Avery inserted his ID card and punched a four-digit number into an electronic security device. Inside, a large cement room about thirty-foot square had three smaller concrete rooms adjoining. The larger middle room was mostly bare with the exception of a few metal pallets, an old beat down forklift and a few five-gallon drums. Most likely, they had once contained hydraulic oil.

The Watchful Eye

Pallets of underwater exercise and training mines painted white with thick orange stripes filled all three of the smaller rooms. Four rows deep and six pallets high, they were stacked with enough space between each row for a forklift to be allowed to maneuver.

Jack recognized the mines from his previous experience in the Navy when he was a member of the elite Seal Team. Two thousand pounds of destruction apiece, MK-67 slimms. The submarine-launched mobile mines, as they were called, were made from old torpedoes that had been partly gutted and converted into underwater mines.

These mines were built for use when utmost secrecy was desired in mining a harbor or other areas determined as needed. First, a submarine would enter a location outside the designated minefield without being detected, and then from a distance, launch the mines as though they were torpedoes.

Upon being launched, the mine would propel itself to a previously programed coordinate by use of an internal gyroscope. After reaching the target area, it would then lay at the bottom of the harbor and patiently wait for the arrival of an appropriate sized ship, unless of course it was programmed to lay dormant for a necessary length of time.

Mostly, Jack remembered stories he had heard from the Navy's Explosive Ordinance Disposal personnel about the many different occasions when they had been called in to disarm one. Because the mine's main purpose was to defend shallow harbors, every once in a while, one would malfunction while speeding to its targeted location and run itself up on the beach like a whale during its mysterious desire for a sun-baked suicide.

Behind the last stack of mines in the small room ahead, they came upon a smaller man-size door. It looked every bit as thick as the larger blast door at the entrance. This door also had a security device to control it. Avery slid his ID into it and then punched in another four-digit code.

"CLANK"

The internal locking mechanism released allowing Avery to push the four inch thick steel door inward.

"Okay," Avery said with an uneasy breath, "If we're stopped for questioning, just say that you're with me to look over a software program pertaining to the MK-83 mine warfare counter-measures."

"First of all," Jack stated. "let's just hope nobody asks. Second, if we do make it to the lab, I hope this idea of yours is well worth the effort."

"You've known me for a long time Jack. You're going to have to trust me on this!"

With that said, the two of them entered a long concrete hallway that sloped down at a twenty-degree angle. It ran a length of about thirty feet.

At the end of that hallway stood another steel door that was also equipped with a security device. When they had reached the end of the tunnel, Avery inserted his card and punched in his code. Next to the security device, a small plasma screen illuminated. Placing his right thumb on the screen, Avery then waited for verification. A voice crackled from a speaker that was mounted in the device.

"Good morning Mr. Harris. Who do you have with you today?"

Avery looked up to a security camera mounted in the upper right hand corner of the corridor. "Lt. Heisen. He's a weapons specialist that's here to look over a virtual software issue."

"Sir, please slide your ID badge into the scanner."

Jack felt a slight chill move down his spine and settle in his stomach as he stuck the false ID into the scanner's slot.

"Okay lieutenant, please remove your card and step away from the door. Mr. Harris, you'll need to bring Lt. Heisen directly to security!"

With a whine of hydraulics, the heavy door slowly lifted straight up and into the ceiling allowing Avery and

The Watchful Eye

Jack to pass directly underneath it. As asked, Avery took Jack down another corridor to the security office.

Behind a large section of bulletproof glass, an armed man in uniform was waiting for their arrival.

"Good day lieutenant, I'll need to see your papers please."

Jack handed over the file folder containing the counterfeit orders.

"Okay," he said while looking them over, "everything seems to be in order." He handed Jack a security badge that was made to wear like a necklace. "This will allow you all level two access, please wait here until I can get a guard to show you to your station."

"Let me save you guys the trouble. I don't mind taking him," Avery stated, "After all, we're both working on the same software program."

"Well, okay," the guard said cautiously as he looked Jack over.

Feeling a wave of relief Jack smiled at the guard in appreciation. "I won't be here for very long and to tell you the truth, I'm anxious to get started."

Handing Jack's file back to him, the guard smiled. "Welcome aboard sir."

With that, the two of them headed toward computer engineering. Along the way, when Avery was sure nobody was watching, he motioned Jack to an elevator where they slipped inside. As soon as the doors closed, Avery reached into his lab coat and pulled out a level six security badge. He handed it to Jack who switched it with the level two badge that he had been issued previously.

"Where did you get this?" Jack asked.

"It's an old one that's no longer valid. As long as we don't get stopped for questioning it should work just fine. Perception is everything so look like you know what you're doing."

Slowly dropping, the elevator took them four levels deeper into the earth.

"Okay Jack, this is our stop," Avery said nervously.

The doors opened into a brightly-lit hallway. Avery peered out down both sides of the corridor. "Good, nobody's around. Let's go!"

Walking casually, although both could feel the other's unsettled energy, they made it to Section Twelve without being stopped. Jack felt helpless.

At their destination, another high security electronic device had to be cleared in order to enter the small lab room that the scientist had been working in. Avery explained his ideas to Jack.

"Every one of these Impret devices," Avery said referring to the security device by the door, "that require a thumb print verification, is also hooked to an EMFD." He pointed to another small electronic device mounted above the door.

"What's that?" Jack asked.

"It stands for Electro Magnetic Flux Detection."

"Yeah?"

"It's an electronic search coil if you will. Anyway, all people naturally carry a small amount of electrical current. It's what allows us to walk, talk, and think. Without it we wouldn't be able to function. The earth, however, has lines of electromagnetic flux surrounding it. Think of it like an energy shield. Anyway, the EMFD to make a long story short, constantly measures the earth's flux field. When something passes through it, in this case a person, those lines of flux are slightly bent. That's the best way I can describe it although it's actually much more complicated than that."

"Okay, so what does it do?" Jack asked.

"After the EMFD takes a reading, it matches my ID number to my known electrical field. If the match is good, no alarms will be activated."

"Well that sounds great," Jack said somewhat sarcastically, "but how do you plan on getting me in there, or am I supposed to just stand out here until I get hauled off by security?"

"Hold on a minute. I've already got that part figured out."

Avery inserted his ID, punched in his code and placed his thumb on the plasma screen. The door opened.

"Swoosh"

"Wait here for a minute. I'll be right back!"

Avery stepped into the lab and the door quickly closed behind him. Before Jack could assess how stupid he felt in his present circumstance, the door opened and Avery stepped back out. He was carrying a brown paper sack.

"It gets even better," Jack commented nervously looking at the paper sack. "What are we going to do now, sit down on the floor and have a nice little sack lunch while I wish like hell I never let you put me into this situation."

"Nope, even better! Try this on for size."

From the paper bag, Avery handed Jack a thin grayish-tan suit that felt cold and clammy to the touch. If he were asked to describe it, he would have say that it almost felt like dead skin.

"What is this?" Jack asked. "It feels sort of creepy."

Avery tried unsuccessfully to hide a grin that stretched across his face from ear to ear. He had worked long and hard to complete the suit before Jack's arrival and was quite proud of it. Short lived, his noble smile was quickly replaced by an egotistical pride and a burning need to tell Jack all about this newest accomplishment.

"Actually, there's nothing creepy about it. It's just a suit I've been working on."

"Just a suit huh? Sorry to have to say this," Jack nervously joked while pulling the suit on over the uniform, "but I believe I'll be looking for another tailor. Who's corpse did you use to make this thing anyway?"

"Come on, it's not that bad," Avery proclaimed. As Jack put on the suit, Avery slid his ID card back into the Impret device.

"What's this thing made of anyway?" Jack asked.

"I mixed $Cs2$, and $Pb3$ and created Tripantalide Cesfite, being careful not to inhale the fumes. Then, I mixed it with Adenosine Triphosphate and Lithium Stearate and added a touch of…"

"Slow down, this is me you're talking to. How about throwing some English at me."

"Oh, I'm sorry. It's simply a silicon-glucose compound impregnated with a lead based gelatin. That's the best I can do to break it down for you."

"Well now that I know what it's made of, what's it going to do, make me invisible?" Jack glanced down the corridor to his left and right to be sure nobody was coming.

"Actually, you're not far off," Avery said. "The outer portion of the suit should reflect any magnetic flux it comes in contact with which will prevent the lines from being bent, while the inner portion of the suit absorbs your personal energy field. As far as the Impret is concerned, you no longer exist."

Avery placed his thumb on the plasma screen and the door opened. *"Swoosh"*

"But then that's just theory, I haven't actually had the opportunity to test it yet." Avery grabbed a hold of Jack's arm and started through the doorway with him. "Until now!"

"Swoosh." The door closed behind them without sounding off the alarms.

★★★

Once inside the lab, Jack removed the grotesque suit and followed Avery over to what looked like a huge professional version of a child's chemistry set.

The Watchful Eye

"I knew it would work!" Avery said cheerfully.

Grinning, he looked at the suit that Jack had set on a chair without folding first. "Take care of that it's your ticket out of here."

"Don't worry it's not going anywhere! So tell me everything you've learned at this point. What do you mean by bug?"

Avery walked over to a table that was covered with a plastic sheet of some sort. Removing it, he uncovered several beakers that contained different colored liquids and a machine that looked as if it belonged in an insane asylum where it would be appreciated for its shock value. All of the equipment and materials on the table made about as much sense to Jack as Chinese scripture.

"What is all this stuff?" he asked while examining the equipment.

"First of all, this is one hell of a bug you sent me. Where did you get it?"

Remembering what had happened to Dr. Clemens Jack replied, "I don't want to sound ungrateful to you, because I truly appreciate everything you're doing, more than you'll ever know, but I don't think we should talk about that."

"Don't worry about it," Avery said with a reassuring smile, "I'm already one step ahead of you. I might not know who you got it from, but I can tell you where that person got it."

Jack stared at Avery with an intense curiosity. "You've got my attention!"

"It came from this very facility!"

Jack looked bewildered. "Are you telling me that the military is involved in this! That can't be possible."

"No I'm not saying that the government has approved this thing as a weapon system, but I do believe that the military might be funding the project without actually knowing about it. That's what happens when you put a few greedy scientists anywhere near a laboratory that's funded with dirty money. You know, the kind of scientists that have completely screwed up morals." The look on Avery's face said it all. He sincerely despised those men without morals.

"Weapons system?" Jack asked.

"Possibly," Avery answered.

"So what is it? What does it do?"

"It's very high tech. I've never seen anything like it. Here's the first of the two you sent me."

Using tweezers, Avery held up a tiny blob that looked like nothing more then a cooled drop of melted solder.

"I destroyed this one by accident," he said as he handed it over to Jack. "It took me a while to figure out what I did wrong. Then, after thinking about it and analyzing the fluid it was packed in, I realized that it has to be in an electrolytic solution with conductivity between 13ms and 15.5ms. Very similar to that of human blood. Once injected into a host, it receives infinitesimal electrical currents from the blood stream. It's kind of like charging a battery for example. Upon being activated or charged, it looks like this."

Avery pointed Jack to a beaker that was filled with a green solution. Covered in the fluid and suspended in the middle of the beaker by transparent mesh, was an active bug. It was less than two millimeters in length and about half that wide. Jack looked through a microscope that was set up over the beaker of fluid.

"How did you destroy the first one?" Jack asked.

"That's what happens when it's not encased in an appropriate solution. From the pen, it has to be injected into a conductive solution like the blood of a host. Because of this, after it's been injected and activated, it's impossible to remove."

This was something Jack couldn't bear to hear. Sharon had been injected with one of these things and there had to be a way to remove it. Avery continued.

The Watchful Eye

"Once it's activated, which only takes about thirty seconds from the time of injection, it has to remain in the host for life. If removed from the conductive solution, or overcharged with static, it releases an extremely acidic toxin that literally melts the transmitter and paralyzes the nervous system and brain function of the host."

"What do you mean by overcharged with static?" Jack interrupted.

"Well, for example the tweezers. If you were to try and retrieve one of these things, you would most likely destroy it and its host in the process. It's probably a security measure that was built into the transmitter during manufacturing. If you can't retrieve it, how can you ever prove that it exists?"

"So there's no possible way to remove one of these from a person once it's been injected?" Jack asked melancholically.

"Not that I can think of," Avery confirmed. "To try and remove one of these things would most likely kill the host. At best, it would leave them in a state of coma."

Jack tried to remain calm although he couldn't accept what he was hearing. If what the scientist was saying was true, then there was no hope for helping Sharon.

Upon closer inspection through the microscope, Jack noticed four small spikes protruding from the tiny device. Hoping to find a helpful clue in the information he was receiving, Jack prompted Avery to tell him more.

"What exactly does it do, and what are the purpose of the spikes sticking out of it?"

"Well, at this point I've confirmed for the most part, that it's a transmitter for a GPS type satellite tracking device. Its shell is made mainly of a silicone type material, and the spikes are a zinc, silver and titanium alloy. I presume the silicone along with the combination of metals allow for better transmission of the current they carry while preventing scar tissue from forming, thus closing the circuit.

If you look closer you'll notice tiny hook-like apparatuses at the end of each spike. I believe their purpose is to allow it to attach itself to the vessel wall like a parasite therefore preventing any clotting of the artery. After the shell is submersed, it collects electrical energy until its charge is strong enough to deploy the spikes. At that time, it attaches itself. Then, the spikes are used as a more powerful conductor for receiving current. They also use the conductivity of the host's blood stream as a makeshift human antenna. That way, it can increase its own signal for satellite location. To make a long story short, the transmitter stays charged by collecting electrical impulses from the host. As long as it's in a host it will never lose power, which allows whoever is receiving the signal to track the host from the time it becomes active, till the day the host dies. At that time, the bug loses power which causes its own destruction."

"If what you're saying is true, then anyone that's been injected with one of these things can be located by the use of a satellite?"

"No matter where they are on the face of this earth," Avery confirmed.

Jack thought about Sharon. No matter where she went or how hard he tried to hide her, someone would always know exactly where she was. Not only that, but if her transmitter ever malfunctioned it would kill her? But why would someone do this to her?

"And this one is active right now?" Jack asked referring to the transmitter in the beaker.

"I know what you're thinking. Don't worry, the room we're in is shielded with lead. It was built into the walls as a safety measure for building explosive actuators that are used in the underwater mines. Therefore, this little thing can transmit a signal till hell freezes over and nobody would ever be able to pick it up."

The Watchful Eye

Jack was relieved to hear that government men in black SUV's wouldn't soon be breaking down the door after tracking down the transmitter's signal.

"So if it's a transmitter for the most part, what other functions does it serve? Didn't you say there was more to it?"

"This is where it gets fascinating!" the scientist said.

Jack understood the scientist's captivation for the technology in front of him, but couldn't find a thing himself to be excited about. He thought about Sharon. Without her consent, she was carrying this iniquitous piece of technology around inside of her. That idea didn't fascinate Jack by any means.

"After melting the first transmitter, I was very careful not to make the same mistake with this one. I hooked up this digital data logging meter," Avery said referring to the machine that looked as if it would be better placed in a pre-lobotomy nuthouse. "With it, I can keep a constant eye on the solution's conductivity and also supply a constant .05 millivolts to keep the transmitter charged. At the same time, the machine constantly measures millivolts throughout the liquid."

Avery the scientist stopped talking for a moment and allowed Avery the friend to take over. He knew at this point that Jack's immense interest in the transmitter was fueled in part by personal anxiety, he just wasn't aware of the extent. Keeping that in mind, Avery continued with a less solicitous tone of voice and tried to leave behind his natural scientific interest in the matter.

"About every eighteen hours, there's a pulse increase in millivolts from .01 to .25 over the .05 millivolts that I'm supplying with the data logger."

Jack stared at the beaker containing the transmitter, and then looked at Avery. He still didn't know for sure what his friend was getting at with this new information, but he could tell by the scientist's new tone of voice that it was only going to get worse.

Jack did his best to remain professional and sound neutral when he asked his next question. "Have you determined the reason for these electrical pulses yet?"

"Without the proper equipment to determine the frequency and duration of the pulses, I can't really be positive as to their purpose," Avery carefully replied.

Hearing the scientist's answer, Jack was certain that Avery had already narrowed it down but was trying to show courtesy through a constrained sense of optimism.

"It's okay, I can take it," Jack said trying to relieve some of the burden in dishing out bad, to worse, to horrible news.

Avery continued, "Like I said Jack, without the proper equipment, I'm only guessing."

"Well then what's your best guess?"

"In my opinion, the pulses are neurological and are used for assisting brain function in one way or another."

"What?"

From the minute Avery had said brain function, Jack thought about Sharon's blackouts. That was the connection. That was why her blood work and CAT scan had both come back negative. All of her spells had been caused by the transmitter!

"Swoosh"

From behind him, Jack heard the automatic door open. Turning around, he saw the Director, Frank Thomas, enter followed by two of the weapons station guards.

"What are you doing here sir?" Jack asked.

"I was told I might find you here. Tell me Mr. Kurts, who's your friend." Jack made introductions.

Not quite sure how to react, Avery shook the Director's hand. Probably in his early to mid sixties, he had a very distinguished look about him. His gray hair complimented the intelligent look in his bluish-gray eyes. Looking into

The Watchful Eye

them, Avery felt a strange sense that the Director could see right through him. He was immediately humbled under Mr. Thomas's knowing glare.

"I see you've been busy at work," Mr. Thomas said looking around at all of the equipment that occupied the room. Jack found the question to be odd, along with the Director's semi sarcastic tone of voice, or at least that's what Jack thought he had heard.

"Actually I have," Jack replied, "I was planning on sending you a report in the next few days but not until I had enough information to give you."

Listening to Jack, but not making eye contact, Mr. Thomas walked around the table and picked up the tweezers and with them, picked up the small remains of the destroyed injection. Squinting, he studied it.

"That won't be necessary Mr. Kurts," he said still studying the dead transmitter.

"No? But this is huge! I think we should report it as soon as we can. There are a lot of lives at stake here."

"I said that won't be necessary!"

Placing the tweezers and their catch back down on the table, the Director scowled at Jack as though he were disobeying a direct order.

"Why not?" Jack asked sensing a strange tension that came from the Director.

"Because I already know everything I should. What you've been looking at is of my own creation. What could you possibly tell me that I don't already know."

Jack held a look of puzzlement. "If *you* know so much, then how come I haven't been informed until now? I think it's time you tell me what's going on here," Jack demanded.

"It's a game Jack. It's all been nothing more than a game."

"I don't understand."

"Your job. Everything you've been doing. It's all been a game. From the minute the AFA was started, it's been nothing more than...I don't know...a quality assurance program so-to-speak."

"Quality assurance?"

"Exactly! When I found out that my project was going to be investigated, I had to do something about it. Thank God I was the one that was approached with the idea. Then, in order to keep a lid on the project and what it's capable of, I helped to start and head up the AFA."

"Why would you do that?" Jack asked.

"If an agency was going to be created to watch for signs of the project's existence, who better to run it than me? That way, I could still keep the Watchful Eye Project under tight lock and key. With the information gathered against it being delivered to me, I could use it to better my security and keep from making further mistakes. Of course I gave small tidbits of information to the Congressman, but never enough to cause myself any problems. I made sure he was given just enough information to keep him satisfied, but never enough to go public."

"So you're behind this whole thing? All the work my units have done has been for nothing?"

"I suppose so, if that's the way you want to look at it."

"How could you do such a thing? Think of all of the people you've infected. What about them?"

"Don't give me too much credit Mr. Kurts. I'm no less of a puppet than you are. This thing goes way beyond me. As for the people that have been infected, it's a small price to pay. Once the project is finally finished and out in the open, they'll be proud to have been a part of its making. Just think Jack, with these transmitters we can have total control over the earth's population and create peace throughout the world."

"Peace? I don't know where you come from, but where I come from peace isn't created by terrorizing the people you were sworn to protect. Peace doesn't involve killing. Nor does it involve taking away privacy and the freedom of thought. Do you really think you can create peace with a satellite and some transmitters?"

"Actually yes, I do think so. There's a lot more to it than you realize Mr. Kurts. With these transmitters, we're capable of controlling a person's thought process. By sending out certain frequencies at scheduled intervals, we can control a variety of emotions. Happiness, fear, aggression, loneliness, it doesn't matter; we can control them all. The possibilities are endless Jack. Think of a world that can live in perfect harmony. If everyone on this earth were equipped with a transmitter, there would be no more wars, no more terrorism, no more violent killings, and no more crime. With these transmitters we can stop crimes before they're even committed by simply controlling the emotions of the people who would otherwise commit the crimes. Don't you understand Jack? Who wouldn't want to live in a world like that? No more suffering. No more violence. No more rapes and beatings. Eventually, with the use of these transmitters, we can bring all of the world's countries together to form one unified and perfect Nation. Our Nation Jack, yours and mine. We can control that Nation."

"Yeah," Jack asked, "and at what cost? Freedom? The right to love who we choose, feel the way we feel? Who would want to live in a world where pride in a loved one has to be programed ahead of time via satellite? Do you really think people want to live without the right to make and stand behind their own choices? I know I don't."

"Don't make it sound so bad Jack. After all, you've already benefitted from it," the Director said sharpening his tone. "You didn't really think a girl like Sharon would fall in love with you without help did you? You can thank me for that. Oh yeah," the Director confirmed with a laugh upon seeing the surprise in Jack's eyes. "Love is an emotion that we can control too, but you ought to know that by now."

Hearing those words, Jack almost lost control of himself.

"You know," the Director added, "some say that love is the most powerful emotion in the world."

"Why her?" Jack asked. "Why did she have to be involved?"

"You're not going to believe this Jack," the Director said with a near-honest chuckle, "but she was involved merely by accident. I wanted you at first, but when I had found out that she had been sent to the hospital instead, and then who she was, I couldn't believe the course of my luck."

"Luck?"

"Her father's an extremely powerful man Jack. I couldn't let her go after I realized who her father was. Besides you, he's been the biggest threat to this operation, at least he was anyway. Now that I control his daughter, I can control him. Then, to make things even better, you started showing an interest in her. Your pathetic concern for that girl is a tool that I'm going to use to my advantage Jack. Don't try to hide it, I know how well you and Sharon have been getting along, hell I programmed it. After finding out about your interest in her, I ordered a few 'special' frequency pulses to be sent to her transmitter. She couldn't help but to fall head-over-heels in love with you Jack." Smiling the Director added, "and you just couldn't resist could you?"

"I don't believe you," Jack said.

There was no way he could allow what he was hearing to explain the wonderful bond the two of them had begun to share.

"I can't say that I blame you," the Director continued. "After all, who could possibly resist a woman like her? And do you know what the best part is? You'll never know if she really loves you, or not. She could, but now that it's been programmed into the transmitter you can never be

The Watchful Eye

certain as to what extent. It would seem Jack, that since I have control of her, I have control over her father *and* you!"

If it hadn't been for the two guards at the door with guns, Jack would have pummeled the Director right then and there.

"You know this won't work," Jack said in defiance. "The first chance I get, I'll expose you for what you really are and blow this whole operation of yours out of the water!"

"Come on Jack, your threats are no good here. All that would accomplish is the immediate death of your sweet little girlfriend. Is that what you want? Can you live knowing that she died because of you and your arrogance?"

"She's protected," Jack stated.

"Oh, is that so." The Director turned toward the door and hollered out into the corridor. "Sgt. Stalls, could you please join us."

From out in the hallway, Jack heard a familiar voice answer. "Yes, sir." Immediately after, Ted came into the room wearing a black military uniform.

"What are you doing here?" Jack asked in disbelief. He felt all hope for Sharon's safety slipping helplessly down the drain. Ted didn't say a word. Instead, he stood by the door and crossed his arms proudly. This was the first time Jack had ever truly seen him smile. The Director didn't say a word either. He only glared at Jack in victory.

Seeing Ted for what he really was, Jack couldn't believe that he had allowed this to happen. Both Sharon and Don had expressed a strong distrust in Ted. Repeatedly, he had ignored it while trying to give the bastard the benefit of the doubt. Even *he* had felt discomfort in Ted's presence. Why didn't he at least trust his own instincts if not those of the people he cared so much about? How would he ever be able to forgive himself? As he glared at Ted in anger, his eyes overflowed with abhorrence.

"If you've hurt either one of them, I'll kill you myself," Jack promised.

Ted's wicked smile only broadened. The Director looked at the two weapons station guards and kindly asked them to leave the room allowing the door to close behind them. Silently, he waited until they were gone before he continued.

"Now, now," the Director finally said, "there's no need for hostile behavior. I can assure you that both your friends are alive. Maybe battered a bit, but alive nonetheless. That is as long as you cooperate anyway. Besides, you can't blame Stalls. Even if he was a good guy, he couldn't protect her. No one can Jack, not even you!"

With that, he took a small communication devise from out of his suit pocket.

"All I need is this Jack," he said holding up the devise. "One day soon, this little thing is going to control the whole world. You didn't really think you could hide her from me, did you?" With a sympathetic look of disappointment, the Director shook his head. "In less than five minutes I can find anyone in the world that has one of my transmitters Jack. Then, if I don't like what I see, all I have to do is push a button and I can get rid of them, permanently." Jack gave Avery a skeptical look.

Trying not to bring any more attention to himself than necessary, the scientist quietly nodded his agreement.

"See Jack," the Director said noticing the exchange. "I have a satellite locked onto Sharon right now as a matter of fact," the Director threatened, "I can prove it if you need me to," he said with his thumb looming dangerously over one of the buttons on the device. "Is that what you need Jack, proof?"

Seeing Jack's eyes fill with fear, the Director laughed as though he were involved in a mere childhood game.

"Just think Jack, with the push of a button I can order her transmitter to self destruct. It wouldn't take long you know. In less then five minutes, she'd fall to the ground dead. It's quite painless actually. Soon after the toxins enter her nervous system, she'll drift peacefully into nonexistence. I'm told that it's almost like going to sleep. However," the Director said now bringing on a more spiteful and angry tone, "I'm not that kind of man. I'd rather see her suffer first, wouldn't you?"

Not wanting to partake in the Director's sickening game of power, Jack ignored the malicious question.

"If I send her transmitter repetitive impulses for depression, in less than an hour she'll kill herself. Can you protect her from herself Jack? How do you think she'd do it?" the Director asked tauntingly as if he were trying to make Sharon's death sound like a simple game of chance.

"Do you think she'd use poison or some sort of overdose like that? Maybe she'd walk out onto the freeway or jump off a cliff? I don't know about you, but I don't think she'd look so pretty anymore if she were lying dead in a bathtub with her wrists cut wide open? What do you think Jack, am I making any sense yet?"

In an instant, Jack's chest grew cold and empty upon hearing the Director's connotation. Churning inside with the thought of Sharon suffering, he felt sick to his stomach.

"Are you truly prepared to spend the rest of your life trying miserably to save somebody that you can't possibly protect?"

Dismayed, Jack didn't answer for fear of reprisal.

"Are you Jack?" he asked again more forcefully.

Jack's fearful anger dwindled further into a look of defeat.

"I didn't think so!" the Director said, knowing that he had finally hit the most exposed nerve.

"So what exactly is it that you want from me?" Jack asked.

The Director smiled knowingly as though he had already prepared for the question.

"I want you to continue working for me, on the other side of course. You're a valuable man Jack and I don't want to lose you."

"I can't do that. What about all the people that are suffering because of you? I could never sleep knowing that I'm a part of that."

"The people? Who cares about the people? You've been serving the people your whole life and what do you have to show for it. The people of this so called country make me sick."

In anger, the Director raised his voice. "Hundreds of my comrades died in Vietnam for these self-righteous people you call Americans. They died horrible deaths for a country of people who couldn't even care. You want me to show concern for the same people that spit on me when I returned home after fighting for their way of life. You want to know about the people?" he repeated angrily with disrespect for Jack's obligation.

"My wife was one of those so called people that you care so much about. Can you believe that while I was off at war proudly defending her, she was back at home screwing one of your people? She ended up leaving me for someone else while I was off at war. For a punk who dodged the draft, Jack! A punk with no honor!

This man was too cowardly to fight for his own country, too cowardly to fend for her even but yet he was allowed the freedom to do as he pleased while I was spit on." Thinking back the Director grew furious. "Are those the kind of people you're talking about? Because if you are, you need to seriously reconsider where your loyalties belong. Mine belong with the government, Jack, and I think yours should too.

Our government is the only thing that ever took care of me. Shouldn't you be loyal to the government that took care of you also, or would you rather suffer even more than

The Watchful Eye

you already have for the people? To hell with the people!" he yelled.

"After all of the blood, sweat, and tears you've shed proudly, do you think this Nation and its self-centered population would shed even one single tear for you? I don't think so Jack! Either you can work for me and the government that has always taken care of you, or you can continue to slave away for a bunch of ungrateful, self-righteous, non-deserving bastards that you call people! You do have a choice Jack and this is it. I can't *make* you work for me, but if you choose not to, your girlfriend will die a miserable death! That I promise!" Finished, the Director glared at Jack in anger.

Jack couldn't believe the situation he was being placed in and the choice he was being forced to make. In his own mind, either solution was the worst possible. There was no way he could partake in the destruction of a nation he had worked so hard throughout his life to protect. How could he participate in bringing such a horrible fate upon millions and millions of innocent people?

However, there was no way he could allow Sharon to die in the hands of the Director. Deep in his heart, he knew that he loved her and that she loved him. How could he make a decision that would end her life while managing to live day by miserable day throughout the rest of his?

"I'm getting impatient Jack!" the Director said. He nodded to Ted who already understood his place in helping to guide Jack toward the answer they were looking for.

With malicious intent, Ted withdrew his .50 cal desert eagle and pointed the hellish barrel at the scientist. Acting at the same moment, Jack grabbed the back of the closest chair and flung it across the room at the big man with all of his might. Before the chair hit its target, the cannon released an ear-shattering roar that sent Avery back three feet into the wall behind him. He hit the floor with a thud.

A split second after the shot was fired, the chair crashed against the side of Ted's left shoulder and head. It was immediately followed by a rush from Jack. Upon impact, Jack knocked Ted to the floor where he lost his grip on the gun. As the two men struggled to get to their feet, the .50 cal handgun came to a rest no more than five feet away.

Desperate to reach it first, Ted was halfway to his feet before Jack violently met his face with the instep of his right shoe. Still, Ted got up.

After kicking the big man with all of his strength, Jack was surprised to see Ted get to his feet as if nothing had happened. Launching another assault, he connected a roundhouse kick to Ted's temple. It also seemed to go unnoticed.

Bleeding from the nose and looking like a two hundred and fifty-pound, stir crazed bull on steroids, Ted swung a massive fist at Jack's head.

Seeing the punch plenty in advance, Jack was able to avoid its threat of destruction by ducking underneath it. Coming back up, Jack managed to connect two solid punches to Ted's rib cage followed by another hard kick. This time, he placed it to the side of Ted's tree trunk of a knee.

Instead of going straight to the floor like Jack had hoped, Ted only fumbled before he managed to get a tenacious grip on Jack's shirtsleeve. Pulling back his overgrown fist, with the look of a train wreck waiting to happen in his eyes, Ted slammed his fist directly into the middle of Jack's chest and sent him flying backwards across the beaker cluttered lab table. Had there been any wind left in him after Ted's punch, Jack would have lost it when he hit the floor on the other side.

Smiling with the excitement of pleasure yet to come, Ted shoved the table out of his way and then reached eagerly for Jack who was lying breathless on the floor behind it.

The Watchful Eye

With one hand, he grabbed Jack by the hair and quickly lifted him from the floor and on to his feet. He was pulling back to deliver another massive punch when Jack spun around to deliver a back kick to the middle of the giant man's throat.

If only momentarily, the kick worked. Ted reached for his throat with both hands and began to gasp for air, but instead of seeing the big man's eyes fill with fear, Jack saw their fire rage out of control. Without waiting to see what would happen next, Jack leaped from the ground with a spinning heal kick, again aimed for Ted's temple. It was time to end this once and for all. Instead of connecting, however, Ted caught Jack around the waist in mid-air and threw him down to the floor at his feet. Then before he could move, Ted, along with all of his weight and brute strength, had landed on top of him.

Struggling helplessly, Jack couldn't avoid allowing Ted to grasp the meat edge of his palm and place him in submission. On his stomach with one of Ted's knees planted in the middle of his back and the other one across his neck to hold his face to the floor, Jack struggled to keep Ted from raising his own arm up behind him and then ripping it apart at the elbow by jerking it across the inside of his thigh. In this position, struggling was useless. Ted was just about to rip Jack's arm from its own socket when the Director yelled out to stop him.

"That's enough!"

Not wanting to listen, Ted continued to apply pressure. Jack was certain that the big man had lost control and wouldn't be able to stop until he had shredded his adversary into several different and useless pieces.

"I said, that's enough! Bring him over here."

Slowly, and against his own burning desires, Ted slightly lowered Jack's arm and then twisted his wrist joint in the opposite direction bringing Jack up painfully from the floor and on to his feet.

With one hand keeping Jack in the new submission hold and the other grasping a handful of hair, Ted forced him over to the table where the Director was standing and slammed him face first on top of it.

"Consider yourself lucky for now Jack," Ted said under his breath, "but I can guarantee you this isn't over yet. One of these days I'm going to enjoy the lengthy process of ripping you apart one limb at a time!"

With that, Ted spit on the side of Jack's face and then prevented him from moving as it slowly rolled down his cheek and onto the table.

"Looks like it's time to make a decision Jack!" the director said.

Pulling an inoculation pen from out of his suit pocket, he leaned down to where Jack could see him from the table and twirled it around in front of his eyes.

"I know that I can't make you *want* to do exactly what it is that I'm asking of you, but if you and your girlfriend *want* to live I would strongly suggest that you do!"

Jack fought helplessly as the Director pressed the injection against the side of his neck.

"CLICK!"

The sound was followed by a small but sharp sensation of pain.

"Now Jack, I don't think you have much of a choice. Either you work for me, or you can watch your little girlfriend suffer a horrible fit of suicide. Then, if that doesn't drive the point home, I'll do the same with you. It really doesn't matter, because regardless of how it all works out for you, I'm gonna win. Do the right thing and win with me Jack. Wouldn't it be nice to finally get the girl, and live a life that most people would die for? Think about it Jack."

Finished, the Director dropped the empty injection casing on top of the table and in front of Jack's face as a reminder before he turned to walk away. "You can let him

The Watchful Eye

go now," he said to Stalls who was still finding satisfaction in grinding Jack's face into the table.

Not wanting to, but knowing he had to, Stalls finally let go of Jack's hair and then slowly released the submission hold. Then with one last fit of spiteful fury, he kicked Jack's legs out from underneath him sending him crashing down onto the floor.

As Jack was slowly getting to his feet, Ted took time to laugh at him and then turned to follow the Director from the room.

"Hey you big ape," Jack said as he got to his feet.

Ted stopped in his tracks, wondering what idiot desire a man like Jack would have to be begging for even more punishment than he had already received.

With a good idea as to where Jack was standing by the location of his voice, Ted turned around to meet him with a violent swing. He fully intended on smashing Jack's face.

Although Ted came around tempestuously, swinging for a grand slam, Jack had already expected the big man's reaction and was ready. Before Ted could blind side him, Jack ducked below the punch and counter attacked Ted's throat.

Unaware of what had actually happened, Ted's eyes filled with a look of surprise and then confusion as he heard and felt the side of his throat rip followed by a heavy spurting of blood.

"You were right Ted," Jack said with satisfaction, "It wasn't over yet!" Having grabbed the empty inoculation pen from the table, Jack had used it to penetrate Ted's massive but unprotected throat. Acting like a straw, the syringe opened up a passageway, which allowed for Ted's life-giving blood to pour quickly onto the floor.

Unable to comprehend what had happened, and with little time in which to do so, Ted fell to the floor with little to no struggle at all. He felt a dark weakness rapidly closing in on him. It was nothing like the power he had expected to feel during the many times he had dreamed of this very event.

As the confusion in his eyes was slowly replaced with what appeared to be a sudden fear of dying, Theodore Stalls mumbled, "Honor?" as though it were a question in which he desperately required an answer.

Looking at the dying man without an ounce of pity, Jack replied, "There's no honor in this world for men like you!"

Hearing Jack's response, his eyes flooded with compunction. Then, they lost their self-possession altogether as the last of his life poured out onto the floor.

Jack looked at the Director with hatred and began his pursuit.

Seeing what had just happened, the Director frantically grabbed for the electronic device that he had already placed back in his pocket.

"Don't even think about it Jack! Take one more step toward me and Sharon will die!" he promised holding his thumb over the button.

Staying where he was physically, but destroying the Director in his mind, Jack did as he was told. Against every ounce of revenge pulling fiercely at his bones and pumping furiously throughout his veins, he managed to remain where he was.

"There's nothing you can do Jack, it's over!"

"The hell it is!" Jack asserted with a demand for vengeance radiating from within his steely blue eyes.

"On the contrary," the Director argued. "Calm down and think about it Jack. No matter what you *think* you're going to do, I can assure you, it will only end in your own demise. What are you planning inside your troubled little head, huh? Do you think you're going to be able to kill me and then go to the Authorities? Maybe put end to this whole thing? Sure, I guess you could try to do that, but I promise I can punch this button and put an end Sharon's life

The Watchful Eye

before you can get even one step closer to me. I might die shortly after, but then so will she Jack. Just think about it. It will be almost like you're killing her instead. You don't really want to do that do you? Besides, before you could even get anybody to believe in what you're saying, this project would disappear under mountains of paper work, and for what, the mere cost of your girlfriend's life. Is that what you want to see happen?"

"If that's what it takes." Jack said in anger. Bluffing, he knew the Director was right, but if he let him walk away now, he might never get a second chance to stop him, thus putting an end to the Watchful Eye. Somehow he had to maneuver the Director into making a vital mistake. He had to create an opening in which he could react.

"It's a federal project for Christ's sake Jack. What do you think you're going to do, take on the United States government by yourself? Even if you managed to kill me, someone else would take my place. Think about what you're doing. Calm down and think! You don't have a choice anymore than I do."

Holding the device tightly, with his thumb hovering dangerously over the button that could end Sharon's life, the Director smiled when he finally saw a subdued feeling of helplessness distort the once angry flare in Jack's innocent eyes.

"You'll make the right choice Jack. I have confidence in you. Tell you what, because I'm a good man and I have respect for you, I'm going to grant you some time to think this whole thing through. You're angry now, but with a little time to think it over, you'll come to an understanding. How about twenty-four hours? I'll give you twenty-four hours to see things my way. Then, we can start this new relationship on track. After twenty-four hours, you can either continue to work for me and the government that loves you, or you can sit by helplessly as the people you care so much about suffer horribly before they die. Then you can join them."

Jack just stared at Mr. Thomas knowing that there was nothing he could do to stop him without risking Sharon's life.

"By the way, don't think you're going to screw with me. I'll be monitoring your movements from satellite. There's no way around this Jack. It sort of feels like it was meant to be doesn't it?" The Director smiled and turned to walk off, then stopped.

"Only twenty-four hours' Jack. Don't be late." With that, the Director left the room.

Alone but alive, Jack stood motionless in the wake of a world that had just fallen apart in heart crushing pieces all around him.

Chapter Twenty Five

When the Director had stepped out of the room, a part of Jack wanted nothing more than to chase him down and mop the floor with his head. Instead, he stood where he was and stifled the rage that was begging to be unleashed. Although he couldn't determine how, he was going to have to find a way to stop Mr. Thomas and then put an end to the Watchful Eye program. Thinking about his options, it seemed hopeless. How could he fight a man that had been given so much power?

He pictured Sharon's beautiful face and reflected back on the time they had been spending together. How could he have let this happen to her? It was because of him and his line of work that she was in this mess with him in the first place. He would never be able to forgive himself if anything worse were to happen to her.

Desperately searching for an answer, Jack was unable to find a way out from under the burden the Director had placed on him. It was hopeless. If he did anything other than what he was being asked, Sharon would die.

As much as he despised himself for admitting it, the Director was right. There was nothing he could do to stop what had already been put into motion. His only choice now was to comply. If not, Sharon, along with himself now, would be erased from existence with the simple touch of a button.

From behind him Jack heard a muffled groan. Startled, he turned around quickly with the expectation of finding Ted, soaked in his own blood with a scared and confused look permanently plastered across his face, looming over him and wanting revenge. As he had hoped, Ted was still lying lifeless in the middle of the floor by the table.

Before Jack could contemplate losing his mind, another groan issued from further back in the room.

Upon hearing it the second time, Jack realized that it must have come from the scientist. Avery was still alive.

In the far corner of the room where he had fallen, Avery was leaning back against the wall with his eyes closed. Jack rushed over and knelt down by his side. His white button up shirt and lab coat were soaked with blood.

"Hey," Jack said kneeling down in front of his friend. "Talk to me buddy."

"Are they gone?" Avery asked. His voice sounded weak.

"Yeah, they're gone. How are you feeling?"

The large amount of blood on Avery's shirt made it looked as though he would bleed to death if something weren't done soon.

"Yeah, I think I'll live. I hope so anyway, there's still a lot I want to do." Avery tried to sit up, but Jack stopped him.

"Whoa, hold on a minute. Before you try and save the world let's get your shirt off and look at the damage. If you still have plenty of things you want to do, we're going to need to stop the bleeding so you can do them alright."

Being careful not to hurt the man, but not so careful as to waste precious time, Jack helped Avery remove the lab coat along with the button up underneath it. By the looks of the blood stained clothing, most of the damage was done to

The Watchful Eye

the scientist's right shoulder. When the garments were finally removed, Jack's suspicions were confirmed.

By throwing the chair at the right moment, Jack had caused Ted to flinch slightly in anticipation of being hit. Although Ted's reaction was minimal, it had been just enough to keep the scientist from taking a direct hit. Instead of pulverizing the heart as had been Ted's obvious intentions, the bullet had gone off course and blasted through the scientist's deltoid muscle. Even though the bullet had probably just nicked him, a large portion of the muscle was shredded and missing. Thankfully, the round was a full metal jacket.

"Well pal, looks like your going to get to do all those things after all," Jack said looking at the bullet wound. Compared to what Jack had expected to see underneath the clothing, the mangle of damaged flesh could have been much worse.

Having been knocked off of his feet, Avery had lost consciousness, not due to a lack of blood, but more likely during the hammered fall. Even though a large portion of his shirt was stained red, his complexion didn't appear as pale as Jack would have first assumed. For being shot only moments ago, the scientist looked quite stable.

With Avery lying on the floor guiding him verbally, Jack quickly rummaged through the lab room until he found the first aid kit. Inside, he found the materials needed to make a temporary dressing.

Holding still as best he could, Avery watched in pain as Jack filled the wound with an antibiotic ointment that he had found in the kit. Next, he opening all eight packets of sterile gauze and stuffed them carefully into the scientist's bleeding shoulder. Next, he covered the wound with a generous amount of surgical tape to keep the pressure dressing from sliding off.

"I know this isn't as professional as it could be," Jack said while ripping long strips from the scientist's blood soaked shirt, "but it should hold you together long enough to get you to the hospital."

"The hospital?" Avery asked looking disrupted. "I'm not going to the hospital."

"You sure are," Jack confirmed, "you need medical attention right away."

"I heard what the Director said Jack. We have only twenty-four hours so you better make sure that bandage is going to hold me together for at least that long."

"No, wait a minute. This is my fight Avery. I think you've been through enough already. Besides, he said *I* have twenty-four hours not you. You have to get to a hospital before you bleed to death."

Jack tied the strips of clothing in a figure eight around Avery's neck and under his shoulder to help keep pressure on the dressing.

"Look at me Jack, I've been shot! Now I don't know how that makes you feel, but in my book, I'm as involved in this as I could possibly be. There's no way I'm going to the hospital to lay around in a little bed while that jerk you're working for gets away with this. Besides, whatever you're planning on, you're going to need my help."

"I don't need your help," Jack disagreed. "I need you to go and see a doctor."

"Can you tell me everything there is to know about the transmitter?" Avery asked.

"No."

"Well I could tell you."

Jack thought it over while adding the finishing touches to the scientists dressing. During that time, he was unable to ignore Avery's demanding stare.

"I guess I can't make you go to the hospital if you don't want to," he said to the scientist who was still making his intentions crystal clear by means of eye contact, "but I think you'd be stupid not to."

The Watchful Eye

"Maybe so, but that's a chance I'm willing to take. Besides, if I checked into a hospital, all I'd be doing is assuring myself that the Director would send another one of his goons to finish the job as soon as he realized that I wasn't already dead."

Again Jack considered what the scientist was saying and knew that he was probably right. After being witness to the Director's conversation, Avery wouldn't be safe no matter where he went. After little more contemplation, Jack decided to let Avery help so long as his wound didn't become infected or continue to bleed uncontrollably after he was finished dressing it.

"Okay," Jack said, "but I think you'll need more than this bandage if your going to be of any use to me."

Ripping the lab coat, Jack tied a few more strips of clothing into a makeshift sling and then helped the scientist to rest his arm in it. Then he helped him to his feet and carefully walked him over to where the suit was still lying unfolded on the back of a chair. Removing it, he helped Avery sit down.

"What do we do now?" Avery asked.

"I'm not sure. I don't know if there's anything we can do?" Jack began to slowly pace in circles while trying to think of his options. No matter what he thought of, every solution he came up with ended in Sharon's death. If he went to the authorities with what he knew, she would die. If he fought for her freedom in anyway whatsoever, she would die. The only thing that he could do to save her was to comply.

Feeling sickened by his only option, Jack stopped pacing and ran his hands against the sides of his face while closing his eyes in an attempt to relieve some of the stress. Upon opening them again, he looked down to the floor in front of him and saw the suit. Reaching down, he picked it up off the floor. For as thin as the creepy feeling material actually was, it was surprisingly heavy.

"What did you say this was made of again?" Jack asked with growing interest.

"The long version, or the short?"

"Short."

"It's a silicone glucose compound impregnated with a lead gelatin."

Seeing a glint of hope in Jack's eyes, Avery was startled when he burst into action and began collecting supplies.

"What are you doing Jack?"

"I've got an idea!"

"Yeah, you mind filling me in?"

While Jack explained his idea, Avery sat in the chair and pointed out the supplies he thought he would need in order to make it work.

After gathering everything the scientist had suggested, Jack loaded the supplies into the duffel bag that still contained the manila file folder with the phony orders. Strapping the bag over his shoulder, Jack helped Avery up out of the chair and then the two of them proceeded to leave the lab.

"What about him?" Avery asked as they stepped around Ted's dead body on their way to the door.

"He can lay there and rot for all I care," Jack replied.

"Serves him right!" Avery agreed.

With most of the security guards eyeing them cautiously, the two of them were surprised in how little effort was required in exiting the huge facility. By the looks they were receiving, Jack could only assume that the Director had given the guards strict orders to allow him to leave. Thinking Avery was dead, the Director had probably neglected to mention the scientist, but the guards had automatically assumed that he was to be granted that same privilege. Regardless, the two of them made it out of the facility and to Avery's car as fast as they possibly could before an alarm was sounded or the guards changed their minds.

The Watchful Eye

Once outside the compound, Jack drove directly to a department store where he picked up more first aid supplies along with a fresh change of clothes for the scientist. After that he drove them back to the hotel where he could better clean the wound and then take time to bandage Avery's shoulder properly.

In the store, Jack had also picked up three different brands of over the counter painkillers. Although they weren't as strong as prescription, for these Avery was the most thankful.

Back at the hotel, Jack cleaned the scientist's wound and changed the bandage. He also helped him to wash off the dried blood and change into the new clothes. Wincing in pain during all the required movement, Avery took a few more pain tablets than the recommended dosage printed on the label. He pocketed the rest.

With the exception of having only one arm protruding from his clothing and the other tucked in the sling safely inside his shirt, Avery felt comfortable enough to make the long plane trip back to California with Jack.

On the way to the airport, Jack stopped at a fast food joint and ordered more than enough food for the both of them.

"You must be hungry," Avery said witnessing the large amount of food that had been ordered.

"Not really," Jack replied, "most of it's for you. If you're going to go with me, then I want you to eat as much as you can before we leave. Then when we get on the plane you can get some rest. You're going to need as much down time as you can get."

"Don't worry so much Jack. I'll be fine," Avery said although he knew Jack was right.

Even though the wound had looked a lot worse than it actually was, he had lost a healthy amount of blood. Now that the adrenaline factor was wearing off, he was beginning to feel a little chilly and weak in his knees.

Realizing that Avery was in a very delicate state, but knowing that his intelligence in the matter could possibly make all the difference in the world, Jack felt an overwhelming amount of pride and respect for the scientist that was seated next to him.

"Thanks Avery," he said with the utmost sincerity. "You were right. I couldn't do this without your help."

Knowing people like Avery existed was more than enough to fuel Jacks fire in doing what had to be done and making the difference. Throughout his entire life he had fought for the freedom of people like Avery, and at times like this, felt the rewards for all of his efforts ten fold.

"You fell for that crap?" Avery laughed. "I only said those things to keep from being dumped off. Wow, you're really gullible, aren't you?"

On the drive to the airport, Jack worked on his plan while Avery ate as much food as he could stomach.

★★★

At the airport Jack purchased the two tickets to California while Avery sat resting in one of the many chairs that surrounded the ticket counter. After paying for the flights, he walked Avery through security and then over to the boarding gate. From there, he found a pay phone and tried to call the secure line to the fitness center. Nobody answered.

Concerned that he might have dialed the wrong number he tried again. Again, there was no answer. Then he called Don's cell phone. It also rang unanswered.

Walking back to the departure gate where Avery sat waiting, Jack thought about the interrogation videos that he had watched, and of all the many horrible things Ted was capable of doing. Although terribly concerned for Don and Sharon's safety, he couldn't bring himself to think about what Ted might have done to them. Having to sit and wait twenty hellish minutes for the boarding call, while trying not to allow his mind to wander across all the awful things that might have happened to them, Jack sat through the worst twenty minutes of his life.

Twenty minutes later, he and Avery were on the plane and leaving the runway. He had only nineteen hours left.

★★★

When their last flight finally touched down at LAX, only twelve hours remained. Jack prayed that those twelve hours would provide the time he needed to make things right.

As Jack had expected, Avery slept throughout most of the flights and looked as though he was regaining some of his strength and composure.

As fast as Avery could move, the two of them hurried out to the massive parking structure to where Jack had left his car that same morning. Once he had helped Avery get situated and then was in the car himself, Jack reached for his cell phone to try the fitness center again.

Three messages were displayed in his mailbox, and all three were from Don who had tried to warn him about Ted. Jack called the number that Don had left and on the third ring it was answered.

"Hello." Jack would have never thought hearing Don's voice could sound so good.

"Are you okay? How's Sharon, is she hurt?"

"We're both fine considering the circumstances. Where are you? Have you seen Ted? I think he went to Charleston to find you. He's crazy Jack!"

"Yeah, I know. I've already dealt with him, he's dead. I'm leaving the airport right now. Where are you?"

"We're still at the unit."

"What happened to the phones?"

"They've been destroyed so I'm calling through the computer line. A lot's happened since you left this morning, you're not going to believe it."

"Oh, I'm sure I will. I've got a lot to talk about myself."

While listening to the news Don had to give him, Jack started his car and left the parking structure in route to the center. If he hadn't had to deal with Ted himself, Jack would have had a hard time believing the story. All he could think about now, however, was that Don and Sharon seemed to be alive and well. On the drive he thought about what Don was saying.

Shortly after he had left Sharon in Don and Ted's, Ted had gone berserk. At least that was how Don put it anyway.

According to Don, he and Sharon were in the computer room talking about the injections and working on the Watchful Eye program, when Ted came in and closed the door.

At first they thought he wanted to be a part of the group, but then seeing an evil look in his eyes, they quickly realized that that was not the case. Instead, he told them the truth about who he was and what he was planning on doing with them. Immediately, Don had grabbed his cell phone and tried to get a hold of Jack before he was on the plane and gone, but Ted took it away from him and smashed it on the floor. Then, he grabbed Don by the collar and the waist of his pants, lifted him clear over his head, and threw him against the wall like a five-pound bag of crap. Don had fallen to the floor unconscious.

Seeing that, Sharon had tried to run for the elevator where she might be able to ride up to the outside world and get some help, but Ted quickly cut off her escape.

Standing between her and the door with an evil grin, he began to recite a long list of sexual desires he had planned for her after he had properly dealt with Jack. Until then, however, he informed her that she would just have to settle

The Watchful Eye

for the small amount of pleasure she could give him now, before he had to leave for the East Coast.

Lightning quick, Ted reached across the table that she had put between them mid sentence and jerked her across the top of it to where he was standing on the other side. Struggling, she had tried her best to get away while he forced himself against her and then tried to elicit a kiss.

Managing to free one hand, Sharon smacked him three times across the face before he backhanded her across the table and on to the floor.

Yelling at her like a raging lunatic that had missed a months worth of medication, Ted promised her that she would eventually do as he wished. Until she decided to please him willingly, he also promised to share more pain with her than she could possibly tolerate.

From where she was cowering down on the floor, Ted reached down with one hand and grabbed a handful of her hair. With it, he drug her on her hands and knees across the room and back over to the table.

Still holding her by the hair, he lifted her to her feet screaming. Then with little effort, pinned her down on the table with one hand while ripping at her clothes with the other.

Coming to, Don quickly realized what was happening and scanned the room for something he could use as a weapon. Finding nothing of solid value, he grabbed a cup of coffee that had been sitting on the edge of his computer station and threw it in Ted's face.

Still hot but not scalding, Ted hollered out in anger while reaching for his shirt to wipe the burning coffee from his eyes. With the other hand, he managed to keep Sharon pinned down on the table.

While Ted was occupied with wiping his eyes, Don searched the room until he found something more useful. Swinging at the big man with all the strength and speed he could muster, Don shattered one of his keyboards across Ted's head. This time, Ted let Sharon go.

After being hit with the keyboard, Ted forgot all about Sharon and shifted his focus on Don. When he did, Sharon stood up from where he had pinned her and stomped on his right foot with the thick solid riser of her two-inch heel. Ted screamed out in pain. Losing his focus all together, he grabbed for his foot with both hands.

Not wanting to wait around like a spectator entranced by the screaming, one-legged dance Ted was performing, Don grabbed Sharon by the arm and the two of them ran out of the room and down the hall. At first, Don had thought about running to the elevator, but then he heard Ted's heavy footsteps coming down the hall behind them. They would never be able to get to it in time. Even if the elevator doors were waiting wide open and welcoming, they would never be able to get the doors to close before Ted was in the elevator and on top of them.

Instead Don had pulled Sharon into Jack's office at the end of the hall. As soon as she was through the door behind him, he slammed it shut and locked it.

Close behind them, Ted rammed the door at full speed.

Of all four offices that were built in the underground unit, Jack's had been the only one that was equipped with a steel door for the purpose of locking away all the important documents that the room often contained. As it was designed to, the door stood firm against Ted's barbarous attack.

Yelling furiously, Ted slammed the door repeatedly, but it held proudly. No matter how strong he was or how hard he hit it, he would have to have brought little less than a bulldozer to penetrate the security provided by the heavy steel door. For the moment they were safe.

Shortly after, the room grew silent when Ted's door battering fury finally subsided. Without having windows to

The Watchful Eye

look through, Don grew nervous in not being able to determine what Ted's next craze driven tactic would be.

Turning around, he switched on a monitor and then flipped through views provided by three different security cameras before he saw Ted in the hallway. He was still standing on the other side of the office door cursing in rage. Eventually he punched the door and then walked away. Don flipped through the different camera views and watched him as he left.

First, Ted began taking his frustration out on the furnishings. Like a bull in a china closet, he smashed through anything he could get his hands on. For at least ten minutes, Don and Sharon watched the monitor as Ted pulverized every object he possibly could. When he finally felt satisfied with destroying the meeting room, he went over to a small gray box that was mounted on the wall, opened it, and began ripping out handfuls of wire.

Amazed, Don couldn't believe that Ted was actually smart enough to know what he was doing. Sharon and Don watched from the safety of the office as Ted destructively disconnected all the phone lines including the secure line in Jack's office.

When the room was in shambles and Ted was content that Don and Sharon were locked away without a means for finding help, he placed a phone call from a cell phone that he kept in his workout bag. Ten minutes later he stepped into the elevator and left.

Not allowing himself to fall for what might be a simple trick, Don flipped to the camera in the elevator and watched Ted until he stepped out of the elevator and onto the first floor.

Telling Sharon to stand by the door and watch the monitor in case Ted decided to return, Don quickly left the safety of the office and went down the hall to his computer room.

Nervously listening for Sharon's warning, Don quickly pulled up the unit's security file and began working on changing the elevators pass code along with Ted's personal voice command. If he could change the code before Ted decided to return, he would be able to keep him from coming back down to finish the job.

Don was into the elevator's security file and had almost finished changing the pass code when Sharon began yelling at him from Jack's office. Ted had stepped back into the elevator with two more men. Both were wearing black military uniforms and were nearly as big and mean looking as Ted.

Listening to Sharon's impatient shouting, Don worked frantically to verify the new pass code before Ted could get to the control panel. If he couldn't verify the change before Ted began pressing buttons, the control panel would reset to the old pass code and allow Ted to come back down with his new friends. Not having time yet to alter the voice pattern either, verifying the code change was his only hope. From the hallway, Sharon was now screaming for him to return to the office.

Finished, Don hit enter on the keyboard at the same time Sharon watched Ted through the monitor, punching his code into the elevator's control panel. Don ran out of the computer room and down the hall as fast as he could.

If the pass code change *had* been disrupted from inside the elevator, he might not have time to make it back to the office where Sharon was waiting for him before Ted could step out of the elevator and grab him.

Not knowing if he had succeeded or not, Don ran toward the office as fast as he could, while keeping an eye on the elevator doors. He prayed that they wouldn't open to spill out Ted and his death squad.

Shouting for Don to run even faster, Sharon glanced back and forth from the hallway to the monitor as Don approached at a run. As soon as he was through the

The Watchful Eye

doorway and in the office, she closed the door abruptly and engaged the lock.

Panting heavily from the combination of fear, adrenaline, and exertion, Don smiled through heavy breaths as he watched Ted on the monitor. He was still pushing buttons on the control panel in frustration. Don had succeeded in changing the pass code and keeping Ted upstairs and out of the unit.

Realizing what had been done, Ted grabbed a gun from one of the soldiers and used the butt end to smash the panel into pieces. If he couldn't get down to them, he would make sure to cut off their only means of escape.

Don and Sharon continued to watch the monitor as Ted handed the soldier's weapon back in anger. He appeared to be shouting orders at both men as though it were their fault he had failed in accomplishing his task. Then as he finished, he walked away from the elevator and out of sight. Both men in uniform stayed behind. Although they hadn't been able to hear Ted's shouting, Sharon and Don both realized that the guards had been assigned the duty of keeping watch over the unit and its occupants while he was gone. If that were the case, they were trapped inside until Ted could return with a better solution.

"Are they still there?" Jack asked.

"Haven't moved an inch!" Don replied.

"I should be there in about twenty more minutes. Can you get a hold of Dr. Clemens?"

"Sure, he called this morning right after you left to thank us and let us know that everything was going fine. He had wanted to talk to you so I had him leave the number to the lodge he was staying at."

"Good, I want you to get a hold of him as soon as we hang up."

"What for?"

"I want him on the next flight back."

"Why?"

"I'll explain it to you later, just make sure it happens."

"Okay, what about the guards? How are any of us going to get past them?"

"I'll worry about that. You just make sure Clemens is on the next flight to Los Angeles."

Jack glanced at his watch in regret. He knew there was no way the doctor could make it back in time.

"I need him here in less than nine hours Don."

"That's almost impossible Jack!"

"Do whatever you have to do. I don't care if you hijack an entire airline, just get him here!"

"I'll do my best." Don hung up.

Fifteen minutes away now, Jack had to think of a way to get past Ted's guards and then get Don and Sharon safely out of the center.

Chapter Twenty Six

Knowing his car would be recognized if seen, Jack pulled over to the curb a few blocks from the fitness center and parked.

"What are we doing?" Avery asked.

"Wasting our time most likely."

"Huh?"

"Now that I have this transmitter floating around inside of me, they're probably watching my every move and already know I'm here, but just in case, I'd like to have the element of surprise."

Thinking about the transmitter along with his new loss of privacy, Jack had to suppress a variety of negative emotions in order to concentrate on what needed to be done.

"So what should we do?" Avery asked.

From behind them, a steady thump of music grew louder in the distance. Competing with it, Avery had to raise his voice in order to be heard.

Less than a block away, a low rider with a monstrous sound system was slowly making its way down the street. With its stereo system turned up to a ground shaking level, it clearly and inconsiderately advertised its occupant's taste in bass-driven music.

While waiting for the ear-pounding vehicle to pass them by, Jack tried to think of a plan. Doing so, he watched through the side view mirror with annoyance as the music-thundering car slowly approached them from behind. The thumping vehicle's reflection began to shudder with vibration.

On low-profile, white wall tires that circled aimlessly around brightly polished chrome rims, a deep black seventy's Monte Carlo with windows tinted to match, appeared to float only inches off the pavement as it slowly made its way past them and down the street. Because of the heavy tinting, Jack was unable to make out the vehicle's occupants. Coming up with a plan, he started his car and then pulled out onto the street behind it.

Coming only inches from the Monte Carlo's rear bumper and then holding the distance, Jack flashed his headlights repeatedly until the car came to a stop in the middle of the road.

"What are you doing Jack?" Avery asked in disbelief. His facial expression displayed his unease as he watched four tough-looking men in their early twenties step out of the still thumping car. They appeared to be rather angry at having been disturbed.

"Don't we have enough problems without pissing off the local gang members?"

"I've got an idea," Jack said as though he had completely ignored the warning. "Why don't you hang tight a minute?"

Jack stepped out of the car and shut the door.

Watching nervously, Avery rolled down the window as Jack confidently approached the four angry looking men. In a frightened curiosity, he was hoping to hear what was being said although he knew it wouldn't be possible over the boisterous thumping bass that echoed heavily down the roadway. To Avery, all four men looked like a nasty heap of trouble just waiting to happen.

The Watchful Eye

Of the four, two were of a rather large build and couldn't have had a combined tattoo total of less than a dozen. Wearing muscle shirts, both puffed up arrogantly with the anticipation of a fight as Jack came closer to where they were standing.

Of the other two, one wore an oversized flannel shirt that clashed frumpily with his baggy pants and Converse tennis shoes. In Avery's mind, he fit the part of a would-be drive-by-shooter perfectly. By the look in his hardened eyes, those that were now focused unwaveringly on Jack, there was no doubt in Avery's mind that the man had probably participated in just that type of activity on more than one occasion. Shooting a living being, was probably nothing more than a game to him.

The fourth guy wore blue jeans and a T-shirt with a hair net that gave him a slicked-down-tight look. Leaning comfortably against the car as though confrontation was a daily occurrence, something he had grown accustomed to over many years of gang type living, he reached through the driver's window of the Monte Carlo and finally turned down the mind-numbing clamor of music.

"What's up holmes', you got a death wish or what?" one of the muscular men asked Jack who was now standing right in the middle of all four.

Considering the man's tone of voice along with his threatening body language, Avery was positive that punches would soon follow the question, before Jack was even allowed time for an explanation.

What was Jack's explanation anyway? Avery wondered.

As far as Avery could tell, Jack most surely did have a death wish. Why else would he call attention to himself in front of thugs like these?

Because Jack's back was to him when he answered the contention-provoking question, Avery wasn't able to hear his reply.

"And what do I get?" the man asked looking a little less angered by Jack's response.

Avery watched from inside the safety of the car as Jack pulled out his wallet, showed the four of them his ID, and then handed each of them something that he had retrieved from inside it. As far as Avery could tell it wasn't cash.

Bewildered at what he was witnessing, Avery cursed Jack under his breath for being so thoughtless as to flash something as intriguing as his wallet in front of four angry hoodlums.

Still expecting punches to fly, Avery nervously searched his mind for a way to defend himself if the need arose. He couldn't simply roll up the windows and lock the doors, leaving Jack to fight all four of the gangsters by himself. Furthermore, even if Avery were a fighter, which he wasn't by any means, there was no way that he and Jack could take on all four of these men at the same time. By the looks of them they were probably not only carrying unregistered weapons, but also itching to use them. All Avery could think about when it came to his own defense was his bum shoulder. The last thing he wanted to do at the moment was use it to throw punches of some sort. What was Jack thinking?

With all four men curiously following him, Jack walked back to his car where he retrieved his keys. Then he waited patiently as the muscular man he had been talking to walked around the vehicle as if he were conducting an inspection.

"Are these for real?" he asked noticing the small holes torn through the right front fender that were made by bullets meant for Clemens.

"As real as it gets." Jack replied.

Smiling at the idea of whatever offer had been made to him, the muscular man looked once again at the card Jack had given him upon introductions, then at the car and smiled. In acceptance of Jack's offer, he held out his hand.

"You got a deal hombre."

The Watchful Eye

In trying to shake the man's hand, Jack was corrected shortly after he had started. Watching with amusement, the three other gang members laughed as their muscular friend complained about Jack's upbringing while demonstrating the proper ghetto handshake that would be required to seal the deal.

After going through the motions, Jack handed the muscular man his car keys and then signaled for Avery to get out of the mustang. Once he was out, all four of Jack's new friends gathered around him and asked to see the bullet wound in his shoulder. Peeling back the collar of his shirt and nothing more, Avery revealed the semi-bloody bandage while allowing all four men to get a closer look.

"Damn holmes'," one of them said with disgust, "you really got popped huh?" Avery just smiled in his confusion.

Although the wound under the bandage had been minimal, the rather large, blood stained dressing made the affliction appear much worse than it actually was. Showing the bandage, Avery began to feel a slight sense of camaraderie. Most likely, the four men now revered him as a tough guy, maybe even one of their own. It was amazing what a stray bullet could do for a man's ego.

Handing the keys that Jack had given him to the man in jeans and T-shirt, the muscular guy that appeared to be in charge gave his friend instructions as to where he wanted him to take his new bullet riddled Mustang. Then he got into the driver's seat of the low-rider-made Monte Carlo. Avery had already sat down in the backseat with the two remaining gang members. Getting into the passenger seat next to the driver, Jack watched with discomfort as the fourth gang member revved up his Mustang and then peeled away from the curb. Like a bat out of hell, the mustang raced down the street and out of sight.

"Are you okay?" Jack asked Avery who was half squished uncomfortably between the two gangsters.

"Sure, I guess." Avery answered from the crowded back seat looking every ounce as uncomfortable on the outside as he felt physically and mentally on the inside.

Sitting up front where he would have the best view, Jack closed the passengers' door as the muscular guy named Jose started the car. Without the help of the massive stereo system, the Monte Carlo rumbled to life beneath them.

Showing pride in his car, Jose bragged about the time and money he had spent on the engine, paint and interior, during the slow, impatience provoking drive to the fitness center.

Once in High Velocity's parking lot, Jack asked Jose to drive even slower than he already was as he peered out the dark window in search of a black SUV. The parking lot was unusually empty. Not finding one, he then instructed Jose to drive around back.

Next to the fitness center's dumpster, Jack saw the SUV. As Jose crept the car down the alleyway and then in front of it, Jack looked it over carefully to be sure that nobody was sitting inside. As he had hoped, the SUV was empty.

Jack picked up his cell phone, dialed the front desk, and then handed it to Jose.

"Ask for Nancy." he instructed.

When the phone was answered, Jose did what he was asked and then handed it back to Jack.

"It's me Nancy," Jack said when the phone was handed back to him.

"Don't say my name."

"Okay," she answered.

"Are you alright?" he asked.

"Could be better."

"Are there men in the building with guns?"

"Yes."

"Have they hurt you?"

The Watchful Eye

Nancy hesitated as though she were trying to define the exact definition of the word hurt and then answered, *"No, we're closed today for repairs."*

"How many are there?" Jack asked not sure of her response.

"Yes, sir, we closed today around two o' clock."

"Only two of them?" he confirmed making sure he was getting the gist of the conversation.

"Yes, that's right. Two o' clock."

"Are they there for me?"

"I can't tell you for sure sir, but I think so."

"I take it they're in the lobby with you?"

Again she hesitated, *"We should only be shut down for one day sir. We had a water pipe break in two different places, but we're hoping to have the mess cleaned up sometime today."*

"Only one of them is in the lobby with you?"

"That's right sir."

"Do you know where the other guy is?"

"No sir, I can't tell you for sure what time we'll be reopening."

"Don't worry Nancy, I'm going to get you out of there as soon as possible alright?"

"That sounds wonderful."

"If you can, I'm going to need you to turn off the alarm system so I can get in the building through the back door. Can you do that for me?"

"Yes, sir, that would be fine. Sorry for the inconvenience."

"Thanks Nancy, you're the best."

"Sure, sorry I couldn't be of more help to you Mr. Hurry. Have a nice day!" The line went dead.

"What now?" Jose asked.

Jack reached into his pocket and retrieved the loose keys that he had removed from his key chain prior to giving away his car. Singling one out, he handed it to Jose and then asked him to stop the car.

"As soon as I get out, I want you to drive around to the front entrance and walk into the gym like you own the place. If you have to use it, this key will unlock the front doors. Now there's two men in there with guns and they're probably not afraid to use them."

At the mention of guns, Jose smiled with the excitement of a challenge.

"What I want you to do," Jack continued, "is create some sort of distraction so I can get in the back door unnoticed. The secretary is supposed to shut off the alarms for me, but in case she's not able to and it goes off, I want you guys to make a run for it while you still can."

"Run? I know I didn't hear you ask me to run," Jose said in disbelief. "Jose don't run from no one!"

"Not that you have to," Jack added while getting out of the car, "but I just don't want to see you guys get hurt."

Jose frowned and blew off the comment as though he were made of steel. In his opinion, the possibility of actually getting hurt was non-existent.

"What about me?" Avery asked still crunched between the two gangsters in the backseat.

"You just stay in the car until I come out and get you. I think you've been through enough already."

Being left behind with three guys that most likely prayed for trouble on a daily basis, Avery couldn't decide whether the stick he had just received was the long one or the short.

Closing the door, Jack made his way toward the rear entrance as Jose drove the Monte Carlo around the corner and out of sight. As soon as it had rounded the corner of the building, Jack heard a rumble of bass kick up and then echo back through the alley as the car's stereo system was cranked up loud.

The Watchful Eye

Laughing to himself, he thought about what was happening, what he was about to do and about the people he was now counting on to help him pull it off. He also chuckled when considering whether Avery was enjoying the new style of music that was being forced into his brain at ear-shattering decibels.

Standing at the rear entrance, Jack waited about three minutes after hearing the music come to a stop in front of the building before he tried the door.

★★★

"Look man," Jose said to the armed man that was in the lobby, "I came here to get my workout and I'm not leaving until I do! You see this asshole," Jose continued handing the man in uniform the year round pass to the fitness center that Jack had given all four of them previously. "This says I can come and go whenever I want. That's why it has VIP stamped on it. Didn't they teach you the alphabet in the army?"

Glancing over at Nancy who was standing behind the receptionist counter looking every bit as afraid of him as she was of the armed man in uniform, Jose gave her a wink.

"I don't care what this says, the fitness center is closed until further notice and that includes VIP's." The guard tried to hand back the year round pass.

"I don't want that." Jose said in rebuttal. "If I can't use it whenever I want like it says right on the card, then I'm not leaving until you give me a refund or something."

The guard looked perturbed. "Listen piss for brains, the center is closed! Do you see anybody else here? I don't think so. I'll give you five seconds to leave on your own before I send you out of here in a body bag. Get it!"

After shoving the pass against Jose's chest in an effort to get him closer to the door, the guard removed the small leather strap that was used to lock his handgun down in the holster. The look in his eyes made it clear that he was prepared to use whatever force was necessary to back his demands.

Acting angry at the way he was being treated, and most likely so after having his life threatened by the guard, Jose shoved the uniformed man backwards with both hands. With his two gang friends backing him on both sides, Jose followed the staggering guard further into the lobby.

"What now, are you threatening to shoot me! Huh?" Jose shouted in anger as though the guard had thoroughly offended him with what he actually considered to be an idle threat.

Before the guard could regain his balance and was able to draw his holstered weapon, Jose's friend in the flannel shirt had drawn his own gun and had the barrel only inches away from the dismayed guard's forehead. Speaking in Spanish, he yelled at the guard who froze in his tracks with the anticipation of being shot.

"You shouldn't have done that cabro`n," Jose laughed. "He's begging me right now to let him shoot you. Maybe I should, huh?"

In the back of the center, Jose noticed the second guard. Having heard the commotion, he had drawn his weapon and was sneaking his way toward the lobby. Stopping halfway, he began readying himself to fire off a shot from behind a Nautilus machine when Jack crept up from behind him with a ten-pound dumbbell. Before the guard could squeeze the trigger, the dumbbell came down upon his head with an earth jolting crash. Knocking the guard unconscious, the weights could be heard throughout the lobby as they clanked against each other in the midst of finding their target.

As the second guard hit the floor, Jose punched the first guard in front of him with a solid left hook that sent him back a few feet and into dreamland.

The Watchful Eye

Rushing to the lobby, Jack had seen what had happened and reached out to shake all three of his new friend's hands.

"Thanks guys, I couldn't have done it without you."

"All you had to do was tell us what kind of jerks you were dealing with and we would've done it for free." Shaking Jack's hand, the other gangsters agreed.

After performing the new handshake he had learned with all three of them, Jack reached across the counter and gave Nancy a hug. She looked frightened half to death and stressed beyond her wits.

"I think you've had a rough day. Why don't you go home and take a few days vacation on me."

"What's going on Jack? Who were those guys?" she asked.

"Sorry you had to go through this," he exclaimed, "I'll tell you all about it when you get back. Take as much time as you need, okay?"

Still wanting answers, but too afraid to stick around and demand them, Nancy quickly gathered up her purse and car keys.

"Are you going to be okay Jack?" she asked with concern for what had just happened along with concern for the company he was keeping.

"Everything's fine," he assured her. "Go home and get some rest. Don't worry about me."

After Nancy left the building, Jack and the three gangsters bound the two uniformed men to a couple of Nautilus machines with a mixture of duct tape and packing tape that they found in the front office. Then after the two guards were secure, he walked Jose and his friends out to the Monte Carlo where Avery was still waiting patiently in the back seat.

"Give me a few weeks and then come by as often as you want. My place is yours." Jack said as the three men got into the Monte Carlo.

WESS REED

"If you have any more trouble look me up," Jose said smiling, "I'll be driving around in a cherry Mustang."

"Take care of it for me."

"Like I own it." Jose confirmed.

Jack and Avery walked back to the fitness center's entrance as the bass thumping Monte Carlo slowly drove away.

"You've lost your mind Jack." Avery said.

"They weren't so bad," Jack disagreed. "You really should've gotten to know them better." Avery just shook his head.

Once inside the center again, Jack double checked that the two guards wouldn't be going anywhere for a while and then took their two way radios with him and the scientist to the elevator. From there he called down to the computer room with his cell phone.

Listening to Don, Jack worked his way through the busted control panel until he had found the right wires to cross together. After he had connected what he was asked to, Don entered the pass code from his computer and the elevator began its decent.

Once the elevator had made it down to the underground portion of the center and the doors had opened to reveal the meeting room, Jack couldn't believe the mess he saw. In a fit of anger and frustration, Ted had performed his last workout on all of the inanimate objects he could get his hands on.

From out of the hallway, Sharon and Don came in a hurry to meet Jack and tell him about everything he had missed. First, Sharon met him with a full-on hug.

"I'm so glad you made it back in one piece."

Holding her in his arms, Jack thought about what the Director had said. *You didn't really think a girl like Sharon would fall in love with you without help did you? You can thank me for that.* Although those discomforting thoughts cluttered his mind, Jack held Sharon as close to him as possible anyway.

"Are you hurt?" he asked noticing the bruise that Ted had left across the side of her face.

"No not really, just my pride. I never want to see that evil man again as long as I live. He was awful Jack."

"I know. I'm sorry I didn't listen to your intuitions better than I did, I hope you can forgive me."

"It wasn't your fault Jack, you only did what you had to do. Just promise me that I'll never have to see that man again."

"You have my word. You'll never have to look at or worry about him again. I promise."

Looking into her eyes and trying to imagine how she must have felt, Jack couldn't find words to express how horrible he was feeling for what had happened to her. How he wished he would have listened to her concerns when it had come to being left behind with Ted. Holding her close while burying his face in her soft blond hair, he would have liked to never let her go again. How could one person treat another so inhumanely? That was a question he knew he would never know the answer to.

"It sure is good to finally see you boss," Don said joining the two. "How did you get past the guards upstairs?"

"I had a little help actually," he said letting go of Sharon but giving a whole hearted expression of apology cast by a lingering look of sympathy into her beautiful oceanic eyes. "Lets all sit down at the table, if we can find the pieces that is," Jack said looking at the mess on the floor all around him, "we have a lot to talk about."

After Jack and Don had picked up the big meeting table, set it upright and then gathered the scattered chairs, all four of them had a seat and began discussing what had happened and what would have to be done at this point to create a solution.

"What about the doctor?" Jack asked, "were you able to get him on a flight?"

Don looked at his watch. "He should be leaving the Canadian runway in about fifteen more minutes. I had to go through a lot of hassles to get him on a direct flight from Toronto, but he should be arriving in around six more hours."

Looking at his own watch, Jack was worried that the doctor wouldn't arrive in time to possibly help. After almost an hour of precious time had already been wasted on getting past the guards that Ted had left behind, there were only seven hours left of the Director's deadline.

Turning back to the conversation and trying not to waste anymore time than was necessary, Jack continued with the planning and discussion. Sadly he looked to Sharon who was sitting directly across the table from him and told her the majority of the conversation he had had with the Director, Frank Thomas.

"Well, at least we finally know what was in the injection," she said trying hard to sound positive. "What do we do now? I mean, it sounds like there's not much we can do."

"There's got to be something we can do. What about your father? For some reason the Director felt like he was a big threat to the program."

"My father?" she asked as though she was questioning her mind. "He's a politician if that helps any."

"Can you get him on the phone?"

"Sure, but didn't the Director warn you about talking to anybody?"

"Yeah he did, so we're just going to have to make sure he doesn't find out about it."

"Both lines to my computer are secured," Don added. "We could get him on one of those as long as there's no one listening in on the other side."

The Watchful Eye

"As big of a threat as the Director considers him, there has to be someone assigned to him that works both sides." Jack considered.

"You mean someone like Ted?" Sharon asked.

"Exactly like Ted," Jack replied.

"We can't take that chance. If the Director even suspects that you're trying to inform someone, especially a politician, you might as well give the whole thing up. He'll kill you Jack. He'll kill both of you." Avery said, firmly stating his disagreement toward Sharon and Jack's conversation.

"You can though," Jack said looking back at scientist with a newfound interest. "As far as the Director's concerned, you're already dead. It's worth a try anyway."

"I suppose so," Avery agreed still thinking over Jack's suggestion. "But if the Director does find out somehow, I don't want to feel responsible for the terrible things that would happen to the two of you."

"What terrible things?" Sharon asked.

So far Jack had told her everything that had been discovered about the transmitter except for the fact that it was capable of sending signals to its host, signals that could drastically effect emotions if not, cause it to self destruct, which in turn would release the toxic acid.

"You know the thing better than I do," Jack said to Avery. "Why don't you explain it?"

Not having the heart to inform Sharon of the extent to which her life had been taken away from her, not to mention how helpless he might be in doing anything about it, Jack sat back and listened as the scientist did his best to explain all of the transmitter's functions in a professional and scientific manner.

Listening to the scientist's explanation, Don seemed to come to life word by informative word as he converted what Avery was saying into computer lingo, lingo that he could apply to the Watchful Eye's computer program. When the scientist had finished explaining how the transmitter worked with what he himself had discovered along with what the Director had confirmed, Don got up from his chair and scurried down the hallway toward the computer room.

"Where are you going?" Jack asked as Don hurried out of the room.

"I think I've got it!" Don shouted as he vanished through the doorway and into his office.

In their own curiosity, the three of them got up from the table and followed.

By the time the others had made it into the room, Don was already sitting in front of the glowing monitor with his fingers hammering away at the keyboard. In no time at all he was knee deep into the Watchful Eye and surfing through a number of screens different than any of those that Jack had already seen. Avery watched in amazement.

"What's going on?" Jack asked when Don stopped at a particular screen and then began manipulating its numbers.

"These are all of the satellite's tracking functions," Don replied still hammering away on the keyboard yet taking time to point out different groups of numeric codes that were being displayed on the screen.

"And those are?" Jack asked.

"Those are used to control satellite positioning," Avery answered as he pulled up a chair and sat close to the monitor on Don's left.

"Right," Don said with amazement confirming what the scientist had said. He seemed to be impressed with Avery's understanding of the computer codes.

Watching with interest as Don worked his magic by way of the keyboard, Avery continued with his own explanation.

"By assigning a target or a set of coordinates, meaning a specific location or even a person in this case, that target can then be located and viewed in only a matter of minutes

The Watchful Eye

by the program's corresponding satellite. How many are there?" Avery asked.

"As far as I can tell, there's at least three. This one is the closest," he told Avery referring to the satellite's screen that was now on display.

"How many what?" Sharon asked not sure if she understood what the two of them were saying.

"Satellites," Don answered.

"Can you obtain control of them with your computer?" Avery asked.

"Not at the moment. See this?" Don said pointing out two groups of numbers on the screen that were not only flashing in sequence, but also changing in value as though they represented the satellite's odometer.

"This satellite is already active. The numbers are coordinates and they're changing because the satellite is slowly moving into an assigned position."

"So you can't control it until after the task it was already assigned has been completed?" Avery confirmed.

"Well, that's not completely true. I have figured out the program's override and lockout sequences."

"So you can override what has already been imputed into the program?" Jack asked.

"Sure, but not for long. Even though I can override the main control panel's direct input, they still have at least two more satellites to work with if not more. Before you know it, they'd have one of them pinpointing my location while working on a way to lock me out of the program. If so, I'd probably lose my connection permanently along with my life as soon as the troops showed up. They'd swat us like flies, Jack."

"Let's say you did override the program. How long would it be before they could find you?" Jack asked.

"I don't know," Don contemplated, "less then three minutes."

"And before they could regain control of the program?"

"That would be a little tougher. We'd probably have at least twenty minutes before they could shut me out," Don answered. "Why, what do you want me to do?"

"Nothing yet," Jack said while concentrating on the new information Don had given him.

"Can you link into the active satellite without being noticed?" Avery asked.

"I'm not sure," Don replied with curiosity. Until being asked, he hadn't even considered the possibility of bridging the link to an active satellite for fear of being discovered and then shut out of the system permanently. "Should I try?" he asked.

"If you think you can do it without getting caught," Jack answered.

As the others watched him work, Don began manipulating a few of the columns that would link him to the active satellite. When he was satisfied with what he had done, he gingerly reached for the enter key.

"Are you sure?" he asked looking to Jack with skepticism.

"You're the wiz kid. You tell me."

"Here we go. Cross your fingers."

With enough anxiety for the four of them combined, Don carefully hit the button and entered his commands.

The monitor blacked out.

"Oh crap!" Jack said with anxiety. He was expecting Don to rush over to an adjacent keyboard like he had had to do the last time this happened. Instead, he stayed where he was seated with his full attention focused on the blank monitor in front of him.

The monitor lit up again to show a slowly scrolling view of a city. It was eerie to think that the image they were looking at on the screen was being transmitted to the computer so clearly from a satellite that was so far away in space.

"Everything's fine," Don reassured them while flipping on a second monitor that displayed the satellite's previously looked at coordinate screen. "It's maintaining the same path. I didn't do anything to change it"

Just as Don finished his sentence, the screen went black. Then almost as abruptly, it lit up to show a close up of the fitness center. Looking at the monitor and the image of High Velocity, Jack went into a panic.

"It's tracking us Don. How can you consider that to be fine?"

"All I can tell you is that it wasn't me." Don assured him.

The screen blacked out again. This time, it didn't light up again immediately.

"What's happening Don?"

"I don't know. It just stopped." On the second monitor, the two sets of numbers that displayed the satellite's longitude and latitude for imagery stopped varying and then stopped flashing all together. Then as the first monitor finally lit up again, a third row of numbers was highlighted next to the now still coordinates on the second monitor.

"Oh my God," Avery said looking at the image that had popped up on the first monitor.

The screen showed an almost transparent black and white photo of the fitness center's structure. Although it wasn't actually, the image looked very similar to that of an X-ray photo. Inside the center, the monitor showed all four of them gathered in the computer room. As if the fitness center itself was invisible, the satellite placed each one of them exactly where they stood by locking onto their heat signature. Studying the monitor closely as it flashed an updated version of the same photo every couple of seconds, Don noticed that one of the heat signatures was blinking under what appeared to be a green cursor of some sort. Speechless he looked at everyone around him and then back to their displayed locations on the monitor. The flashing cursor was over Jack.

"What does it mean Don?" Jack asked. Although his words were soft and quiet, they clogged up inside his throat as if they were demanding that he no less than force them out.

Don looked again at the second monitor and the new set of numbers that had been highlighted. He compared the amount of digits with those on the pages that he had printed only days ago, whereupon he noticed that the highlighted set on the monitor had the exact amount of numbers as the inoculation numbers that had been assigned to the various people that were listed by Social Security and Birth Date.

"Somebody must have programed the satellite to lock onto your transmitter," Don replied with a measurable amount of dejection.

Without hesitation, Jack grabbed for a pen and notepad and then quickly copied down the highlighted number group from the second monitor, his inoculation number. As he was finishing, his cell phone rang.

"Hello," Jack answered.

"Time's up!"

Chapter Twenty Seven

Hearing the surprise in Jack's voice, the Director couldn't help but laugh with amusement.

"Sorry to have to tell you this Jack, but since you've killed my right hand man, I'm going to be needing your services sooner than expected. Surely we've come to an agreement by now?"

"Doesn't seem as though I have a choice, does it?" Mr. Thomas could hear discontentment in Jack's voice.

"Oh come on Jack, I gave you a few options. Are you in or out?" the Director asked while watching the four heat signatures that were displayed on the large overhead monitor.

"I'm not sure I like it, but I'm in."

"That's my boy. Don't worry so much about it. Before long, you'll realize that you're doing the right thing."

The Director waited momentarily in silence while trying to feel out Jack's reaction. Jack didn't make a sound.

"Who are your friends Jack?" the Director asked referring to the three heat signatures displayed around him.

"Just that, friends." Jack's reply sounded somewhat uneasy.

"Oh don't fret, as long as we've come to an agreement, they won't be bothered. You have my word. I see there's two more people in the building. Who are they, friends as well?"

"They're a couple of your guys that got in my way. They don't seem to be very bright. Maybe you could send them back for a little more training."

"Impressive, that's why I need you Jack. You're the kind of man that can get things done, make the difference. You know, the kind of guy that can accomplish anything he sets his mind to. The kind of guy I want working for me."

"What do you want?"

"Let's get straight to the point, huh?" the Director said happy to hear an abiding tone in Jack's voice. "I need you to lead a group of men on a mission. Be at the air field in an hour and I'll have a chopper waiting for you."

"Where am I going?"

"That's not something you need to know right at the moment. One of the men you'll be meeting is Private Stanton. I've already informed him that you'll be in charge. You just show up at the airfield and he'll have everything you need including a uniform and operating orders. If you have any questions I'll be available on my secured line."

"What kind of operation?"

"Oh, it's just a training exercise. It's called Operation NightHawk. Stalls was in charge of it, but since you were so thorough in taking care of him, I'm now handing it over to you. Everything you need to know will be in the operating orders. You are in charge Jack, but don't think my men won't be watching you."

"Fair enough," Jack replied. *"What about these two idiots in my facility? What do you want me to do with them?"*

"I'll send somebody over to pick them up right now. They'll be out of your hair in no time at all. See Jack, everything is going to work out just fine."

The Watchful Eye

"What about Don and Sharon? I don't want anything happening to them while I'm gone. If one of your guys so much as lay a hand on either of them, this whole agreement of ours is over."

"Not to worry Jack. As long as you do as you say, they'll both be fine. Don can continue to work for you. Of course we'll have to inoculate him in the near future, and you can keep the girl for as long as you like. If you get tired of her let me know," the Director said with a laugh, "we can always get you a new one." Mr. Thomas intended to hit a nerve with the comment as well as make sure his point was heard loud and clear.

"Oh, and one more thing," Jack demanded.

"Yes?"

"I want your word that you're not going to be sending any impressionable signals to my transmitter. If I'm going to be in a threatening situation of any kind, I want to know that I can rely on my own intuitions."

"That's why I picked you Jack. You can count on it." the Director stated honestly.

"That goes for Sharon also." Jack added.

"Excuse me?" The Director was beginning to feel rather irritated with all of Jack's requests. "You realize that you're making more than your fair share of demands don't you?"

"That's the deal." Jack said standing his ground.

"Okay, anything else?" the Director asked sarcastically.

"Nope, I'll be at the airfield in an hour. I'm going to do this like you're asking me to, but if anything I don't agree with happens to one of my friends while I'm gone, and I will be checking in, I'll be sending a few of your men home to you in body bags."

"I fully understand and appreciate your concerns Jack and I've already agreed to leave your friends out of it, but that will be the last threat I'm going to be taking from you. I do hold all the cards Jack and don't you forget it! The next demand you make is going to cost you dearly, understood?"

"Understood."

"Make sure you're at that airfield Jack!" The Director terminated the connection.

"Keep an eye on him. If he's not at the airfield and on that chopper before it takes off, destroy him and his transmitter immediately!"

"Yes, sir," one of the technicians answered while watching his own personal monitor.

"I'll be in my office if you need me. Let me know when he gets to the airfield."

"Yes, sir."

The Director, Frank Thomas, walked out of the large, computerized operation center's main network station and down the hall toward his own office. As he left, the three technicians that sat at the satellite's main correspondence control panel, watched the monitor closely while periodically adjusting the location coordinates.

The room's six uniformed guards stood at attention as Mr. Thomas passed them by and then returned to a ready stance with his departure.

"Don't forget to call me!" he reminded threateningly as he left the room.

Chapter Twenty Eight

"You can't be serious? What are you going to do?" Don asked with astonishment after hearing Jack agree to the Director's demands.

"I'm going to do exactly as he's asked me to do'" Jack said while writing a message on the note pad.

"I thought you had twenty-four hours? There's still six left." Sharon said in rebuttal to the Director's impatient calling.

"I suppose he's changed his mind," Jack calmly answered, handing Don the notepad.

After reading what Jack had written, Don quickly left the room and came back with a black leather bag the size of a lunch box. Unzipping it, he took out a small electronic devise and plugged a pair of headphones into it. Sharon watched curiously as he began walking around the room while pointing a small probe at every crack and crevice that he came upon. After carefully probing the room, he signaled "no" with a shake of his head and then left. Interested in what Don was doing, Avery quietly followed.

Less than five minutes later, Don came back and informed Jack that a listening devise had been planted in his office.

"You're sure?" Jack asked quietly.
"Absolutely, what do you want me to do with it?"
"Leave it right where it is. Did you close the door?"
"Sure did."

Jack was astounded that Ted would have the nerve to plant a bug in his office. After all, every unit in the AFA was probed by one of its employees on a three-week schedule as per policy. Ted must have been desperate in order to take that much of a risk.

Knowing they wouldn't be listened to, Jack closed the door to the computer room and began discussing his plan.

★★★

When the elevator doors opened shortly after on the first level, Jack carried the duffle bag over to where the two guards were still heavily taped to Nautilus equipment and then searched them for keys. Don, Sharon, and Avery were still underground working on the final details of his plan. Around the same time he was supposed to be leaving the small airfield in the chopper, they would be leaving the center.

Ignoring the guard's muffled cursing while searching through their pockets, Jack found the keys to the SUV, left the center, and then drove to the airfield.

★★★

Upon arriving at the airfield, two men were waiting for him in a black helicopter. Parking no less than fifteen feet from the lifeless blades of the chopper, Jack grabbed the duffle bag from off the passenger seat and exited the vehicle.

As he walked over to the chopper, Jack carefully looked over the two men and tried to determine which one was

The Watchful Eye

Stanton. Neither of the men made an effort at this point to greet him. Sitting in the cockpit glaring, they didn't look at all happy to see him.

Coming up on the passenger compartment of what appeared to be a Siborsky, H-76 Eagle, Jack studied the helicopter's sleek contours. Built during the Vietnam era, the helicopter was designed for troop transport as well as being an exceptional attack aircraft. As Jack walked up and placed a hand on the aircraft, one of the men stepped out to confront him. The other miked a radio in which he could report Jack's arrival.

"You must be Stanton," Jack asked introducing himself.

Although not as big or ugly as Ted had been, Stanton appeared to be a formidable opponent. More than three inches taller than Jack, he also outweighed him by at least thirty pounds. *What do they feed these guys?* Jack wondered. Stanton, as well as the man behind the controls, wore the same black uniform that Ted had been wearing when he died. The same type uniform the two guards left tied up at the fitness center had been wearing.

"That's right," the man replied odiously as he quickly pulled out a handgun and pointed it at Jack's forehead.

"Is there a reason for this?" Jack asked dubiously.

"Yeah, there sure is. I don't like you, and I don't trust you."

Holding him at gunpoint, Stanton ran a hand over Jack's clothing in search of a weapon. Jack stood still and allowed for being frisked. When Stanton felt comfortable that Jack wasn't carrying, he demanded to see the contents of the duffle bag.

Holding out the bag, Jack took advantage when Stanton looked down and reached out in acceptance. Rushing in and closing the distance, Jack wrapped his left arm over Stanton's right, tucking the gun and the man's wrist up under his shoulder while applying a threatening amount of pressure to the back of Stanton's elbow in an arm bar maneuver. At the same time, he slammed the man back against the side of the helicopter and rammed his forearm into Stanton's throat.

"Drop your gun," Jack demanded while adding a considerable amount of pressure to the man's elbow. Although wincing in pain, Stanton refused the orders. Jack applied as much pressure as he felt he could without actually severing the joint. Furthering the abuse, he forced his full body weight against the Stanton's throat.

"I said drop the gun." Reaching his threshold for pain, Stanton finally did as he was asked.

Upon realizing what was happening, the pilot grabbed his handgun and bailed out of the helicopter. Rushing to where the commotion was, he loaded the chamber and pointed the weapon at Jack. From the corner of his eye, Jack had seen him coming.

Kneeing Stanton in the gut, Jack released the arm bar. As Stanton hunched over from the blow, he grabbed the left side of Stanton's shirt collar with both hands, circled his neck with his arm, and then jerked him between himself and the armed pilot. Using Stanton's collar as a tourniquet, along with the vise like pressure he was applying with his forearm, Jack cut off Stanton's airway as well as the blood flow to his head. Threatening to kill his partner, Jack ordered the second man to disarm himself.

When the pilot didn't oblige, but instead looked for an opportunity to get off a well placed shot, Jack applied a horrendous amount of pressure to Stanton's neck. Stanton's face was changing color due to his lack of blood and an airway.

"Drop it now, or I break his neck!" Jack demanded.

Not being able to take the shot he had hoped for, the pilot dropped his weapon.

"Step away from it!"

Slowly, the man stepped sideways putting distance between him, the helicopter, and his weapon. As he did,

The Watchful Eye

Jack continued to apply pressure to Stanton's throat. Seconds later Stanton went limp. Jack dropped him to the ground and picked up his handgun. Aiming it at the pilot, he walked over to where the second gun had been dropped. He retrieved it as well.

"Get over there!"

Jack motioned the pilot over to where Stanton was lying on the ground. Showing less confidence than he had previously, the pilot hurried over to his partner. Still holding him in his sights, Jack followed.

✯✯✯

"Should I send the signal?" the technician asked restlessly after watching what had happened on the monitor.

"No, not yet," the Director replied. He also watched with interest. "Let's see how it all pans out."

Having been called into the main room as Jack arrived at the airfield, Mr. Thomas had watched the brutal introductions unfold over the large overhead monitor. In his excitement, he was curious to see what Jack would do next. If he were trying to be deceptive, he would simply have to die. However, if Jack could pull this off and somehow manage to find his place among Stalls' men as a leader, he will have passed the first test to becoming the valuable asset Mr. Thomas knew he could be. Smiling with delight, the Director watched the monitor patiently.

✯✯✯

"Uuurrrrg!" Stanton grunted when Jack kicked him the second time.

"I said get up!"

Still holding the pilot at gunpoint, Jack stepped back and allowed Stanton room to move.

"We don't have all day here, get up!"

When Stanton had finally shaken off the remaining stupor associated with being unconscious, Jack instructed him and the pilot both to their knees.

"Contrary to popular belief, I'm in charge and I expect to be treated as such! Do you understand!" Both men remained silent to the question. Not liking the response, Jack fired a round into the ground between them.

"I said, do you understand?"

"Yes, sir." they answered taking the question more seriously.

"From now on, you'll treat me as your superior at *ALL* times. Not when we're standing face to face, not when you feel I'm listening, not when you're by yourself, in my presence, but at *all* times. Am I making myself perfectly clear?"

"Yes, sir." Stanton said. The pilot once again refused to answer.

Knowing he would have to convince both men, Jack rushed over to the pilot, grabbed him by the collar, and jerked him forward. He landed face first in the dirt.

"You seem to have a hearing problem. What's your name tough guy?"

"Perry."

"Perry what?" Jack demanded with a well-placed boot to the pilot's shoulder.

"Perry Jackson, sir."

"That's better Mr. Jackson. It's nice to see you're finally learning to speak. If you're lucky, we can teach you to crawl next. From now on I'll be expecting a proper response every time you address me, got it!"

"If so," Jackson mumbled with his face in the dirt, "you better never let go of that gun!"

"Really?" Jack replied questioningly, "well, today's your lucky day. Looks like you're gonna get to learn how to crawl after all."

Putting all of his eggs and livelihood in one basket, then praying with all of his heart that he wouldn't drop it, Jack removed the clips from both guns.

Although it could cost him dearly, Jack knew he would have to gain respect in order to stay alive in the future. Unfortunately, there would be only one way to earn that respect from these men.

Placing one of the clips in his pocket and throwing the other as far across the airfield as possible, Jack tossed both weapons under the helicopter and then backed away from the pilot.

"Well, now's your chance Mr. Jackson," he said readying himself for the confrontation, "Get up! Let's see what you've got!"

Getting up from the ground, Perry dusted off his uniform and glared into Jack's eyes smiling.

What am I doing? Jack though to himself although it was too late to back out now.

As Perry neared, his smile broadened. He obviously couldn't believe the opportunity that had been given to him. He turned around to look at Stanton who was still kneeling on the ground.

"What are you doing? Come on, this is our chance."

Stanton's lack of excitement clearly showed his disinterest. Holding his throat and looking placid, he held his position by the helicopter as he had been instructed.

Seeing this, Jack felt a rush of relief. Keeping it well hidden, he couldn't believe this new turn of events, as neither could Perry. At first, Jack had been hoping that a tremendous amount of confidence on his part would be enough to bluff his way into control over Stanton and Jackson. If not, he would have to do his best to defeat the two of them, even though he didn't actually see it as a possibility. Now that Stanton had declined the confrontation, however, his odds of success were drastically increased.

Seeing his comrade cower, Perry's smile slightly dwindled as well as his own confidence. Notwithstanding however, he rushed Jack and threw three quick punches.

Pumped with sheer adrenaline, Jack managed to dodge the first two swings but caught part of the last punch in the middle of his chest. Reacting quickly, he grabbed hold of Perry's arm and pulled him off balance, then spun around backward and planted a sidekick to the pilot's rib cage. The kick was solid, but Perry quickly recovered.

Trying a different approach, Perry yelled in anger and rushed Jack for a tackle. Falling to his back mid-collision, Jack placed his left heel in Perry's mid-section and used it to launch Mr. Jackson up and over him. Quickly, Jack got to his feet.

"Had enough?" he asked as though Perry's attack had been mere child's play. In truth, his chest, already sore from the abuse Stalls had delivered, now felt as if Perry's punch had been launched from a cannon. Jack wasn't sure how much more he could withstand. Thankfully, Stanton was still kneeling on the ground by the helicopter.

In a rage, Perry got to his feet and tried to collect his thoughts. Then without warning, he threw two more punches followed by a kick meant for Jack's kidney.

Able to parry the two punches, Jack responded with pure instinct as he cross-blocked the kick and then tucked Perry's ankle in the nook of his arm. Twisting it to the outside, he managed to throw Perry off of his feet and then landed knee first on the pilot's groin.

Keeping the majority of his weight on his knee, Jack locked his arms around Perry's lower leg and used the leverage to take advantage of a pressure point located on the inside of Perry's shin bone. The pilot hollered out in pain.

"Okay, okay, okay, I've had enough!"

"Had enough what?" Jack insisted applying more pressure.

"I've had enough, sir!" Perry shouted out.

The Watchful Eye

"Good," Jack said. Hesitantly, he let go of the pilot's leg. "See to it you don't forget this lesson."

"Yes, sir!"

Getting up, Jack held out his hand in offering. Perry took it and allowed himself to be helped up off the ground.

"Now that that's over, let's get out of here. We have some work that needs to be done."

Following Perry to the helicopter, Jack's knees began to feel weak. He was overcome with the realization of what he had just done and how stupid he was for having done it. Trying not to show weakness, he walked boldly to where Stanton was now standing while Perry Jackson limped over to the helicopter and climbed up into the cockpit. Stanton was holding out Jack's duffle bag and the two handguns that he had retrieved from under the helicopter.

"What should I do with these sir?"

Taking them, Jack retrieved the clip from his back pocket and popped it into one of the guns. Feeling like a lunatic for doing so, he handed it back to Stanton. "I believe this is yours."

Stanton smiled under the assumption of having a bold new leader. "Thank you sir," he said as he holstered the weapon.

The two of them climbed into the passenger bay as Perry Jackson fired up the chopper. When the engine was ready, Perry lifted the chopper off the ground and they flew away.

✯✯✯

"I knew he could do it," the Director said excitedly as he watched the helicopter depart over the monitor.

"Should I follow them sir?" a technician asked from behind the satellite's relay control panel.

"I don't think that will be necessary," the Director replied. "Mr. Kurts has too much to lose. From now on, why don't you check in on his location every thirty minutes and keep me updated as to what's happening. I'll be in my office."

"Yes, sir."

★★★

Shortly after take off, Stanton reached over and handed Jack a large government issued ditty bag that contained his uniform and operating orders. Taking it, Jack dug out the orders and began to shuffle through them, thankful that he had something, other than the two men riding with him to occupy his time. It was going to be a long and uncomfortable flight.

According to the orders, a temporary base camp had been set up two hundred miles east of Lexington, Kentucky where he would have to change into his uniform and then meet with five more of Ted's soldiers in order to brief them in the mission at hand.

Looking at the orders, he couldn't conceive how he was going to survive the night. At the moment, he felt lucky to be alive, never mind the fact that he still had to prove himself to five more thick headed soldiers who probably devour violence on a daily basis.

Letting go of those weakening thoughts, Jack concentrated on the task at hand while the H-76 chopper cut its way noisily through the night.

★★★

Seven hours had passed since Mr. Thomas had watched the H-76 helicopter leave the small California airfield when a technician knocked on the door outside his office.

"Come in."

The Watchful Eye

"They've made the location sir," the technician said opening the door just wide enough to peer inside.

"Good work Jack," Mr. Thomas said to himself. "Keep him on the monitor, I'll be down in a minute."

"Yes, sir." The technician closed the door.

Walking down the hallway from the Director's office, Stan Morris couldn't wait to get back in front of his monitor where he could watch the action as it took place.

As amazing as it was, he was the only technician who hadn't seen one of the Ghost Army's operations. Considering the countless shifts he had endured, staring at multitudes of boring satellite imagery, he couldn't believe that he was finally getting to watch a secret operation first hand. Not only that, but after seeing what the new guy had done to the two soldiers at the airfield, Stan knew it was going to be good.

Pulling up his chair, he sat back down at his work station, double checked the satellite input, and then leaned back to watch the monitor as if he had front row seats at a Knicks game.

"Is the Director coming?" Jim asked.

Jim was one of the technicians that shared the same rotation with Stan. He was somewhat pompous and as far as Stan was concerned, lacked personal hygiene. Not only did his breath stink, but often enough his hair left speckles of dandruff on his clothing that could be seen from at least ten feet away. Tonight Stan was working with Jim and Tom. He didn't care for Tom much either, although he didn't really know him.

Tom wasn't usually on the same rotation with Stan and Jim. Although Tom was probably a nice guy, every time the three of them ended up working together, Stan always felt as though he were being left out. For some reason, Tom never seemed to want to hang out or get to know him. When Stan had to spend his shift with Jim *and* Tom, he might as well have just been working by himself. That's how it always felt anyway.

"Yeah, he said he'd be here in a couple of minutes."

"Can you watch my station for a minute so Tom and I can get something to snack on?"

"Sure, I guess. But if Mr. Thomas comes in before you get back, I'm not going to cover for you," Stan warned.

"We'll be back in plenty of time."

"Bring back something for me," Stan added as the two technicians walked away.

Watching his monitor, Stan punched in a command that would engage the satellite's thermal scanner. Following a momentary darkening of the screen, he was then able to watch all eight soldiers as they took their position around the Kentucky residence. According to the imagery and heat signals, only two people were in the house and both appeared to be laying in bed asleep.

Knowing that Jim and Tom would be back soon, Stan punched the new guy's tracking number back into the program and then waited for the satellite to send its new imagery. When the screen finally lit up, the new guy was displayed with flashing green cursor. He was positioned on the south side of the house with one of the soldiers and was most likely dishing out the orders. Several men were gathered around the front of the residence and looked as though they were preparing to storm the house.

Stan watched the screen impatiently until Jim and Tom finally returned.

"Think fast," Jim said as he tossed a candy bar at Stan. Instead of catching it, which was something he had never been good at, Stan missed the candy bar as it flew past his outstretched hand and hit him in the face.

Watching his awkward attempt to catch the flying chocolate, and then seeing the candy bar pelt him on the forehead, Jim and Tom lost themselves in a short fit of uncontrolled laughter.

The Watchful Eye

"Okay guys, the joke's over," Stan asserted while picking up the assaulting bar of wrapped chocolate off the floor.

Taking their seats behind the workstation, Jim and Tom continued to chuckle at Stan's embarrassment. Doing his best to ignore them, Stan pealed back the wrapper and pushed his glasses back up to the top of his nose. Taking a bite, he continued to snub his co-workers unamusing comments. He looked again to the screen where the real action would be but couldn't find the flashing green cursor. Upon closer inspection, he realized the new guy was gone.

Glory is not without great sacrifice. It is an aftermath from the suffering that is bittersweet. As eternal as a snowflake before melting. As refreshing as a drink of water to parched lips. Glory is a moment in time before the next trial begins.

H.R.R.

Chapter Twenty Nine

"What do you mean, *He's gone?*" Mr. Thomas bellowed in anger.

"I don't know, he just disappeared somehow?" Stan answered in a panic.

In a frantic search for the new guy, Jack, Stan, Jim and Tom punched commands into the satellites control panel feverishly while riffling through its various imagery capabilities. Jack had to be out there somewhere.

"How could he just disappear?" the Director demanded. "Are you trying to tell me you lost him?"

Frightened, Stan concentrated on his control panel while occasionally glancing up at the monitor in front of him. He didn't dare look at the Director or the two technicians beside him for fear that guilt would be displayed in his eyes. How could he have lost the new guy? One minute he was on the screen next to the house and the next, he was gone. Stan had to find him. If only Jim hadn't thrown that candy bar and distracted his attention, he might have seen what had happened.

"Maybe there's a malfunction in the program," Stan answered although he knew that wasn't the case. Flipping the satellite image to infra red again, he was able to locate all seven soldiers plus the two unsuspecting victims that were asleep in the house. Jack was simply gone. Even when he called up the inoculation number and assigned it as the primary target, the satellite wasn't able to locate him.

"Jim!" the Director shouted looking for conformation to Stan's premise.

"Everything's working as it should be sir. All seven soldiers are accounted for including the residents."

"Then how do you explain what happened? Where's Jack?"

Stan cowered in his seat under the Director's vociferated voice. He knew Jim would pin what had happened on him if given a chance. Still bringing the satellite through its many different displays, he answered the question before Jim had the chance.

"Maybe he's dead sir."

Stan hoped the Director would think back to the confrontation at the airfield. Perhaps that was what had happened. Perhaps Jack *was* dead. After all, he did inflict pain and embarrassment on the two soldiers that had been waiting for him. Maybe they had remained patient long enough to take revenge when the new guy was least expecting it.

"Jim?" the Director asked again looking for conformation.

"It's possible sir, however, if he *were* dead, I believe we'd still be able to pick up a heat signature. After only eight minutes his body should still retain enough heat for us to find him."

"Then where the hell is he!" the Director shouted furiously.

"I have to agree sir," said Tom. "Even if he were dead we'd be able to find him."

"How can you be so sure?" Mr. Thomas questioned.

"Well, his transmitter would have relayed a destruction code by now. It's almost like he's disappeared into thin air.

The Watchful Eye

I can't imagine how it would be possible, but it would seem he's found a way to deceive the satellite."

"Who's responsible for this? There's no way I'll believe that one man just disappeared under the direct observation of a multi-billion dollar satellite project. Which one of you lost him," the Director demanded glaring at all three of the technicians accusingly.

For a moment there was silence. Stan shuddered inside knowing his two co-workers would stick together while hanging him out to dry. He should have never allowed them to leave their workstation. How could he have been so stupid?

"Well, who was it!" Mr. Thomas yelled.

Just as Stan was about to step up and take the blame, Jim answered the question.

"It wasn't anyone's fault sir. All three of us were watching closely when it happened. Like Stan said, he just disappeared. I've never seen anything like it. Maybe there *is* a malfunction in the program," he lied. Stan couldn't believe what he was hearing.

"Well if there is, you'd better fix it! I want to know where that man is now!"

"Yes, sir."

"Get Stanton on the line!" the Director demanded.

"Yes, sir," Jim replied as he punched in a communication code.

Several different electronic beeps could be heard over the loud speaker followed by a static hiss. Shortly after, rustling could be heard as someone answered the line.

"Stanton here?"

"This is Mr. Thomas. Where's Kurts?"

"He has the south position with Smith."

Looking to the heat signatures displayed on the overhead monitor, the Director saw only one body to the south side of the residence. It appeared to be lying on the ground awaiting orders.

"There's only one man to the south," the Director replied. "Put a hold on the objective until you find Kurts. I'll keep the line open."

"Yes, sir."

Over the loud speaker, Stanton could be heard relaying the orders over his two-way radio. On the overhead monitor, men could be seen scrambling to the south side of the residence. One by one, they gathered around the single body that was lying on the ground. A stew of voices could be heard over the monitor faintly as Stanton approached the group.

"Well?" the Director called out. There was silence. "Come in Stanton!"

"Smith is dead sir."

"What?" the Director asked as though he hadn't heard Stanton's answer clearly.

"Smith is dead. There's no sign of Kurts."

"He's there somewhere, find him you idiot!" Mr. Thomas shouted in demand.

"Yes, sir."

As Stanton could be heard passing on his orders over the loud speaker, Stan noticed an abrupt but minute change in the satellite's coordinates. As it happened, Jack's tracking number was briefly highlighted. It was as though the satellite had found his signal, and then lost it again. Blinking momentarily, the tracking number was again highlighted and the tracking sequence initiated.

"I have him!" Stan shouted in excitement.

Looking up to the large overhead monitor, Mr. Thomas smiled with wickedness when he realized the satellite had locked onto a signal and was now in the process of locating it. It was closing in on Jack. Then, as if he simply disappeared off the face of the earth, the satellite stopped tracking and came to an abrupt halt.

"What happened?" Mr. Thomas demanded disapprovingly. "Why did it stop?"

The Watchful Eye

"I don't know sir," Jim replied, "I think it's malfunctioning again."

"No, I don't think that's the case," the Director with a contemplating tone, "Smith is dead and Jack is gone. There's nothing wrong with the program or the satellite. Jack's found a way to toy with us."

"But how sir?" Tom asked.

"Oh, with Jack there's no telling. All I know is that it's time to end this game. Destroy him and his transmitter."

Jim turned to his keyboard and punched in the self-destruct code for Jack's transmitter. In less then ten minutes Jack would fall to the ground and begin flopping like a fish out of water. Two minutes after that, his brain would cease to function completely and then he'll die.

The code wasn't accepted.

"It's not working sir."

"What do you mean it's not working?"

"Without being locked on to his signal, the satellite won't accept the command. It wants to know where to send the transmission."

With eyes full of fury, Mr. Thomas looked as though he were about to explode. "I don't want anymore excuses! I want you to find him and then I want him dead! Do you understand me?"

Scribbling down some numbers and doing the math, Stan printed a sheet of paper and jumped up from his chair. He handed Mr. Thomas the piece of paper.

"If my calculations are correct, which I'm quite sure they are, your man should be right about here," he said pointing to a location on the map he had printed.

"How do you figure?" the Director asked spitefully.

Stan explained how he used Jack's last known coordinates, the direction the satellite had been traveling during its last tracking stage, and the approximate distance a man on foot could cover in the twenty two minutes Jack had been unaccounted for.

"Good work," the Director said studying the calculations, "Now find him!"

"Yes, sir."

As Stan gave his calculations to Jim and Tom, the Director gave Stanton the new coordinates over the radio. In a fit of anger, he instructed Stanton to gather his men and begin the hunt.

After quickly looking over the paperwork, the three technicians worked together to call a second satellite over to the area in which Stan had determined Jack would be. Only twenty-eight yards from the position Stan had calculated, the satellite found a heat signature. Jack had made it to the helicopter and was about to lift off.

"Send the signal now!" the Director shouted.

"I still can't get a lock on his transmitter," Jim replied fumbling his fingers across the keyboard.

"To hell with his transmitter," the Director screamed, "lock on to his heat signature! I want him dead!"

As Jim was punching commands into the control panel, the helicopter lifted up off the ground and sped away to the north.

"Kill him!" the Director yelled impatiently.

Jim's fervent battle with the control panel slowed and then came to a stop.

"What are you doing? I told you to kill him!" the Director shouted in anger.

"I can't sir. Now that he's in the air, I can't get a lock on his *exact* coordinates. The helicopter is moving too fast."

Grabbing a chair, the Director threw it across the room in a fit of rage. All three technicians sat in a fear-induced silence.

The Watchful Eye

As the H-76 eagle sliced its way carelessly through the night, Jack fought to familiarize himself with the controls. Although he had learned to fly as a Navy Seal, the years in between had drastically weathered his memory and coordination. It had been over ten years since he had been given the opportunity to pilot an aircraft, and the helicopter jolted in laughter at his attempts. Slowly, his skills returned and the aircraft's disposition calmed in agreement.

Knowing the helicopter was equipped with a locating beacon, Jack had considered several different escape options before taking it. Thinking about the innocent family, however, he had decided that the H-76 was his best option. He wanted to get back to the residence and wake the family in a hurry. After having looked through the orders pertaining to operation NightHawk, he was concerned with their safety and knew that their time on this earth was about to be cut short. Equipped with 7.62mm gun pods, Jack would use the H-76's weaponry to disable the seven soldiers and put an end to tonight's mission.

Flying low in the direction of the ranch house, Jack noticed bright orange flashes of gunfire. Flying over Stanton and the other soldiers, Jack realized that they had been in pursuit and were now trying to shoot him down. Although continuing on his way, he had thought about circling around and opening up the gun pods. In a matter of seconds, he could have annihilated all seven soldiers. Instead, he continued to the ranch house. Even if he did take out the soldiers, it wouldn't put a stop to future operations. Not only that, but he couldn't help but wonder how many of the soldiers had been forced into their situations in a similar manner as he had.

When Jack reached the resident location, he pulled back on the controls and eased down the left pedal. With the blades sectioning the surrounding air in loud thumping strokes, he hovered circles over the ranch house until a few of the windows began to glow from within. When he was sure he had wakened the occupants, Jack dropped the nose of the aircraft and headed east. Jack was sure that tonight's mission had been scrapped on his account. Awake, the innocent that had been targeted would now have a chance to defend themselves.

Leaving the area, Jack knew that he would soon have to ditch the aircraft and find a safer means of transportation. It wouldn't be long before another aircraft of some sort joined him in the night with the intentions of shooting him down.

Jack flipped on the electronic receiver and began listening to federal aviation warnings. According to the gauges he was heading east and would soon be crossing the state line into West Virginia.

★★★

An hour and fifteen minutes had passed since the Director and the three technicians had watched Jack lift off in the helicopter.

"How much longer before he's intercepted?" the director asked impatiently.

"Twenty-eight minutes sir'," Jim answered watching the monitor.

"And how long before he hits that cloud coverage?"

"He'll be out of sight in less than nineteen minutes sir."

"Will we still be able to track him once he's under the clouds?"

"I'm not sure sir. Without being able to lock on to his transmitter, we might end up losing him."

Frustrated, the Director shook his head and chuckled quietly under his breath. "I've got to hand it to you Jack. You're one smart bastard, but I promise you, you're not going to win."

The Watchful Eye

As Jack was entering the storm clouds he began to drop altitude in order to find a suitable place in which to land when a short burst of gunfire ripped through the mid section of the helicopter. Awakened in a heartbeat, he dropped the nose and gunned the turbines.

While the helicopter lurched forward and into a full speed descent, Jack glanced around the cockpit and what he could see of the holding compartment trying to remember if he had seen anything as helpful as a parachute. From what he could tell, there were none.

Steadying his descent, Jack watched for the ground while keeping tabs on the altimeter. As fast as he was moving through the dense cloud coverage, he hoped to find it before it found him. From behind, another short round of gunfire bursted through the fuselage.

Coming close to what he expected to be a sudden impact, Jack pulled back on the controls and began to level off when he finally saw the ground below. He was about sixty feet away from ripping a hole through the earth and closing the gap fast. Coaxing the helicopter with all his might, Jack finally leveled out and began looking for a place to land.

Directly below him, Jack noticed a large body of water surrounded by mesas and trees. About two hundred yards away, he spotted a clearing in which he could set down. Coaxing the rudder, he was turning toward the clearing when another barrage of bullets shredded a piece of the tail section. As though the helicopter had a mind of its own, the controls were ripped from his hand and it began a pivoting decent toward the edge of the lake.

Flying in large uncontrolled circles, Jack fought desperately to regain control of the aircraft. Without responding, it picked up speed as though it was determined to crash itself into the trees at the edge of the water. As his last efforts were ignored, Jack abandoned the controls and exited the aircraft through the open cargo bay. Without a parachute, he fell over fifty feet to the water below.

★★★

"We got him sir!" Jim called out when he heard the F-16 pilot's report. "He went down near a place called Twin Lakes by Cedar Ridge. It's one of the state parks in West Virginia. According to our guy, he went down hard sir."

"Could he have survived?" the Director asked with scepticism.

"Our guy doesn't seem to think so. All he can see of the chopper is a ball of flames."

"What about his transmitter, can you get a lock on it?"

"No sir. It was probably destroyed in the crash." Stan said.

"The pilot is standing by sir. What do you want him to do?" Jim asked.

"Have him circle the crash site a couple more times. I want conformation that Jack is dead. Then call in the state authorities and inform them that one of our men has gone AWOL in case he survived. I want everyone in West Virginia, from the State Police, to the guy that sweeps the floors at the Department of Game and Fish out there looking for him. Inform them that he's armed and extremely dangerous and give orders to shoot him on sight. I also want a group of our guys at the crash site to recover the body immediately. Hopefully they can clean this mess up before the State authorities find a reason to be suspicious."

"Yes, sir." Jim left the room.

"What do you want me to do, sir?" Stan asked.

"Keep looking for that transmitter. If he's alive I expect you to find him."

"Yes, sir." Stan turned to face the control panel and began typing in his commands.

The Watchful Eye

"As soon as you come up with anything call me. I'll be in my office."

It was now eight o'clock in the morning.

✯✯✯

Twelve hours later, Jack was still nowhere to be found. A group of the Director's men had picked apart the crash site to find nothing but smoldering remains of the aircraft. As instructed, the West Virginia State Police had issued bulletins as well as setting up roadblocks in a thirty-mile radius of the crash site.

Having been awake for well over thirty-six hours, the Director walked down the hall and into his office wondering where Jack was. Most likely he was dead, but Mr. Thomas wouldn't be comfortable with that answer until he could look at Jack's remains first hand.

Tired to the point of feeling sick and disoriented, he gathered his car keys and left the building. He had already instructed the new shift of technicians to call him at his house as soon as they had found out something of value.

After making his way through the many security checkpoints, the Director got into his car and shut the door. With a hot shower, a quick bite to eat and at least six hours of sleep, he'd be at his best again and ready to continue the manhunt for Jack. At best, he hoped to receive a call during the night informing him that Jack's remains had been found and his body bag was on a flight back. With that thought, Mr. Thomas smiled pretentiously and drove away.

Chapter Thirty

At four o' clock the next morning, the alarm clock bellowed its irritating wake up call. In a half stupor, Mr. Thomas reached out from beneath the covers and fumbled for the snooze button. Finding it, he choked off the blasphemous wail and then rolled back into a comfortable position.

Last night, after grabbing a quick bite to eat, Mr. Thomas had driven straight home to his bed. Before his head had even hit the pillow, he was half-asleep. Five minutes later, however, he had found himself lying in bed wide-awake. Befit with turmoil, he had thought about the search for Jack throughout most of the night.

Now, feeling nearly as tired as he had before going to bed, he wished for ten more minutes of sleep. Instead of drifting back to sleep, however, the gears in his head began turning as he deliberated the situation with Jack.

Damn that man, he thought. What could possibly have driven him to be so careless and irrational? Mr. Thomas hadn't dreamed Jack would actually try to fight a battle that was impossible to win. How could Jack not know he would die? In a way, the Director couldn't help but feel a small amount of respect for him. To risk his life over something he couldn't possibly change took true courage, not to mention a touch of insanity. Jack was definitely a modern day warrior. Too bad he had picked a battle that would cost him the ultimate price.

Knowing he wouldn't be able to fall back into a slumber, Mr. Thomas pulled back the covers and sat up on the edge of the bed. He reached over to switch on a small lamp on the nightstand.

"Good morning sunshine." The voice came from somewhere in the corner of the room.

In an instant, the Director knew exactly whose voice it was. Instead of flipping on the light, he slowly reached for the drawer. Inside the nightstand was a Smith and Wesson .44 caliber revolver.

"Jack," he said pulling carefully on the handle. "What a surprise. I didn't expect to see you anytime soon. What happened? I was told you had disappeared during the operation."

"And here I am, huh?"

Although he couldn't see for the darkness, the Director spoke to the corner from which Jack's voice had come. Pulling out the drawer and carefully feeling for the revolver, Mr. Thomas continued the conversation hoping to disguise his intentions.

"I had expected you to call some time today, but not like this."

"Kind of makes you uncomfortable to have someone watching over you, doesn't it?" Jack replied.

"Oh, I didn't mean it like that, my boy. I was just worried about you, that's all."

"Worried?" Jack placated.

Slowly feeling through the contents of the drawer, Frank began to worry when he couldn't find the gun.

"Absolutely! I don't know what upset you during the operation, but I know we'll get to the bottom of it. If one of

The Watchful Eye

my men were insubordinate, he'll pay the price Jack. You can count on that."

"Is there something I can help you find?"

"What do you mean?" the Director asked with phony abash.

Reaching over to the nightstand, Jack turned on the light. He was dressed awkwardly in a clammy looking grayish-tan outfit of some sort and was holding the Director's Smith and Wesson.

"Is this what you're looking for?" he asked pointing the large barrel toward the Director's head.

Swollen under both eyes, Jack looked as though he hadn't slept in days. He was definitely worse for the wear.

"I suppose it is," Mr. Thomas laughed as he took his hand out of the drawer and closed it. "I should have known."

"Should have," Jack repeated scathingly. "Now get up and get dressed. We've got a lot to do today, you and I."

The Director smiled as if Jack were involving him in nothing more than a friendly gathering of some sort. "What do you think you're going to do with that? Hold me at gunpoint while I make formal apologies to all of your friends. Is that what you want? Must be," he said with a laugh, "it's too late for anything else."

"Do it!" Jack demanded.

"If you insist, but I'm warning you, you're wasting your time."

"I'll be the judge of that."

Walking over to his dresser, Mr. Thomas retrieved his underwear and socks. From his closet, he removed a nicely pressed suit and then stepped over to the adjoining bathroom.

"You can change in here," Jack insisted.

"You can't be serious," the Director replied as though he were insulted. "Can't you afford me the dignity of changing my clothes in privacy?"

"You of all people shouldn't be preaching privacy. As for dignity, men like you don't deserve it."

"Easy there," Mr. Thomas said not allowing Jack to provoke his anger. "You're definitely all business this morning, aren't you? Why don't you relax a little? Try and unruffle a few of your feathers. By the time we get this whole mess worked out, you'll have forgotten why you were so upset in the first place."

Looking into the bathroom, Mr. Thomas could see the small, satellite uplink devise that was sitting on the counter. Emptying out his pockets, he had left it there before going to bed last night. Somehow, he had to get to it. The Director hesitated. If he could get to the devise without being shot first, he would easily regain control of the situation. Ignoring Jack he took another step toward the door.

"Click!"

"I said you can change in here," Jack warned after pulling the hammer back on the revolver.

Deciding not to risk it, Mr. Thomas turned away from the bathroom and walked over to the bed. Loathing the idea of changing in front of another man, the Director removed his nightclothes in a huff, right down to his underwear. Without removing them, he began putting on the crisp suit. As though they hadn't actually been needed, the fresh change of underwear remained unsoiled on the bed.

"It seems a loss of privacy isn't as grand as you've made it out to be after all, is it?" Jack laughed in noticing the Director's discomfort.

Ignoring the comment, the Mr. Thomas finished getting dressed.

Reaching under his chair, Jack grabbed a duffel bag and stood up. "Where's the duct tape?" he asked.

"What?"

"Duct tape. Where is it?" Jack repeated.

"I think I have some down stairs, why?"

The Watchful Eye

"You're fixing to find out," Jack stated waving the gun toward the door. "I'll follow you."

With Jack following, Mr. Thomas led the way down the stairs and into the garage where he pointed to a small portable toolbox. Opening it, Jack found the tape as well as a bag of zip-ties. Removing the tape and a handful of the nylon zip-ties, Jack instructed Mr. Thomas to drop down on his knees next to the sedan.

"I will not!" the Director claimed. Without sympathy, Jack hit him on the back of the head with the gun.

Weakened from the blow, Mr. Thomas crumbled to the ground. Although he didn't lose consciousness completely, his vision narrowed to a tunnel and he was overtaken with dizziness. From behind him he heard the rip of duct tape as a long piece was being unrolled. Jack began wrapping it around the Director's neck.

"What the hell are you doing?" Mr. Thomas asked in anger while trying to get up.

"Don't move," Jack said shoving him back down to the floor.

Jack ripped off another long piece of the tape and began wrapping it atop the first piece. Then the Director felt something hard and cold press up against the side of his throat. Jack secured it with the tape.

"Rrriiippp!" Jack wrapped another long section of tape around the Directors throat. Finished, he grabbed Mr. Thomas by the shirt collar and helped him roughly to his feet.

Jack walked around the car and opened the passenger door. "Get in," he instructed. "You're driving."

With Jack holding him at gunpoint, Mr. Thomas sat down in the driver's seat and shut the door. As Jack was getting in from the passenger's side, he adjusted the rearview mirror to have a look at his neck. Underneath several layers of duct tape, Jack had secured one of the

M25A2 fragment type grenades to the Director's throat. All of a sudden, Mr. Thomas found it difficult to swallow.

"What the hell are you doing Jack," he cried out.

"Trying to restrain myself from pulling the pin. Come on, start the car. Let's go."

Although the grenade was built to stun, in close quarters, especially being strapped directly to his neck, the Director had no doubts that the explosion would literally take off his head. "Where are we going?" he asked.

"I figured we'd stop by your office so you can show me around the place. Maybe introduce me to some of the guys'."

"I can't take you there Jack. Besides, they'll never let you past the front gate. They'll kill you the minute they see you."

"Is that so?"

"You'd better believe it!"

"I really didn't peg you for someone who cared," Jack laughed sarcastically. "Now quit wasting my time and drive."

With a grenade taped to his throat and a gun pointed at his head, the Director started the car and engaged the garage door opener. With his heart revving higher than the automobile, he backed out of the garage and drove to the operation center.

★★★

Upon pulling into the large parking lot outside the operation center's headquarters, Jack instructed Mr. Thomas to pull over and shut off the engine. Doing as he was asked, Mr. Thomas eased into an available space and shut off the ignition.

Taking the keys, Jack stepped out of the car and walked around to the driver's side where he opened the door. As

Jack motioned him to, Mr. Thomas stepped out of the car and closed the door.

"Face the car and put your hands on top of it."

As he was directed, Mr. Thomas turned around and placed both hands on the hood of the car. Jack kicked the Director's feet apart so as to make it harder for him move quickly.

With Mr. Thomas leaned up against the car for support, Jack grabbed both of his wrists and used the zip-ties to fasten the Director's arms behind his back. Then he pulled off another section of tape and ripped it in half. Jack hooked his index finger through the pin on the grenade and securing it to the pin with the halved section of tape.

"Showtime!" he said pulling slightly on the pin.

With his life depending on it, the Director was quick to follow in whatever direction Jack chose to pull on the pin.

"You're a sick man Jack," the Director said as he was pulled toward the entrance of the facility where a guard was waiting at the gate.

"That makes two of us." Jack agreed.

As they approached the gate, the guard couldn't believe what he was seeing. He recognized the Director immediately and looked befuddled to see a grenade strapped around his neck. He also noticed that Jack had a gun. Reaching for a hand held radio, he called in for support. Jack continued to pull the Director along as the guard then stepped out of his post with an automatic assault rifle.

"Stop where you are!"

Jack ignored the warning.

"Stop now or I'll shoot!"

"Go right ahead," Jack said as he continued on his path, "but you might as well put a bullet in him first. Either way, he's going to die!"

"Hold your fire!" the Director commanded.

Upon the Director's orders, the guard lowered his weapon and stepped back into his post. Picking up the radio and relaying more information, he watched helplessly as Jack led the Director past his post and up to the facility.

On the short walk from the guard post, three black SUV's came screaming out of nowhere and slid to a screeching stop twenty feet away. Four armed men in black uniforms piled out of each one.

"Hold your fire! Hold your fire!" the Director yelled in distress as the men frantically fought for a position in which they could fire upon Jack. Pulling on the pin slightly, Jack smiled at the soldier's confidently as he continued to lead the Director to the facility's front entrance. There was a security device set up beside the two large doors.

"Open the doors," Jack commanded.

"You'll never get back out alive," the Director warned with as calm a voice as he could muster.

"I'll worry about that. You just worry about staying alive long enough to get us through those doors," Jack said pulling on the pin threateningly.

"Open the doors!" the Director shouted.

Before he was forced to ask a second time, the doors opened automatically. Someone had activated them from inside. Pulling the Director behind him, Jack shot two rounds through the door's security device with hopes of disabling it. Entering the building, they came upon six more guards that were armed and on the ready inside the front lobby.

"Are you okay, sir?" one of them asked. Mr. Thomas ignored the question.

The lobby was a large open room with gray vinyl-tiled flooring that reflected its surroundings clearly as though it was polished that very morning. Climbing up to the second story ceiling, the bare, white walls volleyed every sound they came in contact with, thus lending to the room's cold and empty impression.

Toward the back of the lobby, two separate stair cases, built parallel with the wall, provided a vertical pathway to

The Watchful Eye

security offices on the second floor. Underneath them, three different hallways led away from the massive lobby to office spaces beyond. Standing between the entrance and the main portion of the lobby were five rows of metal detectors accompanied by revolving security gates.

"Which way?" Jack asked.

"Down the hall in front of you," Mr. Thomas answered referring to the hallway in the middle. Jack led the Director through the metal detectors, which in turn screamed out in panic. After shutting off the alarm, a uniformed man walked over to the security gates and punched the pass code into a small adjacent control panel, which would allow the Director and his captor to pass through and into the main portion of the lobby. Twelve of the eighteen soldiers followed cautiously at a distance, as Jack guided the Director down the hall.

At the end of the hall, they came upon the operation center's main control room. Jack pressed a call button on a device by the door.

"Pass?" a voice asked over the speaker.

"1876345921," the Director answered.

With a loud audible click the door began to open automatically.

Inside, Jack was amazed at the room's electronic hardware. About the size of a basketball court, it was filed with as much technology as one might expect to find at NASA. There were at least twenty rows of computer banks that were comprised of more than fifteen separate workstations apiece. Each one was equipped with what appeared to be an individual computer system that was also up-linked to the main frame.

In the middle of the room, three technicians in white lab coats sat at a massive control panel. They stared at Jack with disbelief.

"Well, it looks like you made it Jack. Now that you're here, what do you plan on doing? Searching for a large power cord? Unplug it? Hope for the best?" Mr. Thomas laughed with amusement.

"Shut up!" Jack said looking around the room. "I should have taped that big mouth of yours shut when we were back at the car." All three technicians stared in silence.

"Your game has come to an end, Jack. It was awful stupid of you to bring me here. Stan," the Director called out looking at one of the technicians.

"Yes, sir?"

"Let's show him how this whole thing works. Lock on to number 465379."

"Yes, sir!" The technician turned to his control panel and began punching in the numbers.

"Stop!" Jack yelled out pointing the gun at Stan, but the technician continued with what he had been told.

"Jim, Tom, help him out would you." the Director added.

"Yes, sir!" They too turned around to their workstations and began punching in commands.

"Don't tempt me," Jack said glaring deep into the Director's eyes while tugging on the pin threateningly.

"Done," Stan proclaimed.

"Good job. As you can see Jack," the Director said looking up at the large over head monitor, "My boys have locked onto Sharon's transmitter. Let's see where she's at, shall we?"

"Turn it off!" Jack warned as he pulled even harder.

"Oh, it's too late for that," the Director laughed. "The satellite's already on its way. By the way Jack, all three of my guys have the capability of destroying Sharon's transmitter and taking her along with it. All one of them has to do is send the signal. Are you ready," he asked the technicians.

"Yes, sir." they answered.

The Watchful Eye

"On my command, Sharon will die!" the Director warned, "Unless of course you can kill all three of them before one of them initiates her transmitter."

"I don't believe you," Jack said as the monitor blacked out the third time. When it lit back up, it showed a close up view of Sharon's house. A green cursor blinked on the overhead to display her location inside the dwelling.

"Are you really willing to take that chance?" the Director asked. "Can you live with yourself knowing she died because of your arrogance?"

On the monitor above, the view of Sharon's house didn't change. The cursor continued to blink. As far as Jack could tell, Sharon appeared to be in her bedroom. Jack looked at Mr. Thomas with abhorrence and incredulity.

"Kill her!" the Director demanded abruptly while staring into Jack's eyes hatefully.

"Stop!" Jack cried out in protest.

The technicians looked to Mr. Thomas questioningly.

"Drop the gun, Jack," the Director said firmly.

Not willing to take the chance, Jack glanced odiously at the technicians and then at the monitor, then at Mr. Thomas. Defeated by not wanting to see her get hurt, he dropped the gun.

From the back of the room, one of the armed men carefully walked over and kicked it across the floor.

"Good job Jack. I knew you'd see things my way." The Director looked at Stan, "Kill her anyway!"

Hearing the orders, Stan turned around and pressed a button on the control panel. The cursor on the overhead monitor stopped flashing and turned from green, to bright red. Sharon was dying.

"No!" Jack cried out in despair.

Watching the monitor, his heart felt as though it had quickly shriveled only to explode into hundreds of tiny pieces inside his chest. Each piece ripped painful gashes through his cold and empty insides, as though each one were laced with toxic venom. Jack felt as if he were dying a slow death from the inside out as he looked at the bright red cursor. Mr. Thomas laughed at what he saw as Jack's pitiful weakness.

In a fit of anger, Jack pulled on the pin and nearly jerked it out of the grenade. He wanted nothing less than to destroy the man it was attached to. Somehow managing to control himself, however, he tried to focus on what still needed to be done. Even though Sharon was dead, he still had to do what was right for the millions of innocent Americans that had become the victims of the program. He was the only one that could save them and put a stop to the Watchful Eye. Somehow he had to forget about what was happening on the monitor. He had to trust in Don.

Jack reached under the suit and into his pocket. As he did, every armed man in the room wrestled the anxiety to shoot him. Ignoring them, he pulled out his cell phone and hit speed dial.

"Call her if you like," the Director said unsympathetically, "but I can promise you she won't answer. She's dead Jack!" The Director laughed viciously.

"Hello," Don answered.

"Now!" Jack said and hung up.

Dropping his phone on the floor at his feet, Jack began pealing off the grayish-tan suit.

As he did, the overhead monitor blacked out and the number three satellite began a new search. Jack glared into Mr. Thomas's eyes with hate filled resplendence.

"What the hell's happening," the Director barked at the technicians. Stan, Jim and Tom all turned around to their workstations and began typing in commands precipitously.

"Well? What is it?" the Director repeated in bewilderment.

"One of our satellites has somehow initiated a tracking mode on its own."

"Stop it!" the Director commanded.

"I can't sir," Jim answered while typing in commands frantically. "It's unresponsive."

Punching in his own commands, Stan pulled up a list for every active transmitter that was logged into the system. He then used it to cross-reference the inoculation number that satellite three was actively locating. When he found it, he looked up from his station with puzzlement. "It's tracking him sir." Stan said looking at Jack.

★★★

Upon receiving the order, Don had typed a command into his keyboard that allowed him to temporarily override the Watchful Eye program. *Jack had better know what he's doing,* Don thought to himself as he called up the number three satellite.

Next he typed in the inoculation number that Jack had written on the small note pad the previous day.

Watching his monitor, Don sat impatiently as the satellite began the search for Jack's transmitter. When the screen finally lit up the last time, Don printed a copy of the coordinates that were displayed and handed them to Avery. Avery then ran down the hall and into Jack's office where he faxed Jack's coordinates to Sharon's father, Congressman, Jonathon Morgan.

After calling Mr. Morgan to be sure the fax was received, Avery ran back down the hall to where Don was still sitting behind the keyboard.

"Did they get the fax?" Don asked staring at the monitor in front of him.

"They should be on their way," Avery answered.

Earlier last night, Jack had called Don from a small town in West Virginia where he requested a search for Mr. Thomas' residence. Finding the information that Jack had requested, Don had then forwarded that information to Congressman Morgan who had use it to set up a nearby command post and ready the troops. Avery had contacted the Congressman with Sharon's help and told him everything he needed to know.

Calling in a National Emergency, the Congressman had then traveled to Virginia where he would await the transmission regarding the Watchful Eye's control center. If everything went as planned, he, the National Guard, and the West Virginia State authorities would be able to arrive at the operation center in less than twenty minutes after Jack had revealed its exact location. If everything went as planned!

☆☆☆

"I don't care what it's doing, get control of it or you're fired!"

"I can't sir. The program has been overridden somehow. It's not responding."

"Get this damn thing off me!" the Director demanded as he tried to coax one of his soldiers into removing the grenade.

"Stay away or he dies!" Jack yelled.

Ignoring Jack's threats, two of the soldiers began closing the gap with their assault rifles pointed at Jack's head. Jack felt as though he were surrounded by wolves that were slowly closing in for the kill.

In a desperate attempt to regain control of the situation, Jack squeezed the release with his free hand and removed the pin. "One step closer and I let it go!" he shouted, threatening to let it go and run.

"Back off! Back off!" the Director yelled out in fear.

From inside the control room, Jack heard a commotion out in the lobby. Then shots were fired from somewhere inside the building. The calvary had arrived.

While two of the soldiers stayed behind with the Director, the remaining guards evacuated the control room.

The Watchful Eye

As they did, massive gunfire erupted from out in the hall followed by shouting as the National Guard took control of the building.

"Get away from the computer!" Jack yelled to the three technicians who were still trying to get a lock on the source of interference.

"Ignore him!" the Director commanded. Stan, Jim and Tom stepped away from the control panel even as the Director shouted at them in anger.

"Face first. Get on the ground now!" Jack demanded.

"What are you doing?" the Director yelled in disbelief. "Get back to work!"

The technicians fell to the floor and placed their hands out to their sides.

In a fit of gunfire, the battle continued outside the control room.

"Get up now! If you don't get up and get back to work, I'll fire the whole lot of you," Mr. Thomas shouted desperately.

Shortly after, the gunfire had subsided in the hall and a handful of National Guards flooded the control center. "Every body down!" they yelled.

Mr. Thomas continued to scream at the technicians until he realized that he was being surrounded by men with M-16's. With Jack holding on to the grenade, Mr. Thomas carefully kneeled to the floor.

"All clear!" one of the guardsmen reported over his radio.

Minutes later, surrounded by six heavily armed National Guards, Congressman Morgan entered the room. Carefully protected, he walked over to where the two men were kneeling on the floor.

"You must be Jack," he asked noticing the grenade that attached Jack to the Director's throat.

"Yes, sir," Jack replied.

"You look like you could use a hand."

WESS REED

The Congressman nodded to a couple of the guardsmen who quickly removed the grenade's pin from Jack's index finger and carefully placed it back into the grenade. When they had finished, Jack was helped up off the floor. One of the men began ripping the tape from the Directors neck in order to remove the grenade. All three technicians, as well as the Director, were placed in handcuffs.

Looking at his old friend Mr. Thomas, Congressman Morgan couldn't find the words to express his disappointment. "How could you allow yourself to be a part of something like this?"

"But John, you don't understand," the Director pleaded innocently.

"Get him out of here," the Congressman said before Mr. Thomas could have a chance to speak.

"But John!" the Director again pleaded as he was being hauled away, "I can explain everything."

Mr. Morgan turned to Jack and shook his hand.

"I've heard you're one of my best employees. How can I ever thank you for what you've done Mr. Kurts."

"I don't need to be thanked sir. I know we have an awful lot to discuss, but if we can talk later…?"

Jack couldn't bring himself to tell the Congressman what had happened to his daughter until he could actually confirm it. At the moment, he wasn't willing to believe it himself and talking about it would only disintegrate his hopes.

"I understand. There's already a chopper outside waiting for you and a pilot that's willing to take you anywhere you need to go." the Congressman said.

"Thank you, sir." Jack let go of Mr. Morgan's hand and turned to leave.

"I'll expect you in my office within the next couple of days. I'm going to need a full explanation of everything that's happened."

"Yes, sir." Jack said solemnly as he left the room.

Chapter Thirty One

Jack was flown to a nearby naval air station where he then boarded a P-3 cargo flight. From there, he rode the large aircraft straight back to Los Angeles. Weary from the day's events, he managed to fall fast asleep shortly after takeoff and remained as such until the aircraft's wheels abruptly kissed the California runway. After thanking the naval pilots with a smile and a hand shake, Jack exited the aircraft to find two shore patrol guards waiting for him near the runway.

Upon engagement, the two men explained their orders as being instructed to escort him off the installation and to a location of his choosing. With an appreciation for the service the Congressman had provided him, Jack accepted the offer and followed the two naval police to their patrol car. Getting in, he asked to be taken to the fitness center.

Upon their arrival, High Velocity's parking lot was completely empty. Stepping from out of the patrol car, Jack reached through the driver's side window and shook the two

Petty Officers' hands. After thanking them for their generosity and reassuring them that he was where he wished to be dropped, the military police vehicle drove away. As it did, Jack walked up to the fitness center's front entrance and tried the door. It was unlocked.

Stepping through the entrance and into the lobby, Jack had an eerie feeling that something was terribly wrong. Although Don had completed the task of exposing the Director as well as helping to expose the Watchful Eye's main operations center along with its purpose, a task that could easily have ended both his and Don's careers not to mention their lives, Jack had half-expected Don to be back at the center waiting for him. Not that he was expecting him to get straight back to work as if nothing had happened, as far as Jack was concerned, Don had earned as much paid time off as he wished. Nonetheless, he had hoped to arrive back at the center to see Don's friendly face.

After everything he had been through in the last few days, Jack only wished for the comfort of a friend. Most of all, he was feeling an unbearable pain for the loss of Sharon. Jack knew that of all people, Don would not only understand what he was feeling, but could probably use a little consoling himself. After all, in the short amount of time the three of them had spent together, Don and Sharon had hit it off as friends quite nicely.

Jack pulled up a chair at Nancy's desk and sat down by the phone. How would he ever be able to get over knowing that Sharon died because of him? Even though he hadn't actually killed her, Sharon's death felt as though it was solely his fault. If he had only been able to protect her at the beach, or had been sent to the hospital instead that day, she would have never been involved. If only he would have reacted a few seconds earlier, she would still be alive.

Jack picked up the phone and dialed Don's home number, then slammed it back down on the base and threw the whole thing as far as the cord would allow. Leaning on

The Watchful Eye

the top of the desk, Jack placed his head in his hands and attempted to relieve his frustrations through a heavy and methodical exhalation. Had it not been for the distraction of somebody entering the facility, he would have broken down and cried.

"Hello," someone called out from the front entrance.

In an instant Jack recognized Don's voice. He got up from behind the desk and leaned over the counter to look toward the entrance. As he did, Don spotted him and walked over to meet him with a smile.

"I expected this was where I would find you," Don said as he walked around the counter. "Sharon's father told us you were on your way back. It sure is good to see you in one piece."

Taking Don's hand and using it to pull him closer, Jack put his arm around Don and gave him a hug. "It's good seeing you too."

"Easy boss, It's not that good," Don said jokingly. As he did, he returned the embrace knowing that Jack had had one hell of a rough couple of days. He also knew that the next twenty-four hours would be even rougher.

"Did you tell him?" Jack asked.

"Tell him what? Who are you talking about?"

"Mr. Morgan, did you tell him about Sharon?"

"Yeah," Don answered questioningly. "How did you know?"

"I saw it over the monitor."

"Saw what?" Don asked, not sure of what Jack was saying. At the time of the incident, he had been monitoring the satellite that would be locked onto Jack's transmitter while awaiting the phone call. Because of this, he was unaware that a separate satellite had been used to destroy Sharon and her transmitter.

Not wanting to say that he had watched her die, Jack instead asked where her body had been taken and how her father had dealt with the news. "How are you handling it?"

he also asked. For losing Sharon so recently, Don seemed to be taking it quite well.

"I don't think we're on the same page Jack. Sharon is in the hospital right now and she's doing fine."

"You mean she's not dead?" Jack asked in amazement. "I saw them kill her over the monitor. How could she still be alive? Did her transmitter malfunction or something?"

"Of course she's alive. I'm not sure what you saw, but Dr. Clemens and Avery worked together to remove that thing last night."

"How?"

"I don't know all the details, but they're waiting for us at the hospital right now. They're confident that yours can be removed also. As soon as I can get you there, they want to get started."

"So she's alive!" Jack asked needing to hear it again.

"Yeah, at least she was thirty minutes ago when I left to come and get you."

"But I saw her die at her house."

"Oh," Don said with a smile when he finally figured out what Jack was talking about. "Avery took her transmitter and set it up as a decoy in case they decided to come looking for her. After it was removed, he wanted to buy you a little extra time. I guess he must have left it at her house."

"Well what are we waiting for," Jack asked excitedly making his way quickly around the counter. "Lets go!"

Hurrying to follow Jack, Don rushed out the door behind him and then the two of them climbed into his car. Feeling excitement in Jack's new outlook and impatience, Don drove to St. Francis as fast as he safely could.

At the hospital, Jack followed Don to the elevators where they rode up to the fourth floor. According to Don, Avery and Dr. Clemens where both standing watch over Sharon until he could return with Jack.

The Watchful Eye

When the elevator opened on the fourth floor, Jack was out of it and halfway down the hall before he realized that he hadn't yet felt claustrophobic in the hospital's bacterial surroundings. In his excitement to see Sharon, he had forgotten all about his phobia.

On the rest of the way to her room, Jack couldn't help but remember what the Director had said. What if she didn't really love him? What if she didn't even like him? Would he lose her all over again? Smiling, Jack realized those consequences to be of the least importance. He loved her, and all that really mattered now was that she was alive. Alive and well.

As Jack approached Sharon's room with Don close on his heels, Avery stepped out into the hall. He looked as tired as Jack felt.

"There he is," Avery said with a smile when he saw the two of them coming down the hall. "It's about time you got here. We were beginning to wonder if you would ever come back."

"I wondered that a few times myself. How is she? Can I see her?"

"She's asleep at the moment, but I'm sure she'd be pleased to see you. Go on in. Clemens is in there with her." Jack opened the door and stepped into the room. Don and Avery stayed in the hall.

Hooked to an IV of some sort, Sharon looked as beautiful as Jack had ever seen her. Soft, innocent and delicate, she was a sight for sore eyes. Being careful not to wake her, Jack shook hands with Dr. Clemens. He had been giving instructions to a nurse pertaining to Sharon's care.

"Jack, we've been expecting you. You look like you've just fought a war. How are you feeling?"

"Never better," Jack replied looking at Sharon with a smile. "How is she?"

"Oh, she's going to be fine. She's just resting. You can talk to her, but she's just been medicated. I can't promise that she'll make a lot of sense at the moment."

"That's okay," Jack stated, "I'll wait until she wakes up on her own. She could probably use the rest."

"That's a good idea," Clemens agreed. "Besides, we need to focus on getting that transmitter out of you as soon as possible."

Compared to the last time Jack had seen him, Dr. Clemens looked like a new man. Like a man with a renewed purpose in life.

"How do you plan on doing that? I was under the impression that removing it would be impossible. Won't it self destruct?"

"She doesn't have one anymore," Clemens assured him referring to Sharon who looked quite comfortable sleeping on the bed. "Avery, your scientist friend helped me with it. He's a bright man that friend of yours. After sitting down and discussing it together, we realized that it would actually be a fairly simple procedure. As it turned out, it was. We were able to remove hers last night. So what do you say, are you ready?" Clemens asked.

"Yeah, I suppose so. The sooner the better, right?"

"Don't worry Jack. It should be a piece of cake. If I don't feel like I can remove it without causing any harm, I'll leave it where it's at until we can come up with a better solution, okay?"

"Okay," Jack agreed.

As Dr. Clemens was leaving the room, Jack took one last look at Sharon, smiled, and then followed him out the door.

★★★

After being prepped for surgery, Jack carefully stretched out across the small surgical table. He couldn't

The Watchful Eye

help but feel like a lab rat waiting to be dissected for the good of mankind. He watched quietly as Dr. Clemens and Avery studied the X-ray photos one last time.

According to the photos, the small transmitter had been pumped through Jack's circulatory system from the internal jugular vein in his neck, to an artery in his left forearm before it had become active. At that time, it attached itself to the Ulnar artery wall. Because of the information Avery had been able to provide him, Dr. Clemens had already expected to find it somewhere close to where it was. As the two men finished studying the X-rays, an X-ray technician finished setting up a semi-portable Fluoroscope.

"How are you feeling, Jack?" Clemens asked.

"Impatient. Let's get this thing over with."

The technician draped a lead X-ray shield over Jack's waist and mid-section.

Dressed in surgical attire with his own lead shielding, Avery joined Clemens and two OR nurses at Jack's side. "Hang in there, Jack," he said with a reassuring smile, "everything's going to be fine."

As one of the nurses swabbed Jack's arm with beta-dine and finished prepping him for the procedure, the other started an IV. Clemens gave the instrument tray a final inspection.

"What's that for," Jack asked groggily, he was referring to the IV that had been started. Although the morphine had taken effect and Jack wouldn't remember later, Clemens explained the drip anyway.

"We're also giving you a Parenteral dose of Verapamil Hydrochloride, Jack. It's going to slow down your heart rate so we won't chance dislodging the transmitter before we can get rid of it. You might start to feel a little dizzy and sleepy, but that's just the drug working. Why don't you close your eyes and think about what you want to do tomorrow. When you wake up, you can tell me all about it, alright?"

"Alright," Jack mumbled groggily.

When Clemens was ready to begin, he nodded to the technician who flipped on the Fluoroscope. Looking at the monitor, he confirmed that the transmitter was still attached to the artery. It was immobile and in the same location that the X-rays photos had already pointed out. With a scalpel, Dr. Clemens found his mark and then made a small incision on Jack's inner forearm. When he was finished, one of the nurses handed him a small tissue retractor that he used to hold open the incision. A second retractor was placed on the opposite side of the incision. Watching the monitor, Clemens then took a vessel clamp and occluded the artery downstream from the transmitter. He placed a second clamp above it. One of the nurses suctioned the small amount of blood that had begun to pool up around the exposed arteries.

With the transmitter enclosed inside the artery, Clemens quickly clamped it off again with Hemostats and then severed the artery on both sides between the Hemostats and the vessel clamps. Carefully, he removed the small section of artery with the transmitter held in on both sides by the Hemostats and then handed it to Avery. Avery set it on a surgical tray and then carried it out of the room.

With the threat gone, Clemens nodded again to the technician who turned off the fluoroscope. Then with the help of one of the nurses, Clemens placed a small piece of Gortex, graft material between the two sections of artery and began tying it in with absorbent sutures. When he was satisfied with his craftsmanship, he then removed the vessel clamps and performed a final inspection. Pleased with his work, he removed the tissue retractors and began stitching up the wound. Forty-five minutes after the procedure had begun, Dr. Clemens left the room while the nurses stayed behind to clean the patient. Then, he would personally see Jack to his room and wait by his side until he was wide-awake and comfortably recovering.

The Watchful Eye

★★★

When Jack awoke, Avery, Don, Dr. Clemens and Sharon, were all gathered in his room and waiting to talk to him.

"How do you feel?" Clemens asked.

"Like a train wreck. What did you give me?"

"Your headache is a side effect of the Calcium Channel Blocker I gave you to slow your heart rate. Don't worry. It will go away eventually. Would you like something for the pain?"

"No, I think I can manage. Is it gone?" Jack asked with scepticism.

"It's right here," Avery said holding up a beaker of fluid.

"He thought you might want to keep it as a souvenir," Don laughed.

"No, I just wanted to study it a little closer. Who knows, we might be able to find something useful? Something that will help in the future removal of these things."

"Are you sure you don't want something for the pain?" Clemens asked while studying the stitches on Jack's arm.

"Yeah, I'm sure."

"If you change your mind let me know, okay?"

"You got it Doc'. By the way, thanks."

"No, thank you Jack. I wouldn't have been here to help you if you hadn't saved my life." After a warm-hearted handshake and a careful hug, Clemens left the room.

"So what's next boss?" Don asked.

"A few weeks vacation after a couple days of sleep."

"I hear that," Avery said.

Don looked to Sharon who was smiling and then to Avery. "Avery," he asked, "what do you say we go find a soda machine somewhere? It feels a little crowded in here."

"That's a great idea," he replied. After patting Jack on the shoulder, Avery followed Don out of the room. Jack looked at Sharon in silence not sure of what she wanted to say.

"How are you feeling?" he asked.

"Better than you I'm sure. Can I get you something?"

"No, I'm fine."

"I was really worried about you Jack. Thank God it's finally over, huh?" With that, Sharon leaned across the bed and placed her arm across Jack's waist. Laying her head down on his chest, she reached up and kissed him on the cheek.

"I'm sorry I got you involved in all of this, Sharon."

"Nonsense," she said looking up to meet his eyes. "It wasn't your fault. You're the good guy, Jack, and don't you forget that. I just happened to be at the wrong place at the wrong time. How could you think I would hold you responsible for everything that's happened? If it wouldn't have been for you, a lot of people's lives would still be in danger, including mine. If anything, I'm thankful to have met you. I love you, Jack."

With his stitchless arm, Jack held Sharon close and closed his eyes. Life couldn't be any better.

Love is purity, as light powers over darkness. A sensation so marvelous that once possessed by its tenacity, loss is not an option conceivable by the human soul. To be loveless is lifelessness, richness to rags, eternal and shameless. Love has the power to raise to the heavens, but holds a trump of misery played carelessly.

H.R.R.

Chapter Thirty Two

Two years later, Jack sat on the beautiful Hawaiian beach with sand between his toes. He gazed at the ring on his finger. It had been two weeks since he and Sharon had been married and they were now in the process of enjoying their honeymoon. He couldn't have been happier.

After taking a couple weeks vacation, Don had spent a few days behind the keyboard compiling a list of all the victims that had been added to the Watchful Eye program. Having gotten names for all of them, he had found over three and a half million people that had been injected with transmitters.

Avery had gone straight to work on the transmitter and had eventually been put in charge of the fourth floor at the large Naval research facility where the inoculations had been produced. As often as he could, he provided Dr. Clemens with any information that applied to the future removal of transmitters.

Working with government funding, Clemens began in-servicing surgical groups from all across the United States on transmitter removal procedures. As happy as he could be, he had finally found an outlet that would allow him to forgive himself for the terrible part he had played in the conspiracy. After two years, almost eighty-percent of the transmitters had been removed and destroyed from those that had been injected. Sadly, sixty-percent of the victims had been small children under four years old.

"Hey, you." The sound of Sharon's voice broke Jack's methodical gaze.

Walking across the sand to where Jack was sitting, Sharon pulled up some beach next to him and sat down.

"How are you, Mrs. Kurts?"

"Happy, and you?"

"Couldn't be better."

As the sun slowly set over the water, Jack and Sharon sat together by the surf, holding hands and talking about their future.

☆☆☆

Although their words couldn't be heard, Jack and Sharon were captured clearly from miles overhead where a satellite then sent their images back down to the Watchful Eye opetration center.

"Live it up while you can Mr. Kurts. It's not over yet!"

Printed in the United States
1372800001B/34-63